Emerald
Magic

Emerald Magic

GREAT TALES *of* IRISH FANTASY

Edited by Andrew M. Greeley

A TOM DOHERTY ASSOCIATES BOOK

NEW YORK

Emerald Magic: Great Tales of Irish Fantasy
Copyright © 2004 by Andrew M. Greeley Enterprises, Ltd., and Tekno Books

This book is printed on acid-free paper.

A Tor Book
Published by Tom Doherty Associates, LLC
175 Fifth Avenue
New York, NY 10010

www.tor.com

Tor® is a registered trademark of Tom Doherty Associates, LLC.

Library of Congress Cataloging-in-Publication Data

Emerald magic : great tales of Irish fantasy / edited by Andrew M. Greeley.—1st ed.
    p. cm.
    "A Tom Doherty Associates book."
    ISBN 0-765-30504-6
    1. Fantasy fiction, English—Irish authors.   2. Ireland—Fiction.   I. Greeley,
Andrew M., 1928–

  PR8876.5.F35E44 2004
  823'.0876608—dc22

                                2003061477

First Edition: February 2004

Printed in the United States of America

0 9 8 7 6 5 4 3 2 1

Acknowledgments

Introduction, copyright © 2004 by Andrew M. Greeley.

"Herself," copyright © 2004 by Diane Duane.

"Speir-Bhan," copyright © 2004 by Tanith Lee.

"Troubles," copyright © 2004 by Jane Yolen and Adam Stemple.

"The Hermit and the Sidhe," copyright © 2004 by Judith Tarr.

"The Merrow," copyright © 2004 by Elizabeth Haydon.

"The Butter Spirit's Tithe," copyright © 2004 by Charles de Lint.

"Banshee," copyright © 1986 by Ray Bradbury. First published in *Woman's Own*, February 1986. Reprinted by permission of the author and his agents, the Don Congdon Agency.

"Peace in Heaven?" copyright © 2004 by Andrew M. Greeley.

"The Lady in Grey," copyright © 2004 by Jane Lindskold.

"A Drop of Something Special in the Blood," copyright © 2004 by Fred Saberhagen.

"For the Blood Is the Life," copyright © 2004 by Peter Tremayne.

"Long the Clouds Are over Me Tonight," copyright © 2004 by Cecilia Dart-Thornton.

"The Swan Pilot," copyright © 2004 by L. E. Modesitt, Jr.

"The Isle of Women," copyright © 2004 by Jacqueline Carey.

"The Cat with No Name," copyright © 1989 by Morgan Llywelyn. First published in *The Irish Times*. Reprinted by permission of the author.

For Colm O'Muircheartaigh,
Up Kerry!

Contents

❧

Introduction

When I was a small one, my mother told me stories about "the little people" in Ireland, stories she had heard from her own mother. I don't think she believed the stories, at least not that much. Her mother before may have told them at least half in fun. Even if they were not altogether true, they were good stories. So I learned early on in life about the characters that swirl around Dublin's fair city in Diane Duane's first story in this collection—leprechauns and pookas and silkie and banshee and the rest of them. I was surprised that they had all moved to Dublin, but so, it seems, has everyone else. Indeed the largest number of those who speak The Irish as their first language now live in Dublin. The "little people," as my mother called them, go wherever the Irish speakers go.

My mom also explained where the faerie came from. They were

the moderate middle angels in the time of the great war in heaven between Michael and his angels and Satan and his angels. When the matter was settled, and the "bad angels" went off to hell, there was some discussion as to where the "independents" should be sent. They had not fought against the Lord God, so they didn't deserve hell, but they hadn't been on His side either, so they couldn't stay in heaven. The decision was they would be sent to earth, to a place of their own choosing. They opted for Ireland: it was, after all, the place on earth most like heaven! They had the Emerald Isle all to themselves until the Celts came, a variety of humans for whom they didn't have much affection, so they retreated to the west of the island and to their caves and forts and hills and islands in the river and other hangouts. Their situation was made worse when the monks came and replaced the druids. The latter were properly afraid of them, but the Catholic clergy vigorously denied their existence and denounced them from the altars. The Sidhe (whom I call the Shee because few can be expected to cope with the mysteries of Irish spelling) decided that it was not prudent to take on the priests directly and withdrew farther into the ground and into mystery and magic.

In my own story in this collection I try to make peace between the two angelic hosts, an exercise of fantasy, I hasten to add, not theology (lest I be delated to the Holy Office!).

However, at one time the greatest concentration of them was in the County Mayo, whence came all four of my grandparents. Indeed after the famine, it was said, there were more faerie in Mayo than there were humans. So it is fitting that I write this introduction.

Do I believe that one could find the faerie in Mayo today? Well, to tell the truth, I've never looked for them and probably never will, and myself without any psychic sensitivity at all, at all. A prudent man, I would not venture into faerie fields or faerie forts or faerie mounds. You can never tell what you might find. Nor will I spend much time in the "front" room of a Mayo cottage, which by tradition is kept neat and empty except for wakes because on their wild rides around the County, the Troop seems to dash through the front rooms. I've never heard the reason for this belief. Indeed even today, many people are unwilling to talk about the faerie because it is bad luck.

Hence the various euphemisms for them in addition to my mom's "little people." They are variously called "they," "the gentry," and "the Troop." Sometimes people don't call them anything, but merely wink and nod in the general direction of nowhere.

One of my sociological mentors, Everett C. Hughes, told a story about his research in rural Quebec. He asked an old man whether he believed in the faerie. "They're not around anymore, the man replied, but they were in my grandmother's day."

The Irish have no monopoly on the faerie. Mircea Eliade, the distinguished student of comparative religion, once wrote an essay on the Romanian faerie, who, it turned out, were exactly like the Irish faerie, even to the name of Troop of Diana (Tuatha de Danu). So perhaps the legends of the faerie folk are part of an ancient Indo-European heritage. Some will say that it is not surprising that they (or the memory of them) would survive in Ireland, because the Irish are a very superstitious people. In fact, in a survey of thirty nations, the Irish were the least superstitious, less even than the English. The highest rates were in Eastern Europe. So perhaps a study of folklore all along the Danube will unearth remnants of the Tuatha there too. They are at least an improvement on the overweight gods and goddesses who sing in Wagner's ponderous opera and the ham-handed Nordic characters who live in the regions of the North Pole.

The question remains, however, why, if the Irish are the least superstitious of Europeans, they still have so much affection for "them" and indeed why they seem to be so prevalent in this collection of Irish stories, dominating the first half and sneaking into the second half. There are, I believe, a number of explanations. The Irish love stories—they are really the only ones in the world who should write short stories—and "they" are the source of endless good stories. Moreover, they are occasionally somewhat sympathetic to humans, though they usually pay no attention to them.

The so-called "Celtic twilight," which Irish writers in the last century created as an ambience for their stories, does reflect to some extent the mystical bent of Irish culture, even in Dublin. In all the fog and the rain, mixed intermittently with dazzling sun showers, the boundaries between the real and the fantastical do seem a bit porous.

The pre-Christian culture of the land believed that the boundaries between this world and the "many-colored lands" were thin and in some times of the year easily permeable—All Hallows, Brigid's Day, May Day, Lady Day in Harvest (Samhain, Imbolc, Beltane, and Lugnasa). At these four days of the yearly cycle, especially All Hallows, those in the many-colored lands were free to walk among the living—to seek forgiveness, to settle scores, to request prayers, and to express love. The Church, which was very skillful in absorbing pagan festivals in the Celtic Isles, easily baptized these festivals and called them Rogation Days. In some popular Irish Catholicism the blessed in heaven are depicted not as existing in some far-off space but all around us, watching us with affection and pride.

So Ireland is a land of twilight, twilight weather, twilight religion, twilight culture. Small wonder then that fantasy stories of Irish origin and influence are for the most part stories told at twilight time and in twilight perspective by lovers of half-light.

Ms. Duane's story, "Herself," brings the night streets of Dublin alive with mystery and wonder and introduces a very new and very dangerous member of the Troop, who wants to destroy all the others. To deal with this threat she recalls your man back from Zurich and reunites him with his old love, Anna Livia Plurabelle.

Your man lives on also in the stories of Flan O'Brien, who reports that himself survived death in Zurich during the war and works in South County Dublin, where he tends bar and write pious tracts for

Jesuit magazines. O'Brien—ne Brian O'Nolan—is not thought of as a fantasy writer, but only because there was no such thing as fantasy literature in his days and because few read him today. However, he is certainly the greatest of all Irish fantasy masters.

Tanith Lee, whose work I have admired for a long time, admits to only a strain of Irish genes. However, one need only to read one of her stories, any of her stories, to know that she comes from the twilight world and to suspect that this story ("Speir-Bhan") is far more auto-biographical than her many chilling vampire tales. I've never heard of the three fox women before, but they surely belong in the faerie legions, and I would not want to meet them on a dark night in the County Mayo or in London either. Note that in the first two stories, the faerie adjust easily to modern life, walking the streets of Dublin or riding the tube in London.

The next two stories are violent. In the first, "Troubles" (Jane Yolen and Adam Stemple), two branches of the Shee fight one another in a pub on the eve of Beltaine. The good guys, as depicted by the narrator, win the bloody brawl, and the narrator comments that if they did not have the Irish, the fey would have to invent them.

In Judith Tarr's story ("The Hermit and the Sidhe"), the violence is between the Shee and the Church, or rather a rural monsignor who is moved to go on a crusade against them. He fails because the Shee find an ally in a hermit, much to the delight of the townsfolk.

Elizabeth Haydon's "The Merrow" may well be a cousin to the silkie woman who was a key character in John Sayles brilliant fantasy film *The Legend of Roan Inish*. In both cases the seal woman (perhaps borrowed from Nordic folklore) fought for her love, and in both they won, but more gently in the film, where the missing baby is only spending time with "another branch of the family" until his parents decide not to abandon the island. In both this and the previous story, God's love for his creatures is invoked on the side of faerie, a point which Gaby and Mike make in my story.

I've never heard of the Butter Spirit (in Charles de Lint's story "The Butter Spirit's Tithe"), though I suspect he is part of the crowd and not a nice person either, probably one of the bad Shee in the Yolen and Stemple story. However, the gray man is certainly part of the heritage and also a bad Shee, but not without some sense of justice.

Is the wailing young woman out in the cold in Ray Bradbury's story really a "Banshee" (a woman spirit) or is she a ghost or is she a plant that the narrator has used to get rid of his dubious friend? I'm inclined to think that she is the last. The real banshee, is, as everyone knows, an old woman, just as she appears in Duane's story.

Finally, my own efforts to reconcile the Shee with the Seraphs ("Peace in Heaven") is based on two premises—if the angels have bodies (as the fathers of the Church say they do), albeit ethereal bodies, then there must eventually be deterioration and, for the species to survive, reproduction. Gender differentiation is not the only way to do it, but the Other seems to have a certain fondness for this method. The second premise is that in the book of Job, Satan is one of God's court and not a demon. The Seraphs have appeared in some of my novels, but this is the first time they've ever been to Ireland. Like I say, they are fantasy, not theology. Yet, as I also say, I'll be disappointed if in the Other's variegated cosmos there are not beings like them.

The second group of stories are less explicitly tied to faerie lore, though the "Lady in Grey" in Jane Lindskold's story about Maud Gonne and William Yeats may well be faerie too. Yeats was surely the greatest English-language lyric poet of the twentieth century, but I have always felt that he was a creep as a lover and that Maud was well rid of him. Readers of the story will have to decide whether they agree with me.

The two stories about blood, "A Drop of Something in the Blood" and "For the Blood Is the Life" (Fred Saberhagen and Peter Tremayne), are a reference (explicit and then implicit) to another Irish writer who has had an enormous impact on the world, though no one has ever suggested that Bram Stoker, the creator of *Dracula*, was in the same class as Willie Yeats. The encounter between him and Charcot is a dazzling premise brilliantly executed. Peter Tremayne has the most terrifying of the horror stories in this collection, not particularly Irish in its assumptions, but still benefiting greatly from its setting in Dublin.

Cecilia Dart-Thornton's retelling of Lady Gregory's version of the Oisin story is impressive. It is about Irish Faerie and the followers of Finn McCool, and the ultimate defeat of the faerie (though never complete) by Patrick and his crowd. Moreover the faerie woman who takes Oisin away from the Fiana is the daughter of MacLir, who shows up in Dublin to dialogue with Gaby and Mike. Yet the story in its present form is more literary than folkloric, so I put it in the section that deals with fantasy inspired less by folkore and more by more or less contemporary Irish literature (last century and a half).

L. E. Modesitt, Jr.'s lyrical story of space travel could also belong to the early-twentieth-century Celtic revival, an era dense with Irish mysticism. And in this story there's more than a hint of Irish mystical pride. "The universe is thought, wrapped in rhyme and music, and that's why the best pilots hold the blood of the Emerald Isle . . . so long as there are Irish, there will always be an Ireland." And Amen to that.

Similarly mystical is Jacqueline Carey's sad story of the "Isle of Women." It is dense with the melancholy Irish sense of doomed love. I don't think the people of the story are faerie exactly, though the Lady has some magical power. In a way I am surprised that the theme of lost love doesn't recur in some of the other stories.

Morgan Llywelyn's sweet story of Nuala's cat, however, is a fine way to end a book about a fantastic sensibility that constantly plays back and forth between a profound fatalism and a strong sense of hope. I'm sure "The Cat with No Name" was an angel, indeed perhaps Maeve from my story, engaged in renewed work for the Other.

I have written this introduction with the assumption that the authors of the stories are all Irish, but, as far as I know, none of them are. Diana Duane knows Dublin so well that she may well be Irish. Morgan Llywelyn is Welsh, though she lives in Ireland, Tanith Lee claims a strong strain of Irish genes. And while my grandparents were all from Mayo—God help us—I'm a Yank. The Irish sense of the fantastic is so catholic that outsiders can readily fit into its hopeful and fatalistic twilight and write, not like the real Irish would, but at least with enough verisimilitude to sound like they're Irish. The Emerald Magic is available for all who will treasure it.

One final story, or rather the first line of it, which is enough to demonstrate how Catholic Christianity has adjusted itself to the Irish sense of thin boundaries between worlds. The line is, "One cold and windy day in the County Mayo the Mother of God was out walking with himself in her arms." I mean, where else would she be out walking save in the County Mayo, where the people are open to surprise and wonder, where it is always possible that one may encounter a wonder person along the road.

ANDREW M. GREELEY
Grand Beach
June 2003

THE
Little People

Herself

❧

BY DIANE DUANE

I met the leprechaun for the first and last time in the conveyor-sushi bar behind Brown Thomas. It was the "holy hour," between three and four, when the chefs go upstairs for their own lunch, and everything goes quiet, and the brushed stainless-steel conveyor gets barer and barer.

The leprechaun had been smart and ordered his yasai-kakiage just before three. He sat there now eating it with a morose expression, drinking sake and looking out the picture windows facing on Clarendon Street at the pale daylight that slid down between the high buildings on either side.

While I'd seen any number of leprechauns in the street since I moved here—our family always had the Sight—I'd never found myself so close to one. I would have loved to talk to him, but just

· 23 ·

because you can see the Old People is no automatic guarantee of intimacy: they're jealous of their privacy, and can be more than just rude if they felt you were intruding. I weighed a number of possible opening lines, discarded them all, and finally said, "Can I borrow your soy sauce? I've run out."

He handed me the little square pitcher in front of his place setting and picked up another piece of yasai-kakiage. I poured shoyu into the little saucer they give you, mixed some green wasabi horseradish with it, and dunked in a piece of tuna sashimi.

"You're not supposed to do that," he said.

"Sorry?"

"Mix them like that." He gestured with his chin at the wasabi. "You're supposed to just take it separately."

I nodded. "I'm a philistine," I said.

"So are we all these days," the leprechaun said, and looked even more morose. He signaled the obi-clad waitress, as she passed, for another sake. "Precious little culture left in this town anymore. Nothing but money, and people scrabbling for it."

It would hardly have been the first time I'd heard that sentiment coming from a Dubliner, but it hadn't occurred to me that one of the Old People thought the same way. I'd have thought they were above such things. "Do you work in town?" I said.

He nodded. The waitress came back, swapped him a full flask of sake for his empty one, left again.

"Shoes?" I said.

He laughed, a brief bitter crack of a sound. "Have you ever tried to cobble a Nike?" he said.

I shook my head. It wasn't something I'd had to try lately, though I'd had enough job worries of my own. The Dublin journalistic grind is not a simple one to navigate. I had gone from features editor to subfeatures editor at one of the CityWatch magazines, always being hurled from scandal to scandal—they *would* keep publishing badly

concealed ads for the less discreet of the massage parlors and lap-
dancing joints over by Leeson Street.

"That line of work's all done now," he said. "Planned obsoles-
cence . . . it runs straight to the heart of things. People don't want
shoes that last years. They want shoes that maybe last *a* year. My folk,
we couldn't do that. Against our religion."

I didn't say anything, not knowing if it would be wise. I did some
interviewing for the magazine I worked for, and had learned to
appreciate the sound of a subject that the speaker didn't want you to
follow up on.

"It's the death of craftsmanship," the leprechaun said. "Nike and
all the other big conglomerates, they'd sooner have slave labor in
Malaysia than honest supernatural assistance from a first-world
country with good tax breaks . . ." He drank some sake. "No, we're all
in information technology now, or high-end manufacturing, com-
puters and so on. It's the only place left for skilled handworkers to go.
My clan was all out in Galway once: they're all in Fingal now, for the
work. Damn made-up county, nothing real about it but freeways and
housing developments. Name me a single hero-feat that was ever
done in Fingal!"

"I got from Independent Pizza to the airport once in less than
half an hour," I said: and it was all I could think of. It didn't count,
and we both knew it. All the same, he laughed.

It broke the ice. We were there for a few hours at least, chatting.
The belt started up again while we talked, and some more people
drifted in; and still we talked while the light outside faded through
twilight to sodium-vapor streetlight after sunset. The leprechaun
turned out not to be one of those more-culchie-than-thou types, all
peat and poitín, but an urbanite—clued-in and streetwise, but also
well-read. He knew where the hot clubs were, but he could also quote
Schopenhauer as readily as he could Seamus Heaney; and as for culture, he told me several things about Luciano Pavarotti's last visit to

Dublin that made me blink. He was, in short, yet another of that classic type, the genuine Dublin character. When you live here, it's hard to go more than a few days before meeting one. But you don't routinely meet "Dublin characters" who saw the Vikings land.

I ordered more sake, and paused. Slipping into a seat around the corner of the sushi bar from us was someone at first sight more faerie-tale-looking than the leprechaun: a baby teen, maybe thirteen if that, in red velvet hooded sweatshirt and fake wolf-claw wristlet. Little Red Riding Hood squirmed her blue-jeaned, tanga-briefed self in the seat as she began picking at some fried tofu. The leprechaun glanced at her, glanced back at me again, the look extremely ironic. By contrast, he was conservatism itself, just a short guy with hair you'd mistake for sixties length, in tweeds and extremely well made shoes.

"She'd have been a nice morsel for one of the Greys in my day," he said under his breath, and laughed again, not entirely a pleasant sound. "Before the wolfhounds did for them, and 'turncoat' men ran with the wolf packs, getting off on the beast-mind and the blood feast . . . Just look at all that puppy fat." His grin was feral. "But I shouldn't complain. She pays my salary. I bet her daddy and mammy buy her a new computer every year." He scowled.

"Do you really miss the shoes that much?" I said.

It was a mistake. His eyes blazed as he took a plate of the spiced soba noodles, another of the green plates, the least expensive sushi. He didn't have a single blue or gold or silver plate in his "used" stack. "Don't get me started," he said. "Nike, Adidas, whoever: we would have worked with them. *We would have worked with them!* Work is what we live for; good work, well-done, they could have had a labor force like the world never saw. We could have shod the *planet.*"

The leprechaun chewed. "But no," he said. "A decent wage was too much for them. Why should we pay *you* minimum wage, they say, when we can get the work for almost nothing from these poor starving mortals over in Indonesia or wherever, who're grateful for a penny a day? And so they gave us their back."

He poured himself more sake, drank. "We were to be here for you, from the beginning of things," he said more softly; "we were to help you have the things you needed when you couldn't have them otherwise. But your people have made us redundant. Spiritually redundant as well as fiscally. So now, as we can't earn, neither can we spend. 'And who of late,' he said sadly into his sake, 'for cleanliness, finds sixpence in her shoe?' "

"Bad times," I said, looking past the Mercedes and the BMWs and the ladies walking past the sushi bar toward the "signature" restaurants farther down the road, where you couldn't get out the door at the end of the night for less than three hundred Euro for just a couple of you and wine.

"Bad times," the leprechaun said.

"And it's hard to find a decent pint," I said.

His eyes glittered, and I kept my smile to myself. Any Dubliner is glad to tell a stranger, or somebody with my Manhattan accent, where the best pint is. Sometimes they're even right. Sometimes it's even someplace I haven't already heard of. I don't drink the Black Stuff myself, especially since there's better stout to be found than Uncle Arthur's overchilled product in the Porter House brewpub in Parliament Street; but that's not the point.

His eyes slid sideways to betray the great secret, whose betrayal is always joy. "You know South Great Georges Street?"

"Yeah." It was a few blocks away.

"The Long Hall," he said. "Good place. The wizards drink there, too."

"Really," I said.

"That's where most of us go now." There was a silent capital on the "u" that I nodded at. "We go down there Tuesdays and Thursdays, in the back, for a pint. And the wakes," he said. His look went dark. "A lot of wakes lately . . ."

"Suicide?" I said softly. Irish males have had a fairly high suicide level of late, something no one understands with the economy booming the way it's been, and somehow I wouldn't have been surprised to find the trend had spread to the Old Ones.

He shook his head. "Nothing like," the leprechaun said. "None of these people were suicidal. They had good jobs . . . as good as jobs get for our people these days. Coding over at Lotus, hardware wrangling up at Gateway and Dell. They never seem to stop hiring up there in the Wasteland." It was a slang name for the jungle of industrial estates that had sprung up around Dublin Airport, and there seemed to be a new one every month, more and more land once full of Guinness-destined barley, or of sheep, now full of Europe-destined PCs and other assorted chippery.

"But it's not the same," I said, because I knew what was coming. I'd heard it before.

"No, it's not," the leprechaun said with force. "Once upon a time I didn't even know what the ISEQ was! When did our people ever have to worry about stocks and shares, and 'selling short'? But now we have to, because that's how you tell who's hiring, when you can't make a living making shoes anymore." He scowled again. "It's all gone to hell," he said. "It was better when we were poor."

"Oh, surely not," I said. "You sound like those people in Russia, now, moaning about how they miss the good old days in the USSR."

"Poor devils," the leprechaun said, "may God be kind to them, they don't know any better. But it's nothing like what *we* have to deal with. Once upon a time we gave thanks to God when the leader of our country stood up and announced to the world that we were self-sufficient in shoelaces. Who knew that it could go downhill from that, because of too *much* money? But people aren't like people used to be anymore. It's not that the money would spoil them . . . we always knew that was going to happen, maybe. But it's *how* it's spoiled them. Look at it!"

We looked out the window toward the brick façade that the back of Brown Thomas shared with the Marian shrine that also faced onto the street. You could look through one archway and see a painted life-sized knockoff version of the Pietá, the sculpted Lady raising a hand in a "what can you do?" gesture over her Son's sprawled body, her expression not of shock or grief but of resigned annoyance—"Never mind, he'll be right as rain in a few days . . ."—and through another doorway, a few doors down, you could see Mammon in its tawdry glory, all the Bally and Gucci and the many other choicer fruits of world consumerism laid out for the delectation of the passersby. The Pietá was not entirely without Her visitors, but plainly Brown Thomas was getting more trade. Closer to us, the street was full of cars; fuller of cars than it should have been, strictly speaking. There was a superfluity of Mercs and Beemers, and the occasional Lexus, all double-parked outside the restaurant, next to the entrance to the Brown Thomas parking structure. The cold fact of the Garda Pick-It-Up-And-Take-It-Away fleet working its way around the city had plainly not particularly affected these people. They could soak up the tickets and the impound fees and never even notice.

"In God's name, what's happened to us?" the leprechaun said. "What's happened to us that we don't care what happens to other people anymore? Look at it out there: it's nothing much right now, but this street's a bottleneck; in twenty minutes the whole of center city will be gridlocked. And it's worse elsewhere. The rents are through the roof. It's a good thing I can just vanish into one of the 'hills' in Phoenix Park at night. Otherwise, I'd be in a bedsit twenty miles south, in Bray, or somewhere worse—Meath or Westmeath or Cavan or whatever, with a two-hour commute in and back, in a mini-van loaded over capacity. And probably with clurachaun as well.

Have you ever been stuck in a minivan for two hours between Virginia and the North Circular Road with a bunch of overstressed clurachaun trying to do . . . you know . . . what clurachaun *do*??"

Another unanswerable question, even if I had been. "It's tough," I said. "Hard all around."

There wasn't a lot more out of him after that. All the same, I was sorry when he called the waiter over to get his plates tallied up.

He looked up at me. "It's not what it was," he said, "and it's a crying shame."

"We all say that about our own times," I said. "They've said it since ancient Greece."

"But it's truer now than it ever was," said the leprechaun. "Look at the world we were in a hundred years ago. We had poverty, and starvation, and unemployment from here to there, and people being forced out of their homes by greedy landlords. But we still had each other; at least we had a kind word for each other when we passed in the road. Now we have immigrants on the street who're poorer than we ever were; and people getting fat and getting heart attacks from the crap ready-made food that's nine-tenths of what there is to eat these days; and work that kills your soul, but it's all you can get. And forget being forced out of anywhere to live, because you can't afford to get *in* in the first place. The only kind word you hear from anybody nowadays is when you take out your wallet . . . and it's not *meant*. Things are so wrong."

He eyed me. "But you'll say there are good things about it, too," he said.

"You've been here longer than I have," I said. "Maybe I should keep my opinions to myself."

"It was different once," the leprechaun said. "It was different when She ran things." And he stared into the last of his sake, and past it at the black granite of the sushi bar, and looked even more morose than he had before we'd started talking.

He tossed the rest of his sake back in one shot. "Good night to you," he said at last, slid off the cream-colored barstool, and went out into the night.

So it was a shock, the next day, to find that he was dead.

•　◆　•

Leprechauns don't die the way we do: otherwise, the Gardai would have a lot more work on their plates than they already do with the burglaries and the joyriders and the addicts shooting up in the middle of Temple Bar. At the scene of a leprechaun's murder, you find a tumble of clothes, and usually a pair of extremely well made shoes, but nothing else. That was all the Folk found the next morning, down the little back alley that runs from the Grafton Street pedestrian precinct to behind Judge Roy Bean's.

At first everyone assumed that he'd run afoul of some druggie desperate for money and too far separated from his last fix. They may be of the Old Blood, but leprechauns can't vanish at will without preparation: you can get the drop on one if you're smart and fast. Various pots of gold were lost to mortals this way in the old days, when there was still gold in Ireland. But the leprechauns had the advantage of open ground and nonurban terrain into which to vanish. It's harder to do in the city. There are too many eyes watching you—half of a leprechaun's vanishing is skillful misdirection—and, these days, there are too many dangers too closely concentrated. The sense of those who knew him was that he just got unlucky.

I confess it was partly curiosity that brought me to the wake, where I was told all this. But it was partly the astonishment of having another of the leprechaun's people actually look me up at the magazine. There he stood, looking like a youthful but much shorter Mickey Rooney in tweeds, waiting in the place's glossy, garish reception area and looking offended by it all. I came out to talk to him, and he said, "Not here . . ."

My boss, in her glass-walled inner office, was safely on the phone, deep in inanely detailed conversation with some publishing or media figure about where they would be going for lunch. This happened every day, and no one who went missing from now to 3:00 P.M., when the Boss might or might not come back, would be noticed. I stepped outside with the leprechaun and went down to stand with him by the news kiosk at the corner of Dawson Street.

"You were the last one to see him alive," the leprechaun said. I knew better than to ask "who?"; first because I immediately knew whom he meant, and second because you don't ask leprechauns their names—they're all secret, and (some say) they're all the same.

"He was all right when he left," I said. "What happened?"

"No one knows," said the leprechaun. "He wasn't drunk?"

"He didn't have anything like enough sake." Privately I doubted there was that much sake in the city. You haven't lived until you've seen someone try to drink a leprechaun under the table.

The leprechaun nodded, and he looked as grim as my dinner companion had the other night.

"He was murdered," he said.

I was astounded. "How? Why?"

"We don't know. But he's not the first. More like the tenth, and they're coming closer together."

"A serial killer . . ."

"We don't know," said the leprechaun. "Come to the wake tonight." And he was off down Dawson Street, quick and dapper, just one more self-possessed businessman, if shorter than most.

Who would kill the Old Folk, though? I thought. *Who stands to profit? It's hard enough for most mortals even to see them, let alone to kill them. One or two might have been accidents. But ten? . . .*

◆　◆　◆

THERE WERE NO ANSWERS for my questions then. I went back to work, because there was nothing better to do, and when my boss still wasn't back by four, I checked out early and made my way down to the Long Hall.

The place doesn't look very big from the frontage on South Great Georges Street. A red-and-white sign over a wide picture window, obscured by ancient, dusty stained-glass screens inside; that's all there is. The place looks a little run-down. Doubtless the proprietors encourage that look, for the Long Hall is a pint house of great fame, and to have such a place be contaminated by as few tourists as possible is seen as a positive thing in Dublin. If you make it past the genteelly shabby façade and peeling paint, you find yourself surrounded by ancient woodwork, warm and golden-colored, and glossy wallpaper and carved plaster ceilings that were white in the 1890s, but are now stained down by time and smoke to a warm nicotine brown. The pub's name is deserved. It's a narrow place, but it goes on and on, nearly the width of the block in which it resides. There are barstools down the right side, and behind them a bar of great height, antiquity, and splendor—faded, age-splotched mirrors, bottles of every kind racked up to the ceiling, and most importantly, long shelves running the length of the back of the bar, to put pints on.

I wandered in, pushed between a couple of occupied barstools, and ordered myself a pint. This by itself gives you plenty of time to look around, as a well-pulled pint of Guinness takes at least seven minutes, and the best ones take ten. Right now, the front of the bar was full of people who had left work early. It was full of the usual sound of Dubliners complaining about work, and the people they worked with. "So I said to him, why don't you tell him to go to the F ing Spar and get a sandwich and then sit down for five F ing minutes, sure she'll be back then. Oh no, he says, I can't F ing spare the time in the middle of the F ing day—"

I had to resist the urge to roll my eyes . . . yet still I had to smile. This is how, when I return home, I know for sure that I'm in Dublin again. The second you're past passport control in Dublin Airport, you hear it . . . and after that, you hear it everywhere else in town, from everyone between nine and ninety-five. Only in Dublin do people use the F word as casually as they use "Hey" or "Sure" or "Listen" in the US. It's an intensifier, without any meaning whatsoever except to suggest that you're only mildly interested in what you're saying. Only in Ireland would such a usage be necessary: for here, words are life.

I glanced toward the back of the bar. Between the front and the back of the pub was a sort of archway of wood, and looking at it, I realized that it was a line of demarcation in more ways than one. A casual glance suggested that the space behind it was empty. But if you had the Sight, and you *worked* at seeing, slowly you could see indistinct shapes, standing, gesturing. You couldn't hear any sound, though; that seemed to stop at the archway.

It was an interesting effect. I guessed that the wizards the leprechaun had mentioned had installed it. I walked slowly toward the archway, and was surprised, when I reached it, to feel strongly as if I didn't want to go any farther. But I pushed against the feeling and kept on walking.

Once through the archway, the sound of conversation came up to full as if someone had hit the "unmute" button on a TV remote. There had to be about eighty of the Old People back here, which was certainly more warm bodies than the space was rated for; it was a good thing all the occupants were smaller than the normal run of mortals.

There was just as much F-ing and blinding going on back here as there had been in the front of the bar, but otherwise, the back-of-the-pub people were a less routine sort of group. There was very little traditional costume in evidence; all these Old People seemed very city-assimilated. I glanced around, feeling acutely visible because of my height—and I'm only five-foot-seven. Near me, a tall slender woman, dressed unfashionably all in white, turned oblique eyes on me, brushing her long, lank, dark hair back to one side. Only after a long pause did she smile. "Oh, good," she said. "Not for a while yet . . ." And she clinked her gin and tonic against my pint.

"Uh," I said. A moment later, next to me, a voice said, "It's good of you to come."

I glanced down. It was the leprechaun who had come up to the office. "This is one of the Washers," he said.

Even if I'd thought about it in advance, the last thing I'd have expected to see in a city pub would've been a banshee, one of the "Washers at the Ford" who prophesy men's deaths. I was a little too unnerved just then to ask her what her work in the city was like. She smiled at me—it was really a very sweet smile—and said, "It's all right . . . I'm not on duty. Days I work over in Temple Bar, in a restaurant there. Dishwashing."

"Dishwashing??"

She took a drink of her G and T, and laughed. "Most of us give up laundry right away. Won't do their F ing polyester!"

We chatted casually about business, and weather, and about the departed, while I glanced around at the rest of the company, trying not to stare. There were plenty of others there besides leprechauns and bansidhe and clurichauns. There were a few pookas—two of them wearing human shape, and one, for reasons best known to himself, masquerading as an Irish wolfhound. There were several dullahans in three-piece suits, or polo shirts and chinos, holding leisurely conversations while holding their heads in their hands (the way a dullahan drinks while talking is worth watching). There was a gaggle of green-haired merrows in sealskin jackets and tight pants, looking like slender biker babes but without the tattoos or studs, and all looking faintly wet no matter how long they'd been out of the Bay. There was a fat round little *fear gorta* in a sweat suit and glow-step Nikes, staving off his own personal famine by gorging on bagged-in

McDonald's from the branch over in Grafton Street. And there were grogachs and *leanbaitha* and other kinds of the People that I'd never seen before; in some cases I never did find out what they were, or did, or what they were doing in town. There was no time, and besides, it seemed inappropriate to be inquiring too closely about everybody else while the purpose was to wake one particular leprechaun.

They waked him. It wasn't organized, but stories started coming out about him—how much time he spent down around the Irish Writers Center, how he gave some mortal entrepreneur-lady the idea for the "Viking" amphibious-vehicle tours up and down the river Liffey: endless tales of that kind. He was well liked, and much missed, and people were angry about what had happened to him. But they were also afraid.

"And who the F are we supposed to tell about it?" said one of the dullahan to me and the banshee at one point. "Sure there's no help in the Guards—we've a few of our own kind scattered here and there through the force, but no one high up enough to be paid any mind to."

"We need our own guards," said another voice, one of the clurachauns.

"And you'd love that, wouldn't you? You'd be the first customers," said one of the leprechauns.

There was a mutter. Clurachauns are too well known for their thieving habits, which make them no friends among either the "trooping" people like the Sidhe or the "solitaries" like the leprechauns, dullahans, and merrows. The clurachaun only snickered.

"What do you call a northsider in a Mercedes? Thief!" said one of the leprechauns, under his breath. "What's the difference between a northsider and a clurachaun? The northsider is better dressed!"

The clurachaun turned on him. The others moved back to give them room for what was probably coming. But there was one of the People I'd earlier noted, a grizzled, older leprechaun whom the others of his kind, and even the clurachauns, seemed to respect: when he'd spoken up, earlier, they'd gotten quiet. "The Eldest," the banshee had whispered in my ear. Now the Eldest Leprechaun moved in fast and gave the younger leprechaun a clout upside the head. To my astonishment, no fight broke out.

"Shame on you, and the two of you acting like arseholes in front of a mortal," said the Eldest. The squabblers both had the grace to look at least sullenly shamefaced. "Here we are in this time of grief when no one knows what's happening, or who it might happen to next, and you make eejits of yourself. Shut up, the both of you."

They turned away, muttering, and moved to opposite sides of the pub. The Eldest nodded at me and turned back to the conversation he'd been having with one of the merrows, who looked nervous. "I *did* see it, Manaanan's name I did," she said, shrugging back the seal-skin jacket to show that strange pearly skin underneath: it was hot in the back of the pub, with so many People in there. "Or . . . I saw *something*. I was comin' up out of the river the other night, you know, by where the coffee shop is on the new boardwalk. I wanted a latte. And I saw it down the street, heading away from the Liffey, past one of those cut-rate furniture stores. Something . . . not normal."

"What was it?" the Eldest said.

She shook her head, and the dark wet hair sprayed those standing nearest as she did. "Something big and green."

No one knew what to make of that. "Aah, she's got water on the brain," said one of the clurachauns standing nearest. "It's all just shite anyway. It's junkies doin' it."

The Eldest glared at him. "It might be," he said, "and it might not. We don't dare take anything for granted. But we have to start taking care of ourselves now. Everybody so far who's been taken has been out in some quiet place like a park, or in the waste places around housing estates. Now whatever's doing this is doing it in the city. Nowhere'll be safe soon. We have to put a stop to it. We need to start doing a neighborhood-watch kind of thing, such as mortals do."

To my surprise, then, he turned to me. "Would you help us with that?" he said. "We could use a mortal's eye on this. You know the city as well as we do, but from the mortal's side. And you're of good heart; otherwise, the deceased wouldn't have given you a word. He was a shrewd judge of character, that one."

"How can I help?" I said.

"Walk some patrols with us," he said. "That's how we'll have to start. We can get more of our city People in to help us if it's shown to work."

My first impulse would have been to moan about my day job and how I had little enough time off as it was. Then I thought, *What the hell am I thinking? I want to know more about these People*—

"Sure," I said. "Tell me where to meet you."

"Tomorrow night," said the Eldest. "Say, down by the bottom of Grafton Street, by St. Stephen's Green. We'll 'beat the bounds' and see what we can find."

◆ ◆ ◆

AND SO WE DID that for five nights running, six . . . and saw nothing. People's spirits began to rise: there was some talk that just the action we'd taken had put the fear on whatever we were trying to guard ourselves against. It would have been nice if that was true.

We walked, most of the time, between about nine at night and one in the morning: that was when the last few who'd been taken had vanished. I was out with a group including one of the merrow babes—I could never tell them apart—and two more leprechauns from my first one's clan, over on the north side of the Liffey, not far from the big "industrial" pubs that have sprung up there, all noise and no atmosphere. As we went past the biggest of them, heading east along the riverbank, we heard something that briefly froze us all. A shriek—

Herself

As a mortal I would have mistaken it for a child's voice. But the People with me knew better. The three of them ran across the Ha'penny Bridge, past startled tourists who felt things jostle them, saw nothing, and (as I passed in their wake) started feeling their pockets to see if they'd been picked. The People sprinted across Crampton Quay in the face of oncoming traffic, just made it past, and ran up the stairs and through the little tunnelway that leads into Temple Bar. And there, just before the alleyway opens out into the Square, when I caught up with them, I saw them staring at the cracked sidewalk, and on it, the empty tumble of clothes.

It was another of the People, but a clurachaun this time, stolen things spilling out of the clothing's pockets—billfolds, change, jewelry, someone's false teeth. But the threadbare tweeds were all shredded to rags as if by razors.

The merrow began to tremble. She pointed into the shadows, between the kebab place next to us, and the back door of the pub down at the corner.

Something green, yes. A green shadow melting out of the courtyard by Temple Street, turning, looking to right and left . . . and when it looked right, it saw us.

The great round eyes were yellow as lamps, and glowed green at their backs with the reflection of the sodium-vapor lights back on the Quay. Humans walked by it and never saw; and it looked through them as if they were the mist curling up off the water of the Liffey, as if they didn't matter. Massive, low-slung and big-shouldered, swag-bellied but nonetheless easily two tons of hard lean muscle, the size of a step van, the big striped cat put its tremendous round plate of a face down, eyeing us, and the whole block filled with the low, thoughtful sound of its growl, like a tank's engine turning over.

It saw the leprechauns. It saw the Washer. It saw me . . . or at least I think it did, as someone who could see the Old Folk and was therefore of interest. It didn't need us, though, for tonight. It had had enough. It gazed yellowly at us for a moment more, then padded leisurely away across Temple Bar Square into the shadows behind the Irish Film Centre—the lighter-colored stripes, livid green like a thunderstorm sunset, fading into grimy city shadow as it went, the darker stripes gone the color of that shadow already, vanishing into it as the lighter ones faded. Only the shape of the slowly lashing tail remained for a moment under the stuttering light of the streetlamp at the corner of the Square . . . then slipped into the dark and was gone.

A horrified, frozen silence followed.

"F *me*," said the leprechaun at last, when he could speak again. "It's the Celtic Tiger . . ."

◆ ◆ ◆

THE OLD PEOPLE MET AGAIN late that night in the Long Hall, after chucking-out time had officially been called and the mortals pushed (or in select cases, thrown) out into the street. The Old Folk, for their own part, pay no attention to licensing laws, having little to fear from them. There's no point staging Garda raids on pubs open past "time" when between the first bang on the door and the forced entry, everybody inside literally vanishes.

Many of the Old Ones were afraid to say the name of what we'd seen. The idiom had become popular in the early nineties, adopted as inward investment boomed and the economy became the fastest-growing in Europe. It had become a favorite phrase and image for Irish people everywhere, a matter of pride, turning up in countless advertisements. But no one had foreseen the side effects, perhaps not even the Old People. They were seeing them now.

"We should hunt down whoever coined the F ing name and make their last hours unpleasant," said one of the Washers.

"Too late for that now," the Eldest Leprechaun said. "The damage is done. Give the thing a name, and it takes shape. They gave a name and a shape to the force that's always hated us. It's everything we're not. It's New Ireland, it's money for money's sake, brown paper envelopes stuffed full of bribes—the turn of mind that says that the old's only good for theme parks, and the new is all there needs to be. It's been getting stronger and stronger all this while. And now that *it's* more important to the people living in the city than we are, it's become physically real. It's started killing us to take our strength from us, and it'll keep killing us and getting bigger and stronger . . . until it's big enough to breed."

A sort of collective shudder went through the room. I shuddered, too, though it was as much from the strangeness of the moment as anything else. There are no female leprechauns, but nonetheless there are always enough younger ones to replace the old who die. Power in Ireland does not run to mortal's rules, either in reproduction or in other ways. If the Folk said the Tiger could make more of itself, it could. And when the food supply ran out in the city, the Tiger's brood would head into the countryside and continue the killing until there were none of the Old Folk left . . . and none of Old Ireland. What remained would be a wealthy country, the fastest-growing economy in Europe, then as now: but spiritually it would be a dead place, something vital gone from it forever.

"I think we all know who we need now," the Oldest Leprechaun said. "We need the one who speaks to the Island in tongues and knows all its secrets—"

A hush fell. "We don't dare!" somebody said from the back of the crowd.

"We *have* to dare," the Eldest said. "We need the one who died but did not die, the one of whom it was prophesied that he would come back to the Island in its darkest moment and save its people. We need Ireland's only superhero!"

A great cheer went up. Everybody piled out the doors of the Long Hall, carrying me with them.

That's how we wound up heading down College Green in an

untidy crowd, around the curve of the old Bank of Ireland and past Trinity College, heading for the river. Across O'Connell Bridge and up O'Connell Street we went, in the dark dead of night, and late-night revelers and petty crooks alike fled before our faces, certain that we were an outflow of Ecstasy-crazed ravers, or something far less savory. Past them all we went, nearly to the foot of the grayly shining needle of the Millennium Spire, and then hung a right into the top of North Earl Street, catty-corner from the GPO . . . and gathered there, six deep and expectant, around the statue of James Joyce.

• • •

DUBLINERS HAVE AN AMBIVALENT RELATIONSHIP, at best, to their landmarks and civic statuary. Whether they love them or hate them, the landmarks are given names that don't necessarily reflect the desires of the sculptors, but certainly sum up the zeitgeist.

The first one to become really famous had been the statue of Molly Malone at the top of Grafton Street. Some well-meaning committee had set there a bronze of the poor girl, representing her wheeling her wheelbarrow through streets broad and narrow; and popular opinion had almost instantaneously renamed this statue The Tart with the Cart. Within weeks, the bright brass shine of the tops of her breasts (as opposed to her more normal patina elsewhere) seemed to confirm as widespread a friend's opinion that Miss Molly was peddling, as one wag delicately put it, "more than just shellfish" around the streets broad and narrow.

The convention swiftly took hold in Dublin, as all things do there that give the finger to propriety. The chimney of a former city distillery, turned into a tourist attraction with an elevator and a glassed-in viewing platform on top, became The Flue with the View. The attempt to put a Millennium Clock into the river had overnight become The Time in the Slime. And the bronze statue around which we now stood, the natty little man in his fedora, standing looking idly across O'Connell Street toward the GPO—the wild-tongued exile himself, the muse of Irish literature in the twentieth century, James Joyce himself had been dubbed The Prick with the Stick.

And so here we stood around him, none of us insensible to what everybody called the statue—and by extension, the man. We'd *all* done it. And now we needed him. Was this going to be a problem?

The Eldest Leprechaun raised his hands in the air before the statue and spoke at length in Gaeilge, an invocation of great power that buzzed in all our bones and made the surrounding paving blocks jitter and plate-glass windows ripple with sine waves: but nothing happened.

Glances were exchanged among those in the gathered crowd. Then one of the Washers at the Ford raised her voice and keened a keen as it was done in the ancient days, though with certain anarchic qualities—a long twelve-tone ululation suggestive of music written in the twenties, before the atonal movement had been discredited.

And nothing happened at all.

The Eldest Leprechaun stood there thinking for a moment. "Working with effigies isn't going to be enough," he said. "It might be for one of us ... but not for him, a mortal. We've got to go to the graveside and raise his ghost itself."

"Where's he buried?" said another leprechaun. "We'll rent a van or something . . ."

"You daft bugger," said another one, "he's not buried here. He was never at home after they banned his books. It was always Trieste or Paris, all these fancy places with faraway names . . ."

Finally, I could contribute something. "Zürich," I said. "It was Zürich. A cemetery above the city . . ."

"We'll go," said the Eldest. "You'll come with us. And one or two others. We'll fly to Zürich tomorrow . . . wake him up, and at the very least get his advice. If we can, we'll bring him back. Until then," the Eldest said, "everyone travel in groups. Stay off the streets at night if you can. We won't be long."

◆　◆　◆

LEPRECHAUNS STILL HAVE SOME ACCESS TO GOLD, or at least to gold cards: we flew out on Swiss at lunchtime the next day, the direct flight to Zürich. That evening, about five, we were on the ground, and nothing would satisfy the Eldest but that we go straight to the grave, immediately.

I'd been in Switzerland once or twice, and I was against it. "I'm not sure you should do that," I said. "The Swiss are very big on not going into places after they're officially closed . . ."

The Eldest gave me a look.

As a result we immediately took the feeder train from the airport to the main station, and the Number 6 tram from the main station tram depot to the Zürichbergstrasse. At Zürichbergstrasse 129 are the gates to Fluntern Cemetery. We got out and found the place locked and apparently deserted behind its high granite walls; but there was a little iron-barred postern gate that was open—or at least, it opened to the Eldest Leprechaun. We went in.

The cemetery is beautifully kept, and we headed around and up several curving pathways, climbing, for the cemetery is built against the slope of the Zürichberg mountain that leans above the city. Finally, we found the spot. Under a stand of trees, in a sort of semicircular bay, were some tasteful plantings, a bronze of Joyce sitting on a rock and admiring the view, a plaque in the ground saying who was buried there, with dates of birth and death, and a stern sign in German, French, and Italian saying WALKING ON THE GRAVE IS FORBIDDEN.

The other leprechauns took off their hats. Once more the Eldest raised his arms and spoke that long, solemn invocation in Irish. All around us, the wind in the aspens and birches fell quiet. And suddenly there were three men standing there; or the ghosts of three men.

One was tall, one was short, and one was of middle height. They were all wearing clothes from the turn of the twentieth-century— loose trousers held up over white shirts with suspenders. They looked at us in some confusion.

"Where is James Joyce?" said the Eldest Leprechaun.

"He's dead," said the shortest of the three.

The Eldest Leprechaun rolled his eyes. "I mean, where is he *now?*"

"He is not here," said the middle-sized figure. "He is risen."

The tallest of them checked his watch. "And being that it's the time that it is," he said, "why would he still be here at all? He's in the pub."

The leprechauns looked at each other.

"We should have known," one of them said.

"Pelikanstrasse?" the Eldest said to the three shadowy figures.

"That's the one."

"Thanking you," said the Eldest, and we went straight back out of the cemetery to catch the tram back down the hill.

At Pelikanstrasse is one of the bigger complexes of one of the bigger Swiss banks. There, in a little plaza by Bahnhofstrasse, you see a number of granite doorways, all leading nowhere; and past them the street curves down into what seems at first a nondescript arc of shop windows and office doorways.

"Those three guys—"

"They're something from *Finnegans Wake*," said the leprechaun who was walking next to me, behind the Eldest. "Three guys always turn up together with the initials H, C, and E. Never got into that one, too obscure, don't ask me for the details. But the pub's in there too, and in *Ulysses* . . ."

He told me how once upon a time, the bar had been the Antique Bar in the first Jury's Hotel, in Dame Street. There, at a corner table, a little man in round-framed glasses and a slouch hat could often have been seen sitting in front of a red wine and a gorgonzola sandwich, when he could afford them, relaxing in the dim pub-misted afternoon sunlight, while other languages, other universes, roiled and teemed in his brain.

"But someone had a brain seizure," the leprechaun said. "Jury's sold off their old property in Dame Street and arranged to have the hotel knocked down. Urban renewal, progress, all that shite. They wanted the money for the land: that was all. And, they said to themselves, we'll auction off the innards and get a few extra bob for it. If not, we'll just throw it all in the tip, and in any case we'll build a much better bar somewhere else, in a nice new hotel, all covered with lovely Formica." The leprechaun grimaced. "But then along came, would you believe it, the head of the Swiss security services. He was afraid the Russians would invade his country, and he was looking for a safe house in Ireland where the Swiss government could hide if that happened. And wouldn't you know he was a Joyce fan. He found out about Jury's auctioning off the bar, and he got one of the big Swiss banks and some people from the government to buy the whole thing. And then the Swiss came along and took it to bits and numbered every piece, and put it back together in Zürich, and here it is."

The leprechaun lowered his head conspiratorially toward mine.

"The Swiss," he whispered, "are Celts, do you know."

I nodded. "The Helvetii," I said after few moments. "They made cheese. It's in the *Gallic Wars*."

"And why wouldn't they have," the leprechaun said with relish, "seeing that the furious and bloody Queen Maeve herself was killed by being slung at and hit in the forehead by her stepson with a great lump of the Irish version of Parmesan."

Herself

He fell silent.

"Or it might have been Regato," he added.

We came to the door of the bar—a simple wooden door, nothing exciting about it—pulled it open, and went in.

An Irish country-house chef I know once described Zürich to me, under his breath, as "a kick-ass party town." And so it is. It has many sleek, slinky bars, jumping with the sound of the moment, well hidden from the tourists whom such relentless buzz would confuse. But here, in that busy and congenial city, is something completely different—a corner that is forever Ireland. Here Irish-strength cigarette and cigar smoke tangles (ever so briefly) under the lights before being sucked away by the relentlessly efficient Swiss ventilation system. Here voices converse at Irish volume levels, nearly enough to curl the turbine fans on a Concorde. Here Irish craic (if there is such a word) seeps out of the teak-paneled, glinting, polished walls.

And here we found Joyce. He was dead, but he didn't mind, for he was in his local.

He sat at the back corner table, by himself; amazing that the rest of the place was practically pullulating with people, but this one island of quiet remained. His hat sat on the red leather banquette next to him, his cane leaned against the table, and a glass of red wine sat on the table before him. He looked very much the dapper young man of a statelier time . . . though there was something else about him, something in his eyes, that brought the hair up on the back of my neck. It was more than just being dead.

Respectfully we approached him, and the Eldest Leprechaun stood by Joyce's table. "Mr. Joyce," he said, "you're needed."

You would have wondered, if you'd been watching Joyce's eyes earlier, whether he was quite in this time and place, or wandering in mind or spirit to some other time, the twenties or thirties perhaps. Now, though, those eyes snapped into the here and now.

The Eldest Leprechaun spoke to Joyce, quietly and at some length, in Irish. While he did, the narrow, wise little eyes rested on each of us in turn, very briefly. And when he spoke, he sounded annoyed.

"Well, this is tiresome," Joyce said.

Everyone who had the sense to do so, cringed. I didn't. Later I found out that "tiresome" was as close as Joyce ever got to saying F.

"What can be done, sir?" said the Eldest Leprechaun.

Joyce looked thoughtful for a moment. "There is only one hope," he said. "We must conjure the river."

The Eldest Leprechaun blanched.

"We must raise up Anna Livia," Joyce said, "the Goddess of the Liffey, and put your case to Her. Only She can save your people now. She may refuse. She is Herself, and has Her own priorities. But I think She will be kindly disposed toward you. And if anyone can raise Her for you, I can. She and I . . . we were an Item." And his eyes glinted.

"You'll come back with us tomorrow, then?"

"First thing," Joyce said.

•   ◆   •

*A*ND SO IT CAME TO PASS. I have no idea how one handles airline ticketing for dead people these days, but he was right there with us in business class the next morning, Saturday morning—critiquing the Swiss wines on board and flirting with the flight attendants. Two hours later, just in time for lunch, we were home.

A minivan-cab took us back to town. "Bloomsday early this year, is it?" said the cab driver to Joyce.

Joyce smiled thinly and didn't answer. On June 16 of every year the city was full of counterfeit Joyces. "There was a statue of Anna Livia in town, wasn't there?" he said.

"Oh, the Floozie in the Jacuzzi," the driver said. "They moved it."

Herself

"Where is it now?"

"North Quay."

"Then that's where we're going, my good man."

He took us there. We paid him off, and after he'd left, Joyce went over to the statue and looked at it rather sadly.

It had always resembled a dissolute, weedy-haired woman in a concrete bathtub at the best of times, when it had been installed in the middle of O'Connell Street and running with the music of flowing water. Now, though, sitting dusty, high and dry on wooden pallets in the middle of the stones of an unfinished memorial plaza, surrounded by marine cranes and dingy warehouses, the statue just looked ugly.

Joyce looked at it and frowned. "Well, we have no choice," Joyce said. "For this we need the concrete as well as the abstract."

He walked over to the waterside. The Eldest Leprechaun went with him. Joyce took off his hat and handed it to the leprechaun. Then he stood straight, his cane in one hand, and suddenly was all magician . . .

"O tell me all about Anna Livia," he said in that thin, singing little tenor voice: and though he didn't raise that voice at all, the sound hit the warehouses and the freighters and the superstructure of the East-link Bridge half a mile away, and ricocheted and rattled from building to building until the water itself started to shake with it, rippling as if from an earth tremor underneath. "I want to hear all about Anna Livia. Tell me all. Tell me now. You'll die when you hear—"

The water inside the river walls leapt and beat against the banks, soaking us all. I began to wonder if we *would* die: I hadn't seen the river like this since the last hurricane. Joyce spoke on, and the wind rose, and the stones under our feet shook. "Then, then, as soon as the lump his back was turned, with her mealiebag slung over her shoulder, Anna Livia, oysterface, *forth of her bassein came—!*"

"*I hear, I wake,*" said a tremendous voice in response. If you've once heard it, you will never forget it; Liffey in spate, a thunder, a roar between Her banks, lightning trapped in the water, a green-and-white resistless fury pushing everything before Her into the Bay.

She rose up. Those who had the sense to do so, covered their eyes. The rest of us were immediately showered with sodden sneakers, slime-laden Coke cans, ancient tattered plastic Quinnsworth bags, and much other, far less printable detritus of urban Dublin existence. She towered up, towered over us. She was water, water in the shape of a woman: Her hair streamed with water, streamed down and became part of Her again; Her gown was water, and the water glowed. She looked up Her river, and down Her river, and said; "Where am I?"

There was a profound silence all around that had nothing to do with the awe and majesty of Herself.

"Where am I?" said Anna Livia again, in a tone of voice that suggested someone had better F ing tell Her.

One lone voice that raised itself, unafraid, over the dead stillness.

"North Quay," Joyce said.

There was a long, long pause.

"North Quay?" said the gracious Goddess, looking around Her. "What the F am I doin' here? I was in O'Connell Street last time I looked out this ugly thing's eyes, with wee babies playin' in me in the hot weather! When we had it, which was not often. Remind me to destroy Met Eireann when I have a moment to rub together. F ing global warming, *I* know who's responsible, them and their peat-burning power stations, and all these F ing SUVs."

And then She peered down. "Can that be you?" She said in an accent more of the Gaiety Theatre than anything else. "Jimmy, you son of a bitch, my love, my great and only love, what the F are you doing here? You were at peace this long while, I thought, after they put you in the ground far from home, thanks to that F ing deValera—"

She went on for some minutes, splendidly, but ran down at last. "You didn't wake me up for nothing, James my love," She said at last.

"What's to do?"

"There is a tiger eating our people," Joyce said. "A Celtic one. It preys on the Old Ones and tries to kill Old Ireland—"

She was looking around Her at the skyline. Not much had changed in terms of tall buildings—the Irish don't approve of skyscrapers—but much, much else was different, and we were all watching Her face with varying degrees of nervousness.

"Sure I can smell it," She said. "Nasty tomcat stink, they'll always be spraying all over everything. Marking their territory. *Their* territory indeed!"

For a long moment more She stood there, head raised against the blue-milk sky, sniffing the air. "Lady," the Eldest Leprechaun said, "it only comes out at night—"

"It lies up by day," She said. "Aye, can't I just smell it. Hiding won't help it today. Come on—"

Anna Livia strode on down the river, slowly, looking from side to side at Her city, while we pursued Her on land as best we could. She was looking increasingly annoyed as She went. Maybe it was the traffic on the Quays, or the pollution, or the new one-way system, which drove everybody insane: or maybe it was some of the newer architecture. One glance She gave the Millennium Spire, erected at last three years late. That glance worried me—Dubliners are sufficiently divided on the Spire that they haven't yet decided which rude name is best for it—but Anna Livia then turned Her attention elsewhere, looking over the intervening rooftops, southward. Four or five blocks inland stood the International Financial Services Centre, next to one of the city's two main train stations. It was an ugly building, a green-glass-and-white-marble chimera, dwarfing everything around it—a monument to money, built during the height of the Tiger time.

"Yes," She said softly, "there it is, I'll be bound. Kitty, kitty, kitty!"

She came up out of the river, then, and started to head crosstown. What other Unsighted mortals were able to make of the sudden flood that leapt up out of the Liffey, I don't know: but the water got into the underground wiring and immediately made the traffic lights go on the blink, bringing traffic on the Quays to a halt. *Maybe it's a blessing*, I thought, as I ran after the others, trying to keep out of the flood of water that followed the colossal shape up out of the river.

Anna Livia came up to the IFSC and looked it over, peering in through the windows. Then She stood up straight.

"Gods bless all here save the cat!" she said in a voice of thunder.

At the sound of Her raised voice, glass exploded out of the IFSC in every possible direction, as if Spielberg had come back to town and said, "Buy all the sugar glass on Earth, and trash it." From the spraying, glittering chaos, at least one clandestine billionaire plunged in a shrieking, flailing trajectory toward the parking lot of Tara Street Station, missed, and made a most terminal sound on impact: apparently blessings weren't enough. He was followed by his chef, who had fallen on hard times (only recently acquitted of stealing a Titian from his signature restaurant's host hotel) and now fell on something much harder, ruining the no-claims bonuses of numerous Mercedes and BMW sedans parked below.

And in their wake, something else came out—growling, not that low, pleased growl we'd heard the other night, but something far more threatened, and more threatening.

Through the wall, or one of the openings left by the broken glass, out it came. It slunk, at first, and it looked up at Herself, and snarled and showed its teeth. But there was going to be no contest. Anna Livia was the height of the Customs House dome, and Her proportions to the Celtic Tiger's proportions were those of an angry housewife to that of an alley cat.

It did all it could do, as She bent down and reached for it. It ran. Crushing cars, knocking mortals aside, it ran to get as far inland as it could. It got as far as St. Stephen's Green, and dived into the Square, through the trees, and out of sight.

From way behind, I cursed when I saw it do that. By the time we caught up with the Tiger, it would be out the other side of the Green and into Dublin 2 somewhere—

I looked over at the Eldest Leprechaun, then back to see where Anna Livia had gone. She was briefly out of sight, a block or so over now. "Come on," he said, "the Green—"

We went there—it was all we could do. When we got to St. Stephen's Green, all surrounded by its trees, there was no sound of further disturbance anywhere else. "It's still in here—" I said. We looked through the archway at the bottom of Grafton Street and could see nothing but the little lake inside, placid water, and some slightly startled-looking swans.

"Now what?" I said under my breath.

The Eldest Leprechaun gestured. I looked where he pointed. At the top of Grafton Street, by Trinity College, Anna Livia had taken a stand.

She ventured no farther south. She simply raised Her hands and began speaking in Irish. And as we looked back through the archway into the Green, down toward the lake, we saw something starting to happen: water rising again—

"The swans . . . !" the Eldest Leprechaun said.

It wasn't the regular swans he meant. These were crowding back and away from the center of the lake as fast as they could. The shapes rising from the water now were swans as well, but more silver than the normal ones, and far, far bigger. They reached their necks up; they trumpeted; they leapt out of the water, into the greenery, out of sight.

A roar of pain and rage went up, and the Celtic Tiger broke cover and ran up out of St. Stephen's Green into Grafton Street, down the red bricks, in full flight, with the Children of Lir coming after him fast. It may not sound like much, five swans against a tiger: but one swan by itself is equal to an armed knight on horseback if it knows what it's doing. Five swans fighting, choreographed, in unison, are a battalion. In a city street lined with chain stores, and with plate glass everywhere, when you hear the whooping whooshing uncanny sound of swan wings coming after you, you think: *Where can I hide?* But five giant swans who are also four pissed-off Irish princes, and their sister, worth all the rest of them put together . . . if you were a tiger with any sense, you'd leave the country.

This one didn't have quite that much sense. Maybe it was bloated with its own sense of its power—for hadn't it had its way all this while? It turned, roaring with fury, and leapt back down the street toward its pursuers—

A swan's wing caught it full across the face. The Tiger shied back like a horse struck with a whip across the eyes, then was battered by more wings, merciless. The Tiger turned and ran again, back the way it had been going first, around the curve in Grafton Street, with the Children in hot pursuit . . . and ran, in turn, right into Anna Livia.

She reached down and picked it up, yowling and howling, like a woman picking up a badly behaved housecat. Herself turned and walked past Trinity, the flood that had been following Her carefully containing itself, and She made her way north toward O'Connell Bridge, the waters roaring, the Tiger roaring, the horns of frustrated drivers honking all up and down the Quays as She went. *What are they seeing?* I wondered, as in company with the leprechauns I followed Herself as best I could. I had a feeling that the next day there would be stories in the *Irish Times* about flash floods, water main breaks, anything but the truth.

The truth was mind-bending enough, though, as we looked at the River Herself standing on O'Connell Bridge and looking north up the street.

"Yes," She said, and Her voice rumbled against the buildings. "Yes, that'll do nicely—"

In Her hands, as She walked up O'Connell Street, the Tiger writhed and splashed and yowled desperately to get away. But there was no escape. Slowly it was borne up the street, shoulder high to Herself, spitting and clawing in terror, until She stood right across from the GPO, just in front of the Millennium Spire. Slowly She lifted the Tiger up over Her head.

"So you would kill Old Ireland?" Anna Livia said. "You would kill yourself, for without Old Ireland, you wouldn't be. And as we brought you about . . ."

In one hard gesture She brought the Tiger down.

"So we can end you," She said, "or the badness in you . . . if we have the sense."

She turned and made Her way back to O'Connell Bridge. Traffic was in an uproar, and Gardai were rushing in every direction. No one noticed a guy and a few leprechauns and a little slender man in turn-of-the-century clothes standing there by the water, watching the huge woman's shape that eased down into it again . . . if they saw that last at all.

"Not dead yet, boys," She said, as She subsided gently into the water; "not dead yet." She threw a last loving glance at Joyce.

He took his hat back from the Eldest Leprechaun and tipped it to Herself.

The waters closed over Her again. Joyce, or his ghost, vanished as She did. Overhead, we glanced up at the sound of swans' wings, heavy and dangerous, beating their way down the air over the river.

And then I looked back over my shoulder, north up O'Connell Street, and had to grin. There, at the top of the Spire, impaled like a limp hors d'oeuvre on a cocktail stick, and not burning at *all* bright—hung something green.

Speir-Bhan

BY TANITH LEE

This I offer to the memory of my mother,
my unmet grandfather and great-grandfather—who never,
so far as I ever heard, reneged on any bargain.

I

This story, if that's what it is, is written in two voices. Both are mine. My blood is mixed, fire with water, earth with air.

⋄ ⋄ ⋄

I WAS NEVER in Ireland, though from there I came.

The answer to this riddle is simple enough. I am mostly Irish, genetically and in my blood, but was born in another country.

My mother it was who had the Irish strand. Her eyes were dark green—I have never seen elsewhere eyes so dark and so green, save sometimes now, with those who wear colored contact lenses.

She it was who told me of that land where, too, she'd never gone.

O'Moore was her maiden name. She said the weather there was "soft"—which meant it rained, but a rain so fine and often warm, a sort of mist, accustomed as the air. They came from the Ghost Coast, the O'Moores of my mother's tribe, the haunted west of Ireland, where the rocks steep into the sea, harder than hearts. My mother's father had a Spanish name, Ricardo. She used to speak of him lovingly. *His* father, her grandfather, was a gallant man called Colum. He lived to be over a hundred, and died in his hundred and first year from a chill, caught while escorting his new wife, a young lady of forty-five, to the theatre in Dublin. Ah the soft weather then wasn't always kind.

Ireland is the land of green—emerald as her eyes, my mother. She has gone now, to other greener golden lands under the hollow hills. But one day, searching through her things some years after her death, I found my great-grandfather Colum's book. It wasn't any diary, or perhaps it was. It seemed the book of a practical man who is a poet, and cares for a drink, the book of a canny liar who will tell stories, or it is the book of one who speaks the truth. All of which, with arrogant pride and some reticence, I might say also of myself, saving the book and my gender.

There arrived a night when, having found his book, I met my great-grandfather Colum, for the first, in a dream. He was a tall, thin man, who seemed in his sixties, so probably he was about eighty, for at ninety-nine I had heard, he had looked ten years his younger.

"So you found it then," he said.

"So I did."

"Where was that?"

"In a box that had my mother's letters and some of *her* mother's things."

"Tucked up among the girls," he said. "Why should I complain."

I didn't mention my grandmother's fox-fur cape, also in the box—I had been afraid of this cape when a child, and last week, locating it again, had sent it to a charity.

In the dream, Colum told me of his house that was of stone, and had a narrow stone stair. The windows looked across the valley to the sea, where the sun went down at night. It was not the Dublin big house of later years, this, but where he had been a boy.

In the dream, we walked, he and I, through that valley of velvet green. We climbed up inside the house and watched the sunset. Birds cooed, settling on the roof, and in the yard was an old well, full of good water.

Nearby—that was, maybe, seven miles along the shore—stood ruinous and supernatural Castle *Seanaibh*, or Castle Sanvy as the tourist guide has it.

In his book, Colum says that he was there all one night. In the dream he told me that, too.

We drank whisky, the color of two garnets in amber, and the red sun set, and a magpie flew over the stone house in the valley, chattering its advice.

But all this I dreamed had been written in Colum's book anyway. Along with a story, between two lists of things, one of which is a list of fish caught from a boat, and the second a list of likely girls he had seen in town.

◆　◆　◆

In those days, Colum was twenty, tall and slender and strong, with hair that was black, and eyes that were grey, with the smoky ring around the iris no one, who does not have it—they say—can ever resist.

He worked at a desk in the family business, which was to do with leather goods, nor did he like it much, but it left him time and gave him money to go to the dances, and once a week to drink until he could call to stars, and they would fly down like bees. It was on a night just like that, having danced for five hours and drunk for two, that Colum set off along the road to get home. It was about a mile along that road, to the house. On either side the land ran up and down, and trees stood waning in the last wealth of their summer leaves. The full moon was coming up from her own boozy party, fat and flushed and not quite herself. So Colum sang to her as he walked, but she only pulled a cloud across her face, petulant thing. Oh, there were girls like that, too.

A quarter way along the road, Colum stopped.

It felt, he said, as if he had never been on that road, not once, in all his days, when in fact he had traveled it twice a week for many years, and often more than twice. Since he was an infant he had known it, carried along it even, in his mother's belly.

Boulders lay at the roadside, pale, like sheep that dozed. That night he felt he had never seen one of them, though he had carved his name in several.

It was not, he reckoned, a special night, not a night sacred to any saint that he could think of, or to any fey thing, not Samhain, nor Lug's night either. He stood and blamed the pub whisky, or the fiddler in the hall, for the way the road had altered.

And then there they were. Those Others.

He said, in the dream, "It wasn't like the magical effects they do now, with their computer-machines for the films." He said, one minute there was just the empty road under the cloudy moon, and then there was something, as if vapor had got into your face. And then you saw them.

They were of all kinds. Tall as a tall man, or a tall house, or little as a rabbit, or a pin. They trotted along the road, or walked, or pranced, or rolled. There were horses, with flying manes, but they were not horses, you could see that plainly enough; they had human eyes, and human feet.

None of them had any colors to them, though they looked solid. They were like the stones at the roadside, only they moved, and all of them in front of him, and none of them looking back.

Another man would have dropped down by the boulders. Another again would have run off back to the dance hall and the public house.

Colum fell in behind the travelers, at a mild, respectful distance.

He had learned two things in his young life. First, he could not always get or have everything he would like. Second, he could have and get quite a lot.

He thought anyway, none of *them* would turn to see him. They were the Royal Folk, some band of them, and what they were doing out he didn't know, for they had no business to be. He was not afraid. As he told me, if he had danced and drunk less, he might have been— but that was to come.

So he followed them up the road, and soon enough it turned in at a wood. There was no similar wood in the area that he recalled. The trees were great in girth, and thick and rich with leaves, and moon-washed. The road was now a track. They and he ambled along, and presently the track curved, as the road never had, and then they were climbing up and up, and where the tree line broke, Colum saw the fish-silver ocean fluting down below. They must all have covered seven miles by then, and done it in record time, for next up ahead he beheld the castle called Sanvy. But it was not a ruin that night, it was whole and huge, and pierced with golden lights like spears.

It was haunted, naturally, this castle. Every castle, crag, cot, and byre is haunted, it seems, along the Ghost Coast of Ireland. So Colum thought it was the ghosts who had tidied up and lit all the lamps, and he waited for some coach with headless horses, or running fellow with hell's fire all over him, to come pelting down the track. But instead there came a walking woman, with a burning taper held high in her hand.

Ah, she was lovely. Slim and white, but *colored in*, not like the others, for her hair, which was yards long, was like combed barley, with stars in it and her eyes, he said, like the gas flame, blue and saffron together.

She let the Host pass her, bowing to some, and some in turn nodded to her. Then, when they had gone by and on toward the castle gate, her gas-flame eyes alighted on Colum.

Colum, well he bowed to the ground. He was limber enough and drunk enough to manage it.

She watched him. Then she spoke.

"Do you know me, Colum?"

"No, fair miss. But I see you know me."

"I've known you, Colum, since you were in your cradle, kicking up your feet and sicking up your milk."

Colum frowned. You did not like a pretty girl to remind you of that sort of thing.

But at his frowning, she laughed.

She came down the track and touched him on the neck. When she did so, it was the coldest—or hottest—as ice will burn and fire seem icy—touch he had ever felt. He paused, wondering if she'd killed him, but after a moment, he felt a strange sensation in his neck.

"It was as if an eye opened up there—as if something looked out of me, out of my throat."

After that, he found he could speak to the woman on the track in another language, that he had never known, though perhaps he might dimly have heard it sometimes, among the tangle of the hills and valleys.

"What night is this, fair miss," he said, "when the Folk are on the road?"

"Your night, Colum," she said.

Then she turned and moved back toward the castle of *Seanaibh-Sanvy*. And he realized, in that instant, what and who she was. She was a Speir-Bhan, his muse. So he ran after her as fast as he could. But, just before he raced in at the gate, he threw a coin away down the rocks into the sea, for luck, and since no others were left now save that water, and the moon, to watch his back.

Then he was in the gate, across a wide yard, and up among the lights.

◆　◆　◆

WELL, HE WROTE this in his book—wrote it in years later, obviously, in another ink. It says: "I have seen a motion picture in color. An American gentleman showed me. It was like that, when I went in there."

He said, coming in from the yard to the castle's hall, it was as if a rainbow had exploded, and the sun come up out of the night without warning.

If there were a hundred candles burning, there were a thousand, nor did they resemble any candles he had ever seen before, but were stout, and tall like a child of three years. In color they were like lemon curd. And behind, torches blazed on the walls, and showed tapestries hanging down, scarlet, blue, and green, and thick with gold. The Royal Folk had taken on color too. He could see the milk-whiteness of their skins and the berry-red of their women's lips, and how their hair shone like gold or copper. Their clothes were the green of water or the purple of lilac, as the trees are, half of them, they say, in the Lands beneath the hills. But that was not all, for all around, in the body of the castle, which had suddenly gone back in time and back to life, sat the human persons who had once dwelled there, kings and princes from countless centuries, in their finest finery. And the fey horses with human feet walked couthly up and down, white as snow, with silver manes, and the tiny little creatures bounced and rang against the walls like bells, and white dogs with crimson eyes and collars of gold lay still as statues. Yet one thing now was all the same with them. Every eye in that great place was fixed on Colum.

Colum was a handsome man, and used quite often to being made much of. He was accustomed to going into a room, or a dance hall, to a crowd of eyes that turned and whispers behind hands.

But never from such as these.

He turned to stone himself, stood there growing sober as a pain.

However, she, his Speir-Bhan, she turned and took both his hands in her cold-fire fingers.

"Now, Colum, it's your night. Haven't I told you. What is that you're carrying?"

And looking down, Colum saw that now in his left hand, which she no longer held, was a small curved harp of smoothest brown wood, with silver pegs and strings the light had gilded.

"Fair miss," said Colum, "if I'm here as the harper, you'd better know, I can play 'Chopsticks' on my granny's piano, and that's the sum of my parts."

But she only shook her head. And by then, somehow, they had got to the centre of the room.

Directly before Colum on four great chairs knuckled with gold, sat two kings and two queens. No mistaking them, their heads were crowned. "I have never known enough of the history to describe those clothes they wore," said Colum, "but I thought they were from the far-off past, before even the castle had come up there out of the rock. And one of the queens, too, she that had the creamy golden hair falling down to her little white shoes, I think she was not only earthly royal, but of the Royal Folk, too."

"Well, Colum," said the king to the right, "will you be after playing us anything, then?"

Colum swallowed.

Then he found his hands—the hands the Speir-Bhan had held—had each opened, like his neck, an eye—not visible, but to be felt. And he put both hands on the harp and a rill of music burst glittering into the many-colored room, and everywhere around was silence, as *they* listened.

This was the song that Colum sang, written as it is in his book:

Woman veiled with hair, shaming the gold of princes,
In your sun-bright tresses dwells
A flock of sun-bright cuckoos,
That will madden with jealous unease
Any man yearning to possess you.
So long and fair your streaming crown,
It is a golden ring,
And your face set in there like a pearl,
And your eyes like sapphires from a lake.
This is your finest jewelry,
These yellowest ringlets,
Which have caught me now in their chains,
Shackled, your thrall indeed.
No wonder then the cuckoo
Winters in the Underlands,
To sleep in the heaven
Of your veil of hair.

Colum struck the last chord. The silence stayed like deafness. And in the quiet, he heard over in his mind what he had sung—the musicality of his voice and art of his own playing—and the unwiseness of his words that none could doubt he had addressed to a woman of Faerie, sitting by her lord.

Now is the time, thought Colum, *to take my leave.*

He had forgotten the right of harpers to praise the beauty of any woman, royal or not.

Then the applause came, hands that smote on tables, feet that stamped, and voices that called. He saw the Royal Ones were amused, not angry.

The king to the left got up. His tunic was the red of blood, and his cloak was made of gold squares stitched by scarlet thread to yellow. He was, Colum thought, a human king, and from long, long ago.

"You are the one to do it, Colum," said this king, "as heroes have before you."

Colum, who had blushed with relief, and pride, changed over again in his mood.

"What would that be, that you want doing by me, your honor?"

"Why, that you rid the land of the threefold bane that's on it. For only through a song can it be done."

Colum gazed round wildly.

The Speir-Bhan poised at his elbow, cool as Sunday lettuce.

"What do I say now?" he asked her. "Tell me, quick."

"Say yes."

Colum cleared his throat. She was his muse, but he knew some of the old tales, in one of which he seemed presently to be snared. A "bane" could only be something bad, some fiendly thing, and it was "threefold" as well. And he was to tackle it?

Before he could speak, either way, the noise in the hall, which was still coming and going like waves, died again in an instant. The hall doors shot open, and in trudged a group of men, and they too were patched in bloodred, but now it was not any dye, and it was wet.

"They are out again," cried one.

Another shouted, "My wife they have killed! My lovely wife, and my child in her body!"

"And my living son!" cried another.

Then all the group roared out examples of death, even of whole villages laid waste, doors and roofs torn away, and babies dragged out on the track, rent and devoured.

"No pity, they have none."

Shadow fell in the gleaming hall of *Seanaibh*. The candles faded. Colum stood in the dimness, and the fey woman he had sung to, she with the hair of golden shackles, she stood there before him, one last torch that blazed.

"Those they speak of are three uncanny women, Colum, that with every full moon become three black foxes, each large as a boar. They roam the hills and do as you have heard, killing and eating humankind. The one geas on them they must obey, makes them love the music and song. If any goes where they are that has great skill in these things, he will live. Oh, warriors have gone out against them, with swords, and been brought home in joints, what was left. But you are the harper. Once they were slain before, in this way, this *sort* of way. Listen, Colum, if you will do this, I will gift you a sip of Immortality from under the hills. You shall live a happy hundred full years in the world of men, and die soft and peaceful in your bed."

◆　◆　◆

It was at this point in my great-grandfather's story that I had to turn a page of his book. What should I find on the other side, but this:

"I woke at the roadside in the dusk before the dawn. My head was sore and the road looked as you would expect. So I knew I had dreamed it."

And then; "Next week, in the town, I noted a very taking girl. Her name is Mairi O'Connell."

There follows the list of young women I mentioned before.

◆　◆　◆

When I read this, over the page, I thought at first other pages had been torn out. But there was no evidence of that.

Then I thought, *Well, he spun his tale but had no idea of how to go on with it. So he leaves it in this unsatisfying way—as if someone had set a rare old meal in front of you, with meat and fruit and cakes and cream, tea in the pot, wine in the glass, and a little something stronger on the side, but as you pull up your chair, the feast is carried off, a door closes on it, and there you are, hungry and thirsty, the wrong side.*

Madly I thought, *If it was a dream, still he did it.*

For she promised him a hundred years of life, and he wrote of

that in the faded ink of his youth, as of the promise of a soft death—
and both of them he had.

Then, that night when I had my own dream that I met Colum in
Ireland, in the stone house, he told me this, the very matters that
should have been there on the following pages.

He said, once the fey woman had spoken, the castle faded like its
light, and all the people with it, human and un, and there instead he
was, on the savage hills that ran behind the cliff. The moon had put
off her handkerchief, and was round, and pale as a dollar.

Up from the ancient woods of oak and thorn there ran three
shapes, which cast their shadows before them.

He thought them dogs, then wolves, then giant cats. Then he saw
they were three black foxes, black as the night, with white tips to their
tails and eyes that smoked like sulfur.

And he struck the harp in a panic, and all that would come out of
it was a scream, the very one you can hear a fox give out in the country on a frosty autumn night, the cry that makes the hair stand up on
your head.

No one else was there with Colum. His muse, he noted, had
deserted him, as sometimes, in the worst extremity, they do.

It seemed to him that after all the royal lord in the castle had sent
him here to punish him for his impertinent song, and Goldehair herself, she had been glad enough to see him off. And all the while, those
three black, long-furred *things* ran nearer and nearer up the hill, and
they screeched as the harp had done, a cry like the Devil himself, and
Colum's hands were made of wood, and his throat shut.

"It was plain fear woke me up," he said, as we drank the
dreamwhisky in his house, "So I believe. I could no more have stayed
there in that mystic horror—be it sleep or truth—than held myself
down in a pool to drown."

"Yet," I said, "she gave you your hundred years."

"I'll tell you," he said, "I was no harper, no poet. Speir-Bhan though that one was, she went to the wrong fellow, so she did. And for that, I think, they let me wake, and gave me a present for my trouble. But you," he added to me, "now you have the means."

"What means?" I said.

"Is it not," said Colum, sad and resigned, "that you can play and sing a little?"

I scoffed. I said, pointedly, "But the Speir-Bhan is the muse of *male* poets and bards. And all the heroes are men."

"There is Maeve," said my great-grandfather, "riding on her raids in her chariot. There is the nun, Cair, who sang like the angels on her isle."

In *my* dream, the magpie was on the roof again. I heard what it said now. "Give it up! Give it up!"

So giving up, as Colum did, I woke.

◆   ◆   ◆

THE FLAT IS IN BRANCH ROAD, ten minutes walk from the last stop of the underground train at Russell Park Station.

I work in English London four days a week, a dull job to do with filing papers, making and taking calls, and preparing coffee for my betters. It pays enough to keep the flat, and leaves me free on Thursday night till Monday morning. Those between-times then, I go to play in the clubs and pubs—by which I mean play music. It isn't a harp I carry, but my guitar, shiny brown as a new-baked bun. The name I use for myself on these occasions, is Neeve, which should be spelled *Niamh,* nor is it my given name. But there we are.

This life of mine is curious. It feels like a stopgap, a bridge. As if one day something will change. But I've passed my thirty-ninth birthday, and nothing has, so perhaps it never will.

It was Thursday night, and I was coming home on the tube from

London, deep in the hollow underground that catacombs below all the city and half its suburbs.

I was sitting there with my bag of groceries, reading my paper and thinking how the world was going to hell in a hurry, just as it always has been, since the Year 0. Then the lights flickered, as they do, and there in the tunnel, also as they do, the train halted. As I say, that happens. There was a small crowd left on the train, for we were still five stops from the end of the line. The visiting tourists take a stalling tube in their stride, used to the efficiencies of the New York subway and the Paris Metro, but we locals look about, uneasy, distrusting what is indigenously ours.

After a moment, the train started up again with a cranking hiss. That was when the old woman came staggering between the seats and sat herself down beside me. I thought she was drunk, she smelled of liquor, I thought. I have some sympathy. In my bag there waited for me, with the bread, cheese, and fruit, a green bottle of gin. On the other hand, when she turned her face to me and spoke, I deeply regretted she was there, let alone *drunk* and there, and myself her chosen victim.

"It's cleaner they are now, the filthy worms."

I smiled, and turned away.

Insistently the old woman put her claws on my arm. "The trains it is, I'm meaning. Like worms, like snakes, running through the bowels of the earth. Look there, a paper on the ground—" And leaning over she scooped it up. It was the wrapper from a chocolate bar. She read the logo ponderingly, "Mars," she breathed. Not for the first, I confess, I, too, considered the notion of a chocolate named for a planet or god of war. A delicious smell rose from the wrapper—but died in the wall of alcohol that hung about the old woman and now me. Everyone else, of course, stayed deep in their books, papers, thoughts. They weren't going to see the old woman. She was my problem.

For a moment I wondered where she had come from. Had she been on the tube all this while, and just got up and come staggering along to me on a whim? She spoke in the musical lilt of the green land, but I do not, for I'm only an Irish Londoner.

Then off she goes again.

"What's there in your bag? Is it of use? Sure, it looks nice to me. A rosy apple and a bottle of green glass. Well, we'll be dancing, then."

We?

I read my paper, the same paragraph, over and over. And she kept up her monologue. It was all about me, and the bottle, and what the train was like, and how it was a snake, and that *we* would soon be home, so we would.

Well, I thought of calling the police on my mobile when I stepped off the train at Russell Park, and she came lurching off with me, clutching my free arm to steady herself. Should I ease away? Should I push her, shout at her—or for help? No. Nobody would pay attention, besides she was a poor old inebriated woman, in quite a good, clean, well-made, long coat, and boots of battered leather. And her long grey hair was a marvel, thick as wool and hanging to her waist; and if it was all knotted and tangled, no surprise, she would need to groom such a mane every day, like a Persian cat, to keep it tidy, and obviously she'd had other things on her mind.

Before I could think, we were on the escalator, riding up toward the street, and her still on my arm as if we were close friends, going to the cinema in 1947.

Embarrassed, I looked around and noticed two or three Goth girls were on the escalator behind us. They had the ferocious, look-at-me beauty of the very young, all in their black, and liquid ink of hair. They wore sunglasses, too, the blackest kind—all the better not to see us with. I only gave them a glance, relieved really they'd have no interest in me or my companion.

"Where is it you need to get to?" I asked her, politely, as we arrived in the ticket-hall.

"Here I am," she said.

"No, I mean which station do you need? Or is it a particular road here you want?"

"Branch Road," said she, in a stinging puff of whisky.

Oh my Lord, I thought, oh my Lord.

But it wasn't until I went through the mechanical barrier with my ticket, and she somehow slipped through *exactly* with me, which is impossible, emerging the other side—not till then that I began to see. But *even* then, I didn't. I just concluded she was criminally adept, though drunk as a barrel.

So out we go on the street. And the dusty summer traffic roars by, and she clicks her tongue in fascinated disapproval.

"Well, now," she says, "well, now, *cailín*, let's be going where we're to go."

Then she winked. Her eyes were blue, but as she closed one in the wink, they gave off a flash of daffodil yellow. So then, I had to know, didn't I. It was only seven days before, mind you, I had found and read Colum's book and talked to him in my dream.

◆   ◆   ◆

Outside the flat, the trees in the street were a green bloomed by dust and pollution, but they filled the front windows like flags of jade. All was as I had left it, messy, cleaned four weeks ago and not since, the washing machine full of washed and dried washing, the cupboards fairly bare.

I put my bag down and watched the Speir-Bhan as she pottered around, peering into this and that, craning into the tiny bathroom, lifting the lid of a pan of baked beans left on the stove. When she managed to undo the washing machine and most of the load fell out on the floor, I made no move. I couldn't have kept her out of the flat. I couldn't stop her now.

"What do you want?"

I knew. But there.

She was at the fridge by then, cooling herself with sticking her head, tortoiselike, forward in among the salad.

"Well now, look at this, they keep winter in a box. That's clever," she congratulated me. Then she shut the fridge door and turned and looked at me with her blue-saffron eyes. "Ah, *cailín*," she said. She, too, knew I knew what she was there for.

"Calling me 'colleen' isn't enough," I said. I added, "Your Highness—" It's as well to be courteous. "I've never been over the sea to the Isle. Colum made a bargain, or you did. It isn't mine."

"Yes," she said. "How else did you get your talent? Oh, it was there in him, but he wouldn't work for it. He preferred the desk behind the leather shop and then the boss's desk at the factory in Dublin. Oh, the shame and waste of it, when he might have made his way through his voice, and by learning a bit of piano in his grandlady's parlor. He kept his music for talk, to woo the women. Well and good. He was not the one. But it's owed, my girl, for that night."

I hovered in the kitchenette. I said, "And when he was on the savage hill, and *they* came running, where were you?"

"Where should I be and all? Up in his fine skull, waiting for him to hear me inspire him."

"There's the gin," I said. "Have a drink."

I went and ran a bath. I knew she would never come in to plague me there, nor did she. She was from a forthright yet modest age. But when I was out and anywhere else in the flat, there she was.

She sat, like my own geas, across from me at supper, eating apples. She sat by me on the couch as I watched TV, drinking gin. She lay down at my side—somehow, for the bed was narrow—when I tried to go to sleep. And all night long as I stretched rigid like a marble figure on a tomb, she chattered and chanted on and on to me, telling me things that filled my head so full, I myself couldn't move about there. Near dawn after all I slept, hoping to find my great-grandfather again and have a word. But if I dreamed, I didn't recall.

The next night I was to go to sing and play at a pub in Kentish Town. Waking up, my throat was as sore and hoarse as if she, the old hag, had been strangling me in my sleep. Yet no sooner had I croaked into the phone and canceled my gig, than my throat was well, as if from the strongest antibiotic known to man.

"I won't," I said.

But she only opened the fridge door again, and spoke to the winter within, of ice and snows and berries and belling stags, and low sun and the lawless winds of the *Cailleach Bheare*, the winter goddess from the blue hills.

I must pay her no heed. There was nothing to fear. Ignored, in the end she would leave me alone.

◆　◆　◆

$\mathcal{A}$LL FRIDAY, all Saturday, there we were, we twain.

Saturday afternoon I went out to the shops, and she went with me, hooking her loathsome, withered, iron-tough arm in mine. A tourist herself from another time, another country, another dimension, oh such pleasure she had among the market stalls, and in the supermarket. No one else either saw or heard her, but once or twice, when I forgot and spoke to her, as when I told her to leave the cabbages alone, then I got the funny looks the crazed receive.

Perhaps that was it. Had I gone crazy?

"Hoosh," said she, "that is not your fate, my soul."

When we were coming back from the shopping, she dragging on my arm like a bundle of whisky-damp laundry, the next thing happened. In fact, it had happened before, and I knew it had and that it must, if not quite yet what it was.

"Who are they?"

"Who do you think, my soul?" said she.

"The Faerie Folk?"

"Hush, never call the Gentry that, keep a wise tongue in your head, so you must. But no, nor they are."

At which I *must* know, for what and who else was left then that they could be?

They darted through the crowds, the three of them, silken-lithe and gorgeous. I recollected I had seen them before on the escalator, and today in the market, and taken them, as you would, for three Goth girls of unusual beauty. They were clothed in fringed black down to their ankles and to their little black boots, and on their hands were black gloves and bracelets of gold that might be Indian, and off their milk-pale faces, the black hair poured like three black rivers to black seas, and to the backs of their very knees. Unlike my old woman, these were not truly invisible. Some people did see them, and turn and look admiringly at them, but I doubt in that case any-one noted their sunglassless, kohl-ringed eyes, just as I never did till we were nearly at my door. For if any had—

"Run—run, old lady—"

So we ran, and she, bounding along at my side, the eldritch wretch, as if she staggered *now* on the limber springs of a kangaroo. Up the steps, in the door, away and away into the upper rooms of the flat. Door slammed and locked. From the window I squinted down. There they were still, out on the hot summer pavement of London's Russell Park. Three beautiful young girls, loitering.

Irish eyes—I said: Who, that doesn't have them, can resist. *Put in by a smutty finger*, they call that smoky ring around the iris. Colum had it, and my mother did, and her father, too, and I. *She* had it, the *Speir-Bhan*—And *they* did, down there, the trio of Goth girls in black, who were not. For inside the smoky rings, the irises of *their* eyes were sulfur-smoking-red—the fleer-fire optics of foxes in a nightmare I had once as a child, about that fox-fur cape of my grand-mother's.

Scathing eyes, cruel eyes, *heartless, mindless, soulless* eyes—no-pity eyes that would tear you up in joints and eat you blood-gravy hot—if they had no teeth to do the service for them instead. But they had teeth. They smiled them up at me from below.

The Speir-Bhan brought me a cup of tea, strong, with gin in it. I'd never known a poet's muse could make tea. I suppose they can, if they can haunt you to claim back a family bargain for the Fair Fey Folk, do anything they please.

◆　◆　◆

"WHAT ARE THEY?" I whispered. "*What—what*? Do you know?"

City dusk had come down. The moon was up. It was one night off the full, and never till now had I remembered.

I was lying down with my head in her lap, the Speir-Bhan. It was as if I had my mother with me again, and my grandmother as well. Though they had not been so exacting.

She told me the story, and I listened, for outside on the pavement, under the rustling dusty English trees, they still idled, the three fox-vixens, with their rows of glinting teeth.

The Speir-Bhan told me of two heroes, sons of the gods or the Fey Folk, and of how one sat harping on a hill, and the three devilish women came to hear. They were, by birth, the daughters of some sort of demon in a cave, but in those days, their shapeshifting was to a kind of wolf—a werewolf, no doubt—human, or passing for it all month, but not on the night of the full moon, when they would change their skins and prey on everything they could find that lived. It occurs to me now, that by Colum's day, no wolves were left in Ire-land, only foxes. And maybe the foxkind was angry with mankind, as wolfkind had been, seeing as how foxes were hunted by then instead, and made into coats and capes.

Whatever it was, one hero harped, and he persuaded the demon-girls to put off their wolf-skins. And then they sat as human to hear him, one beside another, elbow to elbow, the story said.

"No doubt they were fair to see," sang my muse to me, "fair as three dark lilies on a stem. But no doubt of it either, between the long teeth of them was the rose-red blood of what they had slaughtered, and matted in their sloughen skins and raven locks, the bones of babies."

So while the women were tranced by the music, and songs that were so flattering to them, the second hero, standing below the hill, took his longest, sharpest spear, and slung it, as only heroes can. Up it flew, and passed in at the arm and shoulder of one girl, straight through her heart to the body and heart of the second, and through her into the third, body and heart, and came out at her neck. Then all three were there, spitted on the spear like three beads on a thread.

Did I ask her why that had needed to be done while they were in human form? Was that the only sorcerously potent method to be sure of them—or had it been easier to kill a woman than a beast? I think I never asked. I have no answer.

All I have is the story, which she then concluded. "After which, he took off their heads with his sword, he did." So crooned my Speir-Bhan. She was uncivilized and cruel, too, of course—what could you expect of a muse? Yet not so bad as young girls who rip lambs and children apart with their fangs. The heroes had only done as they'd had to.

"Then it's a job for two strong men," I said.

"It's a job for one that's cunning," said the Speir-Bhan. "But first there must be the song, or they will never stay."

"They're out there on the *street*," I snapped. "They've *stayed*."

"Sing to them, and you live. Without a song, they'll tear you up the first."

"Or, I could stay in. Bolt the door. Wait till Monday—the waning moon. What then?"

"They'll always be there, patient. Till *next* full moon," the old horror murmured, in that honey brogue I can't speak at all. "And next after that next, and next for ever." Not whisky on her breath—*uisege beatha* and flowering heather.

"Why?"

"You found Colum's book."

"Hasn't anyone ever read his bloody book before?"

"You have," said she, "eyes in your eyes. You see what others don't. The curse of your kind it is. And your blessing."

We remained as we were, and the fat moon came up. It glided over the window. That was Saturday. Tomorrow the fat moon would be full.

•   •   •

THAT SATURDAY NIGHT I SLEPT, but had no dreams. I had other experiences. The Speir-Bhan did me the great kindness of sleeping on the couch. Twice I got up. The first time it was about 4 A.M. Outside, down on the pavement, I couldn't tell if *they* were there or not, among the tree shadows and the orange bluster of the streetlamp.

Then, near sunrise, a noise—something—in the garden-yard behind the flats—and I got up again. I went to the back windows now to see, and saw. Shapes . . . shapes in long sombre gowns, circling the single tree that grows there among the rough grass. A glimmer of bangles, spangle of eyes—oh as if their bracelets and their eyes together sprang right at me so I started back. The eyes were red, redder than the lamps over the wall. For a moment as I stood there on the floor, the memory of their red gaze locked with mine—it seemed to me *my* eyes were just the same, bloodred, like *theirs*.

Minutes passed. I made myself creep back and look again. The dancing figures by the tree were merely someone's washing, hanging on the makeshift line that now and then appears there, and the gleam of gold and red—some trick of my vision in the fugitive dark.

It was like the dentist's. You can only put up with it, put it off so long. Something has to be done once the thing's gone wrong.

◆　◆　◆

WHEN I WAS A KID, I used to travel on the tube with my mother. She would hold my hand as I climbed laboriously on. I recollect journeys, and her wearing the French perfume she wore then, called *Emeraude*—Emerald. She told me stories on trains. They're gone; she told me so many, just wisps and drifts of fantasy and idea left behind, which mold quite often the things that I create. In her teenage years, before there were teenagers, she'd written songs and sung them. She had a wonderful singing voice, I've heard, but I never heard it, for by the time I was born, somehow it had left her.

To my embarrassment, I don't even know if they have an underground system in Ireland. Surely they must? Lord help them if they do. Because it will pass, won't it, through all the hollow hills, through all the supernatural caves—in and out of the Many-Colored Land, which is the Hereafter, or Faerie—or both.

This time, the Speir-Bhan did not hang heavy on my arm. She walked unaided with a steadier and more sprightly middle-aged tread. She had become, too, more assimilated. Her hair was less knotted, and shiny. Like me, she had on jeans and a T-shirt, though she'd kept to her old boots and her long coat. There were earrings in her ears. They looked to me like polished diamonds, or, more likely, stars. Maybe, maybe. Her wardrobe was psychic, of course, and she could put on what she wanted.

I carried my guitar in its case. I'm used to taking it on the tube. It's alive, but I never need to buy a ticket for it, because no one else *sees* it's alive—and so with the Speir-Bhan. We slipped through the robot barrier on my ticket like melted butter out of a crock. Then down the escalator, she and it and I, into the hollows under London.

◆　◆　◆

UNDER THE TUBE, *around* the tube, are Roman remains, ancient banqueting halls, plague-pits. I've never heard of fey things there, but naturally there are ghost stories. Like the castle then, Castle Sanvy, where Colum went that night, among the ghosts and Lordly Ones.

We sat facing forward.

After four or five stops—I wasn't counting or looking—the lights flickered. The train halted. I glanced about. The carriage, apart from ourselves, was vacant. Then it was full of something else—clouds, I'd say, clouds on the underground. They tell you, she comes from the sky, *a* Speir-Bhan, Speir Bhean, *Shpervan* . . . her name means something like that, to do with beauty and the firmament—she is Heaven Sent.

We three, she, it, I, were out in the tunnel next, soot-black and echoing with trains. And then the tunnel, too, was no more.

I have said, I've never been in Ireland. I meant, never in the flesh, to visit the actual place. Where now I went, I believe, was the genetic Ireland in my blood and physical soul. *There.*

◆　◆　◆

WHETHER AT SUN'S RISE OR EVENING, *by land or water, though I know I must die, thank God, I know not when* . . .

It was night.

I was on a hill. The Speir-Bhan had vanished. She had said she would sit in the brain to inspire, as she must. So perhaps she did.

This then must be how I *imagine* Ireland, or so I suppose. That is, the Ireland not only of its own past, but of its own eternity, behind the cities and the accumulating modern ways, the trains and graves and Euro currency.

Over there, the cliff edge, not even a castle on it now, but the late-summer dash of the sea over and beyond. The sun was sinking to the ocean. The water was like wine. The land was green and everywhere rolled the woods of yew and oak and rowan and thorn. Hawks sailed away down the air inland. Bear moved like brown nuns through the thickets. It was very quiet. I could smell wild garlic, flowers, and apples.

For myself, my clothes had altered in some incoherent way, but my guitar had not become a harp. I tuned it as I waited for the dark to begin, and the round moon to rise above the woods. As I waited for *them* to come running, with their barking shadows before them. I was lonely, but no longer afraid. Can I tell you why? No, I don't know why it was.

◆　◆　◆

𝒜FTER THE MOON CAME UP, I waited still. Then I began to play, just some chords and showy skitters over the strings. I knew they were coming when the guitar itself barked out in their vixen scream, the sound that puts the hair up on your head. Colum hadn't known what it was, how the harp had done that. But I had guessed. It was calling them in, that was all. The way you sometimes say to the crowd, what tune will you have?

I watched them run out of the woods. Not girls now, but three black beasts, too big for foxes, far too big, thick-furred, and neon-eyed.

My hands played and the guitar played, and up the hill they sped.

I could smell them. They didn't smell of animals, even the feral sort, but of summer night, like grass and garlic and blooms, but also they reeked of uncooked meat and blood.

They circled me, panting a little, their long, black tongues lying out, so the spit sometimes sparkled off them to the ground.

Speir-Bhan

Part of me thought, *They are weighing it up, to see if they like the music well enough to sit down, or if they'll prefer to kill me and have dinner.*

But the other part of me started my voice. I began to sing to them a melody I had made for them in my head.

I'm used to awkward audiences. Noisy ones and restless ones, the chime of glasses and raucous laughter, to keeping on, weaving the spell if I can, and making the best of it if I can't. But these creatures, they, too, in their own perverse way, had the blood of the green land. Presently they gave over their circling. They sat down before me in a row, closed their jaws, and watched, with their ears raised like radar bowls. What I sang them was this:

Women veiled with hair, shaming the black of the raven's wing,
In your night-deep tresses dwell
A murder of crows,
That will madden with delight or envy
Any, be they woman or man,
Seeing you go by.
So long and be-glamoring your streaming crowns,
That glow like the blue-burning coals,
And your faces set there like three white flames,
And your eyes like sparks from the fire.
This is your finest jewelry,
These midnight ringlets,
Which catch the moon herself in their chains,
So she must serve you, shackled,
Your slave indeed.

No wonder then the crow
Can prophesy to men.
Since he lives in the starry heaven
Of your veils of hair.

It was Colum's song, of course, or the song he had been given to please the Faerie woman at Sanvy, and which I had adapted for these three daughters of the dark, to flatter and cajole. As it seemed it did.

When I ended the song, and only went on lightly playing little riffs and wanderings, they were still there on the hillside before me. But they were not elbow to elbow, nor human.

Then I did what the first hero did. Over the music, I said to them softly, winningly, "Oh, how beautiful you are as foxes, my highnesses. But I know that, as human women, your beauty is beyond the beauty of the moon herself. Never forget, I saw you, even in your female mortal shape." Then I paused, playing on, and said, musingly, "It occurs to me, as you exist mostly in your human form, you'd hear my songs to you better with your human ears." Did I speak the Gaelic to them? I shall never know.

The guitar certainly would do anything I wanted. I could fashion things with it, things of light and air, that I had never been able to call up before, and never would again. My voice, too, which is good enough, was that night on the hill of Other-Ireland, the voice you hear sing only in your own head.

Presently, as in the legend, they removed their skins.

I have seen films, movies with computer effects that are miracles, but never did I see anything like that disrobing. Each of them, one by one, rose up on her hind limbs and drew off her fox-body, as a woman pulls off her dress. Off over their heads they drew the fox-skins, and laid them on the ground. Then they shook themselves and sat down once more, in their white complexions and mantles of ebony hair.

Their eyes, I've said, were awful either way, but now I got used to their eyes, as you can, to anything, yes, if you must, and even quite rapidly. And then, once I was used to their eyes, I learned the real atrocity of them. For these three were the most beautiful beings of any sex I have ever seen, yet there they sat, and I could clearly make out the piles of gnawed bones and the gouting blood, not caught in their hair or teeth, but snarled up in those eyes, mired and stuck deep, like poison, in their ruined astral insides. They were like lovely women riddled with some wasting death for which there is no cure. Except, they never could really die, they must, as now, always somehow eventually come back, and besides, who could, even for a century or so, kill them? They would never be done with this. And, just as I'd become accustomed to them, so *they* had become accustomed to themselves.

Did that mean they liked it? No, for you do not have to learn to accept that which you love. It is a part of you, from the start.

All these facts were there in their sulfurous eyes, like rot in apples. And like the apple skin, they mostly hid it, but only from *themselves.*

I'd sung to flatter them, aiding and abetting their self-deceiving. To flatter them stupid, for perhaps that way, I'd thought, I might be able to strike some new bargain. I hoped some inspiration would come to me, trusting the music, and the muse in my head.

But now I found I sang no more of that. I had begun instead to sing of what I saw lying there, putrid, in their eyes.

Colum had taken his chance, praising the golden-haired woman. Now I took mine. We neither of us had a choice. The poet's right— and curse.

Over and over. Not able to stop. I sang about those dreadful things within them. Till the beauty was all mingled with the stench and terror, and the filth hammered down into the beauty. And there they were, those hellgirls, with their fox-skins lying on the ground, sitting elbow to elbow, listening in a trance.

Now was the hour, like the last time in the legend, for my best friend, or my brother, to stand below us on the slope and cast the spear. Up through arms and hearts and breasts and necks. After which he must come striding with the beheading sword to finish our task. But I have no one like that. All my lovers and kin are under the hollow hills. All I keep is the past, and a Speir-Bhan up in the gallery of my mind. Plus my guitar, which is not a harp.

Yet, singing the horror to them, I saw them change, those three on the hill. Not from fox to girl, but from *beast* to human. I saw their eyes sink like six red suns covered by white skies of lids and thunder-burning clouds of lashes. Then they got up. They stared at me, but now *with their closed* eyes.

I could never have stopped what I was at. The music and the voice came out of me, and I hung up in the air and watched it all.

In that manner, I saw how they began, the tears that slipped out under their lids. They were ghastly tears, as the eyes were ghastly, the color of old, sick blood. Yet tears they were. I heard them, too, maidens whispering, but like dead leaves on a dying tree. They spoke of their father, some demon-lord, I didn't properly catch his name—Artach, or something like that—they spoke of a childhood they had never had, of a mother they had never seen, of wicked things done to them, of misery, and a life like night without stars or a lamp. There was nothing in their voices to match the tears. No sorrow. They had no self-pity, being pitiless, but even so, most evils spring from other evils done, and they were no different in that.

Down their faces fled the soiled tears, then the talk stopped, and in unhuman screams they began their emotionless lament. They rushed about the hill, snatching and scratching at each other, yet avoiding the spot where I sat as if it would scald them. They shrieked now like foxes, now like owls—and now, worst of all—like children in fear, perhaps the very ones they had preyed on. But they were not afraid, not unhappy—it, too, was worse, they were *damned,* and they knew it.

I couldn't end my song. On and on it went. It made me ache, my hands bleed, throat all gravel, and it broke me down. I could do no other than play and sing, and witness them as they screamed and ran in circles, weeping.

Then, oh then, I understood. *I* had done the work of two. I had tranced them with music, and with music also I had pierced their hearts of steel, and now, by music, too, I took their reason, and they lost their heads.

If there had ever been a bargain at the whim of the Fair Folk, or if demons had only got the scent of Colum, and so of me, these three had no further use for it. They did not care now that they were alive, or what they were. Did not even care to be girls, or foxes that slaughtered.

The wind came up the hill. It smelled of wheat and moonlight, and furled them up like the dead leaves they were. They blew away with it, down the slopes, over the tree-hung heights and valleys of my imagined Ireland. And on the ground they left the fox-skins lying.

Only when their three figures were gone from my sight into unmeasured distance, did the song leave me. I'm glad to say I remember not a word of it. If I did I would, trust me, never write it down.

My numb hands fell off the guitar, which they had covered with my blood.

At last, in the silence under the sinking moon, I dared to pick them up, those flaccid, forgotten skins. They were, all three, briefly like that cape of my grandmother's, which had so scared me in my fourth year, and with the same demonic, frightened eyes of leaden glass. And then, they fell apart to nothing.

The moon though, as she set, blinked, yellow-blue.

◆　◆　◆

I WAS ON THE TUBE, of course. It was very crowded for a Thursday night. My hands were clean and healed, my throat not raw. The Speir-Bhan was shambling down the carriage, an unsober old hag with dirty hair. She plumped herself beside me and said, in ringing tones that made most of the carriage look up at her, " 'Ere, luv, tell us when we gets up Holland Park."

She smelled of port. I explained she was on the wrong tube line.

Philosophically if copiously she swore, and at the next stop, hiccuping, she left the train.

Months later, not even on a night of full moon, I dreamed I put on the skin of a black fox, and ran over the hills of a vague, perhaps-Ireland. And though I avoided killing anything be it a sheep or a man, a rabbit or a baby, with my teeth, yet I learned from this dream the lesson of my success, why Colum had *not* succeeded, maybe why the heroes had. It wasn't only music, but also the spear and the sword. Not only courage, or honor, but unkindness. Not only talent, but the *emptiness* with which talent pays for itself. It is, you see, the mirror that reflects best the flaws it is shown in another.

For them, they never came near me again. Nor she, the Speir-Bhan, though I will suppose she's there, up there in my brain, where they generally sit.

As for Colum's book, I never read another sentence, not even his leather accounts. I burned it that autumn on a handy neighborhood bonfire. A shame, but there.

For the mortal foxes that steal now and then into the gardens at the back of the flats in Branch Road, I remain one of those that feeds them, dog food and brown bread. Their coats are russet, their eyes the color of whisky, the *uisge bheatha*, Water of Life.

Acknowledgments

The legend of Aeritech's Daughters and the heroes with harp and spear is to be found in Irish myth of the twelfth century and earlier; Colum's song, and many other references, are based on Irish sources, poetry and prose, between the ninth and sixteenth centuries. The idea of a Speir Bhean, or Aisling, is still current.

I would like to thank Beryl Alltimes for helping to clear the way to this, and the *Wolf's Head and Vixen Morris* for undoubted inspiration, for invaluable guidance, Barbara Levick of St. Hilda's College,

Oxford, and especially, for his insights on the Gaelic, Professor Thomas Charles-Edwards of Jesus College, Oxford. However, all errors, liberties taken, and flights of fancy are mine.

＊　＊　＊

As is obvious from the dedication of this tale, I do indeed have Irish blood (though less than that of the narratrix, just as I am quite a few years older), and am very proud of my Irish connection. That side of the family hails from what I call the Ghost Coast—the west of Ireland—County Clare. After this, of course, fiction parts from fact, but not entirely. You must judge what is true and what fantasy—as so must I.

Tanith Lee 2002

Troubles

BY JANE YOLEN AND ADAM STEMPLE

The pub stood on the corner of a residential neighborhood like a dirty old man in a raincoat. A decrepit yellow sign advertised, IRSH MUIC NIGHTLY, the letters that weren't missing altogether sagging toward the ground.

I approached the pub cautiously, as I did any new steading, and sniffed the entrance thoroughly before opening the door.

The doorman was old, squat, wrinkled, and toadlike, much as I would appear if I had not taken precautions. He asked me for identification but, as I had none, I waved a hand at him, and we spoke no more of it.

The front door emptied into a well-lit room that had only a long bar and a few pool players mulling about. I didn't see the One I was supposed to meet. But there was no hurry. My kind have infinite patience.

Stepping past the doorman, I went immediately to the bar. The pub was bigger on the inside than I had suspected. The long mahogany bar split the room into two healthy sections: well lit with billiards and a jukebox on one side, dim and dirty with a live band on the other.

"Pint of Guinness," I said to the bearded man behind the bar, and he shuffled away to fetch it.

When he returned with my drink, and I had waved at his request for payment, I moved to the side with the band.

As I scanned the room, I sniffed my drink. They really have no clue how to pour it in this country. But the magic of the black nectar can survive far worse than a long boat ride and an unsteady pour and still be better than most of the swill they peddle in this young land. I took a deep draught and felt almost at home. I scanned the room again.

This time I spotted him, cloaked in darkness, near the low stage. He was absorbing the energy of the band. And there was a fair amount to absorb. They were a three-piece of hairy ruffians, two of them crouched over guitars that seemed too small for their bulk, and one, his right wrist wrapped tight in an Ace bandage, pounding manfully on a bodhran. They finished "The Boys of the Old Brigade" and ripped into a speedy version of "The Merry Ploughboy," stopping in the middle of every chorus for the crowd to shout, "Fuck the Queen!"

Good Republican stuff, if you go for that. But far too loud for me.

I caught the One's attention by blowing a breath of the Old Country toward him. He turned slowly, raised his head, his eyes like lamplights, and motioned me to join him. Shaking my head, I pointed to the band, then my ears. He mimed earplugs. I could have silenced the band, but magic in new surrounds always leaks out around the edges. No need alerting other Powers beforetime. So, in return, I gestured to the front of the bar, but he shook his head.

If we were at an impasse already, it did not bode well for our negotiations. A few more rounds of gestures, and finally he got up, walking toward me, then past me, his cloak still keeping him invisible to the mortals.

I followed him to a stairway in the far corner of the bar, a stairway that I hadn't seen before. We walked down into the basement, which, surprisingly, had a full-length bocce court. Quickly, I scanned the room for signs of Lars or incubo, those familiar spirits of the Latium, but there were none. I smiled to myself. Perfect!

Turning, he dropped the spell of darkness and grinned at my genuine surprise. There, underground, closer to his natural habitat, he grew more substantial. His skin had less pallor, his hair was long and golden, as were his eyes. They glowed with power. He was no mere underling sent to parley but a true prince of the Unseelie Court. I could not decide whether this was a good thing or no.

"*Tiocfaidh ar la,*" he said in Gaelic. His voice was gravel.

"Our day will come," I agreed, careful not to put too strong a stress on the first word. Then I pulled up a chair that was made gray as a toadstool by the dim light, and sat. Negotiations may take a minute or a millennium, but no one ever gets through them on his feet. If this violated protocol, I did not care. Prince or no prince, I was going to sit.

Above our heads, the *thump-thud-thump* of the band and its fans was a bit annoying. But at least it was no longer a dagger in the ear.

"Well," I said.

"Well," he answered.

We were talking. It was a beginning.

◆   ◆   ◆

COMING TO THE UNTIED STATES, as we call it in Eire, takes more than courage for any of the Sidhe. Crossing that amount of water—

by boat or by air—is difficult and painful. Yet airplanes are full of us on every flight. The reason is simple. The world's power center is now here, and no longer on our green isle. If we wish to continue to be a part of the world's destiny, the Long Passage must be endured.

And the Long Negotiations, as tricky a passage as the ocean, must be endured as well. Or so said my superiors who had sent me over.

So there was I, in the dark bottom of a dirty pub, a band of mock Irishmen above me pounding out the old songs with execrable accents and no sense of history.

I cast one baleful eye at the ceiling and began to wave my hand.

My opposite number touched my thumb, halted me. "We need them," he said, "for cover." His own accent was subtly altered, having lived so long here among them. I detected a bit of the Viking in it, a hint of Thor. The twin cities are full of trolls.

About that touch. I do not allow many to touch me and live. And certainly not those of the Unseelie Court. Not even a prince. But these negotiations were about the fate of *all* the Fair Folk, not just some minor border dispute between the courts. This was about the *continuing* existence of the race of the Sidhe. For we are few and humanity many, and even old enemies within the Fey now must unite if we are to remain in this world and under the hill. Or so say my masters.

I pulled my hand down. Muttered under my breath. Pictured my companion's body flayed and bleeding at my feet. The image calmed me.

The band played on, now singing something quieter, a tune I didn't recognize. Hardly Irish at all.

"Well," he said.

"Well," I answered.

The negotiations continued.

Before either of us could clarify these opening gambits, I felt another presence enter the bar like a cold shiver down the spine that ended with a tickle in the loins.

Bean Sidhe, I thought. *Bean Chaointe.* The wailing woman. Squall crow.

My companion felt her, too, and looked alarmed. His eyes widened, and he stood, starting toward the stairs. But he was not as quick as I. A prince he might be, but I had learned my trade from Cuchulainn so that I might be sharp in both the faerie world and the world of men. Before he got a single step up, I grabbed him and pulled us both away from the stairs. It is no touch if I initiate it.

My back to the wall and my bone knife to his throat, I whispered, "Why does the Washer at the Ford come here?" She was neither Seelie, nor Unseelie, presaging doom and destruction to all she sang, regardless of their house. She was without prejudice. Without mercy. I pressed the knife deeper, and he gave a strangled gasp. It was difficult not to just kill him, to pay him back for that earlier touch.

"I . . . I know not." His face had turned the white of a winding sheet. No prince of any court likes to be held to the truth. But a bone knife to the great vein is the strongest of persuaders.

What he said smelled like the truth, but I distrust coincidence. It may work in the stories we send out to the world, but in real life it smacks of treachery. I took the knife away from his throat and pushed him toward the stairs.

"Let us go ask her ourselves then," I said. "The both of us. Together."

I thought he might turn and rush me. His eyes flared, and for a moment his breath stopped. But my weapon was still in my hand, and he had already tasted my speed. I may look like a toad, but I move like a snake. He thought better of it and gave me the back of his head as he stomped his way up.

I palmed the knife and followed close behind, so close I might be the tail of his coat or the shirt on his shoulders. So close I might be skin of his skin. Negotiations were one thing, but trust him? Never.

.   .   .

I WOULD NOT HAVE THOUGHT IT POSSIBLE, but the club had gotten even louder and smokier in our short time in the basement. The band was lost in an improvisation, fingers flying across their fretboards. One guitarist kept the song nailed in E minor while the other jumped from mode to mode, willy-nilly, with no respect for key or meter. The drummer, now playing acoustic bass, followed the lead guitarist closely, his right foot tapping on the offbeats. When they broke back into the chorus, I recognized the song.

It was Scottish.

I gave a mental spit of disgust. Scots are only secondhand Irishmen, and I guessed the band knew no difference. All the while, I continued looking for the *Bean Sidhe.*

Of course, I was expecting to see her usual flowing white robes and streaming hair, and for a moment was flummoxed when I did not spot her. And then, suddenly, I espied her on the small dance floor, oblivious to our presence. She wore a black half shirt emblazoned with the band's logo and jeans so tight, I wondered she could move at all. But move she did. She whirled and wiggled, shook and shimmied, and half the audience—and not just the male half— watched her hungrily.

I spat for real this time. Not a lot but enough. Enough to keep the bad cess on her and off me.

She never noticed, having eyes only for the three on stage, especially the short blond guitarist with his long hair pulled back in a rat's tail.

"My mistake," I said, my voice hoarse with smoke and aggravation and the difficulty of uttering those two particular words. Sheathing my knife, I added, "Apparently, the Washer sees something in these noise-makers that I do not."

My companion, though still white with past rage, now seemed willing to forget about my violence to his person for the good of the negotiations. His eyes glowed once again, but a mellower gold.

"I have heard them before," he said, meaning the band, their banner proclaiming them to be the Tim Malloys, a name that meant nothing to me. "Too loud, but they have talent. And they are good Republicans all. Supporters of the cause." His eyes held a hint of green.

So he was a true believer then, a member of the black-or-white club, the all-or-nothing brigade, the my-side-ever-and-fuck-yours-to-Hell crew. Why any of us should care so deeply about mortal politics was beyond me. But I knew—for my masters had told me when I asked—that there was precedent for this. Why, the Sidhe had played a part in human warfare since the Battle of Clontarf near Dublin in 1014. No time at all in faerie terms, but centuries to the humans.

The Tim Malloys finished their Scottish song with an unbelievably cacophonous final chord, and the crowd squealed with glee.

"Happy Beltane all you pagan bastards!" shouted the big rhythm guitarist.

Is it really Beltane? I thought in surprise. I was not a great one for keeping time and hadn't realized it was May Eve. Why would my superiors send me to negotiate on the eve of one of the three great festivals, when traditionally we of the *daoine maithe* would be fighting in great mobs, though all the humans would see was a great whirlwind lifting the thatch off a roof? Something was not right.

I threw an ingratiating smile my companion's way. There would be time to pay him back for his insult later. But at the moment, I needed to think. "The squall crow does not see us. Let us keep it that way." Then I realized I'd left my Guinness, half-gone and presumably flat by then, in the basement. "We need a drink."

He nodded, and we left the band room and moved toward the bar.

As I ordered two Guinnesses—my companion being once more cloaked and unable to order for himself—I observed three young men saunter through the front door and head for the dance floor. Their heads were shaved, and their bodies were covered with ancient marks I am sure they knew not the meaning of. They wore black tee shirts with death's-heads and crosses on them and they moved as if they expected people to get out of their way. My companion stared daggers at their backs.

More true believers, I thought. But not of the same faith as my companion. Or the band. Or most of the bar comrades. Orangemen at a guess. Or if not orange, at least not of the green, the green of patriots, the green of the Sidhe.

A plan began forming in my mind as the skinheads marched into the band room. Not a plan my masters had ever thought of. Or maybe they had. They had sent me on May Eve, after all, and told me to move with the moment. That moment, I sensed, was upon me. But for what I had in mind I would need more power. A *lot* more power.

I gave a concealed wave of my hand, unseen by any eyes, mortal or Sidhe. This opening was a very small spell, just a nudge really. Merely pushing the head-shavers to do what was natural. Natural— and ugly. But when the real casting came, I would be well gone from here. Necessary, of course. I had to be gone before the Powers were alerted to my presence.

"Are you eyeballing me?" It was a loud and surprisingly tenor voice from the next room. One of the shaved-heads I presumed.

I waved my hand again, and this time I heard the sound of glass breaking next door.

That, I thought, *should be enough to get things started.*

I was surprised to find my companion suddenly racing into the barroom. And not, I assumed, because of any love of music. Then I considered: *If he is distracted by the fighting, that should make things even easier.*

The noises from the other room grew more violent and promising. I heard the sounds of blows given and received, insults hurled, threats offered, and immediately followed through on. The music came to a sudden halt as—I presumed—the musicians either fled or joined in.

It was time. I smiled and spread my arms wide, letting the power born of blood and passion flow over me and through me. The bar had become a battlefield, a spinning turbine of broken knuckles and bloody noses, and I was a battery, drinking my fill. I was supercharged, I was industrial strength, I was growing greater by the second. I was drunk with power, engorged, enlarged, enlivened.

And stupid. Stupid. Stupid.

That kind of rapid growth, fueled by testosterone surges, fear, and anger, made me stupid for the moment. A faerie moment. Which is longer in human time than our time, of course.

I forgot the missing cloaked man, my mission, my masters, and all as I soaked up the human conflagration.

Human conflagration? What I was hearing was more than that. I dropped my arms and raced over to where I could see the action. The shaved-heads who had started things were down already, but the fight had spread like a fire to engulf the entire bar.

And then I understood why. It was May Eve, and apparently most of the patrons weren't human at all. They were Fey.

I must have been too intent on spotting the Unseelie prince and then the *Bean Sidhe* to see through the elementary glamors they had dropped over themselves.

As I said—stupid, stupid, stupid!

Of course none of that mattered, as battle had been joined and all guises dropped. The dance floor was a heaving mass of Fey combatants, and I could not take my eyes off the sight.

As I watched, a fachan hopped into the fray on his sole leg. One-handed, he swung a club hard onto the head of a squat brownie in front of him, splitting it open, then falling to the ground himself, elf-shot through his single eye. Before the elf could notch another arrow, he took a bone knife in the kidney, courtesy of one of the diminutive bogies darting around the edges of the conflict. An urisk, impaled on the horns of a giant bogey-beast, screamed like the goat it half was. Will o' wisps shot overhead like tracer bullets. Even the band had joined the melee, leaving their instruments onstage. But I had been as mistaken about them as I had been about all the others. The bodhran player was in reality a redcap, that old malignant Border goblin, and he was laying about with a bloody axe and bodies were falling every-where. The blond guitarist was clearly a phooka, his long hair cover-ing his entire body, his feet turning to hooves, which he employed with zeal. Only the big Viking with the guitar was fully human, and he joined in with a kind of maniacal glee.

I was about to head into the room myself when the doorman rushed by me with a pistol, yelling, "You fuckers, I've called the cops."

The *Bean Sidhe* began wailing and a shot rang out.

Cold iron.

Time to finish my business.

◆　◆　◆

THE PRINCE—who'd been in the midst of things, turned and saw me. "I thought we were to keep things quiet," he cried. Or meant to. The last few words died before reaching his lips as I reached out with my mind and grabbed him by the throat. That surprised him, I know, for his eyes turned bloodred before closing forever. But he had touched me. And that I would not countenance for long.

Oh, I had been warned by my superiors to play it safe. But they had always known my character. I expect they guessed something like this would happen. *Hoped* it would happen. Why else send me off on

May Eve for a parley. In a pub? Of course, never having exactly told me what to do, they would have what the humans like to call "plausible deniability."

I laughed grimly and let the prince's body drop. A dozen or so of the Fey had already been killed, with more to come. But the Unseelie Court had lost a great prince, the Seelie Court only pawns. My masters would be pleased. I wondered briefly if they were the ones who had sent the *Bean Sidhe*.

And then I forgot everything in the whirlwind that lifted me higher and higher through the roof, as the bar collapsed in fire as if an explosion had rocked the place.

The Irish would be blamed of course. Both sides. As they always are. As they always will be. I screamed with laughter as the whirlwind bore me home. If we did not have the Irish, we Fey would have to invent them.

The Hermit and the Sidhe

BY JUDITH TARR

Bloody hell," said the hermit.

"Language," Pegeen reproved him, slapping a dot of wool over the stinging wound and stropping the razor until it sent off sparks.

Pegeen was a wild Irish rose, with skin like milk and hair as black as an Englishman's heart. Her round white arm was as strong as a blacksmith's, and her will was forged steel.

She had arrived at the hermit's tower that morning with his pail of stew and his loaf of bread and his jar of brown ale from her father's cask, and informed him in no uncertain terms that she was making him fit for a mortal to look at. She had turned a deaf ear to his protests that a hermit should be wild and uncouth and unshorn, just as on previous visits she had scoured the old tower from top to bottom, and never mind the requirement that he live in sacred squalor.

"Squalor is the Devil's province," she had said.

Now she had determined to make him as presentable as his tower, and even his brief fall into the lower vernacular could not give her pause. She shaved him and clipped him and dressed him in a robe that mortified the memory of the old saints with its absolute cleanliness. It might have begun life as a woman's Sunday gown, but judicious stitching, tucking, and patching had lent it a rather convincingly monastic air—except, of course, for its disastrous freedom from dirt, lice, and vermin.

The hermit's own carefully constructed colony thereof, wrapped in threadbare wool and hanging limply from the end of a broomstick, was not even to die a noble death on the tower's hearth. Pegeen burned it in the open air downwind of the tower, so that the wind carried the stench of it away. Then came the rain of heaven to scour the ashes. "And is that not living proof," said Pegeen, "that the Lord has as keen a nose as any woman in Ballynasloe?"

"The Lord is pure spirit," the hermit said as stoutly as he could manage, "and as such, He can have no—"

"If the Lord is a He," said Pegeen, "then there is one part of a body that it seems He does have, and why not a nose, too, after all?"

With that snippet of appalling theology and an air of solid satisfaction, she put on her cloak and hood and gathered up her empty basket and forayed out into the rain. It was a soft day in Ireland, and a little soaking never hurt a body, as she had told him often before.

Long after the squelch and clatter of her brogues on mud and stone had died away, the hermit sat limply by the hearth. Pegeen's presence was a great tax on his spirit. "And why," he asked the air, "could I not have been sent a true and authentic angel to bring me my bread, and not that spawn of a publican and a harpy?"

Once that sentiment had escaped him, he crossed himself quickly and promised the Lord a dozen lashes on his bare back for thoughts unbecoming a man of God. Nor was pique his only sin; for there could be no denying that Pegeen was a glorious specimen of Irish womanhood.

He had come to this place, taking the white martyrdom, to escape just such a temptation. He had almost forgotten the beautiful Emmeline, with her plump white throat and her golden curls. Odes had been written to those curls, and sonnets to that throat—not a few of them his own, and in the humility of his new state, he could admit that some of them had been of less than sterling quality.

"But I had a little talent," he said. "I did. And twelve hundred a year. But she had a cashbox for a heart. She married six thousand a year."

He crossed himself again. Bitterness was a sin. So was memory. He was a hermit, a martyr to the world, a servant of God—the last in all of Ireland, and the first in many a hundred years.

Yet a third time he crossed himself. Pride: that was a sin, too. Everything was a sin, sooner or later. One could simply atone for living, and hope it was enough to open the gates of heaven.

The last hermit in Ireland lay on the floor of his tower and gave himself up to mortification of the soul—the flesh having benefited rather too thoroughly from Pegeen's ministrations. It would be days before he could mortify it again with any conviction at all.

◆ ◆ ◆

For the thousandth time in his thousand days of ministering to the parish at Ballynasloe, Father Timothy glowered at the doorstep of his rectory. For the thousandth time, a saucer of cream stared blandly back.

It was not for the rectory cat, whose tastes ran more toward mice and the females of his species. That much Father Timothy had deduced some while since. Not long after that, he had confronted his housekeeper with the facts of the case. Mrs. Murphy had not even troubled to look up from the potatoes she was peeling. "And why would you be thinking it was for the cat, Father?" she had inquired in her genteel voice. "It's for Them, of course."

"Them?" he had echoed.

"Them," she said, nodding, as yet another perfect coil of peel dropped into the basin. She reached for the next potato, as if the conversation had concluded.

He was not ready to let it go, although it was all too clear by then what she meant. "Are you saying," he said, "that you offer a nightly sacrifice of good cream to a pack of old and discredited gods?"

"Hardly discredited," she said, as serene as ever, "and more than useful, Father, for the little things that ease a woman's lot in the world. A man's, too, for the matter of that, and a priest's if he will. Or were you dissatisfied with the mending of your boot that is your favorite in the world, and the sole half falling off it?"

That was as much temper as she would show, in the thickening of the brogue and the shift to the speech of her countrywomen. He had judged it wise then to retire from the field, for a housekeeper in a dudgeon was a terribly uncomfortable thing, and one in a true rage could make a priest's life a misery.

He had brooded and he had pondered and he had studied. He had watched the people of the village. He saw how every gatepost carried some bit of something odd: a bundle of herbs, a garland of flowers, or a silver coin fastened with a silver nail. He marked how the women took a certain path at certain times of the month and certain phases of the moon, a path that led to the huge old oak tree that stood in a field somewhat apart from the village. He never saw naked rites there, but bits of ribbon and garlands of flowers or greenery and sometimes a silver penny—just as on the gateposts—would appear in the branches of the tree. Or one of the women would take her washing to the river at odd times—moonrise or first dawn or the dark of the moon—and sing while she did it, songs in the old language that he had steadfastly forborne to learn.

Even the men were part of it. They plowed by the phases of the moon instead of by the calendar like civilized men, and the smith was known to quench his best knives in the blood of a bull calf. When black Paddy was hanged for stealing the squire's prize cow, his corpse vanished in the night, but there was a fresh grave at the crossroad and suspicious marks nearby it, as if there had been a rite with nothing in it of Christian doctrine.

That would have been cause enough to concern himself with the welfare of his charges' souls. But he had seen things—heard things. Flickers in the corner of the eye. Faint voices where no human creature was, and ripples of wicked laughter. Tiny fingers would pluck at his cassock when he walked down paths to this cottage or that.

At first he had told himself that it was just the wind, or a catch of brambles, or children's voices carried oddly along a turn of the track. But he was never a man who could lie to himself, however odd or difficult the truth. There was something here, and that something had nothing to do with any Christian thing.

And every doorstep, every one, had a saucer of cream somewhere on or near it, that the village cats were never seen to touch.

He stared at this thousandth bowl on this thousandth morning, and knew in his heart what he would have to do. He must preach a holy crusade against the old but unforgotten gods. As to who should preach it with him, he knew just the man.

• ◆ ◆

"YOU WANT TO do what?" said the hermit.

Father Timothy had not found the congenial colleague he had expected. The hermit was clean, for one thing. Without his saintly

• 103 •

armor of beard and vermin, he looked distressingly like one of the young sprouts of the gentry who infested the hills in hunting season. He had the same accent, too, and the same bland expression.

Nevertheless, Father Timothy persevered. Whatever this man had been before he elected the white martyrdom, he was a man of God now. "This village is overrun with pagan superstition. Why it was not scoured clean a hundred years ago, God knows."

"Maybe it was," the hermit said, "and the scouring didn't stick."

"That's all too likely," Father Timothy granted him. "These people are relentless in their determination to do as their distant ancestors did before them."

"And yet you think you can rid them of their pixies and nixies?"

Father Timothy blinked, startled out of his fine fire of zeal. "I take it you don't agree that the village would be more godly without them?"

"Certainly I deplore superstition," the hermit said, "but you act as if these figments truly exist."

"The villagers believe they do," Father Timothy said.

"Do you?"

Father Timothy shifted on the hard wooden stool. He should be the doubter, man of the modern age that he was, and this relic of an ancient martyrdom should be frothing over the worship of pagan gods. But the truth was the truth, and he was an honest man of God. "I do believe," he said, "that the old beliefs—and yes, the old gods— are still alive in Ballynasloe. It's my duty as a priest and a Christian man to remedy that."

"You've seen them? With your own eyes?"

"I've heard them," Father Timothy said, "and felt them. They are there, watching and mocking, laughing at our modern pretensions."

The hermit was obviously trying hard to keep his face expressionless. "I wish you good fortune," he said.

"You won't help?" said Father Timothy in a bit of a dying fall, but he had to cling to hope.

It was the hermit's turn to be uncomfortable. That was gratifying enough that Father Timothy resolved to do penance for it later. "I—really don't think—"

"Not even for the sake of the villagers' souls?"

The hermit's soft young mouth went thin and tight. "I'm not here to save anyone's soul," he said, "but my own. I'll pray for them. Maybe God will listen."

"I'm sure He will," Father Timothy said, but not as truthfully as he would have liked.

◆　◆　◆

THE HERMIT HAD been praying when Father Timothy interrupted him. When he tried to go back to it, he caught himself thinking instead. He had taken Father Timothy for a man of modern sensibilities and serious intentions. And here he was, obsessed with a bowl of cream on a doorstep.

"Silliness," said the hermit, whose obsession with a fall of golden curls was blurring into a fixation on neat black braids.

He knelt on the hardest and coldest part of the floor, on his bare knees to be sure he suffered enough, and squeezed his eyes tight shut. He prayed in Latin because in his opinion a hermit should, and because it required a certain level of mortification of the brain.

He still could not stop thinking of Father Timothy and the faeries. He gave it up at last and resorted to mortification of the flesh: a brisk hour in his meager bit of garden among the beans and the potatoes. No faeries there. No Father Timothy, either. By the end of the hour he was lustily intoning the *Stabat Mater dolorosa*, as happy as a hermit could be.

◆　◆　◆

FATHER TIMOTHY HAD all his weapons to hand. Bell, book, and candle—and a fire of devotion that burned higher with every day that passed. His flock was as intractable as he had expected. They came to Mass on Sundays as they always had, heard his sermon with their usual blank politeness and the occasional snore, then went straight back home and put out their saucers of cream and put up their charms to placate this spirit or that.

He strode through the village one fine Monday morning, with his bell ringing and his candle burning. At every doorstep he stopped and bowed and prayed, and poured out every bowl of cream.

It was a great waste of good cream, as the widow O'Brien declared in her brass trumpet of a voice. "And is it any less wasted for sitting out in the sun or the rain?" he shot back from the core of his zeal.

That silenced her, which was a miracle in itself, but by evening every doorstep had its bowl back again, and cream in it—even his own.

It took a great mustering of courage to confront Mrs. Murphy, but confront her he did. He led her to the doorstep and the offending object. Words were almost beyond him. "This," he said. "This thing—this defiance—before God, woman, are you determined to destroy me in this town?"

Her face was as serene as it ever was, but the brogue was just a fraction thicker than usual. "Sure and I did nothing, Father," she said.

"Nothing but put this bowl out for the pixies," said Father Timothy.

"I never filled it," she said. "It was empty when I came in this morning, and full when I came out just now."

Mrs. Murphy stood there with her stiff spine and her perfect rectitude, and he could not believe she lied. "Then who is it?" he demanded. "Who did it?"

"No human person, Father," she said, crossing herself devoutly.

"Come inside, Father. I've a nice chop for your dinner. Where's the harm in a bowl of cream, after all?"

"Where's the harm?" Father Timothy sucked in air. "*Where* is——" He coughed and choked. She thumped his back with a surprisingly strong fist, until he could talk again. "There is all the harm in the world! This is a threat to your immortal soul. You shall have no god before God. You shall worship no heathen spirits. You shall not——"

"Come," she said, tugging lightly at his arm. "Come and have your dinner."

"Unhand me, woman!" he thundered. "I will not be treated like a child—fed and put to bed and then forgotten. This village is in mortal danger. The forces of darkness are creeping up on it. I must defend it. It is my duty."

"Surely, Father," she said soothingly, "and a warrior of God needs his dinner if he's to fight the good fight. Come and have your chop before it gets cold."

Father Timothy groaned in frustration. But she was right. He should eat. Then he would pursue this war in earnest.

◆　◆　◆

THE CREAM WAS THE LEAST OF IT. Every jar of milk that came into the priest's house went sour, even if it were brought warm and foaming from the cow. The boots that fit him best in all the world sprang their soles and stayed sprung. His cassock would not stay clean for anything he did. There were vermin in his bed and spiders in his parlor, and when he walked on his rounds with his bell and book and candle, invisible fingers pinched and poked him until he bled.

None of it swayed him in the slightest. The worse the persecution, the more determined he was. He toppled the dolmen in the wood with his own hands, and nothing but a pick and a crowbar—and all the price he paid for it was a mass of tiny bruises that he offered as a sacrifice, and a broken toe that was even better in that regard. That Sunday he said Mass with more conviction than he had since he was first ordained, and his sermon was thunder and brimstone.

Better yet, the village began slowly to shift from gaping at him in astonishment or, at most, calling out to him to stop whatever he was doing. None of them made a concerted effort to stop him. After his glorious Sunday sermon, when he went to exorcise the ghosts from the crossroad, a surprising number of people followed him and joined in the responses.

He came home from that in a flush of triumph, having prevailed upon his audience to renew their baptismal vows—in which they renounced Satan and all his works. He found Mrs. Murphy in the kitchen as usual, tending a savory pot of stew while she stirred a cake that made good use of soured milk.

He came perilously close to hugging her, but her dignity was much too formidable for any such liberties. He settled for a broad smile and a delighted greeting. "A fine day to you, Mrs. Murphy, and aren't we God's favorite children?"

"You are, I'm sure, Father," she said with no sign that she noticed his ebullience. "I'll be leaving early this evening, Father, if you don't terribly mind."

"Oh, yes!" he cried. "Yes, you can go. It's your daughter, isn't it? I'll be baptizing another soul for the parish soon, I'm sure, and God bless her and the child, too."

Her nostrils thinned slightly at the indelicacy of a man referring to a woman's lying-in, but she thanked him civilly.

"You are very welcome," he said. "Go on now, I'm sure you're eager to be by her side. I can watch the cake until it's done, and feed myself, too."

It was a measure of her concern for her daughter that she did not bridle at the suggestion. She left him with most particular instructions, which he promised to follow to the letter. By the time he had repeated them once, then again, the cake was done; she set it on the table to cool, hung up her apron with unruffled tidiness, and excused herself.

He went to bed that night a happy man, replete with cake and stew and the sweet savor of victory. In the morning, he thought, he would begin the next phase of his campaign: going from door to door and taking down the charms, and calling the rest of the strays back to the fold. He fell asleep with a smile on his face and a heart full of anticipation. It would be a glorious morning, and an even more glorious week, in which Ballynasloe at last, for the first time in its existence, became truly a Christian village.

◆　◆　◆

It was raining that Monday morning, with a raw edge to it that spoke all too clearly of winter. The hermit had been up all night burning the volumes of his sonnets—which served, quite incidentally, to keep him warm in the unexpected chill. Pegeen had brought his daily meal while he snatched a bit of sleep: he found the pail and the jar and the basket of bread and apples by the hearth when he woke. The bread and the stew were as substantial as ever, but the ale had fallen off dreadfully. It was thin and horribly bitter. He gagged on the first unsuspecting swallow, and spat it explosively into the fire. The flames hissed and glowed briefly green.

"William," said a voice as sweet as honey in the comb. "William Thorne."

He started at the sound of the name that he had left behind with the rest of his worldly life, and scowled as he spun. "My name is Brother Columbanus!"

"William Thorne," said the uninvited guest. She was sitting on the bench by the wall. He had not heard her open or shut the door, which even after Pegeen's ministrations had a noticeable squeak in the hinges. She was simply sitting there, smiling slightly, dressed in something shimmering and white.

He did not, except for the first fraction of a second, mistake her for an angel. Angels, as any hermit should know, had no gender. This was a female beyond any shadow of a doubt. She looked rather like Pegeen, in fact, with her hair as black as black ever was, and her skin as white as snow on the mountain, and her eyes the color of the sapphire that his lost beloved's husband had given her on their wedding day.

That memory, once so piercingly painful, now barely rippled the surface of his calm. He knew his Plato; he was a Cambridge man. To the blurred and faded shadow that was Pegeen, this was the luminous reality. His memory of the yellow-haired Englishwoman had dwindled away to nothing. Before this vision of glory, he had forgotten even her name.

"William Thorne," said the vision a third time, as if to seal the spell. "A good morning to you, and a fair meeting on this fine wild day."

"Good—good morning," the hermit stammered. He tried to scrape together the fragments of his dignity, but they were lost beyond recall. "How do you know my name? How did you get in? How—"

"So many questions," she said, still with that hint of a smile. "Is that ale in the jar beside you? May I trouble you for a sip? For it's far I've come, and a thirsty journey, too."

"It should be ale," the hermit said. "It tastes like cat piss." He caught himself; he flushed as hot as the fire. "Pardon—pardon—I—"

"Is that the very truth?" his visitor inquired. He had not seen her move, but somehow the jar was in her hand. She sipped from it, paused to savor the sip, then nodded as if in satisfaction. Then, to his startlement, she lifted the jar and drank deep.

He leaped to her rescue—for, by God's bones, she would destroy her stomach with that vile excuse for a tipple. She smiled blissfully at him and surrendered the jar. He raised it to fling the remainder of its contents into the fire, but stopped short as a pair of things intruded on his awareness: one, that the jar was as heavy as if she had not half drained it, and two, that such an aroma wafted from it as must wreathe the casks in Paradise.

In his shock, he could not help himself. He sipped as she had. His eyes went wide. Just as she had, he took a deep and blissful draught. This was the very living archetype of Ale, as she was the archetype of Woman. And when at last he lowered the jar, with his head spinning from the glorious fumes, the brown ale lipped the brim. The jar was as full as it had been when he began.

He was not ready yet to accept what he was seeing. That the priest was right and there was magic in this world, and a being other than an angel could appear to a would-be holy hermit and transform a misbegotten brew into the tipple of the gods.

His uninvited guest arched a brow. "My dear William. You will credit the existence of angels but not of good earthly magic? Is that what it is to be modern—to be all agog over a myth and all blind to the truth?"

"Your accent," he said. "You sound . . . English."

She drew herself up. He had not known she was so tall. "Indeed I am not any such thing! I am a daughter of the Daoine Sidhe, of lineage as old as any in Ireland."

Her indignation was as imposing as her height. It even overwhelmed the fact that she had heard his thought as clearly as if he had spoken it. "I—I'm sorry," he said rather weakly. "I didn't intend—I only meant—"

"Of course you never intended to offend," she said from the height of her dudgeon. "In all your reading of myths and stories, did you never come across the gift of tongues?"

"I came across many things," he said, and for safety's sake: "lady. How can angels be a myth? They're religious doctrine."

"Have you ever seen an angel?"

"Well," he said, "no. But faith requires—"

"Ah," she said. "What you've never seen, you believe. What you see before your very eyes and taste with your very tongue, you call a fancy and a fabrication, because in your vision of the world there can be no such thing."

Her logic was rather deadly. Her eyes were even more so. He could drown in them. "I believe in you," he said dreamily, "but not necessarily in—"

"I suppose that will have to do," she said with studied patience. "Believe in me, then, and listen. I come to you for help."

"For—" He gaped at her. "What can the likes of me do for the likes of you?"

"One would wonder," she said, but kindly enough that he could not take it poorly. "Still, none of us can escape the truth of it. We have a great difficulty and a spreading grief, and all our castings and omens send us to you."

"Why? What can I do?"

"That," she said, "the omens don't say. Only that you are our best hope."

"For what? Against what?"

She nodded as if his sudden sharpness pleased her. He never knew what to do with himself around a beautiful woman. With this one, for a miracle, he could speak. Mostly he stood and gobbled, or blushed until he had to turn and bolt.

When she spoke again, her voice had a stronger music. He heard the lilt of the Irish in it then. "I come from the Daoine Sidhe to the hermit of Ballynasloe, to the last of his kind in all of Ireland. I come in the name of the Dagda and the Morrigan and Maeve the queen, with their strength in my hand and their blessing on my head. We beg that you will hear us.

"Our power is not what it was. The moon has waned too often. The sun is setting fast. We are old, old as our green hills, and year by year we dwindle into the grass.

"Time was when we would have raised war in heaven and riven the earth below, and broken the back of any army that came against us. Now we have shrunk into the little people, the faerie folk, dwellers under the hills. We feed on cream that goodwives set on doorsteps, and perform little magics for those who still, in their dim way, remember.

"We were proud once. We were gods, and mortals worshiped us. That is gone. All gods die; time rules us all, even us who saw this isle rise gleaming out of ocean.

"We are dying, but our time is not yet come. Yet we are being hastened to our end. Our shrines are violated, our workings fouled, our own land turned against us. The faith that sustained us is being eaten away. Cruel spells weaken and destroy us."

"The priest's crusade," the hermit said in a flash of understanding. "He's only one man. How can he—"

"Not one man alone, William Thorne," she said. "Years, centuries of them. Bell, book, and candle drained away our strength year by year, robbed us of the mortal faith that fed us, and narrowed the sphere of our earthly power to one small ring of hills and a valley with a river in it, and an oak, and a Druid wood."

"Ballynasloe," said the hermit.

"Ballynasloe," she said. "All those things, and an old tower that was ours long ago, set above the last of the hollow hills, with the last hermit living in the tower and the last of us living below."

The hermit regarded her in a kind of a horror. "Then I'm destroying you, too. My devotions, my prayers—"

She laughed—astonishing, and ravishing, with her white teeth and her tumbled hair, and the sound of it like water bubbling from a pure spring. "Oh, no! You're not destroying us at all. Such little strength as we have left, you feed, with your innocence and your trust, and your faith in the beauty of women."

"My faith is in God!"

"And is not every woman an incarnation of Her?"

"God is not—" He stopped short. "You're as pagan as Pegeen."

"I'm of the Daoine Sidhe," she said. "The water of baptism would sear the flesh from my bones."

"I'm a man of God," the hermit said. "I *am*."

"Mostly certainly you are," she said. "Will you help us? We harm no one. We'll fade in time; but it should be our time, not that of the man who has taken such exception to our little tribute of charms and cream."

"He says that you endanger the villagers' immortal souls. He's charged with the care of those souls. He has to defend them."

"We are no danger to anyone's soul," she said.

He should not have believed her. If she had been in any way seductive, if she had slid eyes at him or curved her body toward him, he would have known that she was false. But she never moved. Her face was somber. Her words were simple and her eyes steady. She did nothing that a woman would do to tempt a man.

Her existence was a temptation. He signed himself with the cross, desperately. "Get you behind me! Go!"

To his lasting astonishment, she obeyed him. She winked out like a flame in a wind, vanished as if she had never been.

He should have been triumphant. He sank down by the hearth where the fire was dying, and wished he had never been born. Even with faerie women, he was crashingly inept.

◆　◆　◆

Wᴵᴸᴸᴵᴬᴹ ᴛʜᴼᴿᴺᴱ," said the voice that had been haunting his dreams. He had hoped and dreaded that he would not hear it again while he was awake. But awake he most certainly was. He was digging in his garden in a brief bit of sun between a blustery morning and the promise of rain at evening.

She cast no shadow over him as she stood between the poles on which the last of the beans were hanging rather sadly. Her garment was the color of autumn leaves, and her skin was as white and her hair as black as he remembered. In the plain daylight she seemed more real than anything around her.

"William Thorne," she said. "Have you reconsidered?"

Get thee behind me! he meant to thunder, but all that came out was a strangled squeak. His dreams had been full of her. What he had been doing in them, and what she had been doing in return, he prayed she could not see. He had been doing penance for it until his back was raw.

God seemed very remote just then and rather mythical. She was there and real and as solid as the black earth of Ireland.

"If you're dying," he heard himself say, "then why are you so— so—"

"You give me life," she said. "It's a blessing and a miracle. What a rare creature you are, William Thorne!"

"I'm very ordinary," he said. "I'm a terrible poet. I'm worthless with women. I'm not even very good at being a hermit."

"You are excellent at being William," she said, "and at making us stronger. Tell me, William Thorne. What price will you take for your help against us?"

"What—"

"Gold?" she asked. "Jewels? Works of beauty and great worth?"

"Faerie gold turns to dust in the morning," he said. "Even I know that."

"This is real gold," she said, "from old hoards. But if that won't buy you . . . what of fame? You call yourself a bad poet. Would you gain the gift of the bard? We can make you the greatest maker and singer that ever was in Ireland, give you words of power to shake the courts of kings. You'll make men laugh and sing for joy, and weep with the beauty of your verses."

The hermit's heart stopped, then began to hammer so hard he nearly fell over. Gold tempted him not at all—he had plenty of that if he wanted it, back in Somerset. Poetry—to be a true bard—

"Oh, God," he said. "Dear God." But then, with every fiber of his being: "No. No, I will not. It would never be real. It would be yours, and I would always remember that. It wouldn't come from inside of me."

She regarded him with respect, and bowed as if to a lord. "Integrity," she said, "is the rarest of virtues. Tell me then, William Thorne. In return for the salvation of my people, would you take love? Would you take me?"

He groaned aloud. Heaven was in his grasp, beauty beyond mortal, love that would be, he had no doubt, of quite literally legendary splendor. And yet he said, "I am a man of God. I have forsaken love."

"Even love of God?"

He stared at her. Words were nearly beyond him. He was amazed that he had said as much as he had.

"William Thorne," she said so tenderly that his throat tightened with tears. "Did you think that the old hermits had abandoned the beauty that is between man and woman?"

He could answer that, in a breathless croak to be sure, but there were words at hand, and he spoke them. "They gave up everything—all the lures and uses of the world. They lived pure; they lived clean. They devoted their every living moment to the worship of God."

" 'With my body I thee worship,' " she said. "Those words are in your ritual. I've heard them many and many a time from the church door when a woman weds a man. And do believe me, William Thorne, that many a hermit did just that, away in his tower or his bothy, when he needed a more solid proof of devotion than the words of a prayer."

"No," said the hermit. "You're telling falsehoods—wicked lies to win me over. I won't listen. I won't hear—"

"William Thorne," said that sweetest of voices, "I would never lie to so pure a spirit. I would give myself freely and love you truly, for yourself, and because you were the savior of my people."

"I can't," he said. "I swore a vow. That I would never—"

"You swore out of the pain of your heart," she said, "and out of the conviction that, after all, no woman would have you. For who wants a fool and a mooncalf, a bad poet with nothing better to recommend him than a substantial income and a country house in Somerset? Who would truly love you, or want you for anything but what your father has to leave you? Who would want you as you are, with nothing to your name but a half-ruined tower and a borrowed gown?"

Her words were so true, and so cutting, and so exquisitely cruel, that he could only stand and gape at her. He had thought his heart broken when his true love married another—and what was her name again? What had her face been like? When he tried to think of her, he saw only the face of this woman of the Sidhe.

"I would take you," she said, "though you were naked on a hilltop, bereft even of your wits. Even if you could not help us—yes, I would love you."

"Why?" he said. That tongue of his had a life of its own.

"Because you are yourself," she said. "I watched you long and long before I came to you. I saw what a fool you are, and how silly you can be, but also the goodness of your heart. You will help us, if you can convince yourself that it's worth doing."

"Yes," he said, "I will. But not because you bribed me. Because—because I think you're worth saving. Prove to me that you are, and I'll do it. Not that I don't think you are beautiful and perfect and absolutely tempting, but they say the Devil can be dreadfully like you. Why should I turn against Christian doctrine and save the lives of a pack of pagan gods?"

"Why indeed?" she said. She seemed in no way discouraged. "You love beauty, yes? You love the old things, the true things."

"Magic is all sleights and lies," he said.

"Is it? Do you know so much about it, William Thorne?"

"I know enough," he said. "Prayer is true. God is true."

"And did not God make us, too? We are Her first children. She gave us magic, for beauty and for delight. Yes, it could turn to darkness and terror, but that is true of anything in this world." She held out her hand. "Come. Come and see."

The hermit knew that he should not. He had read the stories, heard the warnings. He could go under the hill and come out a hundred years later, and none of this would matter at all.

And yet, in spite of all he knew or thought he knew, in his heart he trusted this woman. He thought he could sense the truth in her, and the lack of deceit, which ran against all the stories, but there it was. Stories were stories. She was there in front of him. He did believe in what he could see, however preposterous he might once have thought it.

He took a deep breath and crossed himself, at which she did not even flinch. He set his hand in hers. She was solid and warm. He had half expected her to be as cold and frail as mist, but that was real flesh against his fingers and palm, and real bone under it. Only the faint tingle of what must be magic betrayed that she was not a human woman.

Her fingers closed about his. "Are you ready?" she asked.

He had no time to reply. The mists were already rising, and the world melting away. He tasted blood where he had bitten his tongue.

Wherever he was going, that taste of iron and sweetness would remind him that he, like it, was mortal; that magic was not his heritage.

◆　◆　◆

Father timothy's army had swelled to a hundred strong. Man and woman alike, they had armed themselves with axes and a fire of holy zeal. They gathered in front of the church in the morning, singing hymns to keep themselves occupied until he was done with the morning office. He had not known so many of them knew Latin, or that these unmistakably secular people could chant as sonorously as an abbey of monks. The long ominous roll of the *Dies irae* escorted him out into the watery sunlight.

He paused on the church steps, giving a last tug to his vestments and firming his grip on the processional cross. For this he had judged it appropriate to appear in full uniform as it were. At the sight of him, the gathering raised a deep-throated roar.

It was a little frightening to see how dedicated they were. Frightening and exhilarating. They were his army—his soldiers of the Lord. He marshaled them with a word and led them out of the churchyard toward the field of battle.

The tree stood in a field beyond the water mill. The Druid wood came up close to it, but the tree stood alone. It was an oak, with a trunk so thick that half a dozen children could barely reach around it with their arms outstretched. Legend had it that a golden sickle was buried deep inside it, grown into the bark since some ancient Druid had left it there. What his reasons were or what had become of him, even legend did not say.

What the legend did say was that it was the oldest tree in this part of Ireland, and maybe in the whole island. It had been sacred before Saint Patrick came, and had clung to that holiness through centuries of Christian rule. Until Father Timothy stopped them, people had been bringing offerings to it, hanging them in its branches, and whispering prayers into its gnarled roots.

The oak was the last unabashedly pagan thing in Ballynasloe. A wind was blowing through its branches, rattling the dry leaves. Yet no wind blew on the army as it advanced. The air was perfectly still everywhere but in the direct vicinity of the tree.

Out of the corner of his eye Father Timothy thought he could see a flicker of shadows. They swirled about the tree and spun upward toward the gathering of clouds over the wan sun.

He raised his cross like a banner and swept it forward. "Onward!" he cried.

"Onward!" they roared back.

They came in ranks with axes at the ready. Seamus the woodcutter had the honor of the first blow. The ancient oak was as hard as iron. It turned the axe-blade even in those skilled hands and nearly took off the head of the man who pressed too close behind.

Seamus cursed in most unsaintly fashion and hefted his weapon again, glaring down anyone who might have thought to move in. He measured the tree with narrowed eyes, secured his grip on the handle, and swung with a much more carefully judged degree of force.

Bark flew. The axe barely bit, but it was a start.

With a hundred of them, some almost as skilled as Seamus, the tree could not hope to win the battle. It tried its best. Between its thickness and the hardness of its bark and wood, it put up a noble fight. Other things helped it, things barely to be seen but clearly to be felt. Cold iron was death to the old things, but they had ways to thwart it nonetheless.

Father Timothy's army was at it for half the day, taking turns and a long rotation. If anyone lost will or strength, or succumbed to the insubstantial horrors of the pagan belief, a dozen came to take his place. They cut down the Druid tree and hewed it into firewood. Father Timothy spoke the by-now-familiar words of exorcism over the stacked wood. It was all good hard oak that would burn well on the hearth this winter—not a hint of rot or softness in it, and that was a wonder in itself.

Danny Murphy the carter was waiting to haul off the wood. He needed two trips to carry it all, with plenty of willing hands to help him load and unload.

Father Timothy looked on in satisfaction. That was it, he thought. That was the end of the cleansing of Ballynasloe. The sunlight was clean, and the earth was consecrated to the proper Faith. The village was as Christian as it could ever be.

And yet as he contemplated the Mass of celebration that he would perform when Sunday came round again, he paused to wonder why he was not more deliriously happy. He could not help feeling that he had missed something. The exorcisms were all done, the prayers all said, the perimeters secured. Surely there was no pagan thing left to trouble him or anyone else.

Maybe Saint Patrick had felt the same way after he drove the snakes out of Ireland—as if he could not have expelled them all. He must have missed one.

He had not, and nor had Father Timothy. The world was clean. It all belonged to God, and God, he imagined, was glad.

◆　◆　◆

JUST AS THE MIST ROSE TO OBSCURE THE WORLD, the hermit pulled his hand out of the lady's grasp. "No!" he said. "I don't need proof. I don't want to go away for a hundred years or a thousand and one nights or whatever it is. I can't afford the time, and if you're telling the truth, neither can you." He looked her in the eye. "Tell me your name. Just do that, and I'll believe you."

He had startled her. That must be hard to do, if she was as ancient as she said she was. "Just like that?" she asked.

"Well," he said, "maybe not just like that. Hold my hand and meet my eyes and tell me your true name. If it's the truth you're telling, I'll do what you ask."

"You know what you're asking of me," she said. "If you gain that power and use it badly, it will go ill for you as well as me."

"You said I was trustworthy," he said. "You'll have to trust me, then, and do as I ask—or," he said, and for all that he could do, his voice quavered, "or go away and never come back."

For his soul's sake he should have wished that she would do exactly that, but his heart hoped devoutly that she would not.

She took his hands as the mist melted away in the pale sunlight, and looked into his eyes. Her beauty threatened to break his poor long-suffering heart. She was even more beautiful inside, he thought as he met that deep blue gaze. "My name," she said, "is Deirdre."

He gaped. "Not *the* . . ."

"Oh, no," she said. "My sorrows are much more recent and less personal."

"Deirdre," he said dreamily. "Beautiful Deirdre. Lady of sorrows." He blinked hard and pulled himself forcefully back to earth. Her gaze kept trying to lure him away again. Never mind whatever journey she had had in mind—one long look into those eyes, and he had traveled as far into enchantment as he ever needed to go.

He was lost, he supposed, and his soul was in dire danger. He could not find it in himself to be concerned about it.

As he stood staring, she gasped and swayed. Her face had gone stark white. She seemed for a moment to lose substance, to become transparent.

He clutched at her hands and willed her back to solidity. Her fingers locked in his. She clung for her life.

"What," he said. "What—"

"The tree," she said faintly. "They cut down the tree. Its roots go deep, so deep . . . it draws up magic. But no longer. It's broken, broken and dead. William Thorne, if you can do anything, I beg of you—"

And that was the trouble. He could not think of a single useful thing to do, except help her into the tower and sit her down by the fire and spoon broth into her from the pot that Pegeen had brought that morning. She did not object to mortal sustenance, nor cast it back up again, either.

While he looked after her, he began to feel odd. Things were fluttering on his skin and flickering just out of sight. The floor suddenly felt . . . full. As if a great crowd had gathered under it.

She read his thought as always. The broth had revived her; she was still weak, but she could speak. "Yes," she said. "They're here. They've all gone under the hill. There's nowhere else that they can go."

"If the priest finds out," said the hermit, "we'll be exorcised with the rest."

Her lips twitched ever so slightly at that *we*. "We can make a stand here. There's still a little power left in us. All together in one ancient place, we'll be able to resist him for a while. We'll go out with honor, at least, and die in battle."

He rose up in protest. "You are not going to die! I'll think of something. Just give me time. I do have a little, I hope?"

"A little," she said with a sigh.

"I'll pray it's enough," he said. He appreciated the irony of that after he had said it, but he did not try to call it back. These were God's children, too. He had convinced himself of it, looking into her eyes. God would listen to a prayer for their welfare.

◆　◆　◆

THE FAERIE FOLK CAME in all shapes and sizes, from the slender height of the Daoine Sidhe to the diminutive sturdiness of the bogles and hobs and leprechauns, and every range between. Kelpies had come to live in the stream that flowed around the foot of the hill, and but for their magic it would have been a tight fit for all of them. But they managed.

How many of the rest filled the halls under hill, the hermit did not try to guess. Many, that much he could tell: more than he might have expected from the lady's laments. If they were but a fraction of their former numbers, in their heyday they must have been as thick as midges in a marsh.

He had all the evidence he needed now of their existence and their various natures. Deirdre's race and rank protected him from the worst of the mischief, and most of the magics slipped harmlessly away when he happened by. Even so, he could not prevent them from turning his tower into an otherworldly palace and his robe into faerie silk. He would rouse from prayer or sleep to find himself decked with gold and jewels or banked in flowers.

The gold was more lasting than the flowers—stolen from old hoards as the lady had said. He did not find it tempting at all—not being an antiquarian except in the matter of his martyrdom, and honestly having no care for such things.

◆   ◆   ◆

THE MORNING AFTER the Sidhe came to his tower, the hermit was up at dawn. He struggled out of his bed of lilies and roses, shedding bloodred petals, and pulled off the rings and armlets and brooches with which he was weighed down. There was nothing to be done about the shimmering glory of his robe but hope that daylight would turn it to plain brown serge again.

There was no sign of the lady. Her relatives seemed all to have retreated under hill, having made an uproarious and nightlong carouse up one side of his tower and down the other. It was a miracle he had slept through it.

His boots were standing by the door. They had been repaired at every point and polished until they gleamed, but they were still their sturdy selves. He pulled them on and tramped out in the pale grey light.

He had not left his hill since he came to it in the spring. It was strange to set foot on the road again, winding down it toward Ballynasloe. The stream that crossed it was empty of wild black horses, magical or otherwise.

By the time he passed the first house of the village, he had lost most of what courage he had. His plan was worthless. He would do much better to stay in his tower, try to keep his multitude of guests under control, and pray that the priest never learned where the faerie folk had gone.

His feet carried him onward. He had nothing to do with it. They brought him to the tavern and deposited him in the empty taproom, face-to-face with a startled Pegeen.

◆　◆　◆

Pegeen believed his story, wilder bits and all. Better yet, she knew exactly what to do about his rickety bones of a plan. "Leave it to me," she said.

He had no choice but to trust her. There was no one else in the village to whom he dared go. She fed him oat bread fresh from the oven and tea with milk that had not quite begun to turn, then sent him back to his fantastically crowded tower.

◆　◆　◆

The bishop's man was peacefully clopping down the road to Cashel, with no thought in his head but his dinner, his pipe, and his well-earned bed. He was shocked to the marrow to be halted in mid-clop by an apparition of power and terror.

The younger of the two women gripped his horse's bridle. The elder sat in the buggy that had been in her family for time out of mind and peered at him through her little round spectacles, just as she had when she was his housekeeper in the parish of Ballynasloe. "Monsignor Edward O'Reilly," she said. "I'd like a word with you, if I may."

Monsignor O'Reilly would never rise so high in the Church that he could defy the will of the formidable Mrs. Murphy. He bowed, as speechless as he had been in his raw and undignified youth.

It was more than a word and more than a moment, and as he heard it, he remembered who he was and what responsibility he had to the bishop and the diocese. When she was done, he said, "A crusade can be a marvelous thing. A crusade without the sanction of one's superiors in the Church . . . that could be another matter."

"It is a great matter," Mrs. Murphy said, "and a matter of some urgency. If you could see your way to speak with the bishop sooner rather than later . . ."

"I'll speak to him this very night," Monsignor O'Reilly said. He meant it, too. The bishop was a great and terrible personage, but Mrs. Murphy was a close relative to the wrath of God.

For a shrinking moment he knew she would announce that she was coming with him to make sure he kept his word. But she nodded briskly and cocked a brow at the buxom lass who restrained his horse. The young woman let go the brown cob's bridle and climbed into Mrs. Murphy's buggy and took up reins. Without another word spoken, she turned the buggy and sent the neat little bay at a fast trot toward Ballynasloe.

◆　◆　◆

THE BISHOP'S MAN ARRIVED in the village on Sunday morning, just as people were walking or driving in ones and twos and families to morning Mass. He left his companions in the yard at the inn, entrusting them to the capable hands of Pegeen's father, and walked alone to the church.

No one knew who he was. He had a greatcoat over his soutane with its telltale red piping, and a big black umbrella to keep off the mist of rain. He looked much like everyone else on that soft day, hurrying toward a roof and a dry place to sit.

Father Timothy was blissfully unaware of the fly in his ointment. He looked out from the sacristy across a sea of faces—a church packed full, with people standing in the back and along the aisles—and knew the contentment of a man whose job is well done. The old pagan things were driven out. Ballynasloe was saved.

His vestments were waiting, with the server beside them, ready to help him into them. He did not just then recall the boy's name. There were so many redheaded, freckle-faced, snub-nosed imps in the village. If he called out "Sean" or "Seamus" or "Patrick," he had as good a chance as any of happening on the right one.

The boy greeted him with a gap-toothed grin. For a moment Father Timothy wondered how old he actually was. Those eyes were much too sly and knowing to belong to a child.

Children these days were abominably worldly and wise. Father Timothy nodded toward the vestments. "It's time," he said.

"Oh yes," said the boy in the broadest brogue imaginable. "That indeed it is."

A movement caught Father Timothy's eye. He looked toward the corner and started.

The hermit was sitting there. He looked terribly young and pale, and in fact rather ill. He had a rose in his hand. Supernal sweetness wafted from it.

The hermit held out the rose. Father Timothy took it without suspicion. He was armored in the Lord. He had nothing to fear from any earthly thing.

A thorn pricked his finger. He hissed at the sting, and licked a drop of blood the exact same color as the rose. Its taste was supernally sweet. It made his head whirl.

Mass was beginning without him. He heard the voices of the choir. Had they ever sung so beautifully? They were like the voices of angels. The wheezy old organ lifted up the cry of trumpets and the shiver of harps.

He moved toward the door into the church. He had no memory of putting on any of it, but he was vested in shimmering white as befit a great celebration, a Mass of the Angels: the feast of the salvation of Ballynasloe.

The procession was waiting. They were all, like the server, vaguely familiar. They were dressed in white and carrying palms, considerably out of season but beautiful to see. Were those wings arching above their heads?

His heart swelled until it was ready to burst. Angels had come to celebrate with the mortal congregation. The church was full of them. They perched on the corbels of the arches and wreathed the pillars with heavenly garlands. They floated over the altar, a dense and whirling wheel of them, singing the *Te Deum*.

He lifted up his arms and sang with them, floating down the aisle in his escort of heavenly visitors. He danced and dipped and whirled, giddy with supernal joy.

◆　◆　◆

FATHER TIMOTHY WAS STILL SINGING in his pleasant baritone as the monsignor's companions helped him into the wagon. The straitjacket was just a precaution, the bespectacled medical man had assured the hermit. "It's unlikely he'll turn violent," he said, "but the journey's somewhat long, and he's clearly not himself. Better be safe than sorry."

"Do you think he'll get better?" the hermit asked in honest concern.

The medical man shrugged. "Who's to tell? Sometimes they do, sometimes they don't. It's in the hands of God."

Maybe, thought the hermit, and maybe those hands had nothing to do with the Christian Deity in Whose name the priest had driven the faerie folk out of Ballynasloe. He said a prayer, and not just because it was his duty, that Father Timothy would come out of it in the Lord's good time and be his old self again—without the urge to preach a crusade.

A good number of the priest's former crusaders, now greatly chastened, stood watching the downfall of their leader. The Monsignor had taken them under his ample wing. The sermon he had preached while his men dealt with the priest had been short but powerfully effective. It had restored the people of Ballynasloe to sanity in a matter of minutes—and that was quite as magical as anything the hermit's allies could have managed.

Those allies were coming back into the village, quietly and unobtrusively, but he was sensitized to them. He could feel them like a slow seep of water into a dry well. The people could feel it, too—they were standing a little straighter, breathing a little more freely. There was a strong strain of magic in the blood here. Without the old powers in the earth and water and air, they had been subtly and spiritually starved.

He would do penance for what he had helped to do. So would Pegeen and her Aunt Mary Margaret Murphy and maybe the Monsignor, too. Still he could not wish it undone. If that meant his soul was corrupted, then so it was.

It did not feel like corruption at all. It felt like such lightness and freedom and dizzy joy that he could barely keep his feet on the ground. He was lucky there were no men waiting for him with a straitjacket.

A warm hand slipped into his. The lady of the Sidhe stood beside him as easily as a mortal woman, watching as they all watched, while the Monsignor said good-bye to Mrs. Murphy and her brother the tavernkeeper. Pegeen had tried to get the hermit to put himself forward, but he would not. "You take the glory," he had told her. "I'll take the peace and quiet."

"I suppose I will have that," he said to Deirdre as the wagon rattled into motion. The priest was singing at the top of his lungs, as happy a madman as ever made his way to an asylum. "Now that all of you have your homes back."

"I suppose you will," she said, "if you wish it. Or . . ."

"Or?" he asked when she did not go on.

"Or you might have a visitor now and then," she said. "Maybe more now than then."

His heart beat in the old familiar rhythm, fast as a faerie dance under the moon. This time he did not want to stop it. The magic had possessed him. He was fully aware of it. He could cast it out—he knew how; Father Timothy had shown him. But he did not want to.

"In the old days," Deirdre said, "a hermit could be a great friend to us. He could be a lover, too, with no fear of sin and no need of repentance. It was only long after that Rome turned all sour and narrow, and declared love a sin when it had been a sacrament."

She could be lying or stretching a slippery truth. She could be tempting him with diabolical skill. But his heart insisted that this much she did truly mean: she loved him. And he loved her. In her presence he had forgotten even poetry. She was the living essence of it.

The wagon had gone away down the road, with the Monsignor in his buggy behind it. The crowd had melted away. The rain had stopped; the clouds were breaking.

The sun came out as the hermit began to walk toward his tower. His fingers were still laced with Deirdre's. He did not answer her directly, but she could read his smile—none better. Her own smile exactly mirrored it.

They walked hand in hand through the village of Ballynasloe. As they walked, they noticed that certain things had changed since the hermit came through that morning on his way to the church. The charms were back on the gateposts. And on every doorstep was a bowl of cream.

The Merrow

BY ELIZABETH HAYDON

June 2, 1847

Like the other men in his family, young Patrick Michael Martin was color-blind.

Given that he could claim most of the small farming village of Glencar in County Kerry as family, Patrick was in good company in his inability to distinguish red, yellow, purple, or green from the miasma of grey tones that served as the landscape he saw out of his diminished eyes. Aside from the blue sky above, the world appeared to him as one long expanse of colorlessness in varying intensities. Having nothing to compare it to, however, he did not feel the loss.

In the early years of the Great Blight, just before the famine roared through, blackening fields and withering potatoes on the vine, the men of Glencar who worked those fields were at a unique disadvantage, because the initial signs of the scourge were subtle. The "white" Irish potato, originally brought back from the New World by the Spanish, revealed its disease first by going slightly green.

And the men of Glencar could not see the color green.

After many of them sickened and died from eating the blighted crop, the tenant farmers that remained gathered together one evening at dusk in Donovan McNamara's barn to talk about the unthinkable— leaving Glencar and the rocky lands beneath Macgillicuddy's Reeks, the tallest of Ireland's mountains, where their families had farmed for centuries, both before and after the English came.

"The landlords are sending troops to evict anyone who's in arrears in County Limerick," said Oisin McGill nervously. "The village of Coyt is empty, the whole town of Ballincolly has gone to slave in the workhouses of Tipperary."

"They are starvin' down in County Cork, I hear," whispered Eoin O'Connell. "The priests there said there were to be no more burials in coffins, to spare the money for food. Families are to put the dead in the ground in but the clothes they were wearing when they passed."

"Landlord Payne says he will forgive our taxes and pay for our passage in exchange for leaving the lands," McNamara said. "The crop may not be entirely lost yet, but how can we tell the good from the bad? Not one of us has color in his eyes. I've decided we will emigrate to America. I don't know what else to do, and I won't stay here to die on another man's lands."

"Nor will I," Colm Martin, Patrick's uncle, agreed. "I have children to think of. We leave after Mass on Sunday for Dingle. There are ships sailing from there every week or so now."

Patrick's father, Old Pat, cleared his throat. The noise in the barn fell away in the whine of the wind; Old Pat rarely spoke, and when he did, the men of Glencar listened carefully. Old Pat had been a sailor in his youth until two decades before, when he came home to farm his family's ancestral land in Glencar. His wisdom was never doubted, especially regarding the sea.

"Those rickety ships be naught more than floating coffins," he said, his voice gruff. "They're packin' three times the number they should be into 'em. You'll be lucky if half of you live to see New York. I'd rather die here and be buried in the blighted soil of Ireland than be food for fish." He rose slowly to leave, then turned back to his despairing neighbors and younger brother. "But then, that's me. My son is grown, and can decide for himself. Aisling and I will stay. The rest of you, do what you must."

The door of the barn creaked mournfully as it opened, and he was gone.

Patrick rose to follow him, only to be stopped by the hand of Donovan McNamara at his elbow. He looked down; Donovan's hand had withered to arthritic bone covered with sagging skin.

"Young Pat," Donovan said, "you must think of your mother. Aisling's a young woman still; she's not aged a day since your father brought her to Glencar before you were born. Old Pat may be ready to go to sod in Ireland's arms, but your mother, now—"

Patrick nodded. He had been thinking the same.

All the way home in the darkness he wondered as he walked what he could say to his father that could possibly change the most stubborn mind in three counties, knowing full well that no such words existed. The stars winked bright above him in a sky that held no trace of moonlight.

The warm glow of the hearth fire shone in the windows as he came over the hill to his mother's house where he still lived. Old Pat's prized Irish draft horse, Fionnbar, was nowhere to be seen. Patrick opened the door quietly, in case his mother was already to bed.

Aisling sat before the fire, mending Fionnbar's bridle. Her eyes sparkled upon beholding Patrick, and she smiled her customary slight smile, but she returned to her work without speaking. Both of his parents were given to using words sparingly.

Patrick hung his hat on the peg by the door and sat down on the stool near her feet. He watched her for a long time, her delicate hands weaving the leather strands back together seamlessly. Her face was thinner by a breath, no more, and Patrick noticed for the first time how much like the girls of Glencar she still looked, how beautifully shaped were her light eyes, how dark and thick her lashes. Donovan's words came back to him as his eyes roamed over her long hair, freed from the ties that held it bound during daylight, now hanging in rippling waves to her waist.

Aisling's a young woman still; she's not aged a day since your father brought her to Glencar before you were born.

"Mother," he said finally, reluctant to disturb her concentration, "the men concur. We must leave—the blight is spreading. Life, as hard as it may seem to believe, is about to worsen immensely. We should go to America with Uncle Colm and the others."

"Your father will never agree to it," Aisling said softly, her attention still fixed on her work.

"Aye, the Da is a stubborn man, but now stubbornness will lead to death, 'tis for certain," Patrick pressed, gentle in his tone but insistent in his words. "You are hale, Mother; God willing, you have many years ahead of you—"

Aisling did not look up. "Your father will never agree to it," she repeated. She finished her work in silence, then rose and went to the curtain that demarcated their bedchamber. "Good night, Patrick."

Patrick moved to her chair and sat in the darkness, watching the fire die down to coals, until the door opened, and Old Pat came in. He left his boots by the door, hung his hat and neckerchief on a peg, and disappeared behind the curtain without more than a nod. Patrick exhaled deeply and continued to stare at the coals until sleep took him.

Dawn found him there still, in Aisling's chair by the hearth. He woke, feeling the chill of morning, got up and stirred the ashes, hoping to warm the house a little for his parents before leaving to tend to

Fionnbar and the last remaining hen. He was at the well drawing water when Old Pat emerged from the house.

His father glanced around but did not appear to see him. Patrick watched, first in surprise, then in curiosity, as Old Pat made his way furtively behind the house, across the fields out toward the thinly wooded foothills of the high mountain of Carrauntoohil. His curiosity piqued, Patrick followed him, cutting through the sparse glades and high grass in which he had loved to hide since childhood.

There was something about that tall grass that had always pleased his soul, the way it undulated in the wind, even as it gave way to lower, brushy scrub closer to the hills. He had always been able to pass through the grass as easily as swimming through the water of a pond; Patrick hurried through it now, maintaining his distance while trying to keep his father in sight.

He followed him into the forest, taking cover in a grove of alders when Old Pat finally stopped some distance away. Patrick's eyes had always been keen, and he could see the older man's movements, even at a great distance, from his hiding place.

His father glanced around again and, noting nothing untoward, bent at the base of a rock hidden within a ring of trees. Patrick watched as he dug near the base of the rock, then, satisfied, made his way back through the woods again toward home.

Once Old Pat had been gone long enough to assure Patrick that he was not about to return, he emerged from the alder grove and hurried to the place in the tree ring when his father had been digging. The disturbed earth had been carefully covered over with dry leaves and brush, making it all but indiscernible.

He looked with more careful eyes at the place. Around the tree ring a circle of mushrooms grew; Patrick's hands began to sweat as he looked back at the trees, old Irish oaks that must have been miraculously spared from the Tudor axes that two hundred years before had stripped the land clean of them to build Queen Elizabeth's navies, or sprung from the acorns of those trees. He crossed himself hastily.

"A faerie ring," he whispered. "God's nightgown, Da, what are you about here?"

His first impulse was to run. Then worry and curiosity, coupled with fear for his father and a sense that their doom might as well be shared, won out over impulse. Patrick crouched on the cold ground and dug hastily.

He had to burrow beneath more than a foot of earth before his hand struck something smooth and hard. Cautiously, he brushed away the soil.

Within the deep hole was a sailor's chest, bound in tarnished brass.

Patrick's stomach tightened as his fingers ran over the lid, knowing that he was trespassing on something sacred to his father, and at the same time unable to resist. Believing the chest might hold a clue to Old Pat's redoubtable decision to brave the famine rather than leave for a chance at life in America, he swallowed his discomfort, pried the rusty catch open, and lifted the lid.

Inside the small chest were many layers of linen, strewn with tiny clods of earth. Patrick hesitated, then brushed away the dirt and carefully lifted the linen bundle from the chest, sitting back on the grass of the forest floor as he unwound the fabric.

His heart beat heavily in his chest; the wind blew through the glade, rustling the leaves ominously.

At the center of the linen wrappings was a delicate cap fashioned of a dark-colored fabric woven with pearls. Nothing more.

Patrick sat, lost in thought, while the wind whipped all around him, pondering the significance of what he had found. Finally, unable to make sense of it, he took out his handkerchief and painstakingly wrapped the fragile cap in it, stowing it in his pocket. He then rewound the linen and returned it to the chest, which he quickly reburied, obscuring the hole once more.

◆   ◆   ◆

By NOON THAT DAY Patrick had still not come to peace about his quandary. The handkerchief burned a hole in his pocket, his mind itching to make sense of it, why his father considered the pearl cap to be such treasure. And why had he not sold it, when he sold everything else of value they owned but Fionnbar? The beautiful horse was awaiting his leave-taking as well; Old Pat had offered him to the constable who patrolled the three counties and who promised to come by at midsummer to pay in grain. Money had ceased to be of much use; there was no food to be bought, even when there was coin in the pocket. Old Pat was worried that the constable, when he finally came, would be as empty-handed as everyone else.

At noon Patrick checked the hen. She had been a solid layer before the blight, and was fairly young, so while her eggs were small, she still produced one most days, even now that she was foraging in the grass in the absence of feed. She had laid that morning, and so Patrick was shocked to discover a second egg in the nest, gleaming white with a hint of milky blue, the one color he could distinguish.

This all-but-magical occurrence, and thoughts of the faerie ring, set his mind to thinking about Bronagh, the witch-woman who lived alone at the northern outskirts of Glencar. His uncle Colm had once accused Bronagh of stealing his milk in the form of a hare, back when Colm still owned cows. Bronagh had delivered Patrick, and most of the children in the village. She climbed nearby Carrauntoohil, the tallest peak in Ireland, gathering herbs for medicine and ceremony, and was said to celebrate the pagan feast of Lughnasadh, but still managed to attend daily Mass at Queen of Martyrs, Glencar's tiny church.

Father Flaherty, the pastor of Queen of Martyrs, had publicly declared, after hearing her confession, that she was harmless, a bit daft, perhaps, and without question odd, but not in league with Satan, and therefore should be pitied as the forlorn and lonely woman that she was, to whom kindness should be extended whenever possible. Bronagh, in turn, had tended the priest in his final hours as he lay dying of typhus resulting from the blight, had brought him consolation and a spiced soup that had broken his fever, eased his suffering and helped him to sink into a peaceful, painless sleep until his passing.

Bronagh kept to herself unless a baby was coming, or an illness needed tending. She could sometimes be seen in her tiny, rocky garden, but otherwise remained in her odd hut that backed up to the foothills of Carrauntoohil.

Bronagh knew everything.

Before he could think better of it, Patrick was standing at the gate of her broken picket fence, a blue hen's egg in his hand.

The old woman was hunched over in the corner of her garden, scratching futilely at the dry soil with her walking stick.

"Blight's taken the turnips and the horseradish as well," she said; her voice had the harsh sound of wood beneath the saw blade. She looked up then, and when her eyes lighted on Patrick they gleamed.

"Well met, Patrick Michael Martin," she greeted him, shambling forward to the gate. "You've grown a good deal since we've last shared the wind. What brings you? Is someone ailing?"

"No, ma'am," Patrick said respectfully. "I've brought you a hen's egg." He held it out to her.

The old woman's face hardened slightly as she took the blue egg, turning it over in her hand and studying it. When she looked back up at him her black eyes pierced his.

"What is it you wish to know, Patrick Michael Martin?"

Awkwardly, he reached into his pocket and withdrew the handkerchief, carefully unfolding it to show her the pearl-laced cap.

Bronagh breathed deeply.

"Come into the house," she said.

Patrick took off his hat and followed her into the small white hut. A single stool and a hay pallet covered with a linen sheet were the only furnishings. A rusted black pot hung on a crane over the fire. All about the place were jars and sacks and open mats on which herbs and flowers lay drying. An open doorway out the back appeared to lead to an outdoor root cellar of some sort. Woven reeds forming a St. Bridgid's cross adorned the wall, dressed with dried foxglove. The wind whistled through the open door, raising to his nose a thousand scents, spicy and sweet, sharp and musty, all at once.

Bronagh went to the fireplace and ladled some water from the bucket beside it into the pot over the fire, then slipped the egg into it.

"I can make you root tea if you wish, Patrick Michael Martin," she said, her hunched and bony back to him. "That and a bite of the egg you brought are all I can offer you."

"No, Bronagh, thank you," Patrick said hastily. "What can you tell me of the cap?"

The old woman turned, her eyes dark as tunnels in the backlight of the hearth fire.

"Where did you find it?" she asked. Her harsh voice was softer with import.

"In the forest back of the house," Patrick replied nervously, suddenly wishing he had kept to himself.

"Ah." Bronagh revisited the pot, stirring carefully. She sat on the stool, gesturing to Patrick to take the floor, which he did. "Your father must have hidden it out there, then."

Patrick felt ice constrict in his veins. "Why would you say such a thing, Bronagh?"

The witch eyed him levelly. "Was it in a sea chest?"

"Aye." Patrick cursed himself for the weakness in his voice.

"Then the cap must be your mother's," the old woman said.

"From their wedding? Is that why he saved it?"

Bronagh smiled. "You know that's not the answer without even asking the question," she said. "Within you, you sense that there is more."

"Aye," Patrick admitted, "though what that may be, I'm not certain."

"Do you wish to know the truth, then? I will tell it to you if you want to hear it, though I suspect you'll not thank me for it."

"Go on," Patrick said, laying the cap on his thigh to avoid touching it with hands that were by then covered in sweat.

"That is the cap of a murúch, a merrow," Bronagh said. "A sea creature, part human, with the tail of a fish. You've heard the tales, no doubt—the dream of sailors, the daughters of Cliodhna *Tuatha Dé Danann*—they are real, lad. They live within the waves of the sea a thousand years or more, never aging, soulless; their immortality is in this life, not the next. When they finally die, they but turn to foam upon the waves. Your mother, Aisling Martin, is a merrow."

"My mother is a devout Catholic," Patrick whispered. "And a daughter of Ireland."

"Aye, she may appear to be," Bronagh nodded. "But if she is a merrow, it is naught but appearance. Everything about her that you think you know is an illusion, Patrick Michael Martin.

"The merrow lives in the depths, venturing close to the rocky shore—do you know why? Because deep within her there is a compelling desire to walk upon the land, to see the dry world. It is a desire beyond reason, and there is but one way for her to fulfill that desire." The witch leaned closer to Patrick, who was trembling now as if with cold. "She must entrust her red pearl cap—red this is, Patrick, though you probably cannot see that—to the keeping of a human man, a sailor most often. If she does this, she grows human legs, the webbing between her fingers recedes. And then she can walk the earth and see the sights she has longed to see all her life."

Bronagh rose and went back to the fire. She swung the crane out from the flames, fished the egg out of the pot with a spoon, and returned to the stool, cradling the egg in her ratty apron.

"Once a merrow gives her cap to a human man, however, it is as if she has given him control of what little semblance of a soul she has. The freedom and the joy she once knew in the embrace of the sea is gone, replaced by a meek, compliant nature. She becomes a gentle wife, a patient mother, a woman without a thought for herself. The ocean that is her birthplace and her home is forgotten, along with all the spirit that it once gave her; merrows are creatures of immense passion and humor, daring and full of spit and vinegar in their natural state. Now she is a shell, a hollow shadow of her real self. And the man who holds her cap likes her that way. She tends to his needs, gives him comfort and sustenance, bears his children, keeps his home, all the while remaining ever young and beautiful, even as he ages unto death. It is hard to blame him, I suppose; what man wouldn't want such a thing?"

"You're daft, Bronagh," Patrick said testily. "My father adores my mother."

"No doubt," the witch said dryly. "But he adores her as she is, diminished, obedient, shallow like the landscape you color-blind gossoons see only in shades of grey, willing to believe that this is as the whole world is. It is *not*, Patrick—the world is a place of endless color, of vital, blooming color. Just because you do not perceive it does not mean it is not there." The old woman sighed. "But, of course, in life men hold the reins, just as your father holds your mother's cap in a sea chest buried deep in the forest."

Patrick ran his finger over the tiny pearls in the fabric, white pricks of light against a flat, dark background.

"What if I were to return it to her?" he asked.

Bronagh tapped the egg against the knobby white wall, cracking it. "You will both lose her forever if you do," she said seriously, peeling away the shell. "A merrow only remains with her husband because he has hidden her cap. Should she find it, or be given it back, she would immediately seek to return to her home in the sea. She will abandon house, husband, child, without a second thought. You will never see her again."

"No," Patrick said harshly. "You are wrong, Bronagh."

The old woman's dark eyes met his, and there was deep sadness in them. "You asked for the truth, Patrick Michael Martin, and I have given it to you. I am not saying this to decry your mother. But there is great magic in the sea, a magic much too strong to resist. Your own father knows it; ask yourself why he brought her here, to this rocky place in the lee of the tallest of Ireland's mountains, when all his young life he plied the sea by choice? I suspect that you yourself have never seen the sea. Your father knows what Aisling would do were she to find the cap—every sailor is versed in the lore of the merrow. He took her from the sea. She has forgotten her life there. But if you give her the cap, she will remember, and she will abandon all she knows of this world for a chance to return to it. She has been a prisoner of sorts all of your life, and before, ever since she left the sea. Everything she has done she has done against her will, but she does not know it." Bronagh lifted the peeled egg to her mouth. "Perhaps it is kinder not to tell her."

The only sound that followed her words was the crackle of the fire. Bronagh took a bite of the egg, watching Patrick as the young man wrestled with his thoughts. Finally, he stood and shook out his hat.

"Thank you, Bronagh," he said hollowly. "May God sustain you." He turned and walked to the doorway.

"Wait," the old woman blurted, struggling to rise. "What are you about to do, Patrick Michael Martin?"

"I won't be certain of that until I do it," Patrick replied. "I still believe you are mad. But I think my mother is entitled to the truth. In another time it might not be so; were Ireland hale and fertile, I might be tempted to let things be. But my father's insistence on remaining in Glencar is the weight that unbalances the scale. I cannot allow him to keep her here at the cost of her life, even if that costs him her love."

Bronagh shook her head sadly. "He has never had her love, lad, nor have you," she said. "All you have is her enforced fealty, against her will, nothing more."

"Be that as it may, she has mine," Patrick said. "And if in that I must let her go forever, then I must." He put his hat on his head.

The old woman swallowed the last of the boiled egg and brushed her hands against her torn skirts.

"The day I caught you as you came into this world was a good one, Patrick Michael Martin," she said. "May God grant you as many more good days as He is willing to."

Patrick nodded his thanks and hurried out the door, brushing the sting of the cottage air and the water from his eyes.

◆　◆　◆

HE STOPPED at Donovan McNamara's place on the way home to beg the loan of Donovan's remaining horse. It was nigh on three o'clock by the time he returned to the house.

Aisling stood in the road, waiting to meet him. Her face was serene, but her eyes held a tinge of concern. She said nothing, but eyed Donovan's horse questioningly.

Patrick led the horse to her; he smiled, in the attempt to contain the torment that was clawing at his viscera.

"Is Da home?" he asked as he brought the beast to a halt.

Aisling shook her head.

Patrick inhaled deeply, then reached into his pocket and took out the handkerchief. He placed it in her hand, struggling to maintain his smile.

Aisling opened the linen square carefully, revealing the cap. Patrick watched as she stared at it for a moment.

Then, before his eyes, a change came over her.

She caught her breath, a shuddering inhalation that was part gasp, part laugh. Then she laughed again, a merry, bell-like sound he did not ever remember hearing before. A light seemed to ripple over her face, and when she looked up at him, she was smiling broadly, tears pooling in her eyes and beginning to run down her cheeks.

"Patrick," she said, exhilaration in her voice, "will you take me to the sea?"

"'Tis true," Patrick said in disbelief. "'Tis true what Bronagh said, then. You are murúch—a merrow?"

"Aye," Aisling said, her face shining with excitement. "Aye, Patrick, that I am. Take me to the sea, please! Take me to Bolus Head."

Patrick nodded numbly. "Do you—do you want to pack your belongings?"

Aisling laughed again. "That won't be necessary. Let us be off."

As if in a dream, Patrick helped her mount Donovan's horse. "Do you at least wish to wait until Da returns, so that you can bid him good-bye?"

"No," said Aisling. "Come. Let us not tarry."

◆　◆　◆

THE RIDE SOUTHWEST to the sea was not at all what Patrick had expected.

The heaviness in his heart at the knowledge of what would happen when they reached the end of the peninsula gave way fairly quickly to amazement at the change in Aisling.

She sat before him on the horse, her long hair loose and free in the wind, the sun on her face, chatting merrily, something in all his life he never had known her to do.

All the way she told him stories of the sea, tales of the warm shallows where fish of brilliant colors swam between sharp living rocks, of cold depths where broken ships lay in their graves, their decks, masts, and wheels slowly becoming part of the ocean floor, as if the sea were sculpting them the way an artist transforms stone. She told him of her people and their ways, the lazy merrow men sunning themselves on the jagged cliffs of Connemara or the rocks of Small Skellig, guzzling rum gleaned from the wreckage of those ships, and the schools of seals that swam alongside those of merrow children. And she sang him wordless songs in a voice that both haunted him and caused silver shivers to resonate through his soul. The sheer joy that had taken her over was infectious; it was cherished time, this journey to land's end with a mother he had loved from childhood but no longer recognized.

She never mentioned his father.

Only at night when they slept, or during the moments in daylight when they stopped to let the horse drink and rest, did the melancholy return, deep, abiding sadness at the despair he knew would be the lot of Old Pat for the rest of his life. He prayed silently for wisdom, for forgiveness.

Honor thy father and thy mother.

How do I do both, Lord?

All the things she had made with her hands—the delicate tatted lace, the clothing, the sweaters of worsted wool—she had left behind without a thought; Patrick knew she would not need them in the sea, but the readiness with which she had abandoned everything that had been built over the course of her life as Old Pat's wife, as his own mother, thudded hollowly in his head.

Everywhere along the way were signs of the blight—empty huts and storage silos; bare fields that should have been rich with foliage, but instead held only the blackened leaves and withered crop; potters' fields with row upon row of freshly turned earth mounded in scores of graves. Patrick and Aisling stopped at each long enough to say an *Ave* from atop the horse, particularly the ones outside of what had once been homes where entire families had been buried, the smallest mounds no more than a yard in length. A little church stood empty, its door banging in the wind. Even in the places where people lived still, there was emptiness; the eyes that watched them as they traveled through were hollow with hunger, in faces drawn and shrunken from disease.

Finally, after two days' ride with little to eat but that which could be begged or found along the way, the crash of the waves off Ballinskellig Bay could be heard. Patrick saw ripples of spray rising above the ocean even before the old horse crested a hill enough to catch a view of it. He reined the horse to a stop and slowly slid to the ground, transfixed.

The wet wind slapped his hair wildly as he stared out into the endless blue of the sea, the color of it filling his eyes. Even though it was mixed with shades of grey, subtle tones he could not distinguish, it was still the most vibrant, moving panorama of blue he had ever seen, like the living sky, rolling and crashing against the rocky beach. In the distance, he saw the dark rise of Skellig Michael, wrapped in fog and wind.

"How could he have kept you from this?" he murmured, fighting off the deep sense of longing that was twisting around his soul. "How in the name of God above could he have taken you away from here, and kept you in the shadow of the Reeks?"

As if in response, he heard the whinny of a horse in the distance. Patrick turned to see Old Pat, atop Fionnbar, crest the hill behind them. His father reined to a stop for a moment, then, sighting them, urged the draft horse forward, hell-bent for leather.

Patrick felt the breath go out of his body. Then, in the crushing weight of the air's return to his lungs, he ran back to Donovan's horse and crawled up into the saddle behind his startled mother, kicking the poor beast into a canter, then a rough gallop.

"Patrick," Aisling gasped, "for the love of God—"

"Hold to me, Mother," he said. "Hold to me, and I will get you to the shore."

Mercilessly he urged Donovan's horse on, straining to hold on with his knees, gripping the reins in one hand and Aisling with the other. He rode forward into the sea wind, the breeze whistling through his hair, gaining as much speed from the tired horse as he could, knowing that his father's mount was the better, and not wishing to have to fight his way through, should Old Pat position himself between his mother and the sea.

Finally, the tip of Bolus Head was in sight. Land's end, the farthest point west that they could reach. Patrick rode until the rocky shore was too much for the horse's shoes, then dragged back on the reins and leapt from the saddle. He turned and looked over his shoulder.

Old Pat was within sight, perhaps two hundred yards behind him. His father was pitched forward in Fionnbar's saddle, shouting something into the wind, its noise lost in the howl of it and the clatter of the horse's hooves.

"Come, Mother," Patrick urged, holding his arms out to her. "Make haste."

Aisling allowed him to pull her down from the saddle, then looked behind her to the east, beholding Old Pat for the first time. She brushed the flapping locks of hair from her face, staring into the coming dusk, the sun sinking into the sea to the west lighting her back and shoulders with a bright glow. Then she reached into her pocket and drew forth her cap. The tiny pearls caught the light of the setting sun.

"Mother," Patrick said insistently, seeing Old Pat bearing down upon them, "he'll be on us in a heart's beat. Now for it!"

Aisling continued to watch Old Pat, expressionless, as Fionnbar came to a halt. Then she turned to Patrick and smiled, the glow of joy that he had seen coming over her face once more, lighted by the vanishing sun. She took her son's hand, squeezed it fondly, then placed the merrow's cap in his palm.

"Here," she said simply.

He stared at her blankly.

"Take it, Patrick," she urged, glancing over her shoulder as Old Pat dismounted and began to scramble over the rocks toward the shore.

"I don't understand," Patrick said, his hand growing numb and weak with anxiety.

"Save yourself, Patrick Michael Martin," his mother said, smiling, though tears were starting to well in her eyes. "From the famine, and from all that has held you blind until now."

"Blind to what?"

Aisling's smile grew brighter. "You'll see."

Patrick heard the exerted puff of his father's breath behind him, but he was too thunderstruck to move. Aisling squeezed his hand again, then turned away and went to Old Pat, slipping her arm behind his back as he pulled her close.

"You—young fool," his father gasped, struggling to catch his breath. "Did ya not see what—you were—doing to Donovan's poor old—horse? God in heaven above, boy." The hen, caged in a basket that hung from Fionnbar's saddle, squawked in protest as well.

Patrick shook his head as if the sense in it had collected in the corners. "I don't understand," he repeated.

"What's to understand?" Old Pat asked crossly. "Take your mother's cap, put it on your head, wade out into the sea, and be gone.

There's nothing more here for you now, lad. To stay behind guarantees a struggle to live that is likely to turn out badly; two can share a daily hen's egg, but three can't survive on that. To take to the sea in a coffin ship is to risk your life and your health. There's no good choice but this one."

"You'll be safe in the sea, Patrick," Aisling said, leaning against Old Pat's shoulder. "As my son, you are of the blood as well; take the cap and go to find your kin. They will teach you our ways."

"You knew?" Patrick asked incredulously. "You knew he had hidden the cap?"

"Of course," Aisling said, her brows drawing together in surprise. " 'Tis a highly prized thing, that cap; you didn't think we would keep it in the cottage where the landlord or some other English thug might come upon it and steal it?"

"If you knew where it was, why did you not take it back, then, Mother? Does not a merrow long to return to the sea above all else?"

Aisling looked at his father and smiled. "Not above *all* else, Patrick. 'Tis true I would have been spared from the famine if I had returned to the sea, but I did not wish to be spared if it meant going without your father."

"Did you think you found that chest by happenstance, lad?" Old Pat asked, amused. "You must have known I was leading you there—surely you did not think I would have missed seeing you, followin' so close? You think I'm *blind*, lad?"

"You're—you're in on this together," Patrick said incredulously. "If that be so, why did you give chase, Da? I about met my death from heart failure, trying to outrun you."

"Of course we are 'in on this together,' you young cur," said Old Pat with equal measures of scorn and fondness in his voice. "As we are in everything together; that's the very definition of holy matrimony. We decided that this was the answer the night after the meeting in Donovan's barn. We discussed it in bed that night, as you slept beside the fire. I was to meet you both here. And I gave chase because you *ran*. I came to bid you farewell and take your mother home."

Patrick took off his hat and ran a hand through his hair. "The witch," he said to Aisling in amazement. "Bronagh told me that, should I return the cap to you, you would not be able to resist the magic of the sea."

Aisling smiled again. "Some magics are stronger than others, Patrick."

"Despite being blessed with some uncommon wisdom, Bronagh does not know everything," Old Pat added. "She assumes that what she knows about the lore of merrows and sailors applies to every merrow, every sailor. 'Tis folly. When a sailor drowns, it is often said that he has married a merrow. Faith, I didn't want to do it that way. So I merely asked one for her hand instead."

In spite of himself, Patrick chuckled.

Aisling reached out and took his arm. "Remember, Patrick, you are born of both sea and land. The sea holds a powerful magic, 'tis true. But you are a son of Ireland, the most magical realm in all the dry world. You will be at home in both places. When the time is right, when the famine is over, come back to us. If we be living still, we will welcome you home to the Reeks."

Sadness crept over Patrick's face.

"And if you are not?" he asked.

Aisling squeezed his arm. "If not, then I suppose I will see you in heaven."

"But Bronagh said that you do not have a soul."

"What does anyone but God know of the soul?" his mother said. "I can tell you this for certain, Patrick Michael Martin: wherever your father goes, in this life and beyond, I am ever there. We share a soul—and we are both part of you. That should be enough to lift us all from the waves to heaven, don't you think?"

"Aye, I do," said Patrick, struggling to keep his eyes from overflowing. "Just tell me one last thing, Mother—when I gave you back the cap, why did you change so?"

Aisling blinked. "Did I?"

"Aye," said Patrick. "Your face took on the glow of the sun, and you laughed merrily, in a way I don't remember hearing before. It was magical—or so it seemed to me. I could believe that you were hearing the call of the sea, that magic that Bronagh said you would be unable to stand against."

His mother grinned broadly.

"What you saw was joy, Patrick, joy in the knowledge that the blight will not take my child, this son of land and sea, as it has taken so many other mothers' children. Life here on the land has not been easy of late; in fact, it never has been. It is the life I choose, to stay here with your father, come what may. I know that you will be safe now. Sad as I am that you are leaving my house, how can I but be happy for you? You will now see what you have been missing. Fare thee well."

He came into their embrace and remained there until the sun touched the edge of the sea, spilling its light along the horizon. Then he put on the cap and ventured out in the water with one last glance over his shoulder.

Aisling and Old Pat stood, arm in arm, watching him go. Like all those parents who had sent sons to war, or children to the New World in search of life beyond the coming death, they held to each other, their backs straight against the loss, braced together.

As he moved into the waves he felt a familiar sensation, recognizing it after a moment as the same one he had always felt when moving through the undulating waves of summer grass. There was a welcome to it, as there had been on the land, and in that moment he realized he had felt the call of the sea all his life, even far away in the mountains of Macgillicuddy's Reeks.

When the water crested his shoulders he began to swim, and as he did, he felt his legs melt away, forming a deeper muscle, powerful, moving together as one. Then it was as if he was moving through the air, at home in the element of water, and elation swelled up inside him.

Patrick turned in the sea and looked back to the rocky coast at the tiny shadows still standing, side by side, in the dusk; he thought he saw one of the shadows wave to him, but he was unsure. He lifted a hand in return, a hand with a slight webbing of skin between the fingers now. He looked farther up and suddenly saw the green hills rising, verdant in their splendor, the purple mountains beyond, the summer slopes bathed in a glorious array of the bright colors of the land, scarlets and crimsons, delicate yellows and the palest of lavenders.

In his ears he heard his mother's voice, one last time.

Save yourself, Patrick Michael Martin, from the famine, and from all that has held you blind until now.

Blind to what?

You'll see.

Below him, the ocean swelled, no longer grey, in blue-green splendor, gold below. He knew its deeper treasures were his now, could hear the sea wind calling, heard the song from the depths, the same wordless tune his mother had sung to him on the way to this place, telling him not of what she missed, but what lay in store for him.

He dove into the waves and went off to find it.

The Butter Spirit's Tithe

BY CHARLES DE LINT

1

It happened just as we were finishing our first set at the Hole in Tucson, Arizona, running through a blistering version of "The Bucks of Oranmore"—one of the *big* box tunes, so far as I'm concerned. Miki was bouncing so much in her seat that I thought her accordion was going to fly off her knee. I had a cramp in the thumb of my pick hand, but I was damned if that'd stop me from seeing the piece through to the end, no matter how fast she played it.

So of course she picked up the speed again, grinning at me as we kicked into our third run through the tune. I grinned back, adding a flourish of jazzy chords that I shouldn't have had the space to fit in, but I managed all the same. It's the kind of thing that happens when you play live and was nothing I'd be able to duplicate again. Miki raised an eyebrow, suitably impressed.

And then, just as we came up on a big finish, all the strings on my guitar broke, even the bass "E." I snapped my head back, which probably saved me from losing an eye, but I got a couple of wicked cuts on my chording hand.

Needless to say, that brought the tune to a ragged finish. Miki stared at me for a long moment, then turned back to her mike.

"We're taking a short break," she said, "while Conn restrings his guitar. Don't go away and remember to tip your waitress."

I reached over to the P.A.'s board and shut off the sound from the stage, switching the house speakers back to the mix of country and Tex-Mex that the bar got from some satellite feed. Then I sucked at the cuts on my hand. Miki dropped the strap from her accordion and set the instrument on the floor.

"Jesus, Mary, and Joseph," she said, sounding more like her brother than I'd ever tell her. "What the hell just happened?"

I shrugged. "Guess I got a set of bum strings. It happens."

"Yeah, right. Every string breaking at the same time." She paused and studied me for a moment. "Has it happened before?"

I shook my head. I was telling the truth. But other things just as strange had—no more than two or three times a year, but that was two or three times too many.

I set my guitar in its stand and went to the back of the stage, where I got my string-winder and a fresh set of strings. Miki was still sitting on her stool when I got back to my own seat. Usually she'd be off the stage by then, mixing with the audience.

"So what aren't you telling me?" she asked.

"What makes you think I'm not telling you something?"

"You've got that look on your face."

"What look?"

"Your 'holding back something juicy' look."

"Well, it *was* strange to have them all break at once like that."

"Try impossible," she said.

"You saw it."

"Yeah, and I still don't quite believe it. So give."

I shook my head.

"It's nothing you want to hear," I told her.

She stood and came over to my side of the stage so that I had to look up at her. Though perhaps "up" was stretching it some since she wasn't much taller than me, and I was still sitting down. Her hair was bright orange that week, short and messy as ever, but it suited her. Truth is, there isn't much that doesn't suit her. She might be too small and compact ever to be hired to walk down the runway at a fashion show, but she could wear anything and make it look better than it ever would on a professional model.

That night she was in baggy green cargos and a black Elvis Costello T-shirt that she'd cut the arms off of, but she still looked like a million dollars. She'd kill me if I ever said that in her hearing—because she's probably the best button accordion player I've ever heard; certainly the best I've ever played with—but I'm sure that half the reason we sell out most of our shows is because of her looks. Sort of pixie gamine meets sexy punk. It drew the young crowd, but she was too cute to put off the older listeners. And like I said, she can *play*.

"I just asked, didn't I?" she said.

"Yeah, but . . ."

I'd learned not to talk about certain things around her because it just set her off. I can still remember asking her if she ever read any Yeats—that was in the first week we were out on the road as a duo. She'd given up on fronting a band, because it cost too much to keep the four-piece on the road, and had hired me to be her accompanist in their place.

"Don't get me started on Yeats," she'd said.

"What's wrong with Yeats?"

"Yeats, personally? Nothing, so far as I know. I never met the man. And I'll admit he had a way with the words. What I don't like about him is all that Celtic Twilight shite he was always on about."

I shook my head.

"What?" she said.

I shrugged. "I don't know. It just seems that for a woman born in Ireland, who makes her living playing Celtic music, you don't care much for your own traditions."

"What traditions? I like a good Guinness and play the dance tunes on my box—those are traditions I can appreciate. I can even enjoy a good game of football, if I'm in the mood, which isn't bloody often. What I don't like is when people get into all that mystical shite." She laughed, but without a lot of humor. "And I don't know which is worse, the wanna-be Celts or those who think they were born to pass on the great Secret Traditions."

"Which is a good portion of your audience—especially on the concert circuit."

She had a sip of her draught and smiled at me over the brim of her glass. "Well, you know what they say. Doesn't matter what your line of work, there'll always be punters."

That was so Miki, I soon discovered. She was either irrepressibly cheerful and ready to joke about anything, or darkly cynical about the world at large, and the Irish in particular. But she hadn't always been that way.

I didn't know her well before she hired me; but we'd been at a lot of the same sessions and ran with the same crowd, so I already had more than a passing acquaintance with the inimitable Ms. Greer before we started touring together.

Time was she was the definition of good-natured, so much so that a conversation with her could give some people a toothache. It was her brother Donal who was the morose one. But something happened to Donal—I never quite got all the details. I just know he died hard. Overseas, I think. In the Middle East or someplace like that. Some desert, anyway. Whatever had happened, Miki took it badly, and she hadn't been the same since. She was either up or she was down and even her good humor could often have a dark undercurrent to it. Not so much mean, as bitter.

None of which explained her dislike of things Irish, particularly the more mystical side of the Celtic tradition. I could understand her distancing herself from her roots—I might, too, if I'd been brought up the way she had by a drunken father, eventually living on the streets with Donal, the two of them barely in their teens. But while my background's Irish, I grew up in the Green, what they used to call the Irish section of Tyson before it got taken over, first by the bohemians, then more recently by the new waves of immigrants from countries whose names I can barely pronounce.

The families living in the Green were dirt-poor—some of us still didn't have hot water and electricity in the fifties—but we looked after each other. There was a sense of community in the Green that Miki never got to experience. I'm not saying everyone was an angel. Our fathers worked long hours and drank hard. There were fights in and outside of the bars every night. But if you lost your job, your neighbors would step in and see you through. No one had to go on relief. And my dad, at least, never took out his hardships on his family the way Miki's did.

There was magic in the Green, too. It lay waiting for you in the stories told around the kitchen stoves, in the songs sung in the parlors. I grew up on great heaps of Miki's "Celtic Twilight shite," except it was less airy, more down-to-earth. Stories of leprechauns and banshees and strange black dogs that followed a man home.

And, at least according to my dad, not all of it was just stories.

"Well?" Miki said.

"Well, what?"

"Do you need a bang on the ear to get you going?"

"It's a long story," I said.

She looked at her watch. "Then you better get started, because we're back on in twenty minutes."

I sighed. But as I restrung my guitar, I told her about it.

2

I remember my dad took me aside the day I was leaving home. We stood on the stoop outside our tenement building, hands in our pockets, looking down the street to the traffic going by at the far end of the block, across the way to where the Cassidy girls were playing hopscotch, anywhere but at each other.

"If it was just a need for work, Conn," he finally said, trying one more time to understand. "But this talk of having to find yourself . . ."

How to explain? With four sisters and three brothers, I felt smothered. Especially since each and every one of them knew exactly what they wanted out of life. They had it all mapped out—the jobs, the marriages, the children, the life there in the Green. There were no unknown territories for them.

I only had the music, and while it was respected in our family, it wasn't considered a career option. It was what we did in the evenings, around our kitchen table and those of our neighbors.

I'd tried to put it into the words before that day, but it always came out sounding like I was turning my back on them, and that wasn't the case. I just needed to find a place in the world that I could make my own. A way to make a living without the help of an uncle or a cousin. It might not be music. But with a limited education, and the even more limited interest in furthering what I did have, music seemed the best option I had.

Besides, I lived and breathed music.

"I know you don't understand," I said. "But it's what I need to do. I'm only going to Newford, and I won't be gone forever."

"But wouldn't it be easier on you to live with us while you . . . while you try this?"

I'll give them this: my parents didn't understand, but they were supportive, nevertheless.

I shook my head. "I need the space, Dad. And there aren't the venues here like there are in the city."

He gave a slow nod. And maybe he even understood.

"When you do find yourself a place," he said, "make peace with its spirits."

I guess you might find that an odd thing for him to say, but we O'Neills are a superstitious lot. "Everything has a spirit," Dad would tell us when we were growing up. "So give everything its proper respect, or you'll be bringing the bad luck down upon yourself."

The presence of spirits wasn't something we talked about a lot—and certainly not in the mystical way people do now, where it's all about communicating with energy patterns through crystals, candles, or whatever. It was just accepted that the spirits were there, all around us, sharing the world with us: Ghosts and sheerie. Merrow, skeaghshee, and butter spirits. All kinds.

"I will," I told him.

He pressed a folded twenty into my hand—a lot of money for us in those days—then embraced me in a powerful hug. I'd already said my other good-byes inside.

"There'll always be room for you here," he said.

I nodded, my throat suddenly too thick to speak. I'd wanted and planned for this for months, and suddenly I was tottering on the edge of giving it all up and going to work at the factory with my brothers. But I hoisted my duffel bag in one hand, my homemade guitar case in the other. It was made of scavenged plywood and weighed more than the instrument did.

"Thanks, Dad," I said. "Just . . . thanks."

We both knew that simple word encompassed far more than the twenty dollars he'd just given me and the reminder that I'd always have a home to return to.

He clapped me on the shoulder, and I turned and headed down the street, where I had an appointment with a Newford-bound bus.

◆　◆　◆

THINGS DIDN'T go as planned.

I'd set up a few gigs before I left home, but my act didn't go over all that well. I'm not a strong singer, so I need the audience actually to be listening to me for them to appreciate the songs. But people don't have that kind of patience in a bar. Or maybe it's simply a lack of interest. They've gone out to drink and have fun with their friends, and the music's only supposed to be background.

"You're a brilliant guitarist," the owner of the bar I played on the second weekend told me. "But it's wasted on this lot. You should hook up with a fiddler, or somebody with a bigger presence. You know, something to grab their attention and hold it."

In other words, I wasn't much of a front person. As though to punctuate the point, he didn't book me for another gig.

Worse, I knew he was right. I didn't like being up there on those little stages by myself, and even though I knew nobody was really listening, I could barely mumble my way through my introductions. It was different sitting around the kitchen at home, or in a session. I loved backing up the fiddlers and pipers, the flute and box players. And when I did sing a song, people listened.

So I put the word out that I was available as an accompanist, but all the decent players already had their own, and the people who did contact me weren't much good. It was so frustrating. I ended up taking gigs with some of them anyway, but they didn't challenge me musically or help my bank balance—my bank being the left front pocket of my cargo pants, which I could at least button closed.

I ended up busking a lot—in the market, at subway entrances, down by Fitzhenry Park—but since I didn't have enough presence onstage, where I had the benefit of a sound system, I sure didn't have what it took to grab the attention of passersby on the street, where I was competing with all the traffic and city noise as well as audience indifference. My take after playing was never more than a few dollars. By the end of a month I was out of money and had to leave the boardinghouse where I was staying. I ended up in Squatland, sleeping in one of the many abandoned buildings there with the other homeless people, keeping my busking money for food.

I could have gone home, I guess. But I was too proud. Though not too proud to find another way to make a living.

I finally found a job as a janitor at the Sovereign Building on Flood Street. I got the gig through Joey Bennett, this cab driver I met when I was busking at the gates of Fitzhenry Park. He'd stand outside his cab, arms folded across his chest, listening to me while he waited for a fare. He was a jazz buff, but we got to talking on my breaks. When he heard I was looking for work, it turned out he knew a lawyer who had an office in the Sovereign, and the lawyer got me the job.

I guess it wasn't much different than getting a job through an uncle or cousin, except Joey and the lawyer were my connections. I'd done it on my own.

I didn't mind the job that much. I like seeing things put to order and kept clean, and it's very meditative being in a big building like that, pretty much on my own. There are other cleaners, but we each have our own floors, and we don't really see each other except at break time.

Now here's the thing.

I'd paid my respects to the spirits at the boardinghouse, and later my squat—feeling a little foolish while I talked into thin air to do so. No one answered, and I didn't expect them to. But I never thought about doing it at work. So, when I saw the kid tracking muddy footprints down the hall I'd just spent a half hour mopping down, I wasn't thinking of house spirits and respect. I just told him off.

When he turned in my direction, I saw that he wasn't really a kid—more a kid-sized, little man with brown skin and hair that looked like Rasta dreadlocks. He was wearing a dark green cap and shirt, brown-green trousers, and was barefoot—unless you counted the mud on them as footwear. Over his shoulder, he had a coil of rope with a grappling hook fastened to one end. In his hand, he carried a small cloth bag that bulged with whatever it was holding.

It was raining outside, so it wasn't hard to figure out where the mud had come from. How he'd gotten *into* the building was a whole other story. Used the grappling hook to get up the side of the wall, I suppose, then forced a window.

He glared at me when I yelled at him, dark eyes flashing.

"How'd you get in here, anyway?" I demanded.

He pointed a gnarled finger at me.

"I give you seven years," he said in a gravelly voice that felt like it should have come from a much larger person.

"Yeah, well, I'll give you thirty seconds to get out of here," I told him.

"Do you know who I am?"

Until he said that, I hadn't actually considered it. Not after my first impression when I thought he was just some kid, nor when I realized that he was a weird little man who'd somehow found his way into this locked office building. But as soon as he asked, I knew. And my heart sank. I'd done the very thing my dad had always warned us against.

Though I'll tell you, while I grew up with his stories of faeries and such, accepting them the way you do things that are spoken of in your family, I'd never really believed in them. It was like any other superstition—spilling salt, walking under ladders, that kind of thing. Most people don't believe, but they avoid such situations all the same, just in case. Which is why I'd paid my respects to invisible presences in the boardinghouse and my squat. Just in case.

"Listen," I began, "I didn't realize who—"

But he cut me off.

"Seven years," he repeated.

"Seven years and what?"

"You'll be my tithe to the Grey Man."

My dad had stories about him as well. How the brolaghan known as Old Boneless was like a Mafia don to the smaller faeries, offering them his protection in return for a tithe—the main protection he offered being that he himself wouldn't hurt them. The tithe could be anything from tasty morsels, beer or whiskey, to pilfered knickknacks and even changelings. It just had to be something stolen from the human world.

Dad's stories didn't say what the Grey Man did with any of those things. Being a creature of mist and fog, you wouldn't think he'd have any use for material items. Maybe they helped make him more substantial.

I certainly didn't want to find out firsthand.

"Wait a sec," I said. "All I did was—"

"Disrespect me. And just to remind you of my displeasure," he added.

He pointed that gnarled finger at me again, and my pants came undone, falling down around my ankles. By the time I'd stooped to pull them up, he was gone. I zipped up my fly and redid my belt.

They came undone, and my pants fell down once more.

I suppose that's what really convinced me that I'd just had an encounter with a genuine faerie man. No matter how often I tried, I couldn't get my pants to stay up. Finally, I sat down there in the hall holding them in place with one hand while I tried to figure out what to do.

Nothing came to mind.

And the worst thing about it, there was this totally cute girl named Nita Singh that I'd been spending my breaks with. She worked the floor below mine, and while I hadn't quite figured out yet if she was seeing anybody, she was friendly enough to give me hope that maybe she wasn't. She certainly seemed to return my interest.

So of course she had to come up looking for me when I didn't come down at break time.

"Are you okay?" she asked as she came down the hall from the stairwell.

Nita was almost as tall as me, with shoulder-length, straight dark brown hair tied back in a ponytail. Like all of us, she was wearing grubby jeans and a T-shirt, but they looked much better on her.

"Oh sure," I said. "I'm just . . . you know, having a rest."

She leaned her back against the wall, then slid down until she was sitting beside me. She glanced at how I was holding my jeans and grinned.

"Having some trouble with your pants?"

I shrugged. "I think my zipper's broken."

From the first night I'd met her, all I'd ever wanted was to be close to her. But right then I just wanted her to go away.

"Maybe I can fix it," she said.

In any other circumstance, could this have played out any better?

"I don't think so," I told her.

I couldn't believe I had to say that. She was going to think I was such a dork, but instead she gave me a knowing look.

"Had a run-in with the local butter spirit, did you?" she asked.

Butter spirits were supposed to be a kind of house faerie related to leprechauns, but much more thieving and malicious. Back home they especially enjoyed fresh butter and would draw the "good" of the milk before it was churned.

I blinked in surprise. "How do you know about that kind of thing?"

"Daddy-ji's Indian," she said, "but my mum's Irish. There was a big to-do when they hooked up. You know, son disowned, the whole bit."

"I'm sorry."

She shrugged. "Not your fault. Anyway, Mum was forever telling stories about the little people."

"My dad did, too."

"I just never thought they were more than stories."

"But you do now? Have you seen him?"

She nodded. "Not up close. But I've caught glimpses of him and his little grappling hook that he uses to clamber up the outside walls. I think he pilfers food and drink from the bars and restaurants in Chinatown. I've seen him leave empty-handed, but return with a bag full of something or other."

"You never said anything before."

"What was I going to say? I thought you'd be telling me about him soon enough. And if you didn't, what would you think of me, telling you stories like that?"

"Has anyone else seen him?"

She laughed. "How do you think you got this job?"

"I don't understand."

"I've been working here for almost nine months and you've lasted the longest of anybody who's worked this floor in all that time. How long have you been here?"

"Almost a month."

"Most people don't last a week. There's almost always an opening for the job on this floor. Management tries to shift some of us to it, but we just threaten to quit when they do."

"So that's why it was so dirty when I first came on."

She nodded.

"And it's the butter spirit that scares people off?"

"Most people just think this floor is haunted, but you and I know better."

"They got on the wrong side of him," I said. "Like I just did."

"Don't worry," she told me. "Whatever he's done—"

"Fixed it so my pants won't stay up."

She grinned. "It doesn't last."

"Well, I can work in my boxers, but I don't know how I'm going to get home."

"If it's not gone by then, we'll see if we can rustle up a long coat for you to wear."

3

"So I'm assuming it wore off," Miki said when I was done.

I nodded. "Before I left the building at the end of my shift."

"Then what was tonight all about?"

"He likes to remind me that the tithe is still coming due."

Miki got a hard look. "You see what I mean about how this is all shite?"

She looked off the stage, trying to see if the little bogle man was in view, I assumed. He wasn't. Or at least he wasn't visible. I knew, because I'd already checked.

"It's not shite," I said. "It's real."

"I know. It's shite because it does no one any good. There's a reason the Queen of the Faeries gave Yeats that warning."

"What warning?"

"He was seeing this medium and through her, the Faerie Queen told him, 'Be careful, and do not seek to know too much about us.' But do any of the punters listen?"

"I wasn't trying to find out anything about them."

She nodded. "I got that. My point is, any contact with them is a sure recipe for heartache and trouble."

She had that much right.

"You don't seem any more surprised by this than Nita was," I said.

"I'm not. Messing about with shite like this is what got Donal killed."

"I didn't know."

"Well, it's not something I'm going to shout out to the world." She paused a moment, then added, "So what happened with Nita? She sounded nice from what you had to say about her."

"She's wonderful. But that little bugger made her allergic to me, and *that* spell hasn't worn off yet. Whenever she gets physically near to me, her nose starts running, and she breaks out in hives. Sometimes her throat just closes down, and she can't breathe."

I finished tightening my last string, dropped the string-winder under my stool, and plugged my guitar into my electronic tuner.

"We seem to still be able to talk on the phone," I added.

"Is that who you're always calling?"

I nodded. I didn't have a better friend in the world than Nita. And at one time, we'd been far more than that. But the butter spirit thought making her allergic to me would be a good joke—especially when he didn't let the enchantment wear off. Talking on the phone was all we had left.

"I always thought it was one of your brothers or sisters," Miki said.

"Nita's *like* a sister now," I told her, unable to keep the hurt from my voice.

Miki gave me a sympathetic look.

"So it's not just breaking guitar strings and pulling your pants down," she said.

"Christ, that's the least of it. Mostly things happen in private. Shutting off the hot water on me when I'm having a shower. Or fixing it so that the electricity doesn't work—but only in the room where I am. It's the big jokes that I dread. Once I was in a coffee shop and he curdled all the dairy products just as I was halfway through a latte. There were people puking on the tables that day, and I was one of them."

Miki grimaced.

"And then there was the time I was downtown, and he vanished all the stitches and buttons in what I was wearing. It's the middle of a snowstorm, and suddenly I'm standing there trying to cover myself with all these pieces of cloth that once were clothes."

"And you've never said anything about it."

I gave her a humorless smile. "Well, it's not something I want to shout out to the world either."

"Good point," she said. She paused for a moment, then added, "We're just going to have to find a way to turn the little bugger off."

I didn't want to feel the hope that rose at her words, but I couldn't help it.

"Do you know a way to do it?" I asked.

She shook her head, and my frail surge of hope fled. But that was Miki. Determined, tough.

"Only that doesn't mean we can't find out," she said. "You wouldn't know this butter spirit's name, would you?"

I shook my head.

"Too bad, but I suppose that would have been too easy."

"What use would his name be?"

"There's power in names," she said. "Don't you pay attention to the stories? Just because it's all shite doesn't mean it isn't true."

"Right."

I was having trouble relating to our conversation. I mean, to be having it with Miki, of all people. Who knew that behind her disdain, she was such an expert?

"When's the tithe due?" she asked.

"April 30."

She gave a slow nod. "Cally Berry's night."

"You've lost me."

"They call her the Old Woman of Gloominess. She's the blue-skinned daughter of the sun and rules the world between Halloween and Beltane. On the last day of April she throws her ruling staff away and turns into stone for the next half of the year—why do you think there are so many stone goddess images louting about in Ireland? But on that night, when she gives up her rule to the Summer Goddess, the faeries run free—like they do on Halloween. Babies are stolen and changelings left in their cribs. Debts and tithes are paid."

"Lovely."

"Mmm. I wonder if we have a gig that night . . ."

She took out her Palm Pilot and looked up our schedule.

"Of course we do," she said. "We're in Harnett's Point at the Harp and Tankard, from the Wednesday through Saturday. Close enough to Newford for trouble, though I guess distance doesn't seem to be a problem with him, does it?"

I shook my head. We were halfway across the country in Arizona at the moment, and that hadn't stopped him.

"Actually, that can work to our advantage," she went on. "I know some people living close to Harnett's Point who might be able to help. We'll put together some smudgesticks . . . let's see . . . rosemary, rue, blackthorn, and hemlock. That'll be pungent to burn indoors, but it'll keep him off you."

"You really think you can stop him?" I asked. "I mean, it's not just the butter spirit. There's the Grey Man, too."

She nodded. "Old Boneless. Another of those damned hard men that we Irish seem to be so good at conjuring up, both in our faeries and ourselves. But I have a special fondness for the bashing of hard men, Conn, you'll see. Now tell me, how intimate were you and Nita?"

"Jeez, that's hardly—"

She held up a hand before I could finish. "I'm not prying. I just need to know if you have a bond of flesh or just words."

"We were . . . very intimate. Until he pulled this allergy business."

She gave me another one of her thoughtful nods.

"What are you thinking?" I asked.

"Nothing. Not yet. I'm just putting together the pieces in my head. Setting them up against what I know and what I have to find out."

"Not that I'm ungrateful," I said, "but you seem awfully familiar with this kind of thing for someone so dead set against it."

The grin she gave me was empty of humor. It was a wolf's grin. Feral.

"It's the first rule of war," she told me. "Know your enemy."

War, I thought. *When did this become a war?* But maybe for her it was. Maybe it should be that way for me.

"So what's Nita doing these days?" Miki asked.

"She's a social worker. She was working on her degree when I met her at the Sovereign Building."

"Is she with the city?"

I nodded.

"And you still love her? She still loves you?"

"Well, we're not celibate—I mean, it's been six and a half years now. We had six months together before the butter spirit conjured up the allergy, but . . ." I shrugged. "So, yes, we still love each other, but we see other people." I paused, then added, "And you need to know this because?"

"I need to know everything I can about the situation. You do want me to help, don't you?"

"I'll take any help I can get."

"Good man. So, are you all tuned up yet?" she asked, abruptly shifting conversational gears. When I nodded, she added, "Then I think it's time to start playing again."

I was going to have to fight the tuning of my guitar for the rest of the night as the new set of strings stretched. But better that—better to lose myself in the mechanics of playing and tuning and the spirit of the music—than to have to think about that damned butter spirit for the next hour or so.

Except I never did get him out of my head. At the very least, throughout the set, I carried the worry of my strings snapping on me again.

4

Miki wasn't at all forthcoming about her plan to deal with the butter spirit. The first time I pressed her harder for details—"Hello," I told her. "This concerns me, you know."—she just said something about the walls having ears, and if she spoke her plan aloud, she might as well write it out and hand it over the enemy.

"Trust me, Conn," she said.

So I did. She might get broody. She might carry a hard, dark anger around inside her. But it was never directed at me, and I knew I could trust her with my life. Which was a good thing because if the Grey Man ever did get hold of me, it was my life that was forfeit.

◆　◆　◆

THE MONTH WENT BY quickly.

We finished up our gigs in the Southwest, did a week that took us up through Berkeley and Portland, and then we were back in Newford and it was time to start the two-hour drive out to Harnett's Point for our opening night at the Harp & Tankard.

The Butter Spirit's Tithe

Harnett's Point used to be a real backwoods village, its population evenly divided between the remnant of back-to-the-earth hippies who tended organic farms west of the city and locals who made their living off of the tourists that swelled the village in the summer. But it had changed in the last decade, becoming, like so many of the other small villages around Newford, a satellite community for those who could afford the ever-pricier real estate and didn't mind the two-hour commute to their jobs.

And where once it had only the one Irish bar—Murphy's, a log and plaster-covered concrete affair near the water that was a real roadhouse—now it sported a half dozen, including the Harp & Tankard, where we were playing that night.

Have you ever noticed how there seems to be an Irish pub on almost every corner these days? They're as bad as coffee shops. I can remember a time when the only place you could get a decent Guinness was in Ireland, and as for the music, forget it. "Traditional music" was all that Irish-American twaddle popularized by groups like the Irish Rovers. Some of them were lovely songs, once, but they'd been reduced to noisy bar jokes by the time I got into the music professionally. And then there were the folks who'd demand "some real Irish songs" like "The Unicorn," and would get all affronted when first, you wouldn't play it for them, and second, you told them it was actually written by Shel Silverstein, the same Jewish songwriter responsible for hits like Dr. Hook & the Medicine Show's "Cover of the Rolling Stone."

Miki and I played an even mix of bars, small theatres, colleges, and festivals, and I usually liked the bars the least—probably a holdover from when I was first trying to get into the music in a professional capacity. But Miki loved them. It made no sense to me why she kept taking these bookings—she could easily fill any medium-sized hall—but they kept her honest, she liked to say. "And besides," she'd add, "music and the drink, they just go together."

When we got to the Harp & Tankard that afternoon, we were met out back where we parked our van by a Native American fellow. Miki introduced him to me as Tommy. I thought he was with the bar—after all, he helped us bring in our gear and set up, then settled behind the soundboard while we did our soundcheck—but he turned out to be a friend of hers and in on her secret plan. After we got the sound right, he lit a pair of smudgesticks, then he and Miki waved them around the stage until the area reeked. They weren't sweetgrass or sage, but made of the herbs and twigs that Miki had told me about back at the Hole: rosemary and rue, blackthorn and hemlock.

The smell lingered long after they were done—which was the whole point, I suppose—and didn't make it particularly pleasant to be up there in it. I wasn't the only one to feel that way. I noticed as the audience started to take their seats that people would come up to the front tables, then retreat to ones farther back after a few moments. It was only when the back of the room was full that the closer tables filled up.

The audience was part yuppies, part the local holdover hippies, with a few of the longtime residents of the area standing in the back by the bar. You could tell them by their plaid flannel shirts and base-ball caps. There were also a number of older Native women scattered throughout the room, and I wondered why they didn't sit together. I could tell that they knew each other—or at least they all knew Tommy, since before he got back to the soundboard, he made a point of stopping and chatting with each of them.

"Do you know the song 'Tam Lin'?" Miki asked.

Tommy was back on the board now, and we were getting ready to start the first set.

"Sure. It's in A minor, right?"

"Not the tune—the ballad."

I shook my head. "I know it to hear it, but I've never actually sat down and learned it."

"Still you know the story."

"Yeah. Why—"

"Keep it in mind for later," she told me.

Her mysteriousness was beginning to get on my nerves. No, that wasn't entirely fair. What had me on edge was the knowledge that tonight was the night the butter spirit meant to make me his tithe to Old Boneless.

"Don't forget now," she said.

"I won't."

Though what "Tam Lin" had to do with anything, I had no idea. I tried to remember the story as I checked my foot pedals and finished tuning my guitar. It involved a love triangle between the knight Tam Lin, the Queen of the Faeries and a mortal woman named Janet, or sometimes Jennet. Janet loved Tam Lin, and he loved her, but the Faerie Queen stole him away and took him back with her to Faerieland. To win him back, Janet had to pull him down from his horse during a faerie rade on Halloween, then hold on to him while the Faerie Queen turned him into all sorts of different kinds of animals.

It was hard, but Janet proved true, and the Queen had to go back to Faerieland empty-handed.

Fair enough. But what did any of that have to do with my butter spirit and him planning to make me his tithe to Old Boneless?

Apparently, Miki wasn't going to tell me because she just called out the key of the first number and off she went, blasting out a tune on her accordion. In a moment, the pub was full of bobbing heads and tapping feet, and I was too busy keeping up with Miki to be worrying about the relevance of old traditional ballads.

Miki was in a mood that night. The tunes were all fast and furious, one after the other, with no time to catch a breath in between. Most of the time, when we got to the end of one of our regular sets, she'd simply call out a key signature and jump directly into the next set.

I didn't really think of it as peculiar to this particular night. Once she got onstage, you never knew where Miki would let the muse take her. Having a long-standing fondness for jazz tenor sax solos, as well as a newfound love for Mexican *conjunto* music that she'd picked up on our tours through Texas and the Southwest, she could as easily slide from whatever Irish tune we might be playing into a Ben Webster solo, or some *norteño* piece she'd picked up from a Flaco Jimenez album.

But that night it was all hard-driving reels, and we didn't come up for air until just before the end of our first set. I took the momentary respite to kill the volume on my guitar and give it a proper retuning, not really listening to what Miki was telling the audience. But I did note that they all had the same, slightly stunned expression that I was sure I was wearing. Miki in full tear on her box could do it to anyone, and even playing onstage with her, I wasn't immune.

I got the last string in tune, then suddenly realized what Miki was telling the audience.

". . . have to ask yourselves, why these stories persist," she was saying. "We've always had them, and we still do. I mean, alien abductions—that's just a new twist on the old tale of people getting taken away by the faeries, isn't it? Now I don't want to go all woo-woo on you here, but tonight's one of the two nights of the year that these little buggers are given complete free rein to cause what havoc they can for us mortals. The other's on Halloween.

"Anyway," she went on, smiling brightly at the audience in that way she had that immediately made you have to smile back, "whether you believe or not, it can't hurt to wish a bit of good luck our way, right? So while we're playing this next tune, I want you to think about how everybody here should be kept safe from the influence and malice of these so-called Good Neighbors. What do you think?"

She cocked her head and gave them a goofy look, which got her a round of laughter and applause.

"Key of D," she told me, and launched into "The Faeries' Hornpipe."

"Remember," she said over the opening bars, directing her attention back to the audience. "Faeries bad. Us good."

I looked out at the crowd as I backed Miki up. People were still smiling, some of them clapping along to the simple rhythm of the tune. And I'd bet more than half of them were doing what she'd said, thinking protective thoughts for everybody inside the pub.

This was Miki's big plan? I found myself thinking.

Don't get me wrong. I appreciated whatever effort she might have made to solve my problem, but this didn't seem like it would be all that effectual. And I sure didn't see the connection to that old ballad, "Tam Lin."

But then I realized that the Native women I'd noted earlier were all standing up, backs against the various walls. One after the other, they lit smudgesticks and soon that pungent scent of herbs and twigs was drifting through the pub, only this time, except for me, nobody seemed to notice.

And then I realized something else. While the audience continued to clap and stomp away to the music, while I could still *hear* the music, I wasn't playing my guitar anymore. I looked over at Miki and there seemed to be two of her, superimposed over each other. One still playing away on that old box of hers—she'd switched to a tune that I recognized as "The Faerie Reel"; the other regarding me with a serious expression in her eyes.

The sound of her playing and the crowd was muted. Actually, my sight felt muted, too, like there was a thin gauze hanging in front of my eyes.

"It's up to you now," the Miki who wasn't playing said. "Go outside and deal with him."

"What . . . where *are* we?"

"In between. Not quite in the world, not quite in the otherworld, where the spirits are stronger."

"I don't understand. How did you bring us here?"

"I didn't," she said. "They did."

I didn't have to ask who she meant. It was the Native women, with their smudgesticks and something else. I heard a low, rhythmical drumming, under the music, under the noise of the crowd. Mixed with it were the sounds of rattles and flutes, keeping time to Miki's tune, but following their own rhythm at the same time. I couldn't see the players.

More spirits, I guessed. But Native ones.

"And I'm not really with you," Miki added. "You're on your own."

"I don't understand—" I began, but she cut me off.

"There's not a big window of time here, Conn. Get a move on. And remember what I told you."

"I know. Think of the ballad. Why can't you just *tell* me what you've got planned?"

She smiled, but there was no humor in it. Only a kind of sadness.

"You'll know what to do when the time comes," she said. "One way or another, you can finish this business tonight."

You know how in a dream you find yourself doing things that don't make sense in retrospect, but in the dream they're perfectly logical? That's what this felt like. I got up and put my guitar in its stand, then made my way down from the stage and through the tables to the front door of the pub. No one paid the slightest attention to me except for Tommy, who gave me a smile and a thumbs-up as I passed the soundboard where he was sitting.

I thought of stopping to see if he could tell me what was going on, but then I remembered Miki saying something about there not being a lot of time, so I continued on to the door. Considering how weird everything else had gotten, I didn't really expect Harnett's Point to be still waiting for me outside. But it was. And that wasn't all that was waiting for me.

I stepped out into the parking lot, then stopped dead in my tracks. Nita stood there, waiting in an open parking spot between an SUV and a Volvo station wagon. She looked as gorgeous as ever, and my heartbeat did a little skip of happiness before my chest went tight with anxiety. I looked to the left and right, searching for some sign of the butter spirit, but so far as I could tell we were alone. Which I knew meant nothing.

"Nita . . ." I said, stepping closer to her. "What are you *doing* here?"

The smile she'd been wearing faltered. "Your friend Miki . . . she asked me to come. She said we had to do this, then everything would be all right."

I shook my head. *What* had Miki been thinking?

In the light from the bar's signage behind me I could see that her eyes were already getting puffy and her nose was beginning to run— her allergy to me kicking in.

"I shouldn't have come, should I?" Nita said. "I can tell. You don't really want me here."

The sadness I saw rising up in her broke my heart.

"No, it's not that," I told her. "It's just . . . oh, Christ, Miki couldn't have picked a worse night to have you come."

She started to say something, but a voice to the side spoke first.

"Using words like that will just make it worse on you, Conn O'Neill."

I turned and this time I spotted him. He was perched on the roof of an old Chevy two-door, one car over from the Volvo. The butter spirit with his hair like dreads and that glare in his eyes.

"I'm not afraid," Nita told me. "Miki told me all about it."

"I wish she'd told me," I said.

The butter spirit jumped onto the roof of the Volvo and grinned down at me.

"Don't know what you've got planned here, my wee boyo," he said. "I just know it's too late."

Nita and I both felt it then, a sudden coldness in the air. Looking over her shoulder, I was the first to see him: a fog lifting from the pavement of the parking lot that became the figure of a man with a cloak of wreathing mist that swirled about him. The Grey Man, his features sharp and pale, framed by long grey hair. Old Boneless himself. He didn't seem completely solid, and I remembered my dad telling me how he sustained himself on the smoke from chimneys and factories, on the exhaust from cars and other machines. That had never made sense until that moment.

His gaze had none of the butter spirit's meanness. Instead, he appeared completely indifferent, and in him, that struck me as far more dangerous.

"Get away, girl," the butter spirit told Nita. "Or you'll suffer the same fate as your boyo."

Nita ignored him. She moved closer to me.

"H-hold me," she said.

She could barely get the words out, her allergy to me closing up her throat.

"But—" I began, but couldn't finish.

She tried to speak, only she didn't have the breath anymore. Swaying, she would have fallen if I hadn't stepped forward and taken her into my arms. I lowered her to the pavement and knelt there, holding her tight, my heart filling with hopelessness and despair.

"Let her go," the butter spirit said.

I wanted to. I knew I should get as far away from her as I could so that she could recover from the allergy attack. But Nita still had the strength to grip my arm and she wouldn't let go. I knew what she was trying to tell me. So I looked down into her face, and I kissed her instead.

Her skin changed under my lips. When I lifted my head, I found myself holding a corpse. Nita's lovely brown skin had gone pallid and cold, and her gaze was flat. Empty. Her lips moved, and a maggot crept out of the corner of her mouth.

I might have pushed her aside and scrambled to my feet in horror, except somehow I managed to remember Miki's cryptic reminders about the old ballad. So I held her closer. Even when the flesh fell apart in my grip and all I held were bones, attached to each other by bits of dried muscle and sinew. I held her even closer then, tenderly cradling the skull against my chest. Wisps of what had once been her thick brown hair tickled my hand.

I still didn't really see the connection between the ballad and our situation. I was the one in peril with faerie, not her. I should be the one changing shapes. But I knew I wouldn't let her go, never mind the gender switch from the ballad.

None of this made much sense anyway, from the butter spirit's first taking affront to me, through the years of petty torment to this night, when the tithe he owed the Grey Man was due. None of it seemed real. It was all part and parcel of that same dreamlike state I felt I'd entered back on the stage inside the pub. I suppose that was what let me continue to kneel there, holding the apparent remains of Nita in my arms, and still function.

"This man is yours," I heard the butter spirit say. "My tithe to you."

Before the Grey Man could do whatever it was he was going to do, I lifted my head and met his flat, expressionless gaze. I still felt disconnected, reality floundering all around me, but I knew what I needed to do. It wasn't Miki's advice I needed to take, but my dad's.

"I'm honored to make your acquaintance, sir," I said, falling back on the formal speech patterns I remembered from Dad's stories.

For the first time since he arrived, I saw a flicker of interest in the Grey Man's gaze.

"Are you now?" he said.

His voice was a voice from the grave, deep and husky, filled with cold air.

I gave a slow nod in response. I was no longer trying to figure out what Miki's plan had been. Instead, I concentrated on the stories from my dad, how in them, no matter how malevolent or kind the faerie spirit might seem to be, the one thing they all demanded of us mortals was respect.

"I am, sir," I said. "It's a rare privilege to be able to look upon one so grand as yourself."

"Even when I am here to eat your soul?"

"Even then, sir."

"What game are you playing at?" he demanded.

"No game, sir. Though in all fairness, I feel I should tell you that your butter spirit actually has no claim to my soul. That being the case, it puzzles me how he can offer me up as his tithe to you. It seems to me—if you'll pardon my speaking out of turn like this—rather disrespectful."

The Grey Man turned that dark gaze of his to the butter spirit. "Is this true, Fardoragh Og?"

The butter spirit spat at me. "Lies, my lord. Everything he says is a lie."

"Then tell me, how did you gain a lien on his soul?"

The butter spirit couldn't find the words he needed.

"Well?"

"He . . . I . . ."

"If I might speak, sir?" I asked.

The butter spirit wanted to protest—that was easy to see—but he kept his mouth shut when the Grey Man nodded. I explained the circumstances of the butter spirit's enmity to me, and how when I'd realized my mistake, I'd tried to apologize.

"And where in this sorry tale," the Grey Man asked the butter spirit, "did you acquire the lien on this man's soul?"

"I . . ."

"Do you know what would have happened if I had taken it in these circumstances?"

"N-no, my lord."

"For the wrongful murder of their son, I would have been in debt to his family for eternity."

"I . . . I didn't . . . I never thought, my lord . . ."

"Come here, little man."

With great reluctance, the butter spirit shuffled to where the tall figure of the Grey Man stood. I didn't know what was coming next, but I knew that if I could get Nita and myself safely out of the situation, the last thing we'd need would be the continued enmity of the butter spirit, magnified by who knew how much after the night's ordeal.

"Sir?" I said. "May I speak?"

The Grey Man's gaze touched me, and I shivered. "Go ahead."

"It's just . . . this all seems to have been a series of unfortunate misunderstandings, sir. Couldn't we, perhaps, simply put it all behind us and carry on with our lives?"

"You ask for clemency toward your enemy?"

"I don't really think of him as an enemy, sir. Truly, it was just a misunderstanding that grew out of proportion in the heat of the moment. And I should never have disrespected him in the first place."

The butter spirit actually gave me a grateful look, but the Grey Man appeared unmoved. He grabbed the butter spirit by the scruff of his neck.

"You offer a commendable sentiment," he told me, "but I care only for the danger he put me in. It's not something I can afford to have repeated."

With that, he pulled the little man toward him. I thought, how odd that he would embrace the butter spirit in a moment such as that. But the Grey Man didn't draw him close for an embrace, so much as to devour him. The butter spirit gave a shriek as the foggy drapes of the cloak folded over him. And then he was gone, swallowed in the cloak of fog, with only the fading echo of his cry remaining before it, too, was gone.

"Now there is only one last problem," the Grey Man said, his dark gaze returning to me.

I swallowed hard.

"I am still owed a tithe from your world," he said. "Some human artifact or spirit. But I stand before you empty-handed."

I didn't reply. What was I going to say?

"I can only think of one solution," he went on. "Will you swear fealty to me?"

I had to be careful.

"Gladly, sir," I told him. "So long as my doing so causes no harm to any other being."

"You think I would have you do evil things?"

"Sir, I have no idea what you would want from me. I'm only being honest with you."

For a long moment the Grey Man stood there, considering me.

"I owe you a favor," he finally said. "I know you spoke up only to save your own skin, but by doing so, you prevented me from an eternity of servitude to your family."

"Sir, it was never my intention to—"

He cut me off with a sharp gesture of his hand. "Enough! You've made your point. You're very respectful. Now give it a rest." He sighed, then added, "Burn a candle for me from time to time, and we'll leave it at that."

I knew he was about to go.

"Sir," I said before he could leave. "My friend . . ."

He looked down at the bundle of bones in my arms, held together with sinew and dried muscle.

"It's only a glamor," he said. "Seen by you, felt by her."

And then he was gone in a swirl of fog.

I'd managed to keep my soul. The butter spirit would no longer be tormenting me. But I still knelt there with bones in my arms where Nita should be.

At that moment there came a roar of applause from inside the bar. I turned in the direction of the door. It seemed so inappropriate that they would be cheering the Grey Man's departure, but then I realized that it was only that Miki had ended her set.

I started to get to my feet, not an easy process because those bones weighed more than you'd think they would. But I refused to put them down.

I was still trying to stand when the door opened and one of those tall Native women I'd seen inside the bar came out into the parking lot. A moment later and the others followed her, one by one, nine of them in all. The last of them was an old, old woman with eyes as dark as the Grey Man's. When her gaze settled on me, I felt as nervous as I had under his attention.

"You did well," one of the younger women said—younger meaning she was in her forties. I couldn't tell how old the oldest of them was. She seemed ageless.

When they started to walk across the parking lot, I called out after them.

"Please! Can you help me with my friend?"

The old woman was the closest. She reached into her pocket and tossed what looked like a handful of pollen into the air, then blew it in my direction. I sneezed. Once. Twice. A third time. Blinked to clear my eyes.

By the time I was done, the Native women were gone. But Nita was in my arms—the real Nita, seemingly unaffected by allergies. Her eyelids fluttered, and she was looking up at me. A small smile touched her lips.

"I had the strangest dream," she said.

"It's okay. It's all over now."

"Did . . . did we win?" she asked.

I wouldn't call it winning. I don't know what I'd call it. But at least it seemed we were free.

"Yeah," I told her, settling on the easiest reply. "We won."

5

Strong whiskey was the order of the day when we got back inside, because Lord, did I need a drink. Jameson's in glass tumblers, no ice. I had the waitress leave the bottle at the table where Nita and I sat with Miki and her friend Tommy. We still had a half hour before Miki and I had to start our next set.

"I can't believe you let me go into that so blind," I told Miki.

"Shut up and drink your whiskey."

"No, really."

"I told you why. It was so that the butter spirit wouldn't get a hint of what I had planned."

"But how could you know the Grey Man would swallow him and let me go?"

Miki shrugged. "I listened to your story, then I talked to Nita about it. I knew the butter spirit didn't have a hold on you except for his malice. He couldn't offer you as a tithe. But if I'd mentioned it to you, he could have heard and made a different plan."

I was only half-listening, my attention now focused on the other thing that had been so troubling to me.

"And I can't believe you put Nita in that danger," I told her.

"I had to make sure you were both free of his spells. She had to be here for that. Besides, although you won't get them to admit it most of the time, the spirits are big on courage and true love. I figured with the two of you there, you'd show both."

"It's okay," Nita said, putting her hand over mine and giving it a squeeze. "Once she told me how it would go, I agreed to it."

I shook my head and used my free hand to have another sip of the whiskey. I knew I'd be playing very simple chords when we got back onstage for the next set.

"I don't even know how she got hold of you," I said.

"Oh, that was dead simple," Miki told me. "Once I knew she worked for the city's social services, it was easy to get her number."

I glanced across the table at Tommy. Of the four of us, he was the only one not drinking the whiskey. He had a ginger ale on the table in front of him.

"You don't seem much surprised by any of this," I said to him.

That seemed to be the tag line of this whole sorry affair. Maybe I should have been more surprised by people not taking it all at face value.

He shrugged. "I grew up on the rez with the aunts. There's not much that surprises me anymore."

"I never got to thank them."

"I'll pass it on for you."

"So, are you happy?" Miki asked.

She looked from me to Nita, beaming with the look of someone who'd not only got the job done, but got it done well.

"Very," Nita assured her.

"And will you be together now?" Miki asked.

I met Nita's gaze and saw the love shining in her eyes, just as I knew it was in my own.

"Of course you will," Miki went on before we could answer. "Lord, I love a happy ending. I should go back to Ireland and take up matchmaking. It's a respectable profession there, you know," she told Tommy.

"Yeah," he said. "I saw the movie."

"What movie?"

"*The Matchmaker.*"

"Oh, please."

I gave Nita's hand a little tug, and we left the two of them to go on at each other while we went outside to get a breath of air. It was a gorgeous night, the sky so full of stars that even the electric aura of the lights of Harnett's Point's couldn't put a damper on them.

"It's hard to believe we're finally free of that little bugger," I said. "I didn't think we'd ever be able to do anything but talk on the phone."

"Stop wasting time," Nita told me.

Then she wrapped her arms around my neck and drew me down for a long, deep kiss.

Banshee

BY RAY BRADBURY

Ⅰt was one of those nights, crossing Ireland, motoring through
the sleeping towns from Dublin, where you came upon mist
and encountered fog that blew away in rain to become a blowing
silence. All the country was still and cold and waiting. It was a night
for strange encounters at empty crossroads with great filaments of
ghost spiderweb and no spider in a hundred miles. Gates creaked far
across meadows, where windows rattled with brittle moonlight.

It was, as they said, banshee weather. I sensed, I knew this as my
taxi hummed through a final gate, and I arrived at Courtown House,
so far from Dublin that if that city died in the night, no one would
know.

I paid my driver and watched the taxi turn to go back to the living city, leaving me alone with twenty pages of final screenplay in my

pocket, and my film director employer waiting inside. I stood in the midnight silence, breathing in Ireland and breathing out the damp coal mines in my soul.

Then, I knocked.

The door flew wide almost instantly. John Hampton was there, shoving a glass of sherry into my hand and hauling me in.

"Good God, kid, you got me curious. Get that coat off. Give me the script. Finished it, eh? So *you* say. You got me curious. Glad you called from Dublin. The house is empty. Clara's in Paris with the kids. We'll have a good read, knock the hell out of your scenes, drink a bottle, be in bed by two and—what's that?"

"Tell you later. Jump."

With the door slammed, he turned about and, the grand lord of the empty manor, strode ahead of me in his hacking coat, drill slacks, polished half boots, his hair, as always, windblown from swimming upstream or down with strange women in unfamiliar beds.

Planting himself on the library hearth, he gave me one of those beacon flashes of laugh, the teeth that beckoned like a lighthouse beam swift and gone, as he traded me a second sherry for the screenplay, which he had to seize from my hand.

"Let's see what my genius, my left ventricle, my right arm, has birthed. Sit. Drink. Watch."

He stood astride the hearthstones, warming his backside, leafing my manuscript pages, conscious of me drinking my sherry much too fast, shutting my eyes each time he let a page drop and flutter to the carpet. When he finished he let the last page sail, lit a small cigarillo and puffed it, staring at the ceiling, making me wait.

"You son of a bitch," he said at last, exhaling. "It's good. Damn you to hell, kid. It's good!"

My entire skeleton collapsed within me. I had not expected such a midriff blow of praise.

"It needs a little cutting, of course!"

My skeleton reassembled itself.

"Of course," I said.

He bent to gather the pages like a great loping chimpanzee and turned. I felt he wanted to hurl them into the fire. He watched the flames and gripped the pages.

"Someday, kid," he said quietly, "you must teach me to write."

He was relaxing now, accepting the inevitable, full of true admiration.

"Someday," I said, laughing, "you must teach me to direct."

"*The Beast* will be *our* film, son. Quite a team."

He arose and came to clink glasses with me.

"Quite a team we are!" He changed gears. "How are the wife and kids?"

"They're waiting for me in Sicily, where it's warm."

"We'll get you to them, and sun, straight off! I—"

He froze dramatically, cocked his head, and listened.

"Hey, what goes on—" he whispered.

I turned and waited.

This time, outside the great old house, there was the merest thread of sound, like someone running a fingernail over the paint, or someone sliding down out of the dry reach of a tree. Then there was the softest exhalation of a moan, followed by something like a sob.

John leaned in a starkly dramatic pose, like a statue in a stage pantomime, his mouth wide, as if to allow sounds entry to the inner ear. His eyes unlocked to become as huge as hen's eggs with pretended alarm.

"Shall I tell you what that sound is, kid? A banshee!"

"A what?" I cried.

"Banshee!" he intoned. "The ghosts of old women who haunt the roads an hour before someone dies. *That's* what that sound was!" He stepped to the window, raised the shade, and peered out. "Sh! Maybe it means—us!"

"Cut it out, John!" I laughed, quietly.

"No, kid, no." He fixed his gaze far into the darkness, savoring his melodrama. "I've lived here ten years. Death's out there. The banshee always *knows*! Where were we?"

He broke the spell as simply as that, strode back to the hearth, and blinked at my script as if it were a brand-new puzzle.

"You ever figure, Doug, how much *The Beast is* like me? The hero plowing the seas, plowing women left and right, off round the world and no stops? Maybe that's why I'm doing it. You even wonder how many women I've had? Hundreds! I—"

He stopped, for my lines on the page had shut him again. His face took fire as my words sank in.

"Brilliant!"

I waited, uncertainly.

"No, not that!" He threw my script aside to seize a copy of the London *Times* off the mantel. "*This!* A brilliant review of your new book of stories!"

"What!" I jumped.

"Easy kid. I'll *read* this grand review to you! You'll love it. Terrific!"

My heart took water and sank. I could see another joke coming on or, worse, the truth disguised as a joke.

"Listen!"

John lifted the *Times* and read, like Ahab, from the holy text.

"'Douglas Rogers's stories may well be the huge success of American literature—'" John stopped and gave me an innocent blink. "How you like it so far, kid?"

"Continue, John," I mourned. I slugged my sherry back. It was a toss of doom that slid down to meet a collapse of will.

"'—but here in London,'" John intoned, "'we ask more from our tellers of tales. Attempting to emulate the ideas of Kipling, the style of

Maugham, the wit of Waugh, Rogers drowns somewhere in mid-Atlantic. This is ramshackle stuff, mostly bad shades of superior scribes. Douglas Rogers, go home!' "

I leaped up and ran, but John, with a lazy flip of his underhand, tossed the *Times* into the fire where it flapped like a dying bird and swiftly died in flame and roaring sparks.

Imbalanced, staring down, I was wild to grab that damned paper out, but finally glad the thing was lost,

John studied my face, happily. My face boiled, my teeth ground shut. My hand, struck to the mantel, was a cold rock fist.

Tears burst from my eyes, since words could not burst from my aching mouth.

"What's wrong, kid?" John peered at me with true curiosity, like a monkey edging up to another sick beast in its cage.

"John, for Christ's sake!" I burst out. "Did you have to do *that*!"

I kicked at the fire, making the logs tumble and a great firefly of sparks gush up the flue.

"Why, Doug, I didn't think—"

"Like hell you didn't!" I blazed, turning to glare at him with tear-splintered eyes. "What's *wrong* with you?"

"Hell, nothing, Doug. It was a fine review, great! I just added a few lines, to get your goat!"

"I'll never know now!" I cried. "Look!"

I gave the ashes a final, scattering kick.

"You can buy a copy in Dublin tomorrow, Doug. You'll see. They love you. God, I just didn't want you to get a big head, right. The joke's over. Isn't it enough, dear son, that you have just written the finest scenes you ever wrote in your life for your truly great screenplay?" John put his arm around my shoulder.

That was John: kick you in the tripes, then pour on the wild sweet honey by the larder ton.

"Know what your problem is, Doug?" He shoved yet another sherry in my trembling fingers. "Eh?"

"What?" I gasped, like a sniveling kid, revived and wanting to laugh again. "What?"

"The thing is, Doug—" John made his face radiant. His eyes fastened to mine like Svengali's. "You don't love me half as much as I love you!"

"Come on, John—"

"No, kid, *I mean* it. God, son, I'd kill for you. You're the greatest living writer in the world, and I love you, heart and soul. Because of that, I thought you could take a little leg-pull. I see that I was wrong—"

"No, John," I protested, "hating myself, for now he was making *me* apologize. It's all right."

"I'm sorry, kid, truly sorry—"

"Shut up!" I gasped a laugh. "I still love you. I—"

"That's a boy! Now—" John spun about, brisked his palms together, and shuffled and reshuffled the script pages like a cardsharp. "Let's spend an hour cutting this brilliant, superb scene of yours and—"

For the third time that night, the tone and color of his mood changed.

"Hist!" he cried. Eyes squinted, he swayed in the middle of the room, like a dead man underwater. "Doug, you hear?"

The wind trembled the house. A long fingernail scraped an attic pane. A mourning whisper of cloud washed the moon.

"Banshees." John nodded, head bent, waiting. He glanced up, abruptly. "Doug? Run out and *see*."

"Like hell I will."

"No, go on out," John urged. "This has been a night of misconceptions, kid. You doubt *me*, you doubt *it*. Get my overcoat, in the hall, jump!"

He jerked the hall closet door wide and yanked out his great tweed overcoat, which smelled of tobacco and fine whiskey. Clutching it in his two monkey hands, he beckoned it like a bullfighter's cape. "Huh, *toro*! Hah!"

"John." I sighed, wearily.

"Or are you a coward, Doug, are you yellow? You—"

For this, the fourth, time, we both heard a moan, a cry, a fading murmur beyond the wintry front door.

"It's waiting, kid!" said John, triumphantly. "Get out there. Run for the *team*!"

I was in the coat, anointed by tobacco scent and booze as John buttoned me up with royal dignity, grabbed my ears, kissed my brow.

"I'll be in the stands, kid, cheering you on. I'd go with you, but banshees are shy. Bless you, son, and if you don't come back—I loved you like a son!"

"Jesus," I exhaled, and flung the door wide.

But suddenly John leaped between me and the cold, blowing moonlight.

"Don't go out there, kid. I've changed my mind! If you got killed—"

"John," I shook his hands away. "You *want* me out there. You've probably got Kelly, your stable girl, out there now, making noises for your big laugh—"

"Doug!" he cried in that mock-insult serious way he had, eyes wide, as he grasped my shoulders. "I swear to God!"

"John," I said, half-angry, half-amused, "so long."

I ran out the door to immediate regrets. He slammed and locked the portal. Was he laughing? Seconds later, I saw his silhouette at the library window, sherry glass in hand, peering out at this night theatre of which he was both director and hilarious audience.

I spun with a quiet curse, hunched in Caesar's cloak, ignored two dozen stab wounds given me by the wind, and stomped down along the gravel drive.

I'll give it a fast ten minutes, I thought, worry John, turn his joke inside out, stagger back in, shirt torn and bloody, with some fake tale of my own. Yes, by God, *that* was the trick—

I stopped.

For in a small grove of trees below, I thought I saw something like a large paper kite blossom and blow away among the hedges.

Clouds sailed over an almost full moon, and ran islands of dark to cover me.

Then there it was again, farther on, as if a whole cluster of flowers were suddenly torn free to snow away along the colorless path. At the same moment, there was the merest catch of a sob, the merest door hinge of a moan.

I flinched, pulled back, then glanced up at the house.

There was John's face, of course, grinning like a pumpkin in the window, sipping sherry, toast-warm and at ease.

"Ohh," a voice wailed somewhere. ". . . God. . . ."

It was then that I saw the woman.

She stood leaning against a tree, dressed in a long, moon-colored dress over which she wore a hip-length heavy woolen shawl that had a life of its own, rippling and winging about and hovering with the weather.

She seemed not to see me, or if she did, did not care; I could not frighten her, nothing in the world would ever frighten her again. Everything poured out of her steady and unflinching gaze toward the house, that window, the library, and the silhouette of the man in the window.

She had a face of snow, cut from that white cool marble that makes the finest Irish women; a long swan neck, a generous if quivering mouth, and eyes a soft and luminous green. So beautiful were those eyes, and her profile against the blown tree branches, that something in me turned, agonized, and died. I felt that killing wrench men feel when beauty passes and will not pass again. You want to cry out: Stay. I love you. But you do not speak. And the summer walks away in her flesh, never to return.

But now the beautiful woman, staring only at that window in the far house, spoke.

"Is he in there?" she said.

"What?" I heard myself say.

"Is that him?" she wondered. "The beast," she said, with quiet fury. "The monster. Himself."

"I don't—"

"The great animal," she went on, "that walks on two legs. He stays. All others go. He wipes his hands on flesh; girls are his napkins, women his midnight lunch. He keeps them stashed in cellar vintages and knows their years but not their names. Sweet Jesus, and is that *him*?"

I looked where she looked, at the shadow in the window, far off across the croquet lawn.

And I thought of my director in Paris, in Rome, in New York, in Hollywood, and the millraces of women I had seen John tread, feet printing their skins, a dark Christ on a warm sea. A picnic of women, danced on tables, eager for applause and John, on his way out, saying, "Dear, lend me a fiver. That beggar by the door kills my heart—"

I watched the young woman, her dark hair stirred by the night wind, and asked, "Who *should* he be?"

"Him," she said. "Him that lives there and loved me and now does not." She shut her eyes to let the tears fall.

"He doesn't live there anymore," I said.

"He does!" She whirled, as if she might strike or spit. "Why do you lie?"

"Listen." I looked at the new but somehow old snow in her face. "That was another time."

"No, there's only *now*!" She made as if to rush for the house. "And I love him still, so much I'd kill for it, and myself lost at the end!"

"What's his name?" I stood in her way. "His *name*?"

"Why, Will, of course. Willie. William."

She moved. I raised my arms and shook my head.

"There's only a Johnny there now. A John."

"You lie! I feel him there. His name's changed, but it's *him*. Look! Feel!"

She put her hands up to touch on the wind toward the house, and I turned and sensed with her and it was another year, it was a time between. The wind said so, as did the night and the glow in that great window where the shadow stayed.

"That's him!"

"A friend of mine," I said, gently.

"No friend of anyone, ever!"

I tried to look through her eyes and thought: My God, has it always been this way, forever some man in that house, forty, eighty, a hundred years ago! Not the same man, no, but all dark twins, and this lost girl on the road, with snow in her arms for love, and frost in her heart for comfort, and nothing to do but whisper and croon and mourn and sob until the sound of her weeping stilled at sunrise but to start again with the rising of the moon.

"That's my friend in there," I said, again.

"If that be true," she whispered fiercely, "then you are my enemy!"

I looked down the road where the wind blew dust through the graveyard gates.

"Go back where you came from," I said.

She looked at the same road and the same dust, and her voice faded. "Is there to be no peace, then," she mourned. "Must I walk here, year on year, and no comeuppance?"

"If the man in there," I said, "was really your Will, your William, what would you have me do?"

"Send him out to me," she said, quietly.

"What would you do with him?"

"Lie down with him," she murmured, "and ne'er get up again. He would be kept like a stone in a cold river."

"Ah," I said, and nodded.

"Will you ask him, then, to be sent?"

"No. For he's not yours. Much like. Near similar. And breakfasts on girls and wipes his mouth on their silks, one century called this, another that."

"And no love in him, ever?"

"He says the word like fishermen toss their nets in the sea," I said.

"Ah, Christ, and I'm caught!" And there she gave such a cry that the shadow came to the window in the great house across the lawn. "I'll stay here for the rest of the night," she said. "Surely he'll feel me here, his heart will melt, no matter what his name or how deviled his soul. What year is this? How long have I been waiting?"

"I won't tell you," I said. "The news would crack your heart."

She turned and truly looked at me. "Are you one of the good ones, then, the gentle men who never lie and never hurt and never have to hide? Sweet God, I wish I'd known you first!"

The wind rose, the sound of it rose in her throat. A clock struck somewhere far across the country in the sleeping town.

"I must go in," I said. I took a breath. "Is there no way for me to give you rest?"

"No," she said, "for it was not you that cut the nerve."

"I see," I said.

"You don't. But you try. Much thanks for that. Get in. You'll catch your death."

"And you—?"

"Ha!" she cried. "I've long since caught mine. It will not catch again. Get!"

I gladly went. For I was full of the cold night and the white moon, old time, and her. The wind blew me up the grassy knoll. At the door, I turned. She was still there on the milky road, her shawl straight out on the weather, one hand upraised.

"Hurry," I thought I heard her whisper. "Tell him he's needed!"

I rammed the door, slammed into the house, fell across the hall, my heart a bombardment, my image in the great hall mirror a shock of colorless lightning. John was in the library drinking yet another sherry, and poured me some. "Someday," he said, "you'll learn to take anything I say with more than a grain of salt. Jesus, look at you! Ice-cold. Drink that down. Here's another to go with it!"

I drank, he poured, I drank. "Was it all a joke, then?"

"What *else*?" John laughed, then stopped.

The croon was outside the house again, the merest fingernail of mourn, as the moon scraped down the roof.

"There's your banshee," I said, looking at my drink, unable to move.

"Sure, kid, sure, unh-huh," said John. "Drink your drink, Doug, and I'll read you that great review of your book from the London *Times* again."

"You burned it, John."

"Sure, kid, but I recall it all as if it were this morn. Drink up."

"John," I said, staring into the fire, looking at the hearth where the ashes of the burned paper blew in a great breath. "Does . . . did . . . that review really exist?"

"My God, of course, sure, yes. Actually . . ." There he paused and gave it great imaginative concern. "The *Times* knew my love for you, Doug, and asked me to review your book." John reached his long arm over to refill my glass. "I did it. Under an assumed name, of course, now ain't that swell of me? But I had to be fair, Doug, had to be fair. So I wrote what I truly felt were the good things, the not-so-good things in your book. Criticized it just the way I would when you hand in a lousy screenplay scene and I make you do it over. Now ain't that A-one double absolutely square of me? Eh?"

He leaned at me. He put his hand on my chin and lifted it and gazed long and sweetly into my eyes.

"You're not upset?"

"No," I said, but my voice broke.

"By God, now, if you aren't. Sorry. A joke, kid, only a joke." And here he gave me a friendly punch on the arm.

Slight as it was, it was a sledgehammer striking home,

"I wish you hadn't made it up, the joke, I wish the article was real," I said.

"So do I, kid. You look bad. I—"

The wind moved around the house. The windows stirred and whispered.

Quite suddenly, for no reason I knew, I said. "The banshee. It's out there."

"That was a joke, Doug. You got to watch out for me."

"No," I said, looking out the window. "It's there."

John laughed. "You saw it, did you?"

"It's a lovely young woman with long black hair and great green eyes and a complexion like snow and a proud Phoenician prow of a nose. Sound like anyone you ever in your life knew, John?"

"Thousands." John laughed more quietly now, looking to see the weight of my joke. "Hell—"

"She's waiting for you," I said. "Down at the bottom of the drive."

John glanced, uncertainly, at the window.

"That was the sound we heard," I said. "She described you or someone like you. Called you Willy, Will, William. But I *knew* it was you."

John mused. "Young, you say, and beautiful, and out there right this moment . . . ?"

"The most beautiful woman I've ever seen."

"Not carrying a knife—?"

"Unarmed."

John exhaled. "Well, then, I think I should just go out there and have a chat with her, eh, don't you think?"

"She's waiting."

He moved toward the front door.

"Put on your coat, it's a cold night," I said.

He was putting on his coat when we heard the sound from outside, very clear, this time. The wail, then the sob, then the wail.

"God," said John, his hand on the doorknob, not wanting to show the white feather in front of me. "She's *really* there."

He forced himself to turn the knob and open the door. The wind sighed in, bringing another faint wail with it.

John stood in the cold weather, peering down that long walk into the dark.

"Wait!" I cried, at the last moment.

John waited.

"There's one thing I haven't told you," I said. "She's out there, all right. And she's walking. But . . . she's dead."

"I'm not afraid," said John.

"No," I said. "but I am. You'll never come back. Much as I hate you right now, I can't let you go. Shut the door, John."

The sob again, and then the wail.

"Shut the door."

I reached over to knock his hand off the brass doorknob, but he held tight, cocked his head, looked at me, and sighed.

"You're really good, kid. Almost as good as me. I'm putting you in my next film. You'll be a star."

Then he turned, stepped out into the cold night, and shut the door, quietly.

I waited until I heard his steps on the gravel path, then locked the door and hurried through the house, putting out the lights. As I passed through the library, the wind mourned down the chimney and scattered the dark ashes of the London *Times* across the hearth.

I stood blinking at the ashes for a long moment, then shook myself, ran upstairs two at a time, banged open my tower room door, slammed it, undressed, and was in bed with the covers over my head when a town clock, far away, sounded one in the deep morning.

And my room was so high, so lost in the house and the sky, that no matter who or what tapped or knocked or banged at the door below, whispering and then begging and then screaming—

Who could possibly hear?

Peace in Heaven?

BY ANDREW M. GREELEY

No one in The Commons that Samhain night could have imagined that they were witnessing the possible end of a war in heaven.

The Commons is an elegant and excellent little restaurant in the basement of Newman Hall, site of the original Catholic University and unhappy home for several years of both John Henry Newman and Gerard Manley Hopkins. Just across the street on the Green is the marble bust of your man who wrote the dirty books. On that particular Sunday evening the diners were refined and polished disciples of the Celtic Tiger who had for the most part come downstairs after Mass in the chapel. No one would confuse the Sunday night crowd in The Commons with a crowd in a soup kitchen, not that there were any such in the city by the black pool anymore, or a pub on Sean MacDermott Street.

These discreet haute bourgeoisie would never stare at anyone. Quite the contrary—when someone appeared who might merit a stare, they would lower their eyes, much as novices of both genders had been taught to do in an earlier form of Irish Catholicism.

Yet when the last two couples entered the dining room, everyone else violated the behavior code of their culture and stared, particularly at the two women. They were, truth be told with the usual sigh, well worth staring at. The woman in the first couple was tall and statuesque, with burning red hair piled on top of her head. She wore a form-fitting white cocktail dress, sustained in place by thin straps on her shoulders. Her husband was even taller, silver hair, searing blue eyes, devilishly handsome in a flawless dinner jacket and a blue cummerbund. Someone very important whom you knew you had seen recently on the telly. But you couldn't quite remember his name.

They were followed in five minutes by a second couple, even more striking. The man was black, very tall, and with a diamond in one of his earlobes and a scarlet cummerbund as though he were a cardinal. By the solid build of him, an athlete, again someone you'd seen on the telly, maybe in a film (pronounced the correct way "filum") in which he was the leader of the good ones. His consort was the most striking of the four, snow-white hair flowing to her shoulders, arctic blue eyes that took in everyone in the room in a quick blink, flawless buttermilk skin on which rested a pale gold pendant, a strapless pastel blue gown that clung to her full-figured body, and a faint smile that suggested that she was in charge. She might have stepped out of a Celtic revival painting of Irish antiquity.

As the other diners returned to their conversations and focused their eyes on the salad and the hock in their glasses, they wondered in whispers who the four were and, most important, how old they were.

They were not children or adolescents or even young urban professionals. They had reached a certain age, probably between forty-five and sixty, but had the time and the money to take care of themselves. They were bushed and smoothed and shaped—exercise and diet and cosmetics and well-fitted bras and support garments and certain kinds of reconstructive surgery, aristocrats of one sort or the other, probably not Irish even if they spoke to the maitre d' in the finest upper-class Dublin English—finest English in the world, it is often said.

When seated at the table they began to talk a foreign language, magical in its soft and melodic hum, not The Irish, not anything remotely like The Irish, yet somehow peaceful and reassuring like The Irish as it was spoken on the far reaches of the Gaeltacht where the waters from Newfoundland washed up on the sands.

The men among the other diners tried their best to keep their eyes off the two women, a challenging task. The women diners noted with some curiosity that the formalities when the two couples met, the kisses and the handshakes, were a bit strained, almost artificial, as though there might have been a difficult history among them and some doubt that the future would not be equally difficult. It was, one woman who worked for the foreign office thought, not unlike the preliminaries of a meeting about the next phase of the implementation of the Good Friday Agreement.

In that respect she had the right of it. However, she and the other diners were not close to the truth in their estimates of the age of the four and in their guesses about the amount of exercise and corsetry that might have been necessary to turn out the apparently flawless figures of the women. All four handsome people had been around for a very long time and were quite senior among their own kind. While ethereal bodies, like all bodies, do decay, the process is very slow. No one in either constituency had yet died of old age, though that was always a possibility. They knew they would die eventually, one way or the other, as many of their kind had. Till then, however, they would take care of themselves and love as though tomorrow might be the end. Moreover, the wondrous bodies of the women were not exactly their reality. Rather they were surrogates for even more dazzling beauty.

As they sipped Bushmills Green (straight up, of course, because whatever they were, they were not Yanks who put ice in everything), they chatted amiably about the things that Irish men and women discuss at Sunday evening suppers—sports, the latest political scandal, the stupidities of Church leaders, the world news, the idiocies of American foreign policy. Not a word under the circumstances could be said about children. They avoided any mention of the reason for their meeting. Only when the plates had been removed and the sweets consumed, and the coffee and the port served, did they, like all the other Irish, turn to the matter at hand.

"Well now, Mike," said Maeve, she of the scorching red hair, "what's this about reconciliation? We all of us know that question was closed long ago."

Michael lit his cigar and puffed on it thoughtfully.

"You know as well as I do, Maeve, that the Other never closes the door on anyone."

The two couples, you see, represented the remnants of the original war in heaven—Mike and Gaby the side of the Seraphs and Maeve and Mac(Lir) the side of the Shee. Gaby, the smartest and most perceptive of these distinguished folk (not for nothing had she been sent to Nazareth), thought that she would much rather sit down across the table from Ian Paisley than persuade the Shee that peace was possible between the ancient rivals. She loved Maeve and Mac— Seraphs are programmed to love, though not fated to do so. Yet there had been so much hurt, so much pain . . .

"We are not all persuaded," Mac said, a touch pompously, "that we want forgiveness. We have been Shee for so long that it seems rather more appealing than being Seraphs."

Gaby had told the Other in no uncertain terms that it had been a mistake to send the Shee to Ireland. "They've been there so long," she had argued, "that now they think and act like they're Irish. They never say what they mean, and they never mean what they say."

Many of the Seraphs said that Gaby was the Other's favorite. Hence she could say more than anyone else would dare to say, and the Other would merely laugh, like an amused parent with a winsome little girl. Gaby insisted that the Other had no favorites. However, she knew better.

"That's not the issue, Mac." Mike sipped his cognac thoughtfully. "You don't have to become Seraphs . . . In fact, you couldn't even if you wanted to."

"Why is the Other suddenly so interested in forgiving us?" Maeve demanded, her face turning red. "We've been out of favor for a long time? Why can't he leave us alone? Why has He changed his mind about us?"

Gaby pictured the Other as a She, not a He. However, the Other combined the perfections of both. Yet as she often said, if you've ever held a newborn offspring, you know that's how the Other feels about all Her creatures.

For a millennium of millennia the Shee had complained about being outcasts. Now they were arguing that they liked being outcasts. Typical. Gaby wanted to respond furiously that implacable forgiveness was in the very nature of the Other. However, she tried to contain her displeasure.

"The Other hasn't changed, Maevie. You've never been out of favor."

"Do you call endless exile in this soggy, foggy island favor?"

"But you picked it," Mike pointed out. Gaby's companion was a great and good being, but logic was not what the discussion required. Gaby had warned the Other that the Shee had absorbed the Irish love of an argument for the sake of arguing.

"Much choice we had!" Mac joined the argument. "The Other said it was time to go to work running this crazy universe and that if we didn't choose to work, we'd have to leave our home and go live on earth. We saw this green island down here, as green as home, and said we'd go there because it was the place on earth most like home. We didn't realize that it was green because it rained all the time. And the Other didn't warn us that we'd have to share it eventually with the Celts—noisy, contentious, drunken savages."

Poor Mac was still angry and still giving speeches. Well, we'd have to let him vent for a while, though it might take him another millennium or two.

There had never been a real war in heaven. And it wasn't in heaven anyway, but in the home where they had all lived in peace and plenty and happiness. Mike had never waved a fiery sword at anyone. The Other had not sent anyone plunging into flames. He had merely made it clear that those who didn't want to work would have to go somewhere else, anywhere else. No one had thought it would ever come to that. But some of the angels had backed themselves into a corner and walked out because they didn't think it was fair. The angels, you see, and especially the Seraphs, tend to pride, and, as they themselves would have said in defense, they have a lot to be proud about. They were also vain, but they had reason to be vain. Gaby was very vain about her human surrogate and was delighted at the attention she attracted.

She tried again, knowing that she was digging the hole deeper. They were replaying the scenario of a millennium of millennia ago. It seemed like only yesterday.

"You can come home," she said, sipping from her jar of Bailey's. "Or you can stay here in Ireland, which will become for you just like home, and we all can visit back and forth."

"Gabriella," Maeve said, her green eyes sparking fire, "you always were a silly little bitch. "The Other wants us to admit that we were wrong. We're not about to settle for that shite."

"That's a little strong, dear one," Mac cautioned his companion. "There is no point in offending the Other."

Maeve took a deep breath, then reached out and touched Gaby's fingers. "I'm sorry I lost my temper. Sure, it's not you I'm angry at."

If any of the other diners had been watching closely, they would have wondered if they had not seen a stunning display of multicolored lights leap back and forth across the table, lights into which the two women were transiently absorbed.

" 'Tis all right, old friend. We understand."

Mike waited till the strength of that sudden blast of love had abated before he spoke.

"We've been separated too long, my friends. It's time to end it."

"I wonder if that's still possible." Mac became the orator again. "It's been a long, long time. You have found your work to be satisfying, even though it's nothing more than correcting some of the imperfections in the Other's cosmos. We, on the other hand, have become content with the joys of Irish country life. Why is not the Other content to let it be so? Surely He doesn't need our help merely because of globalization?"

Filled with love for these two old friends, Gaby tried to cut to the quick.

"Are you satisfied with night rides on your splendid steeds, dancing till dawn in the meadows and scaring the living daylights out of these poor people . . . Besides, do they scare that easily anymore? Has not the Church finally won out? Does anyone believe in the Shee?"

"Does anyone believe in Seraphs anymore?" Maeve shot back.

"Have you seen the angel shelves in bookstores?" Mike asked.

"You are not claiming, are you, that the people who write such books understand what you really are?" Mac said. "The readers are mostly frightened and superstitious people. As are the people in the West. They love it when we scare them. They'd be brokenhearted if we ever stopped."

Gaby tried to return the discussion to the issues. It was a difficult task because the Other had given no hints about the reasons for declaring peace in heaven, a peace the Other seemed to believe had always been there.

"As we all know," she tried to state the question, "the Other often does not reveal His strategies. Now there is to be peace in heaven, peace between you and us and between the Other and you. Or more precisely, the Other wants the existing peace accepted and recognized. That's all."

"Like nothing ever happened!" Maeve was becoming angry again. "What about those who have died? Are they forgiven too? What about the offspring which we have all too rarely? Is the Other going to make all of this retroactive if we are willing to take an occasional assignment?"

Gaby would not touch the offspring question. She had always believed that offspring required passion between companions, and that passion was incompatible with a lazy life. However, it was not the time to suggest that. If the Shee could be stirred out of their lethargy, they would mate more often, and there would be more offspring.

Mike intervened again.

"We have suffered losses too," he said soothingly. "We live with hope and the fidelity of the Other to the Promises. As you know, Gabriella lost her first companion to a sudden burst of negative gravity."

Maeve touch her hand again. "The good Light Bearer. I'm so sorry, Gaby love. So very, very sorry."

Tears sprung into Gaby's eyes, as they always did when the Light Bearer was mentioned. For a moment she felt fury at the Iranian influence on popular Christianity that implied that the Light Bearer was a bad angel, when in fact he had been the best of the angels.

"We will all be together again," she said with a sigh that was almost Irish. "All of us."

Maeve was crying too, her lovely surrogate breasts moving up and down with emotion. Doubtless the male human diners would be stricken with desire by such movement. Well, they could work that out with their wives later. Gaby spread some seraphic dust in the dining room, which would make the humans more attractive to their companions. If they could see life-bearing Seraphs as we really are, she thought, the beauty of our nurturing organs would drive them mad with hunger.

"The Promises were not revoked with regard to you," Mike continued with an even more blinding smile. "Moreover, you have in fact been involved in the very work you said you did not want to do. Unasked, you supervised the Good Friday Agreement. I'm sure the Other was pleased."

"Someone had to do something," Mac waved off the compliment. "On occasion we have done good some things in Ireland of our own freedom."

"Once a Seraph"—Gaby giggled—"always a Seraph."

"That's all the Other expects of us," Mike continued, flashing his absolutely best smile. "The important point is that nothing much has to change. The war in heaven is over, if there ever were one."

"And we're back in?" Maeve said skeptically. "If we want in?"

"Even if you don't want in." Gaby spoke the core truth.

"That's what I don't like at all, at all. The Other doesn't even ask us politely if we want back in or if we are sorry we ever slipped out. Both are assumed. That's not fair."

"And what if the Other did ask both questions?" Mike wondered. "How would you answer them?

"This is the best port I've ever tasted," Mac interrupted the flow of the conversation. "Where's it from? Seraphic vineyards? Are they at home or here on earth?"

"Both places," Mike replied easily. "We'll send you some. We're rather proud of some of our vintages."

Seraphic life givers, like the human ones, were given to boasting at the wrong time, even the shrewd and tough Michael.

"You didn't answer Mike's questions?"

"We might not say no, and then again we might," Maeve answered for her companion. "And we'll not be bribed by your private wine stock!"

Laughter around the table, for the first time.

"Don't you see, Maevie, the Other loves you so much that the return is made easy for you."

"As much as we love one another, Gabychild?"

Seraphs are essentially creatures of love. They liked to think that they were the best sacraments in the universe of the Other's love. Their most intense love was for their companions and their offspring, of course. But their love for others, of either gender, was also overwhelming. They were smart enough to make the proper distinctions, so jealousy was rare among them.

"You know the answer to that Maeviekid."

"The Other's love," Michael laid out the party line, "is implacable. As we all know, the Other wants no one to get away from that love. Or even to think they have. That's why we're meeting tonight."

"To tell us that we're not demons?" Mac asked with a touch of bitterness.

"We have searched much of the cosmos, Mac, not all of it, mind you, but most of it. We have not found any bad angels. There may be such, but we have not discovered them."

"It would be nice to be able to visit home again, Mac," Maeve said sadly.

"We would have a grand party!" Gaby promised. "The best in many millennia."

"We'll have to think about it," Mac said, ending the discussion. "And talk it over with the others."

That was as far as they would get that night, about as far as Gaby had hoped, maybe a little more. The Shee did miss home and their old friends more than they were willing to admit. Progress had been made. The Other presumably would be pleased. The embraces at the end of the dinner were much more passionate than those at the beginning. Again, in the blink of an eye, the dining room was filled with dancing lights. As they left, Gaby scattered more of her love magic on the other diners. This All Hallows Eve would be a night that they would never forget.

Back on the street, they bid farewells. Mike and Gaby reabsorbed their surrogates into themselves. They would surely couple almost at once. Would the leaders of the Shee? Gaby hoped they would, but doubted it.

Then they heard cries from the dark and foggy Green. People were being attacked. Maeve and Mac darted into the Green. Gaby heard two splashes. Someone had been tossed into the pond. Mike and Gaby materialized at the edge of the trees, hidden by the fog. Two young thugs had been dumped into the pool and were shivering in the November cold. A handsome Irish couple was assuring the victims, two traumatized middle-aged Americans, that the two louts would never attack anyone again and indeed would never use drugs again.

Faerie magic.

"Well," said Mike, "it looks like we've made a little progress, doesn't it now? Aren't they acting like Guardian Angels?"

"The Other will be pleased," Gaby agreed piously.

Later, the two of them were dancing on the top of the Millennium Needle in O'Connell Street. Dancing was always a preliminary to lovemaking among the Seraphs. Gaby had an age-old reputation for dance of invitation.

"Well, we're the answer to the question of how many angels can dance on the head of a pin," Mike said as he overpowered her with his magic.

"Point of a needle," Gaby corrected him before she succumbed completely.

LITERARY Fantastics

The Lady in Grey

BY JANE LINDSKOLD

WILLIE

Sometimes, as now when he watched her pouring out the tea for himself and George Russell, Willie found it difficult to remember that he had only met his beloved Maud a few years before.

Meeting Maud had been the transforming experience of Willie's life. From the day she had first come to his father's house in Bedford Park, her beauty, her grace, her passionate involvement with Irish Nationalism had haunted Willie's every waking hour—and many of his sweetest and most troubling dreams as well.

Willie had written poetry to Maud and for Maud, had dragged himself from literary seclusion into public life for her. Yet seeing Maud as he did this day, weighted down with sorrow, her apple blossom loveliness nearly quenched by the unremitting darkness of her mourning attire, Willie felt he knew her as he never had before, and he knew, too, that he loved her as he never had when she was light prettiness surrounded by her birds and dogs.

The waves of sorrow are the waters which shall lap us close, he silently recited, framing the thought for poetry, discarding it, giving the image other words. *This flood tide of tears upon which we sail.*

Better, but not right, though it would be easy to find a rhyme for "sail." Too easy, perhaps. What if he broke the line after "tears"? Two good rhymes, then, building toward an alternating rhyme scheme. Yet he must take care. Would the lines then be too short, too choppy? The difference between doggerel and true poetry could be as narrow as the cadence given when the poem was read aloud. The poet must be in control of all possible readings.

Seeing Maud completely engaged with Russell, Willie made a surreptitious note of the potential line on his shirt cuff. He could not work at poetry just then, even though his finest inspiration was before him, her slender height bending over the teacup cradled in her hand, her voice—a voice he had so frequently heard raised in exhortation—sweet and mellow.

Maud was quizzing Russell about reincarnation, and that good man, so knowledgeable about things on the other side of the veil, was reassuring her that a child who died young was frequently reborn, often into the same family.

Willie opened his mouth, about to express his skepticism regarding reincarnation. Even if reincarnation did exist—and the matter was one open to ample speculation—would a child be reborn to its birth mother or simply into the same family? How might one recognize such a reborn child? Russell had said a child might be reborn "soon," but what was "soon" to a spirit freed of physical referents?

Yet even as Willie shaped the words he would speak so readily in one of the discussions that followed meetings of the Golden Dawn or the Theosophical Society, he realized the pain they would bring Maud were he to speak them aloud. Willie knew that Maud was not questioning Russell at random. She was thinking of the little French child, Georgette, whom she had adopted and who had recently died in France.

Maud had been at Georgette's sickbed, and when the death bird had tapped on the windowpane Maud had sent for doctor after doctor, striving to the end against the death her inner eye had told her must come. Shouldn't Willie permit this woman he adored whatever slim comfort Russell's mystic wisdom might bring her?

Yet, Willie admitted honestly to himself, there was a part of him that envied any—even a dead child—who had so held Maud's love. Would Maud mourn him so extravagantly? Hadn't she refused his proposal of marriage not long before her latest departure for France?

While she had been away, Willie had teased himself with fantasies that she had fled the intensity of her feelings for him, that she had left rather than admit she had been wrong to refuse his proposal, that she would return and confide in him her love and her fear. It was a deflation of his hopes to discover she had gone instead to this child's deathbed.

MAUD

Maud was aware, acutely aware, of Willie listening to George Russell's expostulation on reincarnation.

Willie was unwontedly quiet, by which sign she knew he was brooding. When nervous, dear Willie chattered. He also chattered when he was happy or engaged with an idea. The only times he was silent were when he was composing—and even then he drummed his fingers on the table, trying out meter and rhythm—or when he was unhappy.

When Russell departed, promising to send several books and

articles on reincarnation around to her rooms, Willie maintained his brooding silence.

Although Maud herself was so weighed down with misery that she hardly knew herself (*George, my dear baby, how could I have left you?*) she strove to find some item of interest with which she might distract her friend—as means to draw him from himself and back into the world they shared.

Once before Maud had offered Willie a fragment from one of her dreams. In that dream they had been brother and sister in the Arabian desert, sold together into slavery. Now she began to tell him of another dream image that haunted her, remembering too late that the intimacy created by that first dream confession had led Willie to his very awkward proposal of marriage.

That would be an easy way to make Willie happy—accept him, but that she could never do, not with her sins so heavy on her soul. She could not even bear to tell him the truth about little George— had told him the child who had died was "Georgette," and even that name, once out of her mouth, had seemed too close to the truth.

"When I was small," Maud began without preamble, "I repeatedly dreamed of a beautiful dark woman. She would bend over my cot and look at me. Her eyes were so sad they broke my heart."

She spoke quickly, her inflection curiously flat. Willie stared at her, his ear quick to the difference in intensity between words and tone, but as she had known, the lure of something occult—and more than occult, information intimately linked to her—drove him to pursue the information rather than to query after her state of mind.

"A woman?" he asked. "Old or young?"

"Neither," Maud replied. "A woman grown, not a girl, but not an old woman yet."

"Was this woman someone you knew? Your mother perhaps? I recall you saying your mother died when you were young."

"No. It wasn't my mother. I never saw this woman in life, though I looked for her among my mother's friends and relations. Although I never found her, I felt curiously intimate with her—as if I knew her well."

"This vision was of a modern person then?"

Maud thought Willie seemed disappointed. He did so love the exotic. It would have been more exciting for him had she dreamed of Joan of Arc in her armor or Deidre in her bridal robes. Maud called the image of the dark woman to her mind's eye, unwilling, though she knew not why, merely to invent details.

"Not modern, no," she said slowly. "The woman in my dream wore a grey dress, with grey veil covering the lower portion of her face. Over this veil I saw her eyes, large and dark brown, looking at me intently and with immense sorrow. Those eyes are what I remember most of all."

"Ah . . . I wonder . . . What do you feel for this woman?"

"Pity, I think, and always a peculiar intimacy."

Maud turned away, unable to bear any longer the keen, interested light that had come over Willie's countenance, although she was the one who had sought to awaken him from his brooding. The curtains over the window she faced had not yet been drawn, and the glass cast back a reflection.

Two reflections, one laid over the other, so that the images were intermingled yet curiously distinct. Oddly, neither of the reflections contained Maud herself.

Behind her, Willie had raised his hand and was making several quick, elaborate gestures. Maud hardly registered his odd behavior, so overwhelmed was she by the other image—one she had at first taken as herself, only to realize that the woman reflected there was also the Lady in Grey.

In the reflected image, the black of Maud's mourning had washed to dark grey. The eyes, so like Maud's own in the misery they held, were darker and ringed with sleeplessness. What Maud had before taken for a veil was her own gloved hand, raised to her mouth in horrified recognition.

WILLIE

As Willie listened to Maud's account of her childhood haunting by the Lady in Grey, he heard the strain in her voice. That tightness only grew worse as she sought to answer his simple questions. Intuitively, he knew that they were approaching one of the obstacles to the love he had felt should have been theirs from the very first moment of their meeting.

Overcome with her own emotions, Maud had turned away from him. Willie made up his mind with a swiftness that surprised him, for in all his studies of the occult he had always attempted to remain rational. Indeed, his rational desire to test magical theory was what had led to his expulsion from the Theosophical Society. What he was considering now was hardly the result of careful reasoning, but he felt it was right.

In his studies with the Order of the Golden Dawn, Willie had been indoctrinated into a wealth of magical lore. As surely as if he heard golden trumpets sounding to announce the coming of a king, Willie knew the time had come for him to put that knowledge to use.

Maud speaks of this as a specter from past dreams, Willie thought, rapidly analyzing what would be needed. *Very well. First the sign for the Fifth Element.*

He sketched it in the air, but felt no tremor in the veil between the world we know and those beyond.

Another element must be subordinate to the first, or we shall have no form. Maud is fire, so I shall sketch that . . .

The results were more certain than Willie could have imagined.

Maud had been facing the window. Now she reeled back a few paces as if confronting some figure standing before her. Her lips moved in prayer or entreaty, but Willie heard nothing but a moan of terror.

MAUD

"Who are you?"

Maud had meant the words as a challenge, but they sounded thin and timorous. Oddly, the very weakness of her own voice gave her courage. Hadn't her father told her to fear nothing, not even death? Hadn't she lived her life by this maxim, facing and conquering each fear one at a time until now she feared nothing?

"Who are you?" Maud repeated, and though this time her voice was stronger, she noted that the words did not reverberate in the air but were swallowed, as if she and the Lady in Grey stood within a fog.

The Lady in Grey looked at her, and those eyes Maud had always thought of as sad held a mocking expression.

"You know my face," the Lady in Grey replied.

"It is much like my own face," Maud said, "but you are not me. Who are you?"

"You are wrong. I am you—in a sense. I am more than you and less. I am the myth and mystery of yourself that you have created, Maud Gonne. I am the Irish Joan of Arc, Cathleen ni Houlihan, Queen Maeve of Connaught. I am the Woman of the Sidhe who showers her blessings upon the poor peasant folk and who brings misfortune to their enemies."

"This is not possible," Maud protested, clinging to a rationality she did not feel. "I have caught glimpses of you since I was a child. Those identities of which you speak are more recent dreams."

"Since as a child of four," the Lady in Grey agreed, "clinging to your father's arm in the presence of your dead mother you have seen me. There he said to you, 'You must never be afraid of anything, even of death' and you believed him, though he himself was trembling under the weight of grief and fear. When you took his words to you as a talisman, then I was born. Vows are powerful things, especially vows kept. They are absolutes, and so bring the world of the real to rub against that of the ideal. Today, your idealistic friend and his rituals provided the razor to cut away the barrier and bring us face-to-face."

Maud did not wish to believe these words, yet she could not deny the evidence of her senses. This woman possessed her face, her bearing, and her features. Oddly, in those features Maud saw nothing of the beauty she knew was her own, a beauty she had used to gain her way since first she realized she possessed beauty and that it was not a gift, but a tool. But though the Lady in Grey had Maud's features, she had no beauty. She was as hard as Maud knew her own soul to be.

The Lady in Grey reached out and caressed Maud's face. Her hand was very cold. Strangely, for all the ways they were alike, the Lady was slightly shorter than Maud, but as Maud looked down into those eyes so like her own, she felt none of the confidence that her considerable height usually granted her.

"So Willie has brought us face-to-face," Maud said, stepping back from that cold touch. "Why did he do that?"

"He is sensitive, your young poet, and rightly sensed that I am a danger to you—and even more, a danger to his dreams of someday wedding you."

Maud shook her head, exhaustion, defeat, and sorrow flooding her like a tangible wave.

"Never," she said. "I cannot accept his love."

The Lady in Grey laughed mockingly.

"You fear his love. You fear the disclosures it would force from you. You fear . . ."

"I fear nothing!" Maud interrupted hotly.

"Then why do you lie to Willie so persistently? Why not tell him that the child you mourn is not some little adopted Georgette but your own son, George? Why let kind Willie persist in viewing you as a pure goddess? Why not tell him of your French lover, father of that dead son?"

"It would hurt him!"

"It would hurt you."

The retort was as cutting as a blade.

"It would destroy your myth. Maud Gonne, the Joan of Arc of Ireland, pure and passionate, giving herself and her small fortune to the Cause would be transformed into pathetic Maud Gonne, mistress to a second-rate French journalist, bedmate to a man who would pimp her for his revolutionary cause, yet is so weak he collapses into whining misery if she leaves him."

"That isn't how it is between us."

"You lie if you deny it. I speak only the truth. I am the truth. You, for all your pretensions of fiery honesty and righteous passion are the lie. You are cold with the chill of fearlessness. Only those who fear are brave. You do not fear—not even death. Or so you say . . . Is that lack of fear why you did not hesitate to barter away your father's life? Since death is something not to fear, did you fool yourself that you were doing your Tommy no harm?"

"No!"

Maud's scream of anguish was so intense that it ripped through the veil that separated her from Willie. She saw him move toward her, felt him touch her arm, heard the sound of his words but could make no sense of them. Only the words of the Lady in Grey reached her ears, though she raised her fists to cover them.

"You cannot have forgotten, have you?" the Lady taunted. "Have you forgotten the young girl chafing under the restrictions set by her indulgent father—that same father who gave you and your sister freedom to play wild when others would have bundled you off to some boarding school? That father who taught you not to fear anything— even death."

"I don't want to hear this!"

"Why?" came the mocking reply. "Is there then something you fear?"

Maud could not manage the slightest sound. Her sense of herself was dissolving into minute fragments. The Lady in Grey spoke on relentlessly.

"You called your father 'Tommy,' as if he were a boy your own age. When you were reaching womanhood, you felt strange, perverse pride when Tommy escorted you on some outing. Together you laughed when you—father and daughter—were mistaken for newly-wed man and wife. Yet when Tommy asserted his father's role, when he insisted that you not encourage flirtations, you were angered. Or was it something else that angered you? Something else that made you act against him?"

"No! No! No!"

"Had you learned that your Tommy had a lover?" continued the relentless interrogation. "Had you learned that this woman was heavy with his child? I think you did know this, and that you resented how your Tommy went to this woman to ease his needs. You were angered that he sought to command you when he was not even in command of himself. You were jealous that he could care for another. So what did you do?"

"No! Say nothing more. I demand it."

The Lady in Grey's lips shaped a mocking smile; her words flowed unceasing. "On a night full of storm, storms you did not fear, for you fear nothing, you lingered over the fire, brooding over the restrictions Tommy had placed on you—and on other things. There was a book among your father's belongings, one of those he had collected for its beauty—for he had an eye for beauty in all things . . ."

"No!"

Protest had become plea, and with a cruel smile the Lady in Grey interrupted her narration.

"I will tell it or you will, Fearless," said the Lady in Grey.

"I will tell," Maud said, drawing on the private strength that had always been her own. She saw the Lady in Grey grow taller as she did so, and knew the link between them. But she had promised, so she spoke.

"There was a book of occult writings among my father's treasures. It contained incantations and bits of lore, but he had not purchased it for these. He had bought the book because of the richness of its illuminated engravings and the gilt edge of its bindings. Always interested in building my resources, I had read the book and knew its contents well.

"Among the spells within the book was a prayer for calling upon the Devil and receiving his aid. I spoke that prayer aloud with all the anger in my heart. As I finished the clock struck midnight. I knew then my bargain had been taken. The Devil had become my ally. When my father fell ill some days later, I knew the sickness would be his death, though the doctor had not yet spoken the words 'typhoid fever.' I dreamed of Tommy's funeral in perfect detail and felt nothing more than idle curiosity."

She stopped, but the Lady in Grey was not finished with her.

"As you won your freedom from Tommy," the Lady in Grey said, no approval in her cold eyes for Maud's courage in articulating this horrid memory, "so you later won it from the uncle appointed your guardian, though it meant alienating his own daughter from him, and taking your sister from a quiet life that might have suited her and saved her from the unhappy marriage she later made. No matter the cost to others. You must have again the wild freedom of a child, running with the wind in the heather."

Maud laid her face in her hands and realized that her skin was as cold as that of her adversary.

"Shall we talk of other deaths you have brought, Fearless? Of the men who, inspired by your words, have gone to fight and die? Of the peasants who have been evicted for defying their masters and have later died in ditches? Of little George, whom you mourn now in your costume of black? Would George have grown ill if his mother had spared time for him—but she must deny him in favor of revolution . . ."

"Why are you tormenting me?"

"I am not. If you fear nothing, you cannot fear the truth about yourself. It cannot torment you."

"You are evil . . ."

"You know best."

WILLIE

Willie gazed in horrified fascination at what his magic had wrought. Maud stood transfixed, staring at her own reflection in the window glass, speaking unintelligibly, not hearing when he spoke to her.

When a touch on her arm did nothing, he went past her and pulled the curtain over the glass. She continued to interact with the reflection she could no longer see.

Growing frightened, Willie reviewed his rituals, seeking one that would break the first summoning. When those symbols did nothing, he began drawing signs for a ritual meant to sharpen his own perception of what lay beyond the veil.

The first few sketched symbols had no effect, but then Willie thought of an elaborate combination evoking Maud's birth planet conjoined with Venus followed by his own conjoined with Mars, following the whole with Mercury, for Hermes is the guide to travelers and the patron of magic.

At the conclusion of this ritual, Willie felt a trembling, then a wash of cold and dampening of sound. Then, with outline blurred and substance cloudy, yet clear enough not to be mistaken for a product of his imagination, Willie saw the Lady in Grey.

I have parted the veil, he thought, pride and apprehension mingling in his breast.

He could hear but fragments of the conversation between Maud and the Lady in Grey, the words as faint to his ear as if heard across a broad field, where an occasional word was tossed to him by the wind.

"Maud!" he cried. "Tell me what she is saying!"

MAUD

As a butterfly might feel the touch of a summer zephyr, so Maud felt Willie's mystic workings—she was aware of them, but they did not distract her from her object.

She faced the Lady in Grey and spoke of the cost of truth.

"Parnell," Maud said slowly, "ruined himself and his cause by his actions. He loved well, but not wisely."

"As did you," the other replied.

"The agent of Parnell's ruination was truth—not love."

"And what his enemies did with that truth."

"They would do more to me," Maud said, "for I am a woman, and my sex is held to higher standards. Parnell's enemies forced him into exile. I would not be so lucky. I would be paraded through the streets, and even those who have been helped by my actions would drown me in their poison."

"True."

"Even so, I do not fear for myself or my reputation. I gave up fearing for my petty respectability when I left Uncle William's house and went on the stage."

"That is so."

"The Irish people need those leaders who remain to them more now that Parnell is dead," Maud said. "They need inspiration, or the cause will be lost, buried in the earth even as Parnell has been buried. The factions since his exile have been pulling us apart. Now that Parnell can never return, factionalism will grow worse as his successors seek to claim leadership."

The Lady in Grey picked up the thread, her voice coaxing, "Can you rob the people of inspiration at such a critical time? Can you set the Lady of the Sidhe up for attack when she is most needed? Can you deny them their Irish Joan of Arc?"

Maud shook her head.

"I cannot. I feel that my debasement would end the Irish national cause as surely as if Ireland were sunk into the sea."

They stared at each other in silent consideration. Now Maud heard Willie's voice calling as though across a great distance, "Maud, tell me what she is saying!"

She remembered that Willie knew nothing of who the Lady in Grey truly was. "I cannot tell him who you are!" Maud protested aloud.

"Lie to him," the other sneered. "You're good at that. I warn you. Shape your lies not too far from the truth, for William Butler Yeats is already sensitive, and this rending of the veil will sharpen his ear to lies."

Maud nodded, then turned away from the Lady in Grey. As she pulled closed the rent in the veil, she felt as never before the other's cold hand upon her heart.

WILLIE

At last she heard him!

Maud turned and, stumbling slightly, felt her way into the nearest chair. She reached for her cup of tea, surely cold by then, but drank it thirstily and poured another from the still-warm pot.

Shaking slightly, the slender length of her hand quested after the sugar bowl. Willie took it from her and spooned a liberal measure into the steaming tea, his heart wrung with pity for that tremor in a hand usually so steady.

"Maud," he asked gently, eager to gather impressions while they were fresh in her mind. "What did you see? What did she say to you?"

"The Lady in Grey," Maud murmured as if partially entranced. "She said she was me, a part of me, from a past life."

Willie nodded, his mind racing.

I wonder if Russell's talk of reincarnation colors Maud's memories? That does not invalidate the experience. She mentioned the woman soon after Russell's departure. His words may be what brought the woman to mind. Unconsciously, Maud may have been aware of their connection even before my agency brought them face-to-face.

"A past life?" he prompted.

"In Egypt," Maud replied, speaking more quickly now. "She—or I—was a priestess responsible for oracles in a great temple. She had a lover, a priest, and he persuaded her to give false oracles to serve some purpose of his—for money."

The last phrase was added hastily, and Willie felt a flicker of unease, as if Maud might have said something she did not wish him to hear and had added the words to distract him.

Does she think I would be jealous of this past-life lover? Willie thought. *Perhaps she is right to so dread. I am jealous, but I can hide that jealousy.*

"I don't understand this next," Maud went on, casting him a pretty look of appeal. "The Lady in Grey spoke as to how this betrayal of her sacred trust was so great a violation of her vows that the part of her that had been responsible for the betrayal split off from the greater soul and became a wandering spirit."

Willie felt a surge of satisfaction that quite drowned his momentary jealousy. His studies with the Theosophical Society had included just such theory. Although Maud was interested in psychic phenomena, hers was not a scholar's interest. It was unlikely she had encountered the theory before. Therefore, not only was her report reasonable, it confirmed established thought.

"I have studied this phenomenon," he said, patting her hand. "You must take care. Although rejected by the greater soul, the fragment will always seek reunion. It must always be refused. The generative seed of its being is an evil deed—so evil the soul could not bear to embrace it. To accept the fragment back into the whole, no matter how great the pity you feel for the exile, is to risk being flooded by that evil."

Maud looked at him and smiled strangely.

"Don't worry, Willie. I'm not afraid. Haven't I told you before that I am never afraid?"

She rose, her trembling completely gone, and even the sorrow that had weighted her before her arrival diminished. She looked stronger, and, in that strength, more distant. Willie felt a twinge of longing for the weaker Maud, who had needed his comfort, but he put the feeling from him as selfish.

"I must be going now," Maud said. "Where is my wrap?"

Despite his protestations that they must further analyze her experience, Maud departed soon after, promising to let him call on her the next day. She would not allow him to see her to the street, saying she was perfectly capable of finding a cab.

Willie went to the window to watch her depart. As he pulled back the curtain, he found a face was looking at him from the glass. The cold shock sent him reeling back a pace, the curtain falling limp from his hand, but the face and the woman to whom it belonged remained standing before him.

She resembled Maud and yet was not precisely the same. A veil of some gauzy stuff was drawn across the lower half of her face. He could see her lips, full and beautifully shaped, moving behind it.

"You have never really believed," said the Lady in Grey, and her voice was Maud's, underlaid with a mocking note he had before heard only in nightmare. "If you had believed, you would never have summoned me to face her. I shall give you something to remember me by—and to remind you of the dangers of parting the veil."

Bending slightly, the Lady in Grey extended one hand toward Willie's groin. The cold caress of her fingers slipped through the fabric and touched him intimately, even as he had fantasized in shameful dreams that Maud would touch him. Cold emanated from those elegant fingers, spreading through his masculine parts and lingering long after the Lady in Grey had given him a saucy smile and vanished.

MAUD

Initially, Maud was pleased to have spoken with her other self. Aware that Tommy's cautions about fear seemed to have been the genesis of the Lady's independence, Maud took another of his teachings as her guide when dealing with the Lady in Grey.

"Will is a strange, incalculable force," she remembered Tommy saying. "It is so powerful that if, as a boy, I had willed to be the Pope of Rome, I would have been the Pope."

But Tommy had not possessed a fixed will, and so had achieved little. Maud was determined not to make the same mistake. Her will would be strong enough to make the Lady in Grey her agent.

Maud took to sending the Lady in Grey to infiltrate the dreams of her adversaries and through the Lady's agency persuading the reluctant ones to join Maud's cause. In this way, Maud reasoned, the Lady would do good, and so would not be the evil influence Willie feared.

The Lady in Grey seemed pleased by these missions, going forth in whatever guise would best reach her target's subconscious self: sometimes as Maud herself, sometimes as the devious and lovely

Queen Maeve, sometimes armed and armored as the Irish Joan of Arc. Maud's influence grew. Despite the loss of Parnell, the cause of Irish Independence grew stronger.

Yet there were difficulties between Maud and the Lady as well. For one, though Maud would fain have let the Lady in Grey resume haunting her only with an occasional vision, Willie's parting of the veil seemed to have given the Lady more freedom to appear at her own impulse. Her appearances grew more frequent the more Maud relied on her services.

The Lady in Grey only appeared in certain circumstances, most often when someone who was psychically sensitive was present. After some embarrassing errors, Maud realized that no one but herself could see the Lady. Only the most sensitive seemed even to know she was there.

Soon after the Lady in Grey first appeared, Willie brought Maud to meet the head of the Order of the Golden Dawn. Willie seemed hopeful that the Order might do something to help Maud banish the Lady, but though MacGregor Mathers had been willing to lecture Maud from his copious hoard of odd knowledge, it was his wife, Mina, who seemed to be more aware of the Lady in Grey.

"Beware of her," Mina warned. "I sense she has killed a child, and though she regrets it, there is hatred in her for children."

Maud, who knew too well that the dead child was her own George, killed by her neglect, said nothing. She wondered if the hatred Mina sensed in the Lady in Grey was shared by herself as well, and that her grief was only a sham. Was she perhaps relieved to have the child gone? Had her deepest heart seen little George as an imped-iment to her freedom as Tommy had been?

So horrified was Maud by the thought that she convinced her French lover to lie with her again, this time in the vault under the memorial chapel of their dead son. She prayed that her child would come back to her and show forgiveness, but there was no sign that George had heard.

When the child conceived in that union was born, it proved to be a girl. Though Maud tried to lavish on Iseult the devotion she had not given to little George, her attempts at motherhood were stayed by the mocking face of the Lady in Grey.

"No child, no lover offers you the excitement you crave. Only I give you what you most desire, Fearless, Flawless, goddess who inflames men's passions. This is the price you pay."

Maud and Willie had drifted apart—partly because she could not bear keeping her new secret from him, partly because he was angry with her for quitting the Order of the Golden Dawn. She had told him that this was because she suspected the Order had ties to Freemasonry, which she despised as one of the tools of the British Empire. Her true reason was that the Lady in Grey appeared frequently in their presence, unsettling all.

Maud wondered if Willie's anger at her departure from the Order was not intensified in that what he really felt was relief. The Lady in Grey seemed to have her own bond with the poet, and though Maud could sense nothing of their interaction, she knew well by now the Lady's cruel streak and knew that Willie would be offered no kindness from that quarter.

One night, years after the birth of Iseult, Maud dreamed. A powerful spirit, represented as a towering figure of light, stood beside her bed, beckoning her to follow. Maud rose obediently, and was led into a great throng of spirits, each a living flame possessed of a human shape. Her guide stopped and placed her hand into that of another spirit. When their hands met, Maud saw that the spirit was Willie Yeats.

"You are married now," the great spirit said, and Maud knew it was true.

Then the Lady in Grey, her voice filled with mocking laughter, her flame cold and blue, spoke from among the gathered spirits, "And a great lot of good it will do you."

Maud looked where the Lady pointed and saw that though elsewhere Willie glowed with a pure clear light, the area about his groin was dark and cold.

"You have castrated him," said the Lady in Grey, "for he loves only you, and though he tries to take other lovers, his virility fails him. Now he convinces himself he lives celibate because his love is the pure love of old, but his heart knows the bitter truth."

WILLIE

Willie awoke with a vision of Maud kissing him, her form fading from his sight as if the real woman was slowly stepping back. Unlike those erotic dreams he had had of her—and they were legion—this simple kiss left him with no sense of guilt or defilement.

He whistled as he went about his shaving, and went to meet Maud with a light heart. They had plans to spend the day together, visiting old Fenian leaders and learning what they might for the cause.

Maud greeted him with an odd question.

"Had you a strange dream last night?"

Emboldened by his curious contentment, Willie replied, "I dreamed this morning for the first time in my life that you kissed me."

Maud said nothing to this, but turned the conversation to some mundane matter, but all the day her mood was strange. They dined together that evening and, as Willie was about to take his leave, Maud said suddenly, "Let me tell you what happened. Last night I dreamed a great spirit brought me to you and told me we were married."

Willie hardly knew what to say, and while he was struggling for words, Maud leaned forward and for the first time in their long association kissed him on the mouth. She left him then, and as he walked back to his hotel he imagined that finally she would be his.

And then we will win over you at last, he said in thought to the Lady in Grey.

But when morning came, and Willie went to Maud, he found her cast in as deep a gloom as he had ever seen.

"I should not have spoken to you that way last night," Maud said, not looking away from the leaping flames of the fire, "for I can never be your wife."

"Is there someone else?" he asked, thinking of rumors he had heard.

"There was," she replied, "and there is still, in a way. Sit with me. There is much I should have told you long ago."

Willie took the chair she indicated, and found himself unable to look at her. Instead, he gazed into the flames as Maud told him the truth behind things he had heard rumored and refused to believe. She told him of her French lover, of the son who had died, of the daughter who still lived.

As he listened, his heart twisted in him, and his world shifted around him, for her tone left no doubt that she spoke the truth. Willie had always accepted that others would love his Maud. How could they not? It was harder to accept that she had loved another, and how badly that other had used her.

Without a pause, Maud went from these recent sins to tell him about her belief that she had been responsible for her father's death. At last she ended, facing him for the first time in all that long narration.

"Having done what I have done, having been what I have been, how could you marry me? You would never forget. Better, perhaps, that I should have left you to your grand romance and the poetry you make of it, but I thought I owed you truth instead."

Her gaze dropped, and Willie realized that somehow she knew of the curse put on him by the Lady in Grey, and that she hoped that her honesty would free him—as he realized that her dishonesty had bound him, for the idealized image of herself was what linked them both to the Lady in Grey.

Yet Willie felt no stirring in his loins, though Maud's lovely eyes were upon him. He knew that at this moment Maud would lie with him, even though she would not marry him. He felt no desire, only wrung out and weary—not from the truth Maud had offered him, but because he finally realized that though he might ask a hundred times more, Maud would never accept him.

She fears you, came the voice of the Lady in Grey, *for you offer her a contentment that would rob her of her desire to act—and without action how can she redeem herself?*

"I leave her then," Willie said, and he hardly knew whether he spoke aloud or not, "to you and redemption."

And without another word, he rose and walked out the door.

He knew, however, that Maud had only to speak and he would return, over and over again, until at last death did them part.

A Drop of
Something Special
in the Blood

🕸

BY FRED SABERHAGEN

Monday, 16 July, 1888—

The dream again, last night. I shall continue to call these visitations dreams, as the London specialist very firmly insisted upon doing, and it is at his urging that I begin this private record of events. As to the "dream" itself, I can only hope and pray that in setting it down on paper I may be able to exorcise at least a portion of the horror.

I awoke—or so I thought—in an unmanly state of fear, at the darkest hour of the night.

As before, the impression (whether true or not) that I had come wide-awake, was very firm. There was no confusion as to where I was; I immediately recognized, by the faint glow of streetlights coming in round the edges of the window curtain, the room in which I had lain down to sleep, in this case a somewhat overdecorated bedchamber in an overpriced Parisian hotel.

For a moment I lay listening, in a strange state of innocent anticipation. It was as if my certain memory of what must inexorably follow was for the moment held in abeyance. But that state lasted for a few breaths only. In the next instant, memory returned with a rush. There was a faint sound at the window; and I knew beyond the shadow of a doubt what I must see when I turned my gaze in that direction. *She* was standing there, of course, just inside the window. In my last coherent thoughts before falling asleep, I had begun to hope (absurdly, I suppose, whatever the true cause may be) that the visitations could not have followed me from London.

In the poor light it was as difficult as on the previous occasions to be sure of the color of her long curls of hair, but I thought they might be as red as my own were in my youth. The long tresses fell to her waist round her voluptuous body, that was otherwise only partially concealed by a simple shift or gown.

Though the moonlight was behind her, I thought that her slight figure threw no shadow on the floor. In spite of that, hers was a most carnal and unspiritual appearance. Plainly I could see her brilliant white teeth, that shone like pearls against the ruby of her full lips.

A tremendous longing strove against a great fear in my heart . . . I knew, as had happened on every previous occasion, a burning desire that she would kiss me with those red lips . . .

It is difficult for me to note these things down, lest someday this page should fall under the gaze of one I love, and cause great pain. (Florence, forgive me, if you can! Will I ever embrace you again?) But it is the truth, even if only a true account of a strange dream, and I must hope that the truth will set me free.

I have not yet learned my nocturnal visitor's name—assuming that the woman is real enough to have one. Perhaps I should call her "the girl," for she seems very young. As she approached my bed last night she laughed . . . such a silvery, musical laugh, but as hard as though the sound could never have come through the softness of human lips. It was like the intolerable, tingling sweetness of water glasses when played on by a cunning hand . . .

Overcome by a strange helplessness, I had closed my eyes. The girl advanced and bent over me till I could feel the movement of her breath upon me. Sweet it was in one sense, honey-sweet, and sent the same tingling through the nerves as her voice, but with a bitter underlying the sweet, a bitter offensiveness, as one smells in blood.

I was afraid to raise my eyelids, but could see out perfectly under the lashes. The girl bent over me, and I had the sense that she was fairly gloating. She actually licked her lips like an animal, till I could see in the moonlight the moisture shining on the scarlet lips and on the red tongue as it lapped the sharp white teeth. Lower and lower went her head as the lips went below the range of my mouth and bearded chin and seemed about to fasten on my throat . . . I could feel the hot breath on my neck, and the skin of my throat began to tingle as one's flesh does when the hand that is to tickle it approaches nearer—nearer . . . the soft, shivering touch of the lips on the supersensitive skin of my throat, and the hard dents of two sharp teeth, just touching and pausing there. I closed my eyes in a languorous ecstasy and waited—waited with beating heart.

Suddenly she straightened, and her head turned as if listening for some distant but all-important sound. As if released from a spell, I moved as if to spring out of the bed, but in the instant before the motion could be completed, she bent over me again. The touch of her fingers on my arm seemed to drain the strength from all my limbs, and I sank back helplessly.

"So sweet is your blood, my little Irishman. I think there is a drop of something special in it," the apparition murmured. In my confused state, the idea that this diminutive visitor might call my large frame "little" drew from my lips a burst of foolish laughter.

In response, the girl laughed again, a sound of ribald coquetry, and bent over me to accomplish her purpose.

Then the truth, or what seemed the truth, of what was happening overcame me, and I sank down in a delirium of unbearable horror and indescribable delight commingled, until my senses failed me.

◆　◆　◆

ODDLY ENOUGH, my faint, if such it was, passed seamlessly into a deep and restful sleep, and I slept well until the street sounds of Paris, some cheerful and some angry, below my window, brought me round at almost ten o'clock.

My awakening this morning was slow and almost painful, and it was difficult to fight free of a persistent heaviness clinging to all my limbs. A single spot of dried blood, half the size of my little finger's nail, stained the pillow, not three as on certain unhappy mornings in the recent past. In London I had independent confirmation (from a hotel maid) that the stains themselves are real, which at the time afforded me inordinate relief.

This morning, as before, an anxious examination in a mirror disclosed on my throat, just where I felt the pressure of lips and teeth, near the lower border of my full beard, the same ambiguous evidence—two almost imperceptible red spots, so trivial that in ordinary circumstances no one would give them a moment's thought. I cannot say it is impossible that the small hemorrhage had issued from them, but it might as easily have come from nostril, mouth, or ear.

I take some comfort in the fact that if anyone in the world can help me, it is the physician I have come to Paris to see—Jean-Martin Charcot, perhaps the world's foremost authority on locomotor ataxia, as well as hypnotism. Whether he can possibly help me, either in his character as mesmerist, or as expert in neuropathy, is yet to be discovered. If Charcot can help, in one capacity or the other, he must.

If he cannot, I tremble for my very life. I have already gone past the point of fearing for my sanity.

I must force myself to write down what I have been avoiding until now, the evil I fear the most. If the girl has no objective reality, then mental horrors that I endure are sheer delusion, and the precursor of much worse to come, of an absolute mental and physical ruin. I am in the grip of a loathsome and shameful disease, contracted years ago—if that is so, then what is left of my life will not be worth the living. I only pray God that the source of my agony may *not* be syphilis. It is only with difficulty that I can force myself to pen the word on this white page—but there, it is done.

As far as I know, or the world knows, there is no cure. The more advanced physicians admit that the current standard of treatment, with potassium iodide, has been shown to be practically worthless. I know the early symptoms (alas, from my own case) and have seen the full horror of the tertiary stage expressed in the bodies of other men. Delusions are frequently a part of that catastrophe.

But the beast takes many forms. The first symptom of the last stage, sometimes appearing decades after the first, local signs of infection have passed away, tends to be a weakening or total loss of the ankle and knee reflex. In succeeding months and years the patient's ability to walk, and even to stand normally, slowly declines. Sometimes in medical description the initials GPI are used, standing for general paralysis of the insane, the most dreaded late manifestation. The effects on the brain are varied, but include delusions, loss of memory, sometimes violent anger. Disorientation, incontinence, and convulsions occur often. *Tabes dorsalis* (also known as locomotor ataxia) is the commonest symptom of infection in the spinal cord. Others include darting attacks of intense pain in the legs and hips, difficult urination, numbness in hands or feet, a sense of constriction about the waist, an unsteadiness in walking—all capped by a loss of sexual function.

So far I have experienced only the delusions—if such they are. Horrible as that fate would be, I believe this current torture of uncertainty is even worse. I will go mad if Heaven does not grant me an answer soon.

◆ ◆ ◆

(LATER)—I find it a source of irritation that I will not be presenting myself, openly and honestly from the beginning, to Charcot as a sufferer in need of help, but only as a visiting "celebrity." In the latter category I of course shine solely by the reflected light of my employer. No one here has shown the least awareness of my own small literary efforts; and I would not be surprised to learn that no Parisian has ever read *Duties of Clerks of Petty Sessions in Ireland*.

This concealment of my true purpose is, to a certain extent, dishonesty on my part. But when I consider the unfortunate publicity that might otherwise result, and the risk of harm to others if my condition were widely known, it seems to me the role of honor must include a measure of dishonesty. Desperate though my situation is, I wish to meet Charcot and form my own estimate of the man and his methods (which some denounce, perhaps out of jealousy), before committing myself completely into his hands.

◆ ◆ ◆

EVENING: TODAY I HAVE seen and heard that which frightened me anew, but also that which gives me hope. Let me set down the events of the afternoon as quickly and calmly as I can, before the memory of even the smallest detail has begun to fade.

First, let me state my key discovery: *The girl is real!* Real, and, to my utter astonishment, a patient of Charcot's!

I was certain, from the moment today when our eyes met in the hospital, that she knew me as instantly and surely as I knew her. I suppose I need not try to describe the hideous shock I suffered upon recognizing her among the inmates. There can be no possibility of a mistake, though in the filtered daylight her teeth appeared quite small and ordinary.

I was certain that she knew me from the moment when our eyes met, and I had the odd impression that she might even have been *expecting* me.

We were standing close together in the treatment room, one of the stops on what I suppose must be the regular tour afforded distinguished visitors. Her whisper was so soft that I am certain no one but I could hear it. But I could read her lips with perfect ease. "It is my little Irishman!" And then she licked them with her soft, pink tongue

◆　◆　◆

Bᴜᴛ ɪ ꜱʜᴏᴜʟᴅ set down the afternoon's events in their proper order. The hospital, La Salpêtriére, sprawls over several acres of land not far from the botanic gardens, and houses several thousand patients, nearly all women. (The Bicêtre, nearby, is reserved for men.)

The famous doctor is now about sixty years of age, of small stature but imposing appearance. I have heard it said that he is pleased to exaggerate his natural resemblance to Napoléon . . . he is pale, clean-shaven with straight black hair only lightly tinged with grey, a firm mouth, and dark melancholy eyes that seem to remember some ancient loss.

Our tour began in what seemed routine fashion. Charcot called several patients (by their given names only), and brought them forward one at a time to demonstrate the symptoms of their illness and the means he used to treat it. His comments were terse and to the point. Whatever could not be helped by the power of suggestion must be the result of heredity, and nothing could be done about it.

I paid little attention to the mysterious girl when she first appeared, as routinely as any of the others, called out of her private room, or perhaps I should say cell. Her long, red hair, which first caught my eye, was bound up in a cap, from which a few strands of bright coppery red escaped, and she was decently clad, like the other patients, in a plain hospital robe. I did not even look closely at her until I heard her voice.

Charcot was pronouncing his accented English in forceful tones. "Lucy, this gentleman has come from England to visit us today. He is a famous man in London, business manager of the Lyceum Theater."

Lucy—that is the only name by which I have heard her called—responded to the doctor's questions in English bearing almost the same flavor of Ireland as does my own. From Charcot's first remarks regarding her, it was clear that she has been his patient for only a few days. With a casual question I confirmed that she had been admitted on the very day of my own arrival in Paris.

Stunned by the familiarity of her voice, I gazed intently at her face, and could no longer doubt her identity. There was an impudent presumption in the look she returned to me, and a twinkling in her green eyes that strongly suggested we shared a secret. There followed the whispered words which, though nearly inaudible, seemed to seal her identity as my nocturnal visitor.

The tour was moving on. I wanted desperately to question Charcot further on the background and history of the girl, but I delayed. I admit I feared to ask such questions in her presence, lest she put forward some convincing claim of having known me in different circumstances.

Gradually more facts of her case came out. According to the doctor, Lucy displays a positive terror of sunlight, and has a disturbing habit of refusing to eat the standard fare provided for patients—the quality of which, I note in passing, seems higher than one might expect in this large an institution.

Hers, he said, is a very interesting case. (Ah, if only he knew!) Several days ago Lucy had somehow got hold of a rat—I can well believe that Charcot was livid with anger when he heard of such a creature being found, in what he considered his hospital—and, using her own sharp-pointed teeth as surgical instruments, was delicately draining it of blood, which she appeared to consider a delicacy.

It is also said that she manifests an intense fear of mirrors—as they are practically nonexistent within the walls of La Salpêtriére, this presents her caretakers with no urgent problem.

As it was evident from my repeated questions that I had a strong interest in the patient, Charcot at the end of the tour obliged me by returning to her cell and questioning her at some length while I stood by.

Lucy's manner as she replied was not particularly shy, but still subdued, and somehow distant.

What was her present age? She did not know, could not remember—and did not seem to think it was at all important.

Had she been born in Paris? No—in Ireland, far across the sea—of that she was certain. How, then, had she come to France? Her parents had brought her when they had come to join the Paris Commune.

This was interesting news indeed. The doctor frowned. "You must have been only a very small child at that time. How can you remember?"

"Oh, no sir. I was fifteen years of age when we came to France, and much as you see me now."

Charcot gave me a significant look: The fierce rebellion of the Commune now lies fully seventeen years in the past, and the girl who stood before us today could hardly be more than eighteen at the most.

His voice remained gentle, but insistent. "And you have been here, in Paris, ever since?"

Lucy began to twist her fingers together nervously. "No; the fighting grew terrible in the city, soon after we arrived. My mother was killed, and quite early on I ran away."

"Indeed? You ran away alone?"

There was a hesitation. Then, finally: "No, sir. It was then *he* came to me, and claimed me for his own, and took me away. To be his, forever and ever." As she said this, the girl gave a strange sigh, as of triumph and dread all mingled.

Charcot gave me another look filled with meaning and picked up on what he evidently thought an important clue. " 'He'? Who is this 'he'?"

The question produced evident distress. But however Charcot prodded, even threatening the girl with strict confinement if she refused cooperation, there was no answer.

The doctor's interest in this strange tale, though on his side purely professional, seemed to have become nearly as great as my own. He dispatched an orderly to bring him the girl's dossier, and stood in an attitude of deep thought, chin supported in one hand. "And where did this person take you when you fled from Paris?"

Lucy frowned; her eyes were by then closed, and she seemed to be experiencing some type of painful memory. Her answer when it came was long and rambling and unclear, and I do not remember every word. But the gist of it was that her mysterious abductor, who had evidently also become her lover at some point, had carried her to what she called the dark land, "beyond the forest."

By that time the girl's medical record had been brought to Charcot from the office; on opening, it proved to contain only a single sheet of paper. Turning to me, Charcot read rapidly from it. "She has been telling the same story all along: that she is the child of an Irish-Russian revolutionary couple, brought to Paris by her parents when they came, with others of like mind, to join the Commune in '71. But that is absurd on the face of it, for the girl cannot be more than twenty years old at the very most."

Another brief notation in the record stated that Lucy on first being admitted to the hospital had been housed in a regular ward. There she had displayed an almost incredible skill at slipping away during the night, but was always to be found in her bed again at dawn, the means of her return as mysterious as that of her disappearance. Irked by this disregard of regulations, the doctor in immediate charge of her case had transferred her to a private cell, in the section set aside for patients who are violent or otherwise present unusual difficulties. Even there she had at least twice somehow managed to leave the locked cell at night, so that a search of the hospital wards and grounds was ordered.

"Without result, I may add," Charcot informed me. "But each time, in the morning, she was found in her cell again, wanting to do nothing but sleep through the day. I found it necessary to dismiss two employees for carelessness."

"She seems a real challenge," was the only comment I could make.

By then it was obvious that the doctor was growing more and more intrigued. But his voice maintained the same calm, professional tone as he turned back to the girl and asked, "What did you do in the land beyond the forest?"

The trouble in Lucy's countenance cleared briefly. "I slept and woke . . . feasted and fasted. . . . danced and loved . . . in a great house . . ."

"What sort of a great house?"

"It was a castle . . ."

The doctor raised an eyebrow, expressing in a French way considerable doubt. "A castle, you say."

"Yes." She nodded solemnly. "But later he was cruel to me there . . . so I ran away again."

"Who was it that was cruel to you? What was his name?"

At this the girl became quite agitated, displaying a mixture of emotions . . .

"He who brought me there . . . the prince of that land," she finally got out. Then one more sentence burst forth, after which she seemed relieved. "He made me the *dearg-due*."

"I did not understand that word," Charcot complained briskly. But the girl could not be induced to repeat it, and could not or would not explain.

All this time I said nothing; but I had understood the Gaelic all too well. My hand strayed unconsciously to touch the small marks on my throat.

The questioning went on. Why had Lucy come back to Paris? She had been "following the little Irishman, who is so sweet." (She said this without looking in my direction; and I was much relieved that neither Charcot nor the attendants standing by imagined "the *little* Irishman" could possibly mean me.)

She went on, in a voice increasingly tight with strain, "I am afraid to return to the dark land. And I yearn to go back to blessed Ireland, but I dare not, or *he* will find me, and take me back to his domain, the land beyond the forest . . ."

Thinking quickly and decisively, as is his wont, Charcot abruptly announced that he had decided to try hypnotism. In a few minutes we had adjourned to a small room that is kept reserved for such experiments. There he soon began to employ his preferred method of inducing trance, which is visual fixation on a small flame—a candle against a background of dark velvet.

Lucy was seated in a chair, directly facing the candle. Charcot stationed himself just behind her, murmuring in a low, soothing voice, whilst I stood somewhat farther back. What happened next I cannot explain. It seemed that even as the girl began to sink into a trance I could feel the same darkness reaching for me, as if my mind and Lucy's were already somehow bound together.

I fell, losing my balance as awkwardly as some weak woman in a faint. At the last moment I roused enough to try to catch myself by grabbing the seat of a nearby chair, breaking my fall to some extent but seriously spraining my left thumb.

◆　◆　◆

CHARCOT HELPED ME to a private room where he insisted that I lie down until I was fully recovered from my "faint." Meanwhile, as he provided a rather awkward splint and bandage for my thumb, I had the chance for a private consultation with the famous doctor.

Charcot confessed himself intrigued by my behavior in the presence of the girl. I began to tell him something of my case, and confessed my overwhelming fear.

He nodded, and prepared to give me a quick examination. But another detail still bothered him. "What was that word—neither French nor English . . . something, she said, that her princely abductor had caused her to become."

"It is in the old language of Ireland: *dearg-due,* meaning the sucker of red blood."

"Yes . . . I see." After a thoughtful pause, he added, "Having some connection with her behavior with regard to the rat."

"Yes," I agreed. "No doubt that was it."

Charcot examined me briefly, I suppose as thoroughly as possible without advance preparation. He then gave me some hope, as a world expert on *tabes dorsalis,* by saying that while he certainly could not rule out the possibility in my case, he thought it unlikely that the dreams, or delusions, that I described were due to any organic lesion of the brain.

Instead, Charcot suggests that a kind of displacement has taken place: the girl in the hospital only resembles the one of whom I dreamed, and my unconscious mind has somehow altered my memory of the dream to fit the available reality.

Would that the matter could be so easily explained. But I fear that it cannot.

Tuesday, 17 July, morning—

Lucy came to me again last night, here in my hotel. Before retiring, I had made doubly sure of the room's single window being closed (it is utterly inaccessible from outside, two stories above the street) and locked the door and blocked it with a chair, which has become my nightly habit. This morning after her departure, when I examined the window in broad daylight, after my strange visitor's departure, a thin caking of dust and an intact small spiderweb offered proof that it had not been opened.

If the girl in the asylum be real, as must be the case, can her shade or spirit in my room at night be anything but a figment of my own disordered reason?

In the course of last night's visit, she said to me, "From the moment I first heard you speak in London, my little man, I knew great hunger for your sweet Irish blood."

Flat on my back in bed, I still did not know if I was dreaming. But I was curious. "Where did you hear me speak?"

"It was at the back door of your Lyceum Theater."

"And is it that you love the theater, then? You come to watch my employer, the great Henry Irving, on the stage?"

"Oh aye, he's marvelous. And I love the darkness and the lights, the curtains that can hide so much, the painted faces and the masks . . ."

Still murmuring, she bent over me, and all was as before. It seems that when her touch is upon me, my uninjured hand is as powerless to resist as the sprained one.

Thursday, 19 July, late afternoon—

This will be my last entry in this journal. The business has come to a conclusion in the most startling and amazing way.

A Drop of Something Special in the Blood

Lucy appeared in my room again last night, and events followed their usual frightening course, of grotesque horror mingled with indescribable pleasure—until, at the last moment before our intimacy reached its peak, she abruptly broke off and pulled away from me.

Raising myself dazedly on one elbow, I became aware of a new presence in the room.

Though the tall figure standing near the window was visible only in outline, I could be sure it was a man. Lucy cowered away before him.

Moving silently at first, the new apparition (very shadowy in darkness, hard to see distinctly) advanced toward the bed.

Hardly knowing what to make of this development, I could only stammer out, "But you are real!"

A deep voice answered, speaking English in a strange accent that was neither French nor Irish. "I am as real as life and death."

In the next moment the newcomer turned to the girl, who was still cowering away. His voice was softer, and almost tender. "Lucy, my dear, your sisters are waiting for you at home, in the land beyond the forest. I am ready to take you to them."

"I do not want to go!"

"But you cannot continue in this way." He might almost have been a parent, remonstrating with a wayward child. "Your vanishing from the hospital. Your toying with this man."

She dared to raise her eyes, and pleaded piteously. "He is my sweet little—"

The man took another step toward her, and spoke in a tone charged with menace. "*Silence!* These games you play will bring again the hunters down upon us, with their crosses and their garlic and their stakes!"

When Lucy struggled, he knocked her down with a single blow from the flat of his hand.

That was not to be borne, and the instinct of manhood in me sent me springing out of bed, bent on defending the girl.

Honorable as my intentions were, and sincere my effort, the only result was that the nightmare seemed to close upon me with new force. Seizing me by the throat, in a one-handed grip of iron, my opponent forced my body back upon the bed, meanwhile murmuring something of which the only two words I could hear clearly were "misplaced chivalry."

Meanwhile, Lucy had regained her feet, and she in turn tried to come to my aid. But with his right hand the tall man caught her by the hair and forced her to her knees, saying, "You will see him no more."

Those were the last words I heard from either of my visitors. Struggle as I might, I could not loosen the dark man's grip by even a fraction of an inch. I doubt whether I could have succeeded even had I been able to use both hands, which of course I could not. And once more darkness overcame me.

◆　◆　◆

WHEN I RECOVERED CONSCIOUSNESS THIS MORNING, there were no blood spots on my pillow. But there were bruises on my throat beneath my beard, five small purpling spots that must have been made by the grip of a single hand, a left hand, of overpowering strength—and it is blessedly clear to me that with my own left hand, injured as it is, I could never have done this to myself. Charcot, when I managed to see him today at the hospital, confirmed the reality of the bruises—as indeed the internal soreness of my throat had already done, to my own full satisfaction. To explain them to the doctor I made up some tale of a scuffle with a would-be robber in the street.

I am ecstatic with a sense of glorious relief: the man who with one hand overpowered me was a terrible opponent, fit to inhabit a nightmare—but he was real! So was Lucy, my girlish "succubus," truly in my room, and so were all the visits she has paid me. Nothing that has happened was the product of an infected and disordered brain. Whether or not Lucy is ever to appear to me again, and whatever the ultimate explanation of the mystery, it has nothing, nothing whatever to do with locomotor ataxia.

One might think this knowledge a new occasion for terror, this time of the supernatural. But the dominant emotion it arouses in me is a relief so strong that it is almost terrible in quite a different way.

I do *not*, after all, find myself doomed, hopelessly succumbing to the tertiary stage of syphilis. I can hope to avoid that stage entirely, as do most victims of the disease. Whatever bizarre powers may have intruded in my life, and whether or not they are of occult derivation, my fate is at least not *that*.

◆ ◆ ◆

I FIND I MUST ADD A POSTSCRIPT TO THIS JOURNAL. I visited Charcot again this afternoon, and thanked him for his efforts as I paid his bill. I told him nothing of last night's events. The doctor, as might be expected, sympathizes with my bruised throat. But Charcot remains unable to regard my nocturnal experiences with Lucy as anything but dreams or delusions. He still doubted that a physical lesion of the brain, caused by disease, was likely to be responsible. In this glorious conclusion I heartily concur.

Charcot's parting advice to me echoed that of the London specialist: rest, good food, and exercise. Then: "If these fantasies continue to trouble you, Mr. Stoker, my advice is to continue to record them with pen and ink."

I believe that I shall soon be writing another book.

Fred Saberhagen

Author's Note

Bram Stoker died in London in 1912, of locomotor ataxia, or tertiary syphilis, leading to "exhaustion."

For the Blood
Is the Life

BY PETER TREMAYNE

"For the Blood is the Life"

—advertising slogan for Clarke's Blood Mixture,
The Times (London), Monday, October 3, 1887.

I suppose that I was lucky to get the interview at all.

I stood on the steps of Teach Cluain Meala, a tall and narrow Georgian building, situated in Dublin's busy Harcourt Street, and gazed curiously at the polished brass plate outside the door. AVERTY ENTERPRISES, it read. The name was known not only in Ireland but also throughout the world as one of the biggest international entertainment promotion companies. Averty Enterprises had been on the credits of enough Broadway "Hit Musicals" and television variety shows for it to be immediately recognizable—a sort of entertainment brand name.

Standing there, I had a feeling, not for the first time, of irritation that I had even bothered to waste my time making the journey into central Dublin from Chapelizod in answer to the letter that had summoned me. The letter arrived for me on the previous day, with its embossed company notepaper and its few typed lines, politely requesting me to attend an interview with the managing director to discuss the prospect of a position within the company. I felt it was some silly mistake, for what would an entertainment agency want with a doctor of medicine such as I?

The letter had been sent to me care of the College of Physicians, for as a Fellow of the College, I was entitled to have my mail forwarded from there. The truth being that I was not in practice at that time, having just returned from Africa. I was seeking a position because I could not afford to buy a partnership in a general practice, especially in Dublin where life was pretty expensive. A rural practice was not something I even contemplated.

It was my sister Étain, in whose house I was temporarily living at Chapelizod, who had insisted that I should respond to the letter. Étain knew all about the entertainments business. She was a semiprofessional singer and told me that a company such as Averty Enterprises did not make mistakes.

"Turn down an offer to work for Averty Enterprises? You must be out of your skull!" she had jeered. Although Étain was a few years younger than I was, after our parents died in a traffic accident, it was she who worked to keep a home together. I had been in my final year at medical school. I had felt that I still owed something to her for going round the pubs and clubs and singing to earn a living for the both of us. She was not a great singer, but had a nice, easy voice. She was a balladeer rather than a "pop" singer. Poor Étain. She had made a bad marriage to an irresponsible and impecunious youth named Art Moledy, who had disappeared to America within a year. She became very ill after that and nearly died. I had felt protective toward Étain from then on and took heed of her advice. On this occasion I wasn't so sure that she was right. Surely an entertainments company would need a medical doctor like an opera singer with laryngitis?

But there I was, standing on the steps of the company head office, and decided that I might as well go through with the meeting. I set my shoulders determinedly and marched up the steps to the brightly painted door. In a small hallway beyond, a burly uniformed security guard gazed sourly at me.

"I have an appointment," I stammered as his six feet six inches of height towered threateningly over me.

His eyes narrowed, and he testily demanded, "Got your letter?"

I scrabbled into my pocket and brought forth the letter.

The security man stared at it as if trying to find some fault with it.

"Up the stairs, first right," he eventually ordered in a laconic manner.

Up the stairs, first right led me to a door marked RECEPTION. A bored but pretty-looking girl sat behind a desk on which there was a small telephone exchange, an intercom unit, and a computer. She was doodling with noughts and crosses in a notebook and started nervously as I entered and presented my letter to her. She read it carefully, then, without a word to me, reached for the intercom.

"Dr. Sheehan is in reception, sir."

A muffled voice squawked unintelligibly from the box. The girl regarded me coolly. "Up the stairs, first left," she ordered.

I climbed another flight of stairs, came to an unmarked door, and tapped gently. A male voice boomed, "Enter!" I did so.

"Dr. Joseph Sheehan?" The man was beefy, red-faced, overweight, and oozed *bon diable*. He rose from a massive desk and looked every inch a theatrical entrepreneur, even down to the garish grey-blue suit with the broad stripe. Gold chains jangled from one wrist and his multicolored silk tie would have lit a darkened room.

He pumped my arm like a man determined to get water from a dried-up well. Unhealthy beads of sweat shimmered on his forehead.

"Are you Mr. Ronayne?" I asked. That had been the signature on my letter.

"Sit down, Doctor. I am Ronayne, director of Averty Enterprises. Sit down."

I obeyed. He pulled a sheaf of papers out of a folder and glanced at them. I noted his wheezing breath and wondered whether I should suggest he try an inhaler for the condition. I waited patiently as he peered at the papers.

"Surely there has been some mistake?" I finally ventured after a while. "I am a medical doctor. I know nothing about the entertainment world."

He reluctantly brought his gaze away from the papers and stared dourly at me for a moment.

"Mistake?" he seemed puzzled.

"You cannot be looking for a full-time medical doctor for your company, and that is the position that I am looking for," I added.

"There is no mistake. Let me ask you a few questions—just to confirm some facts. You have just returned to Dublin, right? You've been abroad. You did your training here and are a . . . a . . ." He referred to the papers. "You are a Licentiate of the College of Surgeons and Fellow of the College of Physicians, right?"

I wasn't sure whether the staccato barks were meant as statements or questions. I decided that the word "right?" at the end made them into questions.

"Right," I confirmed.

"For the last three years you have been working in Africa with Médicins Sans Frontières, right?"

"Right," I echoed dutifully.

"Pretty tough work in Africa, I suppose? Famine, malnutrition, and all that, right?"

"Right," I echoed back, then relented. "It was pretty tough. But how did you know that I was back in Dublin looking for a new position? Your letter was addressed to me at the College of Physicians, but they aren't supposed to hand out personal information."

He made a dismissive gesture with his hand.

"We have our contacts, Doctor Sheehan. I suppose that you have had to deal with HIV, AIDS, and all that sort of thing?"

"Oh yes," I said, a trifle bitter by the memory of the suffering that I had seen. "And all that sort of thing."

"I gather that you were working at the Wambiba Hospital specializing in AIDS screening?"

"For a time. I was specializing in blood diseases. Why does all this interest you?"

Ronayne sat back and placed his hands together across his ample stomach. He stared at his desk for a moment. His eyes seemed to focus on a fly that was crawling across the papers in front of him and, for a while, he seemed oblivious to everything else. My sharp cough caused him to jerk up and he refocused on me.

"We do need an in-house doctor. Full-time. We are a big business. Right? We deal with lots of clients. Big names. We need someone who is discreet. Right? We were informed that you had finished your contract abroad and had returned to Dublin. You need a position. Right? We are prepared to offer you that position. The position of chief medical officer to our company. It may mean some travel, to visit our clients abroad, but in principle you will be based in Dublin. We have a small medical facility at Clontarf."

He mentioned an annual salary that was extraordinarily generous, adding, "This doesn't exclude you taking on any private patients so long as it doesn't interfere with your first priority, which is company business."

I was intrigued. It sounded too good to be true.

"What does the work entail?"

"You run the medical facility and we send you our clients for medical checks. We want to know that they are in good health. Right? So we need a thorough examination, blood tests and so on—can't be too careful about druggies and people with AIDS and so on—we have a worldwide reputation to think of. We have to insure all our clients. Your confidential reports come to us. Then we fix up insurance and so on."

"It seems straightforward enough," I agreed. The idea was beginning to appeal to me the more I thought about the financial remuneration and the possibilities it offered. "But who are your clients?" I resisted the temptation to add: ". . . and so on." It was a manner of punctuation that came as naturally to him as other people say "er" and "ah."

"Pop singers, members of bands, groups, and so on. You know the sort of thing. We send groups all over the world. Insurance is crucial, and the insurance companies can wheedle out of anything unless we apply the small print. Right? If we claim someone is healthy, and an accident happens, and it can be proved that they are not healthy, we wind up with egg all over our faces and out of pocket. Understand what I mean?"

It was easy enough to follow.

"What about laboratory backup? If you want all the screening tests to be done, you need a technician and laboratory equipment."

Ronny sat back and shook his head.

"You will have the facilities but, as we need to be discreet, it will be up to you to see all the tests through yourself. That is why we give you full-time employment and a generous salary. Of course, you will have a nurse receptionist, but the rest must be confidential. You might be seeing only two or three clients a week, or even fewer. Therefore, you will have plenty of time to conclude each test yourself. If you want to see the laboratory before making a final decision, I can drive you up to Clontarf right away."

I sat and reflected for a moment.

"Is there a problem?" he prompted, anxiously. "Your dossier says that you were doing all your own testing in Africa."

"There is no problem in that respect," I assured him. "Let me look at the laboratory, then I'll give you my answer."

It was a formality. I had already made up my mind to accept, but I didn't want him to see that I was so eager.

◆　◆　◆

For a whole week I had nothing to do but laze about my well-equipped office and laboratory, which was tucked on the end of Marino Crescent, facing onto the sea. Bríd, the nurse receptionist, was competent, a married middle-aged woman, and a reassuring fixture. Averty Enterprises certainly did not stint on equipment. Some hospitals would have given the collective right arms of their surgery staff to possess many of the diagnostic machines that were at my disposal.

It was Bríd who injected a note of drama in an otherwise hum-drum day by telling me about old Dr. Hennessey, who had been my predecessor. He had taken it into his head to go midnight bathing off the Bull Wall at Clontarf, and his body had never been recovered. He had gone insane, she thought, for the day he decided to take his mid-night dip in the turbulent sea, he had been mumbling about blood being life, or some such phrase.

Toward the end of the week I began thinking seriously about pur-suing the idea of a private practice. Ronayne had assured me that the company would not object to my having private patients if it did not interfere with work for the company. What work? I had a whole week of nothing else to do but familiarize myself with the laboratory and its equipment. Bríd's only strenuous occupation seemed to be read-ing copies of *Ireland's Own* or telling me tales of the eccentricities of old Dr. Hennessey. I discussed the prospects of building up a private practice with her, and she offered to organize the appropriate listings and advertisements to promote it.

It was not until the following week that the first couple of clients were sent by Ronayne. Bríd showed them into my consulting room with a disapproving look.

They were young girls, fresh out of convent school, gawky yet trying to be sophisticated. They were not more than seventeen or eighteen years old.

I tried to put them at ease while I went through the medical checks.

"And what do you do in show business?" I asked gravely.

They giggled.

"Oh," said one of the two, a broad-faced redhead with a fast West Cork accent, "we aren't in showbiz yet."

"We are too!" corrected her blond companion in a snappish tone. She was a thin-faced girl with the harsh tones of south Dublin. She positively reeked with some cheap perfume. Her articulation was punctuated by a certain four-lettered Anglo-Saxon expletive, which she pronounced to rhyme with the word "book." "We are going to be backing singers, and Mr. Ronayne has promised us a season in England. That's why we need this insurance thing. He's sending us to some seaside place—Whitby, I think he said."

"It's our first contract," confessed the redhead.

I busied myself with the tests, wondering if their singing voices were any better than their speaking voices, for I could not honestly say that I picked up any discernible talent there. The stench of the blonde's cheap perfume lingered for two days.

I was able to let Ronayne have my typed reports on the following day.

He was on the telephone after lunch.

"Excellent reports," he breezed. "I just wanted to check that you did carry out all the specified blood tests. Right?"

I felt irritated.

"I would have thought the reports were specific," I replied coldly.

He was conciliatory.

"Right. But these are your first reports. I thought I would just check, right? It's all very important for the insurance and so on."

"Right!" I returned. "But it's down in black and white. All the required tests have been made. You have two healthy girls on your hands. Though I can't vouch for their singing voices."

"Oh?" He seemed sharply interested.

"To be honest, I thought that their voices were pretty unmusical. But, of course, you don't pay me for that opinion. You obviously know your own business."

"Right!" He sounded vaguely amused.

I began to think that I had little appreciation of modern music as, over the next several weeks, a succession of people came through the consulting rooms for examination. They were mainly young girls, though a few androgynous youths paraded before me. Most of them were healthy enough, although I found some with various ailments. Drugs have become a problem in Dublin in recent years. A couple of youths tested HIV positive while another girl confessed that she was a diabetic. Ronayne always seemed pleased when I was able to give a clean bill of health for his potential performers.

Thanks to Bríd's management I even began to squeeze in some private patients, and life was looking decidedly good.

When I went back to Chapelizod in the evenings I would talk things over with Étain. I could see that she was a little envious of the stage-struck youths who, thanks to Averty Enterprises, were setting off on various world tours.

"Aren't you meeting any real stars yet?" She mentioned the names of some well-known singers who were reputedly handled by Averty Enterprises. I shook my head. The would-be talents I described were of no interest to her except to stir her envy.

"From what you say," she sniffed coldly, "I could easily get Averty Enterprises to represent me."

I had to admit that she was right. Judging by the so-called talent I had seen, Étain could have been one of their more professional singers. As I have already mentioned, she had been quite a hit on the pub-and-club circuit. Since she had been on her own, after her husband left, her singing was the only thing that really interested her. She was still in her late twenties, still young enough to make the grade in the music business. I noticed that she was quiet for a few days, but I didn't think any more about it.

Then, one morning, much to my surprise, Bríd showed her into my consulting room.

"A Miss Étain Moledy to see you." Bríd made it clear that she did not realize that we were related.

"What are you doing here?" I hissed in astonishment after Bríd had closed the door.

Étain smiled brightly.

"I'm here for a medical examination, big brother," she replied calmly.

"What?" I nearly exploded, trying to keep my voice low and wondering if she were joking.

"Your famous Mr. Ronayne has sent me."

I stared at her.

She continued in an unconcerned tone: "I went to audition for him. He likes my voice and thinks I have a great talent. He wants to send me on a tour of Australia. It all boils down to his medical examiner giving me a clean bill of health for the insurance, and you *are* the medical examiner for the company."

"This isn't ethical," I protested. "I am your brother. Does Ronayne know . . . ?"

I glanced nervously to the door beyond which my nurse receptionist sat.

"Of course not," Étain snapped. "I used my married name and called myself 'miss.'" Ronayne won't know. He contacted you at the College of Physicians, so he doesn't even know you live in Chapelizod. And you use that goddamn mobile phone, so he wouldn't even associate my phone number with you. In other words, it's up to you. Are you going to blow the whistle on me?"

Of course, I wasn't. I have already said that I felt responsible for Étain, especially after the sad experience with her husband, Art Moledy.

"Is this singing deal what you really want?" I asked.

She smiled eagerly at me and nodded rapidly.

"You know it is. It could lead to good things. Yes, it is what I really want."

I knew Étain, If she had set her heart on something, then there was nothing that I could do to dissuade her.

Ronayne was pleased at the report I sent in. I wished Étain well.

It was a day later that there was a discreet knock at my consulting room door. Bríd showed in two men whose soft hats and raincoats gave them the appearance of refugees from a movie set of a 1940s detective thriller. Indeed, so stereotyped were they that, at first, I thought they were clients of Averty Enterprises. But Bríd coughed hollowly and said, "Two gentlemen," she made clear that she was dubious over the use of the word, "from the Gardaí."

It was only after one of them showed me his warrant card that I realized that she was not joking, and they were, indeed, members of the Garda Síochána, the Irish police.

"I am Detective Halloran," said the one who had showed me his identification. "Dublin Metropolitan Division." He was a stocky man with gloomy features. He did not bother to introduce his colleague, who had simply entered the room, then lounged with his back against the wall by the door, hands in pockets. His jowls worked rhythmically as he masticated chewing gum.

"How can I help you?" I asked.

"Not sure that you can, Doctor," Halloran confessed in a voice that showed he contemplated the worst in life. He fished into his bulky raincoat and withdrew a faded photograph. "Recognize her?" He pushed the print across my desk and seated himself opposite.

I frowned as I stared at a young girl in school uniform.

"I don't think . . ." Then I peered closer. "Does she have red hair, by any chance?"

There was a long sigh as if Detective Halloran had just been told that he was going to face the rest of his life in loneliness and penury.

"She does," he intoned mournfully.

It was the red-haired Cork girl who had been one of my first two clients from Averty Enterprises.

"I did a medical examination for her," I offered.

"When was that?"

"About a month ago."

"Why?"

"Do you mean, why did I examine her?"

He raised his eyes to the ceiling as if it were perfectly obvious what he meant by the question.

I told him the story. He sighed moodily. He had apparently known all along my part in the story and was seeking my official corroboration.

"What's happened?" I asked.

"Her body is missing."

"Her body?" I was startled. "Do you mean," I tried to rephrase the question so that it made sense, "that the girl has gone missing?"

"I do not," the detective protested as if anguished by the suggestion that his use of language was inaccurate. "She died a fortnight ago."

I was shocked and showed it.

"Died? But she was an exceptionally healthy young girl. Was there some sort of accident?"

"The girl died of"—Halloran checked his notebook—"died of virulent anemia in the Bon Secours Hospital."

"You must be joking," I said.

He was not joking, and he reproved me in a carefully phrased sentence for suggesting as much.

He reached into his pocket, pulled out a paper, and thrust it at me. It was a death certificate. The certificate confirmed what the detective had already told me. The cause of death was massive blood loss.

"Her parents came up from Cork to collect the body. When they reached the hospital it was missing." He paused and corrected himself gently. "The body, that is. It had been removed from the morgue."

I stared blankly at him.

"I don't understand."

"Neither do we, Doctor. At the moment we are following up every lead we can. We checked all the burials from the hospital. No one was buried in error for someone else. The only logical explanation we can come up with is that the body was removed for use in an anatomy school."

"Are you suggesting body-snatching in this day and age?" I grimaced with dark humor. "Come on! Burke and Hare are a hundred and fifty years out-of-date."

"Perhaps a simple case of mistaken identity of the body," he suggested smoothly.

"Then you would be left with the body that she was mistaken for," I pointed out logically. "Do the hospital administrators agree with that?"

"They do not. They say it is not possible with their system of checks. But they are most likely covering their backs," he added cynically. "However, the fact is that you are correct, we can't trace any likely form of substitution. The body has simply vanished."

"Things like that don't happen," I insisted. "You just can't mislay a body these days."

Halloran gazed at me with moody speculation.

"I don't suppose you ever carry out anatomy experiments here?" There was a hopeful note in his voice.

"You are perfectly welcome to search in case I have the odd body tucked away," I replied sarcastically. "We keep the choice cuts in the 'fridge."

Halloran took that as a negative and began to rise. I held up a hand to stay him.

"What really intrigues me is how this girl could die of anemia? That would mean a massive blood loss. Death certificates just give the cause of death not the reasons behind the cause. When she was here, the test showed that she was absolutely normal. I don't understand it."

"Well, perhaps if we found the body we might be able to help you," said the detective heavily. "My job is just to find the body. Then we can find out what she died of."

"Have you consulted her friend?"

"Her friend?" His eyes were suddenly bright upon me. "She had a friend?"

I went to my files, looked up the notes, and gave the name and address of the blond girl. He noted them down.

"I thought that both girls were supposed to be on tour in England as backing singers with some pop group . . ."

Halloran frowned.

"First I've heard of it. The redhead was found not far from here, in Artane. That's why she was taken to the Bon Secours Hospital. Mr. Ronayne didn't mention anything about her going on a tour. I'll look into it. Thanks for all your help, Doctor."

That afternoon I was busy with more clients; a sad-looking bass player who was going to America to join some band playing in a casino on the Pequod American Indian reservation in upstate New York. The Native Americans were, by all accounts, amassing large fortunes from old treaty rights by running nontaxable gambling casinos. I suppose it was about time they managed to get those treaties working for them.

When I reached home in the evening I found my sister, Étain, in the hall with a suitcase packed. She was beaming with joy.

"I'm glad that you came home before I left. I tried to raise you on your mobile, but you had it switched off. I was going to leave a note."

"Before you left? Where are you going?"

"It's come through quicker than I thought," she announced. "A singing tour in Australia. A car is calling for me any moment and taking me to the airport. There's another group who are joining me, and we are picking them up along the way."

I was dumbstruck.

"Are you off to Australia *now*?" I demanded. "So soon?"

"It'll only be for three months, Joe," she said. "I know what you did to help me get this job. You know, the medical thing. I appreciate it. I really do."

I shrugged.

"I knew you wanted the job. What's the point in raking up Art Moledy and his problems? But look after yourself. Check with a doctor in Australia when you can."

She leaned forward and gave me a quick peck on the cheek.

A car horn sounded outside.

She was suddenly very excited.

"That's the car. I must go. I'll send you a card. Look after the place while I'm gone."

"Shouldn't I come with you to the airport?" I asked.

"The car will take me there. And we don't want Ronayne, if he is there, to realize that Doctor Joe Sheehan and Miss Étain Moledy are related, do we? At least not until after the tour."

Then she was gone.

I just caught a glimpse of a large black Mercedes drawing away into the evening dusk.

I kept myself busy for a week. The private practice was building up nicely even though I hardly had any clients from Averty Enterprises during that time. There was plenty of time to pursue my own work.

There were no further calls from Detective Halloran, and I wondered if they ever solved the mystery of the disappearing body.

Thinking about it did prompt me to telephone the hospital and speak to the medical examiner who had signed the death certificate.

I explained who I was and that I had made an examination of the girl only weeks before for insurance purposes. I pointed out that there had been no sign of her being anything other than a normal, healthy eighteen-year-old.

"You saw my certificate." The pathologist was clearly irritated. "It was the worst case of anemia I've seen. Not a red corpuscle in her entire body. I can't believe anyone in that condition was healthy just a week or so beforehand. I can only report what I found."

He hung up with a petulant grunt before I realized that he had impugned my professional ability. I decided to let the matter drop.

◆　◆　◆

IT WAS ABOUT THREE O'CLOCK in the morning when my mobile telephone buzzed.

It was Ronayne. I have never heard a man in such a state of distress as he was.

"I need your help, Doctor. Need it desperately and right away. Where are you? My car will be round to collect you as soon as it can get there."

"Are you ill?" I asked curiously, trying to shake the sleep from my head.

"No, not me. Not me."

"Then . . . ?"

"It is the chairman of our company. Right? He is ill."

"Chairman? Doesn't he have his own physician? And if it is that urgent, then the emergency services . . . ?" I began to protest.

He interrupted me with a snarl. "May I remind you that you are the company doctor? Right? Give me your address now!"

A large black Mercedes slid to a halt outside the house, and, clutching my medical bag, I climbed in. Ronayne was in the back. He looked pale and nervous. To be truthful, I was rather grateful that he was so preoccupied. Otherwise, he might have realized the Chapelizod connection with Étain.

"You best tell me something about the patient," I invited as the car purred off into the night.

"Mister Averty? What can I tell you?"

"Mister Averty?" I was surprised. I had not realized that there was an Averty still controlling the company which I knew had been formed back in the music hall days. "What are the symptoms? What is the problem?"

"I think that you'd best wait until you see him for yourself."

We drove across north Dublin to Artane. Artane used to be a sleepy village north of Clontarf in Coolcock barony. Now it is just part of the sprawling mess of north Dublin suburbs. We turned into the secluded grounds of Artane Lodge. It had once been the lodge of Artane Castle, which had been the seat of the O'Donnellans, where Archbishop Allen was done to death in 1533. The gaunt castle had been pulled down to make way for Artane House and Lodge. To my surprise the house was in total darkness. It did not seem to bother Ronayne, who drew out a key and let himself into the darkened building.

"Isn't there any domestic help?" I protested, as Ronayne led the way hurriedly across the echoing hall and through the house. He did not reply nor even wait to turn on a light. Taking a small pocket torch from his coat, he lit the way for me. Surely someone of Averty's wealth was able to have a whole army to look after his needs? Again to my surprise, instead of heading up the winding staircase to where, presumably, the bedrooms were situated, Ronayne opened a small side door and began to climb down into the musty cellars of the house.

The main cellar was lit with a dim, flickering light.

I stood at the foot of the stairs and could not begin to comprehend the sight that met my eyes.

Two large spluttering candles lit the cellar, but the smell of the place was . . . well, I have been in many a plague graveyard in Africa, with putrid rotting corpses By comparison to this cellar, they smelled sweet.

There was a man's body stretched out on a slab in the middle of the cellar. He was clothed in evening dress, a white tie and starched shirt and waistcoat. Even lying there, pale and lifeless, the body seemed to emanate a charisma that commanded attention from his apparently lifeless form. At first I thought he was old, for he had white hair and a long white moustache. His face was etched in sharp features, the nose thin and high-bridged, with strangely arched nostrils. The bushy eyebrows met over the nose. The forehead was high-domed, the lips thin, red, and almost cruel.

"What's the meaning of this?" I asked in distaste as I stared at the candles placed at the foot and head of the apparition as it lay on what appeared to be the top of a stone sarcophagus.

Ronayne made a gesture of dismissal with one hand.

"Mister Averty is an eccentric gentleman," he muttered. "We must respect his wishes."

"Nonsense!" I replied. "If the man is ill, he should be in bed. Who has placed him here in these damp, vile conditions? This is outrageous!"

"Just examine him, please, Doctor. Please! I do not think we have much time."

Reluctantly, I went to the side of the man.

The body was icy cold. There was no pulse in spite of the redness of the lips.

"He is already dead," I announced brutally. "And by the feel of him, he has been dead some hours."

"He cannot die," Ronayne's voice held a frantic quality. "See what you can do, Doctor. Please!"

"We all have to die sometime," I replied, somewhat testy at his presumption.

"But he cannot die," insisted Ronayne in a wailing tone. "He is the Master."

It was then that I began to worry for my employer's mental health. Perhaps Ronayne was having a breakdown or else he was in some curious state of shock. Nevertheless, my first duty was to ensure that the figure of the man in evening dress was beyond my assistance. I would see to Ronayne later. Turning back to the body on the slab, I drew out a syringe from my bag and stabbed the needle into the dead man's skin. There was no reaction. It did not even cause a spot of blood nor stimulate the nerve that I had aimed for. I then cautiously drew out a blood sample and, as carefully as I could, put it in a small phial in my case. It was pale like no blood I had seen before. There were no signs of animation anywhere on the body. The man was clearly dead.

I half turned to get my notepad.

As I turned back I realized, with a tingling disgust, that the skin of the corpse around the mouth was sliding away from the teeth. To my horror, the entire flesh had suddenly taken on a strange consistency, like melting wax. It was slipping from the body. No, not slipping—it was actually rotting, bubbling and dispersing before my eyes. I could only stand there in frozen horror watching as the body began to decompose and wither in front of me.

"What in hell is happening?" I whispered, the skin at the nape of my neck tingling in my horror.

The smell that arose was vile. I began to choke on the fumes.

Soon all that was left was a pile of molding dust among the remains of the now-sodden evening clothes. Even the skeleton had vanished. Where the right hand had lain was a great golden signet ring set with a jewel and a crest. Automatically, I picked up the ring. I do not know what prompted me to do so. I turned it around in my fingers, still staring at the remains that had, a moment before, been a body.

My eye then caught something on the ring. A name inscribed in old fashioned Gaelic lettering. "*Abhartach.*" I realized that the phonetics would be "Averty." But it was the Gaelic form of the name that stirred a distant memory.

I swallowed hard. Then my rational mind took a grip of my confused emotions, and I wheeled round to Ronayne.

"Is this some kind of joke?" I demanded angrily. "If so, it is a joke in bad taste."

Ronayne was staring at the slab as if he could not believe what he had seen.

"It is not possible," he moaned over and over again. "He cannot die."

"You've got some explaining to do, Ronayne," I went on coldly. "I don't like being made a fool of. Are you responsible for this charade?"

He turned to me. There was terror in his eyes. If he was acting, then he was brilliant. I tried to make myself believe that this was some bizarre charade.

"It is not possible!" he almost screamed. "I did everything I could to protect him; to protect the Master. What has gone wrong?"

I backed off from his wild staring eyes. My first thought returned. Ronayne had gone mad. Stark-staring mad!

"You'd better calm down," I coaxed, reaching out a placating hand.

His eyes suddenly fell on the ring I still held in my hand, and he seemed to crumple before me.

"My family has served him down the generations. From the time he was lord of Doire and Ciannachta, when even the Uí Néill would tremble before him. We have served him before the High King Laoghaire converted to Christianity. He was the *Neamh-Mhairbh*! He cannot die."

It took me some time to translate the Old Irish. *Neamh-mhairbh*—UnDead! I had a cold feeling come over me, as I remembered the legend of Abhartach of Derry. He had been an evil prince who was supposedly slain by his people, was buried but did not die. Every time he was buried, he rose from the grave to feed on the blood of the living. I chuckled nervously. It was some practical joke.

"What are we to do?" Ronayne was crying. "He protected us. He must not die. He cannot die!"

Ronayne, I realized, was without doubt in the middle of some nervous breakdown for no one sane could act like this. I began to back away, thinking to use my mobile phone to call an ambulance.

It was then that I heard a sound like the sharp intake of breath. There was a smell of cheap perfume, which seemed strangely familiar. It reminded me of something. There was a swish of a skirt behind me. I turned.

I recognized her at once, in spite of the new whiteness of her skin and the curious staring eyes and redness of the lips. It was the blond girl from south Dublin.

"What are you doing here?" I asked, totally bewildered.

She appeared to shuffle forward. She did not walk normally but had a lurching gait. Her hands were reaching out like claws toward me. Her mouth was opened, showing the teeth, teeth that seemed so white and sharp against red lips, lips that were so red. She gave a chuckle. I have never heard a laugh like it. The lips curled back showing gums and displaying the large white canines. Then she lunged forward toward me.

A silver crucifix was thrust before my face, and I heard a scream of pain. The scream came from the blond girl. Her face was distorted in a fearful expression; she was cowering back away from me, eyes wide on the religious symbol.

Ronayne was holding the crucifix up before me.

"Take this, Doctor," he muttered, suddenly very calm. "Get out of here—quickly. These new sisters often do not differentiate between those who must remain in life to help them and those who are their natural sustenance. Be careful. There are more about. The car will take you wherever you want to go. Get out now!"

"I don't understand any of this," I protested, my eyes unable to leave the cowering blond girl.

"Go now!" Ronayne almost screamed. "Leave!"

Protesting somewhat halfheartedly as I did so, I took the crucifix from him. The blond girl's eyes seemed fixed on it as if something caused them to become attached to the sacred symbol.

"Better you don't understand!" Ronayne called after me.

I hurried up the stairs and back the way that I had come. The car was waiting there outside the main door, and the driver did not even bother to ask me where I was going. We raced back along the road to Chapelizod.

Could what I had witnessed have been real? That was the question hammering in my mind. Was I having some hallucination? Was I drawing on some forgotten childhood fantasy? Some nightmare? The legend of Abhartach—Averty—was one that had scared many a young child, a legend well-known in folklore. I squeezed my hand in agitation and found something hard in my palm, something that I still held. It was the gold signet ring and those awesome Gaelic letters—*Abhartach*. A two-thousand-year-old legend?

Something made me lean forward and call to the driver. "Stop! Turn back and take me to my consulting rooms at Clontarf."

He turned the car without a word, and in a few moments it slid to a halt outside my office in Marino Crescent.

I went in and switched on the light.

I took out the sample of blood that I had taken from the corpse before it had degenerated. It was still normal and had not decomposed like the body. Perhaps removing it from the body had preserved it? I worked quickly. I began to go through every blood test I knew. I found its composition curious. A strange mixture that defied analysis. It seemed to combine all the qualities of A, B, and O blood groups and yet was like none of them at all. It was as I was making the final tests that I discovered that the blood was contaminated by a virus. I had seen the strain of virus many times before, the virulent sort that gives hepatitis B and can be fatal. The toxicity that I was observing was enough to kill an ox, let alone a man.

I put the samples carefully in the office refrigerator, making sure that I labeled them POISON. As I stood up I was aware that I was exhausted. I realized that it was long past dawn and, just as I became aware of the time, I heard a key turning in the outside door of the offices. It was Bríd. She was surprised to see me. I made an excuse about working through the night on some samples and told her to cancel all my appointments and take the day off herself. There was no way I could work that day. Then I asked her to call a taxi and went home to Chapelizod. Even in my fatigued state, my mind was still working. If what I suspected was reality, then I had no words to express my horror. It could not be true. Yet what other explanation was there for what I had seen? And the sample of contagious blood—that was certainly real enough.

If it were true, then it meant that I had to accept what I had previously dismissed as ancient legends, quaint old folklore, and old stories to scare children with. *Dún Droch Fhola*, the castle of evil blood, in the Kerry mountains. The *Deamhan Fhola*, the bloodsucking demons of western Ireland. The great vampire himself—Abhartach. If this were true, then the world must be in deadly danger. But who would believe me? To whom could I turn with such a tale?

I took out the heavy gold signet ring and stared at it as if it would provide the answer.

It was genuine enough. No one, unless they had money to burn, could have such a priceless trinket made up just to sustain a joke. No one.

I fell into my bed. Sleep overcame me immediately.

About midafternoon there came a telephone call. To my surprise it was Ronayne. He seemed calmer, more like his old self.

"You will forget everything that you saw last night, Sheehan," he said in a confidential manner. "Everything. It was just a joke. Right? A joke in very bad taste. You know what people in showbiz are like."

"I know what I saw," I replied, feeling that I was confirming the truth. "I want an explanation. I don't believe it was a joke."

"Believe that no one will believe you. No one," his voice snapped back sharply.

I felt impotent. He was right.

"It's not a thing I want to spread around, Ronayne," I said. "Just for my own peace of mind, however, I should like to know the truth."

He hesitated for a moment. Then his voice was matter-of-fact.

"I suppose you are entitled to that truth since you cannot use it without looking a fool. Between ourselves, then, I shall not deny what happened. You are intelligent enough to work it all out. The company was a means of supplying young girls for his nourishment, the Master's nourishment. Something went wrong. He is dead. They are now UnDead. He is gone, but they will live forever."

Having my fears confirmed as reality did not help my nerves. Foolishly, I could only say, "You are mad!" and switched off the phone. Then I lay back, still exhausted yet trying to figure out the implications of the test results. It was thus that I fell back into a troubled sleep.

I was awakened by a sound at the front door.

I shook my head to clear my thoughts and saw that it was already evening and dark.

I went to the top of the stairs, my befuddled mind trying to remember the events of the last twenty-four hours.

"Who's there?" I called nervously into the darkness of the hall.

"It's only me!" Étain"s cheerful voice came up the stairs. "Don't tell me that you were in bed at this hour?"

I breathed a sigh of relief.

"Étain," I cried, hurrying down the stairs. "What the devil are you doing back so soon. I thought that you were going to be in Australia for months."

"Australia? It's a long story." She turned to me and smiled. It was then that the streetlight outside our house flickered on abruptly and shone through the glass panels of the front door, flooding the hall with a shadowy pale light. I had never seen her lips so red, blood red and thin. The teeth so white and sharp. The skin so pale.

A cold horror seized me. Suddenly, it all became clear.

"You killed him?" I whispered aghast. "It was you who contaminated his blood and killed him."

She chuckled coarsely.

"*Droch Fhola!* Bad blood! Ironic, isn't it? The victim becoming the slayer. You passed me as medically fit, in spite of the hepatitis. You knew all about it. You knew that Art Moledy had infected me and made me a carrier. Yet you didn't mention it in your report to Ronayne. You gave me a clean bill of health."

I held my head in my hands.

It was true. Art Moledy had been a carrier of the viral infection, which produced malignant hepatitis B. Étain had been ill with it for a long time and near death. She had recovered but, in turn, she had become a carrier. That was why she had shunned most male friends after Moledy. Moledy had disappeared, leaving her to fend for herself. I knew all about it; knew that was why Étain had seized the opportunity that I had presented to get herself passed as fit for Averty Enterprises to endorse her on the singing tour. And I had done so willingly.

What was it Ronayne had said? The company was just a front to supply the Master with fresh blood for his nourishment. I had been like some glorified food inspector and had passed young girls as fit to be consumed.

I had passed my own sister to him.

She was smiling, as if she had followed the process of my thoughts.

"Oh yes. I was forced to go to him. He drank long and deep . . . and died. He died because of my contaminated blood, and now I am UnDead. Only fresh blood can sustain me. The great *Neamh-Mhairbh* is dead and I am now *Neamh-Mhairbh*. *Bloody* ironic, isn't it?"

She burst into a peal of terrible laughter, which ended abruptly.

She was staring at me. My own sister. Staring deliberately at the pulsating artery in my neck.

I realized that the crucifix was still in my jacket pocket. But my jacket was in the bedroom. She was only a few feet away from me, smiling speculatively with those awesome canine teeth. I would have no chance at all.

Long the Clouds Are over Me Tonight

❧

BY CECILIA DART-THORNTON

Straight and strong was Oisin, the son of the Chieftain of the Fianna. Like a sword of pale bronze, his body was hard and lean. Clean-sculpted was his face, and his eyes were midnight pools from which a startling flash could leap as swiftly as lightning. His hair was a swath of shadow; blackness starred with lustrous reflections, cascading down wide shoulders to the middle of his back. Oisin, the handsomest youth in Ireland, was twenty winters of age when he witnessed an amazing spectacle.

On that morning the young man and his father, Fionn mac Cumhail,[1] went out hunting in the company of many warriors of the

[1]Pronounced: Finn McCool

Fianna. The sky was the breast of a blue bird, plumed with wisps of white cloud. The custom of the Fianna was first to climb the bluff and look out across the Atlantic Ocean, so that they could scan the watery acres for any sign of approaching invaders. As the huntsmen reached the cliff tops of Kerry, the waves pounded on the rocks below, the gulls screamed, the wind came careering cold and fresh, to rush up the precipice. Miniature mosses and sea pinks were clinging in crevices of ruined stonework—some ancient fort had once stood on the headland. The men were clad in shirts of linen, tunics of moleskin, and boots of leather. The salt breeze ruffled their hair as they laughed and chaffed one another. Eagerly, the hounds coursed the ground, their tongues lolling between their fangs and dripping with desire for the chase.

Below the cliffs the sea boiled like gooseberry wine. Scalloped were the waves, and netted with a delicate, filmy lacework of foam that continually tore and reknitted, only to fray again. The water was lucent, as green as cats' eyes, marbled with foam and woven with lank streamers of kelp, begemmed with beads of bubbles. Far below the swirling and the rushing of the waves threaded a distant plaint: a song, perhaps, or was it only a trick of fancy, a plucking of aural nerve endings by the shameless fingers of the wind?

As that famous band of Irish warriors scanned the ocean, they were discussing past exploits. Oisin said, "Centuries from now they will still be singing songs about us. For there have been none like ourselves. The Fianna were but fifteen men, but we defeated the king of the Saxons by the strength of our spears and our own bodies, and we won a battle against the king of Greece."

"We took Magnus the great," rejoined Caoilte, "the son of the king of Lochlann of the speckled ships; we came back no way sorry or tired: we put our rent on far places."

Faolan directed his attention to Fionn mac Cumhail. "Aye, and

we fought nine battles in Spain and nine times twenty battles in Ireland; from Lochlann and from the eastern world a share of gold came
to you, Fionn."

"And of all chieftains you are the most open-handed, Fionn," said
Osgar. "You were generous with that gold; you gave food and riches,
you never refused strong or poor, for your heart is without envy."

"Now the ranks of the Fianna have swelled mightily," Oisin
declared with pride. "We have seven battalions of warriors to defend
Ireland against invasion."

"Fionn, don't you wish you could be hearing those songs they
will be making about the Fianna?" asked Caoilte.

"The poets will have much to be singing about," replied Fionn
mac Cumhail, "but I'd as soon hear the song of the blackbird in Leiter
Laoi, and the very sweet thrush of the Valley of the Shadow, or the
noise of the hunt on Slieve Crot. The cry of my twelve hounds is better to me than harps and pipes."

"Save for the songs of Little Nut," said Caoilte, laughing as he
glanced toward the dwarf standing staunchly beside his chieftain,
"for when he makes tunes he puts us all into a deep sleep."

"I can guess what else you have a mind to be listening to," Oisin
said to his father, "the wave of Rudraighe beating the Strand, the bel-
lowing of the ox of Magh Maoin, the lowing of the calf of Glenn da
Mhail." The young man turned his head to look out across the ocean,
toward the band of white gauze where the water met the horizon.
"The cry of the seagulls there beyond on Iorrus, the waves vexing the
breasts of the boats, and the sound of the boats striking the strand."

"You know the desires of my heart," Fionn said to his son, "for
they are the desires of your heart also."

Oisin felt the benison of his father's pride, and he thought his
heart must split asunder with the swelling of the joy that was in it.
The sun broke through the clouds to dance in glints on the water, and
the young man considered that there was nothing more he could

wish for on such a grand day, than to be striding at his father's side in the company of his brethren-in-arms. The sea wind barreling up the scarp swept exhilaration into him, until his blood fizzed in its pathways, and he silently began to conjure lyrics, for he was as skilled at poetry and singing as at fighting.

The huntsmen descended the slopes of the headland until they were treading along the strand, among the ceramic fans of shells and the convoluted ribbons of cast-up oarweed.

It was then that the astonishing sight manifested itself.

Far away across the sea a tiny smudge evolved on the horizon. Presently, it became apparent that something was approaching, and as it came nearer to the land the blur coalesced into an unexpected form—that of a rider on a white horse. Closer still, and the Fianna could discern there was a girl seated on the horse's back; closer yet, and they perceived she was the most beautiful girl any of them had ever beheld.

Her looks were stunning beyond imagination. The sight of her sent ecstasy piercing through the men; made them forget who or where they were, for a long moment, while their minds struggled to recover from the shocking thrill of witnessing a form, a face so enchanting the vision stifled breath. Hers was a beauty so wondrous it was almost terrifying; so rare beyond the beauty of the world they knew she could not be human.

Her gown seemed made of blossom and raindrops, while a slender band of gold encircled her head. Her hair outshone the gold. The long locks were so purely golden they seemed spun from fibres of sunlight. The wind, racing across the sea to the land, would have lifted its long strands and unraveled them, save that the swift pace of the horse equaled that of the air currents in the opposite direction.

Splendid was her steed, with his shining silken coat and burnished hooves. He traversed the water's surface with no more trouble than a horse trotting on the land. Like a floor of jagged green glass was the ocean, yet the hooves took no harm, nor did the steed sink at all; not even a drop of water beaded the gown of the rider.

She guided her mount into the shallows, and the men, watching in silent awe, heard the splashing as he came up the beach, and the crunch of pebbly sand. The damsel walked her horse up to the spell-bound band of hunters and drew to a halt, and all the men who looked upon her were seized by love.

It was Fionn mac Cumhail who first recovered his voice.

"Lady," he said wonderingly, "who are you, and from what place do you hail?"

She answered in a low sweet voice. "My name is Niamh Chill Óir, and my father is Manannán mac Lir, the king of Tír na Nóg.

"Tír na Nóg?" repeated Fionn in puzzlement. "If I am not mistaken, that name signifies 'The Land of Youth.' An unusual title. What kind of country is it?"

"It is the land of delight and happiness, where no one ever grows old," she said. "In Tír na Nóg the trees are constantly laden with ripe fruit, and flowers bloom all year round."

The Fianna was astounded by her description, but they could only believe it, because they had seen her riding over the water.

Then Fionn said, "Niamh, daughter of Manannán mac Lir, you are welcome to Ireland. Never have I seen you here before."

She replied, "It was not possible for you to see me, but I have seen you many times Fionn mac Cumhail. Many times I have visited Ireland to watch you and the Fianna"—she turned her radiant eyes upon the young man at Fionn's side—"and your son Oisin."

When he heard her speak his name Oisin trembled like an over-tuned harp string, and a furnace spilled hot embers over him from head to toe. The Fianna perceived that she knew the names of their chieftain and his son, even though they had never encountered her previously, and it occurred to all of them that when she spoke Oisin's name her melodious voice adopted an even more mellifluous quality.

"What is the name of your husband in Tír na Nóg?" inquired Fionn.

"I have no husband," she said, and at her words there was a stirring among the Fianna like sudden gusts through a field of barley. "Many are the lords and princes of Tír na Nóg who have asked to wed me, but none have I accepted."

"Then unfortunate indeed are the gallants of Tír na Nóg," said Fionn. "It is a pity for such a beauty as you to withhold your love from all men."

"Not from all men," she replied. "Only from the immortals of Tír na Nóg."

A hush descended upon the gathering, and even the wind faded to stillness. The gulls ceased their mewing, and the sound of the waves on the shore receded, as if to the farthest corners of a misremembered reverie.

"Lady, what is your meaning?" Fionn asked softly, emptying his words into the stillness like water into a profound well.

Once again the comely damsel bent her gaze toward Oisin. His sight was edged with shadow, and her beauty shone at the core of the shadow, and he could not look away.

"I love a man of Ireland," Niamh of the Golden Hair said simply. "I have traveled here to ask if he will wed me, and return with me to Tír na Nóg."

She smiled at the son of Fionn mac Cumhail. The embers of passion melted him as if he were a figurine of wax, and his sinews flowed with fire. Her smile had struck through him like a blade, straight to the heart. Then she leaned down from her saddle and kissed him on the mouth. He did not know whether he stood still or fell through some dizzying gulf, whether he had been smitten by outrageous bliss or unbearable torment. It came to him at that moment that he must go with her or die; that neither the love of his father, nor the friend-ship of his companions, nor the excitement and adventures of the Fianna were enough to keep him in Ireland.

"Ride with me on Capall Bán," Niamh invited.

Without hesitation he vaulted onto the majestic horse behind the faerie damsel, and clasped his arms around her iris-stem waist. At the sensation of enfolding her in his arms, and the caress of her blowing hair across his cheek, his pulse surged. He looked down at his father and the warriors of the Fianna standing on the wave-rinsed shingle, and he saw them raise their hands in a valedictory gesture.

They understood.

"Farewell, my father," said Oisin. "Farewell, my friends. I am sor-rowful at our parting, but I would go with Niamh to Tír na Nóg, and make her my bride."

A light of sorrowful acceptance shone in the gaze of Fionn. "You have chosen well, Oisin," he said. "She will make you a good wife. I am glad for you, yet sadness is on me, that we must part. It is long the clouds will be over me tonight."

His comrades expressed their joy and their sorrow also, while the hounds gathered at their feet, and Oisin's hound, Sceolan, stared beseechingly at his master.

"You must obey Fionn now," Oisin bade the hound, "for I myself am going far away."

Sceolan lifted his muzzle and howled his distress, but the great white horse turned toward the west, and after calling out a final farewell to his father and his comrades, Oisin galloped away with Niamh.

◆　◆　◆

LIKE A VISION from a dream they looked, those two riders on the faerie horse—he the handsomest man in Ireland, she the fairest princess from the Land of Youth. For Oisin, the journey was more fabulous than any dream. The sea unrolled before them like polished onyx, not flecked with foam now, but patterned with reflections of the sky, the forces of currents and wind and restless tides. As clouds swept across the face of the sun, the sea colors shifted through jade and aquamarine to amethyst and indigo. Along the way they passed mountainous islands, upon whose slopes rose lime-white cities and courts, forts, and palaces. Once, Oisin and Niamh saw beside them a hornless deer running hard over the water, and an eager white red-eared hound chasing after it. Later they saw a young girl on a horse going over the tops of the waves, and she was carrying a golden apple in her right hand. A young man riding an ivory horse galloped after her, wearing a crimson cloak and bearing a gold-hilted sword.

But Niamh's incredible steed did not stop. The riders turned their backs to the island forts and palaces, and the horse under them moved quicker than the spring wind on the backs of the mountains. The sun was falling down behind the ocean, a brass penny flaming in a bath of molten copper. The sea seemed to catch fire. Long clouds ranged across the west like aerial volcanoes, and the great white horse, Capall Bán, galloped into the splendor of the skies.

As the day waned, storm clouds drew a curtain across the west. The sky darkened, and a reckless wind rose in every quarter. Next the sun disappeared, and evening scorched the air to ash. Still they rode on, Oisin and Niamh, although the wind eddied around them, whipping the wave crests.

Stars began to prick forth in the south, where the skies were clear. Gradually the clouds rolled away from the west, and the stormy wind abated. Then the firmament looked to be netted in an invisible web that reached right down to every horizon, and the stars were snagged everywhere through it. Against the deep purple of the heavens they glittered with heart-piercingly pure whiteness. How long the night endured, Oisin could not tell, but it seemed only a short while until the new-birthed sun opened like a marigold at their backs. As the new day dawned, they saw before them a vast stretch of shoreline from which climbed the slopes of mountains and hills, their peaks hidden in pale gauzes of vapor.

Oisin said softly into the ear of Niamh, "Is this the Land of the Young?"

"It is," she answered him. "And indeed, Oisin, I told you no lie about it, and you will see all I promised before you . . ." Then she leaned back against him, and whispered, ". . . forever."

Capall Bán cantered on to the beach. Without pause he ran inland, through gorgeous countryside. It was like one gigantic garden; every bush and plant burgeoned with inflorescence, while the trees were simultaneously covered in blossom and luscious globes of fruit; quinces and oranges, figs and plums, apples and pears. From the grassy plains the mountains soared to sharp crags, draped with silver wires of waterfalls. Here and there Oisin saw mansions of shining stones, skillfully built.

Their road began to climb, but Capall Bán cantered tirelessly on, and at length they arrived at a stately citadel on a hill. On the hill's crown stood a palace. Graceful pinnacles and turrets stood up like a forest from its multitude of roofs. The airy mansions of the citadel were adorned with slim columns and filigree, and fashioned from marble of every color.

The horse galloped swiftly up the urban streets. At last, when they reached the gates to the courtyard of the palace, he slowed to a halt, and the riders dismounted.

Tall gates opened wide, and from the courtyard emerged a hundred of the loveliest girls, wearing cloaks of silk worked with gold thread. They were carrying basketsful of perfumed petals, and as they strewed these scented flakes of color upon the ground, they cried, "Welcome, Oisin, son of Fionn mac Cumhail! Welcome to our country!"

In the wake of the damsels a great shining army issued from the gates. Their armor and mail shimmered as if wrought from moonbeams. They were led by a strong, handsome king, garbed in a shirt of yellow silk, his golden cloak flying in the breeze, the jewels of his crown glittering in the sunlight. A young queen followed him, accompanied by fifty youthful handmaidens.

When all were gathered together, Manannán mac Lir took Oisin by the hand, and proclaimed before the assembly, "One hundred thousand welcomes before you, Oisin, son of Fionn mac Cumhail. As to this country you are come to," he said, "I will tell you news of it without a lie. It is long and lasting your life will be in it, and yourself will be young forever. And there is no delight the heart ever thought of," he said, "that cannot be found here. For I myself am the king of the Land of Youth, and this is its comely queen, and it was our golden-haired daughter Niamh that went over the sea looking for you to be her husband."

"Your Majesty," answered Oisin, "I am honored to be welcomed with such ceremony. Greetings and salutations to you and your queen. I thank you with all my heart." He bowed courteously to the royal couple. Then Niamh placed her hand inside the crook of his elbow, and together they approached the royal house. All the aristocrats emerged to meet them, both lords and ladies.

Oisin and Niamh were married on that very day. When the nuptials had concluded, Manannán mac Lir led the newlyweds to the Great Hall of the palace. It was filled with hundreds of tables set with snowy linen and tableware of silver-gilt. Platters and dishes were sumptuously piled with sweetmeats of all descriptions.

"Herewith," said the king of Tír na Nóg, indicating the hall with a wave of his hand, "in celebration of your arrival and wedding, a feast."

The feasting and revelry continued through the length of ten days and ten nights, and afterward Oisin went to dwell with Niamh in their own palace.

• • •

THRICE THE SEASONS TURNED. Seasons did revolve in Tír na Nóg, because eternal sameness grows tedious eventually. Yet, temperate and sunny were the winters and the summers were balmy, while spring was an explosion of flowers and autumn a riot of leaves in scarlet, bronze, and amber.

Three beautiful children Oisin had with Niamh, two young sons and a daughter. Niamh gave the two sons the names of Fionn and of Osgar. The name Oisin gave to their daughter was Bláth: "The Flower."

It seemed to Oisin that three cycles of the seasons numbered three years, for he was accustomed to measuring time, and could not shake off the habit despite that he knew he was dwelling in a land where time had no actuality. He did not feel moments passing, because they never passed, and only at an idle moment did he attempt to calculate the years at all.

But in that idle moment, when he began to consider the passage of hours and days and years, he recalled also the look of sadness in his father's eyes and the dejection on the countenances of his friends when they had parted. And the desire came over him to see his father and his comrades again.

There came a morning when Oisin was walking among the blossoms with his beautiful wife, Niamh, in the company of Manannán mac Lir. The king and his daughter laughed and conversed, as blithe as always, but Oisin remained silent and thoughtful. When they asked what was troubling him, he said, "I long to see, once again, my father and the Fianna."

Then it was the turn of Niamh to fall silent, whereas the king said gravely, "If that is your wish, Oisin, I will not prevent you. Mark you—it is on Capall Bán you must make the journey, for that great horse has the ability to cross back and forth between Ireland and Tír na Nóg."

Following suit, Niamh said to her husband, "You will get leave from me, for I will never prevent your happiness. But for all that," she added quietly, "it is bad news you are giving me, for I am in dread you will never come back here again through the length of your days."

Oisin smiled at her. "Have no fear, my darling. Capall Bán will bring me safe back again from Ireland."

Niamh placed herself in front of her husband, obstructing him, so that he must stop in his tracks and look down into her face, meeting her steady gaze. "Bear this in mind Oisin," she said, "if you once get off the horse while you are away, or if you once put your foot to the ground, you will never come back here again."

He nodded assent. "Your worries are unfounded, because I will only be gone long enough to see my father and comrades, then I will return swiftly. After all, if I am not to dismount, I will not bide in Ireland for more than one day, for it would be difficult to find any rest while couched on the back of a horse!"

Yet she was not appeased. "O, Oisin," she said, "I tell it to you now for the third time, if you once get down from the horse, you will be an old man, blind and withered, without liveliness, without mirth, without running, without leaping. And it is a grief to me, Oisin," she continued, "that you ever go back to green Ireland. It is not now as it used to be, and you will not see Fionn and his people, for there is not now in the whole of Ireland but a Father of Orders and armies of saints."

"I am not deterred," declared Oisin, dismissing her warning. "You do not understand—I know the places where the Fianna are most likely to be found, the places they dwell and hunt. I will go to their favorite haunts, and I will find them, even if the whole of Ireland is filled with clerics as you say. I will find them."

"You will not," she whispered, but he could not believe it, and longed to see for himself.

Along the shores of Tír na Nóg the briny waves rustled, silky as layers of flounced petticoats. They lapped crystallized sands strewn with shells colored like opals, twists of driftwood, seaweed necklaces, luminous scatterings of uncut jewels, and the spiral of a narwhal's tusk. Lying faceup beneath clear skies, the sea was encrusted with winking scintillants. Oisin narrowed his eyes against the flare and flicker, focusing on the east as he strapped the saddle on the back of Capall Bán and tightened the girth strap. Already he had taken his leave of the king and queen. Now he turned to his three children, bidding them farewell and telling them he would return soon.

Last of all he went to his wife. Rare was she, and finer than wild music, as she stood upon the strand. Her gown was a lacework of cobwebs and starlight, and the hem brushed her narrow feet.

"I will be leaving now," he said.

"Alas," said she, "it is long the clouds will be over me tonight."

She was weeping. Never before had he seen her weep, and he looked upon her with wonder, for her tears shone more like pearls than salt water. His heart was moved, and he took her gently in his embrace. "I love you," he said. "I'll come back so swiftly you'll hardly know I was gone."

Niamh wiped away her tears and bestowed upon him such a look of sorrow that he imagined he might die of it. He remembered her look of love the first time they had met, and at that instant he was sorely tempted to abandon his quest, but he thought better of it, for the absence of Fionn and the warriors of the Fianna was an ache beneath his ribs.

"And here is my kiss for you, my darling Oisin," said Niamh, "for you will never come back anymore to the Land of Youth."

Then she brushed her lips against his cheek and turned away.

As he rode off over the sea he looked back and saw her standing on the beach, her golden hair lifted by the breeze, fanning out from her face like the petals of a radiant flower.

◆   ◆   ◆

OISIN'S JOURNEY ACROSS THE SEA back to Ireland was without incident. Indeed, so eager was he to reach his homeland, and so accustomed was he to the supernatural phenomena of Tír na Nóg, that he scarcely took note of any sights or sounds along the way. Through the starry night he hastened, until the sun blazed out in front of him and the bright hooves of Capall Bán were splashing through the shallows of the beach in Kerry whence he had departed. The tireless faerie horse bore him up the slopes and across the meadows, and all the while Oisin was looking about him, for this was a favorite hunting precinct of the Fianna. Every moment he expected to hear the hounds baying, or to witness the hunters making their way across the turf behind the milling hounds.

He saw no one. Not even any stranger to whom he could direct a question.

Therefore without delay he turned his face and went on. To Dún Almhuin he rode. This was a massive fort on the hill of Knaockaulin in County Kildare, which was built by Fionn's great-grandfather Nuada Airgetlámh—Nuada of the Silver Arm, king of the Tuatha de Danaan. As Oisin galloped up the incline he noted weeds had taken root in the road, and the cow pastures were neglected, and the place was deserted. He searched in growing dismay, but found no sign of Fionn's strong fort and his lofty hall except some low piles of crumbling stone among the weeds and nettles.

Terrible anguish seized him then, and he said aloud, "Och, ochone my grief! It is a bad journey that was to me, and to be without tidings of Fionn or the Fianna has left me under pain through my lifetime."

But he had not yet given up hope.

Back down the road he went, and turned his horse's head toward Glenasmole, the Glen of the Thrushes, another favorite hunting ground of the Fianna, near Dublin.

The valley measured one mile across, from north to south, and three miles in length. Grassy walls sloped gently down to the stream flowing along the floor of the glen. Clumps of trees grew at random on the slopes; rowan and hawthorn, beech and wild apple, punctuated with clots of yellow-flowering gorse and rosy briars. Along the banks of the waterway, old willows let down their attenuated showers of green hair.

The soil was thin, and in patches the bare rock showed through. Granite boulders rested here and there, whose surfaces were flecked with mica and tapestried with lichen. Most of these monoliths were small enough for a child to sit on, but some were as large as a bull, and one was taller than a man.

It was there in Glenasmole that Oisin first spied some people. A group of men was struggling to move the largest rock, and on seeing this, Oisin grew puzzled. Any one of the Fianna could have picked up the block with one hand, and the strongest among them would have been able to throw it from the south side of Glenasmole and landed it on the north side. Yet here were ten men shoving and hauling and levering at the rock, and not able to shift it as much as an inch.

Beetles of dread swarmed in Oisin's vitals, and he murmured to himself, "What has happened to the people of Ireland since I departed for Tír na Nóg?"

He rode up to the men, but was unable to recognize any of them. As he took in their appearances he noted that they were small and puny, by comparison to the Fianna. Upon noting Oisin's approach they straightened up from their task, and when he reined in the horse they wished him good health. There was wonder on them all when they looked at him, seeing this stranger so unlike themselves, so tall, so strong, yet obviously no more than twenty winters of age.

The scion of the Chieftain of the Fianna sat erect in the saddle. Proud of bearing was he, powerful of shoulder, hard and lean as a blade of bronze. Flawlessly carved was his countenance, and from beneath dark brows lanced two flashes of brilliance from lakes of shadow. His hair was a spillage of black water infused with points of light, and the onlookers were dazed by his extreme comeliness.

"Greetings, good folk!" said Oisin. "Have you heard if Fionn mac Cumhail is still living, or any other one of the Fianna, or what has happened to them!"

"Fionn mac Cumhail?" one man echoed. "There's no one in these parts by that name, and there never was."

"The Fianna?" repeated another. "Back in days of yore, mothers and nursemaids used to tell tales to frighten naughty children, about a race of wicked giants called the Fianna, who wandered the countryside devouring people."

"But nobody recounts those gests anymore," said a third man. "It must be nigh on three hundred years ago those tales were invented, and after three centuries they've lost their fascination."

It was at that instant, when it was borne in on him by their talk that Fionn was no longer living, nor any of the Fianna, that a cry of sheer desolation seared through Oisin's spirit. It expanded through the core of his being, filled his skull, and escaped from his mouth to fly away like a wounded bird.

All this time he had thought he had been away for three years, but his father and his friends had been dead for centuries. Despair turned his veins to ice, and all of a sudden a tremendous weariness overwhelmed him. Desperately, he yearned after his lost family and friends.

The men stared in apprehension at the young rider, who was

obviously waging some inner struggle. His handsome face was racked with torment, his brow was creased as though he suffered extreme pain, and his shoulders sagged as if the burden of all hopelessness had been laid upon them.

At length Oisin managed to master himself, although his voice was hoarse. "It is a good thing they don't tell those stories anymore," he said with vehemence. "They are lies. I am Fionn's son, Oisin, and I was a member of the Fianna myself."

The men's doubt showed plainly on their faces, and the first one said, "That is hard to believe, for how could you still be young and living?"

"Believe it," said Oisin passionately. "There never was Fionn's equal for strength or bravery or a great name. There ought to be many a book written down," he said, "by the sweet poets of the Gael, about his doings and the doings of the Fianna, and it would be hard for me to tell you all of them. And Fionn had a son, and there came a faerie princess looking for him, and he went away with her to the Land of Youth, and that man is myself."

"It cannot be so," said the second fellow, "for if the Fianna ever existed, which is unlikely, then surely they were brutish ogres."

Anger welled up in Oisin, on hearing Fionn and the Fianna being spoken of so disrespectfully, and by weaklings such as these. "We were not giants," the young man said, contemptuous in his wrath, "but any one of us could have picked up that rock with one hand, and the strongest among us could have hurled it across the valley."

Overcome with loathing for their ignorant sneering he spoke no other word, but turned his horse's head toward the west and Tír na Nóg. As he wheeled about, one of the men yelled, "Prove what you say is true by lifting this rock for us, then we'll listen to your stories of Fionn and the Fianna!"

"I'll do that," shouted Oisin fiercely, "to put right the facts of history. Then I'll go back to Tír na Nóg, for there's nought left for me in this country."

Recalling Niamh's warning about dismounting, he leaned down from the saddle and slid his hand under the huge boulder. However, when he began to lift it the girth of the saddle broke under the strain, and Oisin toppled to the ground. Capall Bán shied and galloped away, leaving him there—maybe in fright, or maybe because the faerie horse knew that now Oisin could never return to Tír na Nóg.

In that moment three centuries caught up with Oisin. He lay on the ground, an old man, weak and spent, wasted, blind, bereft of comeliness, deprived of strength and mental alertness. The glossy filaments of his sloe-black hair fell out of his scalp and shriveled as if torched. His teeth darkened to brown, as if baked in an oven, and several of them dribbled like stones from his puckering lips. The clear lines of his bone structure lost beneath a mass of sagging flesh; jowls, lids, and eye pouches. A wattle like that of a turkey wobbled at his throat. His skin, once pale bronze and flawless, turned freckled with splatters and spots of discoloration. Vacant grew his eyes, and as shallow as muddy puddles. No longer were his shoulders broad, his spine erect; his back was curved like the crescent moon, and skinny wrists stuck out from the sleeves of his rich raiment.

His sunken chest appeared motionless. It seemed he breathed no longer.

The men were terrified. They believed Oisin was dead, until they heard him muttering "Tír na Nóg!" upon which they lifted him up and carried him from the valley of Glenasmole.

"This is no ordinary man!" they said amongst themselves. "What shall we do with him?"

"It is not up to common folk like ourselves to decide such matters. We must take him to the wisest of the wise."

"Saint Patrick?"

"The very one."

Saint Patrick was dwelling in Ireland in those days, and his shelter was a cottage on a hillside, near the place where a church was being built. It was for the purpose of fashioning this church that the stones in Glenasmole were being removed. Already the bell tower had been completed, and the bells installed. Bell ringers hauled on the ropes several times a day, swinging the mighty domes on their axes, their metallic tongues calling people to prayer.

The brazen voices of the bells tolled out across the countryside as the stone-haulers bore the antiquated form of Oisin to Saint Patrick's door. The priest stepped out, dressed in his austere robes. Patrick was no young man himself, but he remained sprightly and keen.

"Who is this grandfather you have brought to me?" he inquired.

"He is a stranger to us, Father, but he declared he is Oisin son of Fionn mac Cumhail."

"Father Patrick, it was the strangest thing. When we first saw him he was a youth. Then he fell from his horse, and in the blink of an eye he turned into the old fellow you see before you."

"It is the most astonishing sight we have ever seen, and the most fearsome."

"What should we do?"

Patrick knew what they were talking about, and he was intrigued. He held great respect for the old traditions and folktales, and he was aware that Oisin was known as the poet and historian of the Fianna, and if anyone could tell him the ancient stories, it was Oisin.

"Bring him inside. Leave him with me. I shall take care of him."

Greatly relieved, the men did as he bade them, and hastened away.

◆　◆　◆

THE FIRST SOUND Oisin heard when he had recovered his wits was the pealing of the bells. He pulled himself up on his elbow and turned his balding head about distractedly. Naught could he see, for he was blind.

"What is that noise?" he shrieked with his cracked and ancient voice. "So loud, so harsh. It is clanging through my skull like hammerblows!"

"Hush," said the priest. "They are the church bells chiming for prayers."

But Oisin moaned, and sank back onto his pallet and would not be appeased. "Och! Here I lie, listening to the voices of bells. It is long the clouds are over me tonight."

Patrick allowed Oisin to sleep in his cottage and gave him food to eat. When Oisin had recovered sufficiently from his terrible ordeal, the priest asked him to relate the old stories so that he might write them down, thus preserving them for future generations.

It came to Oisin that this was the only way to correct the lies that people were telling about the Fianna, so he agreed. But as he related the stories to Patrick, he relived the memories, and he could not help but sometimes break off to give vent to his despair.

"Oh, how I wish I could see my father once more! It was a delight to Fionn, the cry of his hounds on the mountains, the wild dogs leaving their harbors, the pride of his armies, those were his delights. My grief! I to be stopping after him and without delight in games or in music; to be withering away after my comrades; my grief is to be living. If you had been in company with the Fianna, Patrick of the joyless clerks and of the bells, you would not be attending on schools or giving heed to your God."

Clang! clang! The church bells reverberated sonorously across the countryside.

"I would rather hear the blackbird's song," said Oisin, heaving a sigh. "Blackbird of Doire an Chairn, your voice is sweet; I never heard on any height of the world music that was sweeter than your voice. If myself and the Fianna were on the top of a hill today drawing our spear heads, we would have our choice of being here or there in spite of books and priests and bells."

Patrick replied softly, "You were like the smoke o' a wisp, or like a stream in a valley, or like a whirling wind on the top of a hill, every tribe of you that ever lived."

But Oisin continued his lament. "The time Fionn lived and the Fianna, it was sweet to them to be listening to the whistle of the blackbird; the voice of the bells would not have been sweet to them. If you knew the story of the bird the way I know it, you would be crying lasting tears, and you would give no heed to your God for a while. In the country of Lochlann of the blue streams, Fionn, son of Cumhal of the red-gold cups found that bird. Doire an Chairn, that wood there to the west where the Fianna used to linger; it is there they put the blackbird, in the beauty of the pleasant trees.

Clang! droned the bells. The reverberations hummed through the stones, the earth, the very bones of the living and the dead.

"The stag of the heather of quiet Cruachan," whispered Oisin, turning his empty eyes toward the window he could not see. "The sorrowful croak from the ridge of the Two Lakes; the scream of the eagle on the edge of the wood, the voice of the cuckoo on the Hill of Brambles. The voice of the hounds in the pleasant valley; the early outcry of the hounds going over the Strand of the Red Stones. These are the sounds more delightful to Fionn and our fellowship."

But after enduring Oisin's nostalgic plaints for so long, Patrick was growing impatient. "It is a silly thing, old man, to be always talking of the Fianna. Remember, your end is come, and take the Son of God to help you."

With some effort, Oisin rose to his feet, staggering a little and putting out his scrawny hand to steady himself against the chimney-piece.

Dismayed at his own weakness, he grieved anew. "This is not the way I used to be; without fighting, without playing at nimble feats, without young girls, without music, without harps, without bruising bones, without great deeds, without increase of learning, without generosity, without drinking at feasts, without courting, without hunting, the two trades I was used to: without going into battle and the taking of spoils. Ochone! The want of them is sorrowful to me." As he spoke, he groped his way to the door of the cottage. "Without rising up to do bravery as we were used, without playing as we had a mind; without swimming of our fighting men in the lake; it is long the clouds are over me tonight!"

Oisin stumbled forth onto the path beside the weedy turnip patch, and turned his raddled face to the west. Bitter currents of air lifted and combed the last silver threads of his hair. Suddenly his eyes flew wide and he stabbed his finger at the horizon, gasping, "There it is! It lies ahead, where the sea meets the sky!" His eyes stared sightlessly into the distance; his scrawny hands reached out, but grasped only the wind.

"Tír na Nóg is gone," said Patrick, not unkindly. "It disappeared when Christianity arrived at these shores."

"That's ridiculous!" snapped Oisin. "How could it disappear, when it exists forever?"

But he lowered his arm, and two clear drops budded beneath his lids. "Never more shall I see Fionn and the Fianna. Never again shall I behold my sweet Niamh, and my children playing on the hills of Tír na Nóg. For now I am a shaking tree; my leaves are gone from me. I am an empty nut, a horse without a bridle, a people without a dwelling place. I, Oisin, son of Fionn." Lifting his blind visage, he shouted to the skies in cracked and accusing tones, "It is long the clouds are over me tonight! It is long last night was. Although this day is long, yesterday was longer again to me. Every day that comes is long to me!"

Whenever the booming stridor of the bells winged its way across the valley, Patrick would find Oisin in the cottage with his gaze fixed on emptiness. Once he heard him mourn, "I am the last of the Fianna, great Oisin, son of Fionn, listening to the voice of bells."

"Come outside! Do not stay here staring at the walls," urged Patrick.

"It is not walls I see," murmured Oisin.

Despite himself, Patrick felt drawn to approach his guest, and ask, "What is it you do see?"

"I see a horse," answered Oisin, "moving swiftly over the ocean. And he is made of steam that is the color of snow, and his mane streams out along the wind like milk, and his hooves skip lightly across the waves." He paused a moment, before continuing. "But it is without saddle he is, and without a rider. Alone he gallops into the west."

On an impulse, the priest gently placed his hand on the shoulder of the old man. At this gesture of kindness, something inside Oisin seemed to break. As if finally defeated, he bowed his ancient head.

"And oh, Patrick, it is long the clouds are over me tonight."

References and Acknowledgments

This work is inspired by Lady Gregory's famous translation of the history of Oisin. In the interests of authenticity, the dialogue is partially quoted from this source.

The Swan Pilot

⁂

BY L. E. MODESITT, JR.

I eased myself into the control couch of the ISS *W. B. Yeats,* making certain that all the connections were snug, and that there were no wrinkles in anything. Then I pressed the single stud that was manual, and the clamshell descended.

You could call a trans-ship a corade or a cockle guided by will across the sea of endless space. You could, and it would be technically wrong. Technically wrong, but impressionalistically right, and certainly the way it feels when you're alone in the blackness, balancing the harmonics and threading your way from the light matter and through the dark matter and faerie dust of overspace, guiding the ship and all it contains out from light and into darkness and then on to another minute isle of solid warmth once again. Or you could refuse to call it a ship at all, nor the ocean it sails a sea. There is no true sea, the theorists say, just a mist of the undermatter that fills overspace, a mist that stretches to eternity, in which float the brilliant blocks of light matter that can incinerate you in a nanoinstant or the solid dark blocks upon which you can be smashed into dust motes tinier than the stitches on a leprechaun's shoes.

A pilot is more like a light-blinded night bird with gossamer wings that soars across the mists of undermatter against and through the darkness and light that are but the representations of the universe above. Or perhaps those denizens of overspace perceive us as underspace, blocky and slow and awkward. I could call every flight a story of the twelve ships of the Tir Alir, and that would be right as well.

How many ways are there to explain the inexplicable? Shall I try again?

None of what I experience would make sense to, say, François Chirac, or Ahmed Farsi, and what they would experience would not make sense to me, either. But I'm Sean Shannon Henry, born in Sligo and a graduate of Trinity, and in the universe of the trans-ships, that has made all the difference, for the sky roads are not the same for each of the swan pilots, though the departures and the destinations—and the routes—are exactly the same. Nor can there be more than one pilot-captain on a ship. A second pilot wouldn't help, because if a pilot fails for a nanoinstant, the ship is lost as well. Oh, the scientists have their explanations, and I'll leave those with them.

With the clamshell down, I was linked to all the systems, from the farscanners to the twin fusactors, from the accumulators to the converters and the translation generators, and from the passenger clamshells to the cargo holds. I ran the checklist, and everything was green, and both cargo and the handful of passengers were secured.

"Alora," I pulsed to the second, who handles cargo and passengers from the clamshell in the compartment aft of mine, "systems are go."

"Ready for departure, Captain."

A last scan of the systems, and I pulsed control. "High control, *Yeats*, systems green, ready for delocking and departure this time."

"*Yeats*, wait one for traffic in the orange."

"*Yeats* standing by."

Another wedge shape, formed of almost indestructible adiamante composite, so solid in the underspace we inhabit, slipped out from the glowing energy of Hermes Station, out toward the darkness up and beyond, where it would rise through the flames of translation, phoenix-swan-like, to make its way to another distant stellar hearth, and there untranslate, and glide like a falling brick back into the safe dullness of the reality we require.

"*Yeats*, clear to delock and depart."

"Control, delocking and departing this time." After releasing the couplers and giving the faintest touch of power to the steering jets, I eased the *Yeats*—a mere thousand tons of composite and cargo—away from Hermes Station, that islet of warmth in the black sea of oblivion that is space.

Like a quarrel arrowing through space, where there is no up or down, the *Yeats* and I accelerated away from Hermes Station and the world of Silverston. Once we were clear of satellites and traffic, I spread the photon nets, like the butterfly soul of the proud priest of ancient Ireland.

"Stand by for translation."

"Ready for translation," answered Alora.

I *twisted* the energies pouring into the translator. The entire universe *shimmered*, then turned black, and the *Yeats* and I fused into one entity, no longer pilot and ship, but a single black swan flying through deeper darkness.

A deep chime rolled from below, and crystalline notes vibrated from above, shattered, and fell like ice flakes across my wings, each flake sounding a different note as it struck my wings, and as each note added to the melody of the flight, it left a pinprick of hot agony behind.

I continued to fly, angling for the distant droning beacon that was Alustre, with the sure knowledge that there would be at least one timeless interlude. One was standard, two difficult. With three inter-ludes began high stress on both the ship and the pilot, and a loss level approaching 50 percent. Only one trans-ship had been known to sur-vive four interludes; the pilot had not.

Unseen cymbals crashed, and the grav waves of a singularity shook me. Black pinnae shivered from my wings, wrenched out by the buffeting of a black hole somewhere in the solid underspace I flew above/between.

Brilliant blue, blinding blue, enfolded me—and passed—and I stood on the edge of a rock, wingless, now just a man in a mackin-tosh, looking at the gray waves sullenly pounding on the stone-shingled beach less than two yards below. A rhyme came to mind, and I spoke it to the waves on that empty beach.

> "Captain Sean went to the window
> and looked at the waves below
> not a mermaid nor a merrow
> nor fish nor ship would he know . . ."

"So you'd not know a merrow? Is that what you're saying, captain of a ship that is not a ship?"

I turned. To my right, where there had been no one, was a man sitting on a spur of rock. Although he wore brown trousers, and a tan Aran sweater, his webbed feet were bare, and he was not exactly a man, not with a scaly green skin, green hair, and deep-set red eyes that looked more like those of a pig than a man. He had a cocked red hat tucked under his arm.

"It'd seem to me that I know you, by your skin and hair, but mostly by the hat."

"For a drowning sailor, you're a most bright fellow."

"Bright enough to ask your name," I answered, not terribly worried about drowning. Overspace captains drown all the way through every voyage. We drown in sensation, and in the unseen tyranny of underspace that presses in on the overspace where we translate from system to system, world to world.

" 'Tis Coomra, or close enough." He smiled, and his teeth were green as well. Beside his feet was a contraption of wood and mesh. The mesh was not metal, but glimmered as if it were silver coated in light. It probably was. "And your name is . . . ?"

"Sean."

"A fine Irish name that is." He laughed.

"A fine lobster pot that is," I replied, although I knew it was no such thing. I'd prepared for this moment as well as for many others, for to fly/sail overspace, a pilot must know all the stories and all his or her personal archetypes. That is, if he or she doesn't want to drown out there. Or here. I had to remember that interludes were real, as real as life underspace, and just as able to kill me, and all the passengers who rode on my wings.

"A lobster pot? That's what others have called it, but you, Sean Shannon Henry, would you not know better?" The green eyes glittered.

I stepped closer to him, but on the side away from the soul cage. "How old are you? As old as my great-grandfather Patrick?"

"I'm older than any dead man, and any that swim in the sea."

"He's not dead. In fact," I said as I stepped closer, "he's in his second century now, and feeling like he still has years ahead of him."

"You'd not be thinking I was that young, now, would you?"

"He's older than fine brandy," I pointed out, concentrating hard, before producing an earthen jug. That was a trick it had taken years to master, making objects seem real in overspace, because interludes are short, long as they sometimes seem.

"That's not brandy, not in an old jar like that." Still, he cocked his head to the side.

"I wouldn't know brandy. This is old-time poteen."

"And I'm the mayor of Dungarven . . ."

"As you wish it." I pulled the cork and presented the jug.

He did not take it, not immediately.

"I bring you a gift, and you would refuse it?" I asked gently. "Surely, you would not wish to waste good spirits." I shouldn't have made the punnish allusion, but the overspace elementals usually don't catch them.

"You are a hard man with words, Captain Sean Henry, but you are drowning, and drown you will." But he took the jug, and so heavy was it that it needed both his green hands.

In the moment that he had both of them on the jug, I lunged and grabbed the cocked hat.

The jug vanished, but the hat did not, and I held it, with both hands and mind.

The green eyes glittered, with a copper-iron heaviness and malice. "Clever you are, Captain Henry, clever indeed."

"I only ask to keep what is mine, within mine, and nothing of yours."

"So be it." The merrow cocked his head.

Blazing blue flashed across me, and once more I was spin-soaring through darkness, gongs echoing. I almost thought of the gong-tormented, wine-dark sea, but pushed that away. An interlude in Byzantium would not be one I'd enjoy or relish, and probably would not survive. It wasn't my archetype, even with the Yeats connection. Instead, I slip-slid sideways, letting the faerie dust that could have been air, but was not, swirl over my wings, as I banked around a sullen column of antiqued iron that was the gravity well of a star that could have shredded me into fragments of a fugue or syllables of a sonnet. The subsonic harp of Tara—or Cruachan—shivered through my bones and composite sinews.

Once more, I soared toward the shimmering veil that was and was not, resetting us on the heading toward the now-less-distant beacon that was Alustre.

And once more, the brilliant interlude blue slashed across me.

I stood under the redstone archway of a cloistered hall. The only light was the flickering flame of a bronze lamp set in a bracket attached to a column several meters away.

Before me stood a priest, a stern and white-faced cleric.

As any good Irish lad, I waited for the good father to speak, although I had my doubts about whether he was, first, truly a reverend father, and, second, good. His eyes surveyed me, going up and down my figure, taking in the uniform of the trans-ship captain, before he spoke a single word. "Your soul is in mortal danger, my son. You have sold it for the trappings of that uniform and for the looks that others bestow upon you."

It's truly hell when the elementals of overspace—or their abilities—combine with your own weaknesses. I swallowed, trying to regain a certain composure, trying to remind myself that I was in an interlude and that other souls and bodies depended upon me.

"With all your schooling and knowledge, you do not even know that you have a soul," he went on. "Knowledge is a great thing, but it is not the end in life. It can be but a mess of pottage received in return for your birthright."

Mixed archetypes and myths were dangerous—very dangerous in overspace interludes. "If I do good," I said, "does that not benefit everyone, whether I know if I have a soul or not?"

"Words. Those are but words."

Words are more powerful than that, but following such logic would just make matters even worse. I concentrated on the figure in friar's black before me. "Truth can be expressed in words."

"Souls are more than words or truth. You are drowning, and unless you accept that soul that is and contains you, you will be eternally damned." His voice was warm and soft and passionate and caring, and it almost got to me.

"I am my soul." That was certainly true.

"You risk drowning and relinquishing that soul with every voyage across the darkness," the priest went on.

"Others depend on me, Father," I pointed out.

"That is true," he replied. "Yet you doubt that you have a soul, and for that your soul will go straight to Hell when you die, and that will never be when you wish."

"I have also doubted Hell."

"Doubt does not destroy what is. Denial, my son, does not affect reality."

"Then, reality does not affect denial," I countered. "If I have been good, whether I believe in souls or Hell or the life everlasting, my soul should not be in mortal danger. If I have been evil, then belief in Heaven and Hell should not save that soul from the punishment I deserve."

"Are you so sure that you have been that good?" The dark eyes probed me, and the flickering lamp cast doubt across me.

"I am not sure that I have been evil, nor that you should be the judge of the worth of my soul."

"Who would you have judge your soul, if you have a soul?"

Simple as it sounded, it wasn't. The question implied so much more.

"No man can judge himself, let alone another," I said slowly. "No being can judge another unlike himself, for the weight of life falls differently upon each."

The priest stepped forward, and I thought I saw the ghost of wings spreading from his shoulders. The trouble was, in the dimness, I couldn't tell whether they were ghostly white or ghostly black. "If you will not be judged, then you will be in limbo for all eternity, and that is certainly not pleasant."

It didn't sound that way, but it was better than Hell, even if I didn't believe in Hell—at least not too much. "Well . . . perhaps I need more time to consider. You won't have to make that judgment, and neither will I, or anyone else, if nothing happens to me right now."

"So be it." The father made a cryptic gesture.

There was a stillness, without even background subsonics or shredded notes from underspace filtering up. Then, blue lightning flashed, and, for a moment, I could sense and feel overspace. I had been slewed off course, as can happen in an interlude, particularly one that slips into the pilot's weaknesses, but I banked and swept back toward Alustre and the ever-closer-but-not-close-enough beacon.

That was about all I got done because the deep swell of a pulsed singularity rolled toward us, like a black-silver cloud. With it came another sheet of glaringly brilliant blue.

Three interludes? That was the only thought I managed before I found myself standing in a dim room. A woman stood in front of me. From behind what was most noticeable was her hair, although I saw little of it, but what I did see was red and tinted with sun, where it slipped out from the black silk scarf that covered her head.

She faced two men in black. They sat at a round table that groaned under the weight of the gold coins stacked there, yet, with all that weight of coin, not a stack trembled. They looked up at me, and their black eyes glittered in their pale faces above combed black beards. They dismissed me, and their eyes went to the woman who had not even noticed me. The two looked almost the same, as if they were brothers, and I supposed that they were, in a manner of speaking. The only thing that caught my eyes was that the one on the right wore a wide silver ring, and the one on the left a gold band.

The woman was speaking, and her voice was music, silver, gold, yet warmer, and with a core of strength. "You have stolen from me. That does not trouble me. What troubles me is that you stole from me so that the poor would be forced to sell their souls to you."

"We are but traders. No one is required to come to us." The man on the right smiled politely, then added a gold coin to the pile closest to him.

"Any man or woman who has a child that is hungry or suffers and loves that child is required to come to you. Anyone with a soul that is worth your golds will come to you to spare another from suffering. Your words are meaningless. They are false." She laughed.

I liked her, even though I hadn't even seen her face.

"Why are you here?" asked the trader on the left, pointing to me.

"Because I am." That was the only response that made sense.

The woman turned to me, and I understood who she was, if not precisely why I was with her and the two emissaries from the nether-lands. I could also see why the old tales called her a saint with eyes of sapphire. Her eyes were deep, so deep I wanted to swim in them, and I had to swallow to recall I was in an interlude, a *third* interlude, and 50 percent of those were fatal.

"You? Are you one of *them*?" she asked.

"No, Countess . . . I am Captain Sean Shannon Henry." I paused. "You are the Countess Kathleen O'Shea?"

"Kathryn would be more accurate . . ."

I murmured words. From where they came I could not have said.

> *"The countess had a soul as pure as unfallen snow*
> *and a mind that no evil could know . . ."*

"I am not that good. And Gortforge is not so poor as this place here."

"You are a saint," I said.

"No. I care that people do not barter their souls to live—or to keep their children from suffering and hunger. That's all."

Had I done that? Bartered my soul for something? For what? Interludes have a meaning. That's why they're so deadly. If you don't have interludes, the ship never leaves the departure system. If you have too many, it never arrives at its destination—or any destination any have yet discovered.

Her eyes softened. "Souls ride with you, don't they?"

"In a way," I admitted.

"We will add those he is trying to save to the price for yours," offered the second trader, the one with the gold ring on his finger.

"No!" The words were out before I thought.

"You would doom them, then?" asked the first trader.

"No. I would doom your bargain."

"You cannot," Kathleen/Kathryn said. "I have made it, and I stand by it."

"You're a saint," I said again.

"You had best find that out in the world that counts." She vanished.

I felt my mouth open. *That* was the first time that had ever happened to me in an interlude.

"Your soul is not worth a thousandth part of hers," announced one of the traders, "but we will carry you into the depths with us, until the soul of the countess is tendered to the one who paid for it."

"A bargain under duress is not a valid sale," I pointed out. "A soul must be tendered freely."

"She tendered hers freely."

"She did not. As she said, anyone with a soul of worth would tender it to prevent another's suffering, and the One Who Is already has judged that you cannot have her soul."

Both looked at me, and I felt as though I had been skewered by those black eyes.

"And what of your soul, Captain Sean Shannon Henry? Your soul has not been so judged. What is it worth to you?"

"Hers, and more . . ." What I meant was not what I said, because what I meant was that my soul had worth, but, as they had already judged, not nearly the worth of hers. Not yet, anyway.

Something happened, because, before I could say more, the men in black had vanished, and so had the Countess Kathleen . . . or Kathryn . . . O'Shea, and I was in the depths of the ocean, cold and black, water weighing in upon my lungs with such force that all the air I had breathed was forced out in an explosive gasp.

With that, brilliant blue swept across overspace, and black lightnings shattered the blueness.

Then, I was again flying free, banking ever so slightly to avoid the singularity below my left wing tip. Somewhere deep within my swan-form, every part of me ached as I scanned the darkness of overspace, glad that I had emerged from the interlude, but pushing away the questions as I searched for the beacon that was Alustre.

I discovered that we had almost oversoared it and swung into a downward spiral, ignoring the flutter of dislodged pinnae, as we dropped lower . . . and lower—until I could feel the power of the beacon vibrating my sinews/feathers.

Only then did I *untwist* the energies flowing through the translation generators. Instantly, the black swan was no more, and the *Yeats* and I were but pilot and ship.

I passed out briefly from the pain when we reemerged into underspace, normspace for those of us who live in it.

"Captain . . . Captain . . ." Alora's voice finally got to me.

"I'm ... here ... Rough translation," I pulsed, checking, then deploying the photon screens.

"Rough?" A sense of laughter, ragged laughter, came across. "The *Yeats* isn't making any more translations without some serious work."

I hadn't made the evaluations, but the feelings from my body, and the fact that not all the farscreens and diagnostics were even working, suggested a certain truth to her words. Still, I'd untranslated closer than normal, and that was good, given our situation.

◆　◆　◆

"Augusta station, this is ISS *W. B. Yeats*, inbound from Silverston. Authentication follows." I pulsed off the authentication, trying to ignore the aches that seemed to cover most of my clamshelled body, as well as the tightness in my chest, and the feeling that I was still drowning.

There wasn't any immediate answer. There never is, not with the real-time, speed-of-light delay. My head continued to ache, and I had to boost the oxygen to my self-system as we headed down and in-system.

It was more than a few standard hours before the *Yeats*, with passengers and cargo intact, docked at Augusta Station, the trans-ship terminal for the planet Jael of the New Roman Republic. The pilot and ship were less intact than the passengers and cargo.

"Captain Henry, Augusta control here. External diagnostics indicate extensive maintenance required. Interrogative medical attention."

I scanned the ship systems once again, although I knew control was right. The fusactors were both close to redline, and the translation generators were totally inoperative. Two of the farscreens were junk. As for me, my nanetics had told me more than once that I was bruised over 21.4 percent of my body, that I had more than a few subdural hematomas, and that 20 percent of my lung function was impaired. But there hadn't been anything I could have done until we were in-locked.

"Affirmative. Class three removal requested." Class two would have meant half my body would have needed attention. Class one would have come from the ship systems or Alora, because Class one med alerts meant the pilot was dead or close to it.

As I waited for the med crew and shuttle, I downlinked to the Roman infosystems, running through the search functions as quickly as I could. Then, I went up a level, for the information on the other worlds of the New Roman Republic. There was no Gortforge on Jael, or on any of the other Roman worlds, nor anything resembling it in name. That didn't matter. It existed somewhere—and so did the Countess Kathryn O'Shea. Of both I was certain.

The universe is thought, wrapped in rhyme and music, and that's why the best pilots hold the blood of the Emerald Isle. We know what we are . . . and each time we fly, we have to discover that anew.

For, as a pilot, I have always held to my own two beliefs. First, science is not enough to explain all that is in the wide, wide universe, and without magic, science is as useless as . . . a man without a soul. Second, so long as there are Irish, there will always be an Ireland.

After the med crew rebuilds me, again, I will fly the swan ship that is the *Yeats* to as many worlds as I can, and must, until I find the Countess Kathryn.

With whom else could a swan pilot trust his found soul?

The Isle of Women

BY JACQUELINE CAREY

We are nameless in the stories told by men.

Even the Lady, my gracious Lady, who wore her beauty as lightly as a garment of the finest-combed wool, on whose shoulders the mysteries perched like twin doves. It is no wonder they hailed her as Queen, although it was not what she was. For that, there is no word. Lady, we called her. But she had a name, too, although it was seldom spoken aloud. In the stories they told afterward, none of us have names.

I saw them first, from the ramparts. I saw their hide-bound curragh riding the green swell of the waves, a curragh so vast it might have been a small whale, making its way to our shores. Truly, it was a mighty vessel to hold such men; seventeen, bold and fearless, and boldest of all was their leader, Máel Dúin.

I did not know that, then. I did not know if they were kinsmen or
foes, reavers come to wreak violence upon us. Then, I merely picked
up my skirts and hastened down the stairs to tell our Lady. She sat at
her spinning wheel within her day chamber. I knocked and was
admitted. Several of the other maidens were present, carding and
combing. I told them what I had seen.

"Thank you, Cébha." The Lady bowed her head and her fine,
white hands went still. Then she laid down her distaff, and when she
lifted her head, there was a strangeness in her face. "I will ride forth to
see these men. Do you prepare the sacred bath, for it is in my heart
that they are not enemies, and I must make ready to receive them."

All this was done as she wished. While the men of Máel Dúin
drew their mighty curragh ashore and my Lady watched, we labored
outside the walls of the dún. There, where the spring bubbles from
amid the moss-covered rocks, we built the fires to warm the big
hanging kettle. We filled it with pure water from the spring, before it
spills over the rocks into the little brook.

It took three times to fill the bronze tub within the bothy, and
when it was done, she came back. She gave her horse over to Eithne,
who led it to the stable. We eased the richly embroidered robes from
our Lady's white shoulders, and she went straightaway into the bothy
to bathe.

That is when I saw that the men had followed her.

They had hung back on the sloping hill, gathered and watching.
All of them with their mouths agape, except for two. And we maidens
watched back, all with our mouths agape, for we had seen few men
since the Lady's consort died, and that was some years ago, when
most of us were but children.

One whose mouth was closed upon his thoughts was Máel Dúin.

By the way he stood, and the other men regarded him, it was clear
he was their leader. And it was at him that the other maidens stared,
for even though he was tossed and draggled by his sea voyage, he

stood straight and tall, hale of limb and proud of sinew. His shoulders were broad and strong. Although his beard was like a wild man's, and his hair was tangled with wind and salt, it shone bright as gold in the sunlight, and there was a fierceness in his face as he stared at the door of the bothy where the Lady had gone.

But I looked at the other man, who saw me looking and smiled.

"Cébha."

It was my Lady's voice. I went inside the bothy, where it was warm with steam. She sat in the bronze tub, pouring water from a dipper over her white skin.

"Go forth on my behalf and make them welcome in the dún," she said to me. "Their leader is named Máel Dúin."

So I was the one who went to give them greeting, picking up my skirts and making my way up the slope, while my sister-maidens watched in envy. Although I was not afraid when I began, my heart beat quicker as I drew near. If they were reavers, they would have fallen upon us at once; still, they were men. I breathed slowly, that my voice should not tremble.

"My Lady gives greeting to you and your men, Máel Dúin," I said to him. "Do you come with me, we will make you welcome."

His eyes were pale blue, ringed in black like a falcon's. Although he was young, a man with such eyes might gaze at the sun until he saw visions. There was wariness in them, but no fear. "Who is your lady that she knows my name?" he asked me, and although his accent was strange and harsh, and there were words that sounded wrong to my ears, he spoke the tongue of Ériu. "What is this place? Does she rule here?"

I gave him the only answer I knew. "She is the Lady of this isle. It is her place."

"I am seeking the sea raider who killed my father, Ailill, who was called Ailill Edge-of-Battle." The pale falcon's eyes did not blink. "Does your Queen know where he is to be found?"

I shook my head. "I do not know, Máel Dúin, what the Lady knows and does not. Will you accept her hospitality?"

He turned to the man beside him. "What think you, Diurán?"

It was the man who had smiled, and he smiled at me again. My ears went hot, and my tongue felt thick and clumsy in my mouth. He was dark where Máel Dúin was fair, with hair as brown as oak leaves and watchful dark eyes. They were eyes that might see visions, too; not in brightness, but in quiet, still places, where other men would not have the patience to wait.

"Máel Dúin, it is not in my heart to refuse the grace of the Lady of this place," Diurán said, and I knew by his words and the music in his voice that he was one of the filidh, who had studied among bards, and not like the others, who were warriors first and foremost. "How could I bring myself to tell the tale if we failed to accept it?"

"Spoken like a poet!" Máel Dúin clapped a hand upon his shoulder, and I saw that there was much affection between them. As for the other men, they eyed the distant maidens and made approving sounds, nudging one another and trying in vain to comb their tangled beards with their fingers. "Lead on, girl."

I led them to the dún and saw from the corner of my eye that my sisters were going on ahead to draw water from the well of the dún and heat it within the walls. Also, I saw the Lady emerge and a glimpse of her fair skin, rosy from the bath, then two maidens slipping the robe over her. And I saw that Máel Dúin looked, too, and a strange smile touched his lips.

Inside the dún, Máel Dúin's men marveled at the strong stone walls and the arching doorways, and I could see it had been many days since they had dwelled out of the elements.

"Come," I said to them. "You will want to bathe before the Lady receives you."

They went without complaining, and some of them exclaimed at the sight of so many steaming tubs. Máel Dúin said nothing. Only

Diurán spoke, touching my wrist with two fingers. "So we do not bathe where the Lady bathes?"

"No." I whispered the word. "That place is sacred."

He nodded and let me go. The pulse in my wrist throbbed.

We made ready for them while they bathed. There were things that had been brought by the isle folk and left for us; brown bread, cheese, and apples, strong ale and a slaughtered pig ready for the spit. I do not know how they knew to do such things, save that the Lady had told them, for she went forth among them every day to hear their concerns and make such judgments as were needed. Such was her duty, and such were her mysteries.

There were great splashes and shouts of laughter from behind the closed door where Máel Dúin's men bathed; we maidens glanced at one another and nodded and smiled, as if to say, yes, that is how men behave, though we knew little of such things.

Then the Lady came among us in raiment fit for a Queen. Her robes were of the purest blue, adorned on the hems and the edges of the sleeves with gold embroidery three handspans deep. Her hair, that was a deep auburn in hue, hung down her back in a gleaming mass of autumn splendor. Two lengths of it had been braided and bound with gold cord, and these were woven into a coronet about her head. Around her throat was a great collar of gold set with blue gems, and gold sandals peeked beneath the hem of her robe.

We all paused in awe to see her in such finery, with such a brightness upon her. Eithne, who was boldest among us, spoke first. "Will you take Máel Dúin as your consort, then, Lady?"

"I will." She smiled, and in my heart I sighed with gladness that it was not Diurán she had chosen. "This night, we shall celebrate it. My daughters, follow your own desires and make such choices as you will; or none at all as it please you."

There was much excited whispering, then, as we laid out the bowls of warm water, soft linen towels and the shears. It did not seem there was anyone among us unwilling to make a choice. I did not take part in it, afraid that if I voiced my desires, some other might voice the same.

"Cébha." The Lady touched my wrist, exactly as Diurán had done. I lifted my head to gaze at her lovely face. There was a shadow of sorrow in it; or of knowing. "Do not give away your heart too fast, little bird. Those who see the most may be the most dangerous to love."

I opened my mouth, then closed it. I had no words.

"Ah, Danu!" She smiled once more, although the shadow had not passed, and patted my cheek. "You are young, and the heart will do as it will. Come and help me welcome our guests."

She stood straight and tall among us as the doors to the great hall were opened, and lamplight played over her hair to make of it a second flame, subtle and muted. Máel Dúin stood at the forefront of his men, looking at her with his falcon's eyes, and I saw desire hit him like a fist. What she felt, I could not say, but everything went quiet as they gazed at one another, those two. Then he looked past her and saw the chairs, the towels, and the shears laid out.

"My lady Queen." A muscle in his jaw twitched. "What is this?"

"Why, Máel Dúin!" She smiled at him, and there was a lilt in her voice such as none of us had heard. "You and your men are as hairy as eremites after your long voyage. Will you not let us make you comely?"

He stared at her a moment, then flung back his head with a laugh. It had been a long time since the rafters of that hall had echoed with a man's laughter. Striding across the rush-laid floor, Máel Dúin sat in the biggest chair. He planted his legs and put his hands upon his knees, tilting his chin.

"Will you shear me like a lamb, my Queen?" he challenged her.

"No, Máel Dúin." Bending over him with tenderness, my Lady laid a linen towel across his chest. She took up the keen-edged shears, and they gleamed silver in the lamplight. "Only as a woman does a man whose face she wishes to behold."

"All right, then. Come, lads!" He grinned as the shears snipped and a tangled clump of golden beard fell upon the linen. "Who's next for the shearing?"

After that there was much milling in the hall. Some of the men were bold, and some of the maidens, too; others blushed and stammered, shuffling on uncertain feet. I stood in one place and shook my head when a man I did not desire approached me. With so many bodies milling, I lost sight of Diurán.

And then he was there, alone, smiling at me. "What is your name?"

"Cébha," I whispered.

"Cébha, little songbird, with lips as red as rowan berries, your bright eyes pierce me to the heart." He brushed a curling lock of my hair with his fingertips. "Little bird in a blackthorn thicket, do you have a gentle touch?"

A hot blush rose along the column of my throat, reddening my cheeks. "I don't know."

"Well, let us find out together." He took a seat in the nearest chair and offered his throat. I had to lean over him to spread the linen towel. A clean scent rose from his warm, freshly scrubbed skin. "Little songbird, would you know the name of the man who puts himself in your hands this night?" he asked me. "I am Diurán."

"I know." My hands trembled as I took up the shears. "I know your name."

"Here." Diurán's fingers encircled my wrist, steadying me. They were strong and callused from many a turn at the oar, but finely made. There was no mockery in his dark eyes, only gentleness. Here was a man who understood there was something more at work here. "I will help you, Cébha."

It seemed to me, then, that everything else went away. I concen-

trated on clipping the tangled locks, dipping a towel in warm water
and wiping loose hair from his chin. As I trimmed his beard short,
the shape of his face came clear, younger than I had thought. His lips
were firm and ruddy. I could hear his soft breathing and see the pulse
beat steadily in the hollow of his throat, and I did not dare meet his
eyes lest he see my thoughts.

So I cut his beard until his handsome face showed, and I cut the
knots from his long hair until I could pull a wooden comb through it,
and his hair lay on his shoulders, fine and shining, like a cape of oak
leaves.

And then solemn-faced Brigit was there, the youngest among us,
holding a withy basket. Inside lay the hair of Máel Dúin's men, red
and black and brown all mixed together, and locks of bright gold that
were Máel Dúin's. I gathered the linen towel that held Diurán's brown
hair.

"Wait." He caught my arm. His dark brows were drawn together
in a frown. "What is it you do here, little songbird?"

I made myself meet his eyes. "Would you have us throw it upon
the fire? What a stink it would make, all this hair!" I teased him, hearing a lilt come into my voice. "I did not think you were a man to fear
making a small offering in this place, Diurán."

Diurán's lips smiled, but his eyes, intent on mine, did not. "And
what will you offer, little songbird, little Cébha?"

I swallowed. "What would you have me offer?"

"Your own hair, Cébha, spread in black ringlets over my pillow.
Your rowan-berry lips, for mine to feast upon." At the expression on
my face, his smile reached his eyes, and his grip upon my arm softened to a caress. "Your white throat, arched like a swan and your
white breasts, a pair of nestling doves cooing in my hands. All of that,
sweet Cébha, and more."

I blushed this time to the roots of my hair.

Diurán laughed and released me. "Take it," he said to Brigit, still holding the basket and watching wide-eyed. "Surely, I will grow more."

So it was done and the shorn locks of his oak-brown hair were piled atop the others. Brigit went away with the basket and we cleared away the towels and shears and bowls of warm water. In exchange we brought platters of food, so heavy the weight made us stagger. The men dragged their chairs to the long trestle table and began to pile their trenchers high with meat and bread, pouring foaming tankards of ale from the jugs we set on the table. Once it was done, we joined them.

The Lady sat in the center and presided over our meal, and Máel Dúin sat beside her. With his beard neatly trimmed and his hair combed smooth, he looked less like a fierce warrior, and more like a young King at her side. There was that air about him that drew the eye.

What had transpired between them, I cannot say, though I may guess well enough. They exchanged glances and touches throughout the meal. Outside the walls of the dún, night was falling. I think they would have hastened its coming if they could.

His men ate with a goodwill, trying not to rush in their hunger; still, hands and faces were soon smeared with grease. I swabbed a piece of brown bread in the juices of the meat and nibbled at it, for I had little appetite. Beside me, Diurán cut his meat into small pieces with his belt knife, eating slowly and with relish. He caught me watching him from the corner of my eye.

"You do not rush like the others," I said to him.

"No." He wiped his knife on a linen napkin. "I am accustomed to fasting."

"You are one of the filidh, are you not?" I asked it quietly.

"I am." Diurán lay down his knife. "It is no secret, little songbird.

I am only of the third caste. Half a poet, no more." He smiled at me. "Máel Dúin sails at the behest of a monk of Duncloone to avenge his father. But it was my master, who is a druid, who told him to build his curragh. We have no secrets from one another."

He told me, then, of the voyage they had undertaken.

It was a terrible and wondrous tale. Their journey was fated from the outset. The druid, Diurán's master, told Máel Dúin only seventeen men might undertake the voyage; but his three foster brothers followed and swam after them. Lest the brothers drown, Máel Dúin had pulled them aboard the curragh.

After, they were blown off course and had been seeking the island where the reaver who had killed Máel Dúin's father lived ever since.

Although they had not found it, they had seen many marvels. Diurán told me of an island with ants the size of horses, and another with birds the size of cattle. On the island of the empty fortresses, one of Máel Dúin's foster brothers sought to steal a collar of gold, and there a little white cat leapt at him like a fiery arrow and passed through him, and he was dead. Another of his foster brothers was lost on a strange island, where the folk wept and lamented without cease; when they tried to rescue him, he wept and covered his face and would not come.

Strange to tell, the third foster brother met a fate much the same, on an island where a company of men laughed and played without cease, and would speak to no one unless he join them. Máel Dúin had to sail without him, and that was the last of his foster brothers, though his fate happier than the others.

When Diurán finished speaking there was silence, for all around the table had fallen to listening to his poet's voice, and Máel Dúin's men mourned their lost comrades, filling their cups and toasting to their valor.

"Such is the price of vengeance," the Lady said softly, laying her white hand on Máel Dúin's. "Perhaps that is the lesson the druid meant to teach you, for surely he knew your foster brothers would follow."

Máel Dúin did not answer for a long time. "My Queen, I do not know," he said when he did. "But I am weary to the bone, and glad enough to tarry here with you."

At that his men laid aside their grieving for a fearsome jollity, for such is the nature of warriors, who cannot afford to dwell upon the slain. They began to bang their cups upon the table, praising the solace of women and calling upon my Lady and Máel Dúin to make the nuptial toast as surely his foster brothers would have wanted, they said; for those lost comrades were no fools when it came to women's beauty and grace, even if they were fools in the matter of obeying druids.

On it went until the Lady laughed and ordered a cask of good red wine to be breached and the two-handled loving cup to be brought forth. This was done, and wine poured into it until it foamed pink. Each grasping a handle, they drank; first her and then him.

Afterward her gaze was tender and bright upon him, and something in his falcon's stare had eased into softness. His men shouted and cheered, and we cheered, too. I marked how Diurán raised his cup with the others and offered a toast, but when the Lady and Máel Dúin rose to leave the hall, he gazed after them, and his brow was furrowed.

Then he turned to me and smiled, and the smile smoothed his brow. "What do you say, Cébha my songbird? Shall we stay and make merry? Or shall we go forth and conclude the offering?"

The heat of his smile warmed me in unfamiliar places, and I blushed and nodded, unable to make an answer. He took my hand in all gentleness, and some of my sister-maidens gazed on me with envy, having heard his poet's voice. I paid them no heed, and Diurán let me lead him forth from the hall, down the winding corridors of the dún to my own chamber.

It was a small room, but I shared it with no one. There was a narrow window that let in slanting rays of light from the rising moon. I stood in it as Diurán removed my clothes with his gentle hands, and moonlight silvered my skin.

"Little bird, my Cébha," he whispered, his breath soft and warm on my neck. "Sea lily, pale as frost. Your side is as smooth as the swell of a wave, shining like foam in the starlight. Your sweet breasts are proud as mountains, tipped with dawn's rosy glow. Come to me, hold me in your rounded white arms."

I did, and he kissed me until my head swam. And then he laid me down upon my pallet and unlaced his shirt and his breeches. Naked in the moonlight, he looked like a vision, a man risen out of an enchanted pool. I reached out my arms and the pallet dipped under his weight.

"Sweet Cébha," he murmured, and I shivered to feel him pressed the length of me, his skin so warm. "Love me well, my songbird."

So it was that first night Máel Dúin and his men arrived, and I did not heed my Lady's advice but gave away my heart to Diurán the poet as though it had no more value than a speckled pebble I had found beside the brook.

I did not know it, then. Love sets its barbs like a hook; it does not hurt until the line is tugged. I knew only that his words made my heart sing like the songbird he named me, and his touch made my blood sing. Such were the mysteries we uncovered together that night, the simple mysteries of a man and a woman together, and I was glad to know them at last.

The next day, the Lady went forth on her grey mare as she did every morning, riding inland to hear the isle folks' concerns. Máel Dúin was content to wait in the great hall, and his men were content, too, playing at knucklebones and such games as men invent who have spent much time together. When she returned, she greeted Máel Dúin with a kiss. He caught her arm and begged her to stay, but she shook her head and smiled.

"Would you have me be idle?" she teased him. "You have earned your rest, but I have work to do."

She went then to her day chamber, and I went with her.

It was a formidable job to card and comb all that we had gathered. On my own, I would have lacked the patience for it, and so would my sister-maidens, but our Lady spoke gently to us. Bit by bit, we eased the tangles from the matted fibers, and the pile in the basket grew smaller.

Our Lady began to spin.

That night there was another feast, and revelry filled the hall. Diurán had found a lap harp, and he played and sang love songs for us. Listening to his rich voice, I felt as though I were floating, and I wished the moment might never end.

"Is this not better sport than vengeance, Máel Dúin?" the Lady asked him.

He smiled. "Truly, my Queen."

So it was that night and the next, and when Diurán laid down his harp, I led him back to my chamber and lay down upon my pallet with him, holding him in my arms. After love, we sank into sleep and though his head was heavy on my shoulder, I welcomed its weight. Those moments, too, I wished would never end.

For many days, it was much the same. In the morning, the Lady went about her duties and we went about our chores. During the afternoon, we retired to her day chamber. Day by day, the basket dwindled toward empty; day by day, the length of silken-fine thread increased upon the wheel.

One day, as we worked, we heard footsteps in the corridor outside. They halted at the door to the Lady's chamber. A strange hand tried the door and found it locked.

The other maidens and I glanced at once another. Any one of us would have knocked. We looked to the Lady, whose hands had gone still upon the wheel.

"Let them pass," she said quietly. "It is of no concern."

We sat quietly, and soon there were footsteps, going away.

That night in the hall, Diurán played the harp he had found, but he sang no love songs. Instead he sang a lament for the foster brothers of Máel Dúin, who had died on their voyage. And Máel Dúin's men wept as they listened, but in Máel Dúin's eyes there were no tears. He looked only at the Lady, taking pleasure in the sight of her.

When they had gone, and Diurán laid down his harp, I stood.

"No, Cébha." There was sorrow in his voice. He gazed at my outstretched hand and shook his head gently. "We have tarried too long in this place. I will not be going with you tonight."

"Why?" I whispered.

"Your Lady knows the reason," he said. "If you do not, ask her."

I fled the hall, weeping.

On the day that followed, Máel Dúin's men were restless and muttered to one another, no longer content to idle in the dún playing games as they had done. Instead they tended to the curragh, dragging it farther up the shore and overturning it. A fire was built and the pitch pot set to heating until it smoked, so they might apply a fresh coating to the hide seams of the curragh.

When it was done, the curragh was sea-ready; but Máel Dúin had no interest in leaving, preferring to wait in the dún until the Lady returned to join him in the evening. And that night, Diurán did not sing love songs, but the song of their voyage. He sang of further wonders they had seen; of an island divided in twain by a brazen palisade, with white sheep on one side and black sheep on the other; of an island where golden apples grew and were eaten by swine with eyes of fire, where the ground was so hot it burned their feet; of an island with a miraculous fountain that yielded water and milk.

Máel Dúin's men listened to his songs and said among themselves, yes, so it was. And they told the stories to each other; yes, here are the marks of scorching upon the sole of my shoe, yes, that was the isle where Máel Dúin flung a peeled white birch wand on the black side of the fence, and it turned black and we fled.

But such talk had no interest for Máel Dúin, who wished only to gaze at the Lady. And when I saw this, I remembered how she had made ready to receive him and how he had stared after the bothy where she had gone to bathe, and I understood that an enchantment had been laid upon him.

Once more, I slept alone and wept.

I listened the next morning as Máel Dúin's men spoke to him of leaving. Their voices grew loud and angry, for they were afraid for their leader and loath to leave without him. As Máel Dúin listened, his brows drew together, and something of the falcon's stare came back into his eyes, as if he were emerging from a fog. Then he caught sight of me lurking and smiled, and his features eased once more.

"What, lads?" he asked. "Have you grown tired so quickly of a life of plenty, and fair maidens to attend you?"

In the corner was Diurán, who had said nothing. He said nothing now, but only met my gaze. I left to await the Lady in her day chamber.

The thread she had been spinning came to an end and was finished that day. With no carding and combing to do, the other maidens were gossiping and idle, speaking of the men's restlessness. I sat quiet and watched as the Lady removed the thread from the wheel and wound it into a little ball, her white hands working deftly. It was a mottled thing when it was done, brown and black and red, with bits of gold glinting here and there.

"Lady," I said when she was done, "why do you keep Máel Dúin here against his will?"

After I spoke the chamber went very quiet, for the others were shocked at my boldness, but the Lady smiled and shook her head to show she was not angry.

"I do nothing against his will, little bird," she said to me. "A warrior's pride is a fearsome burden. I have given him leave to lay it down."

And with that I had to be content, for the Lady said no more, but tucked the ball of thread in the bodice of her robe and went forth to greet Máel Dúin in the great hall, and we went with her.

That night, Diurán played the harp and sang of Máel Dúin's father, Ailill, who was called Ailill Edge-of-Battle. And it came that Máel Dúin had never known his father. He had been fostered as a Queen's son and raised in ignorance of his true parents, for Ailill had gotten him upon a nun in a convent who had taken vows against such things. But when a jealous rival taunted Máel Dúin with his lack of knowledge, he went to the Queen, and she brought him to his mother in the convent, who told him where to find his father's people. And that was Duncloone, where Máel Dúin learned how his father Ailill had died, defending a church from reavers who came raiding. But he was slain, and reavers burned the church around him.

There it was that the monk had showed him the burnt and blackened bones of his father and charged him to set forth to find the reaver who had slain him.

And when Diurán laid down his harp, all the men were silent, and I saw there were tears in Máel Dúin's eyes. When the Lady led him from the hall, his steps were slow, and twice he turned to look back at his men.

"Cébha." Diurán held out his hand to me. "Will you have me this night?"

It was in my thoughts to say no, for he had set himself against my Lady's will, but his eyes were dark and sad, and I knew he took no joy in it. So it was that my heart answered, and I said yes.

There were words he whispered into my ear that night, but they were for me and me alone, and not for others to hear. Though it grieved me, I knew it was in his heart to say farewell, and that was why he had come to share my pallet. In the morning, when dawn cast a rosy glow in the narrow window of my chamber, I watched him rise and don his clothing.

"Why must you attempt this thing, Diurán?" I asked him. "You know there is no harm in this place, nor in the Lady."

In the act of settling his belt, he paused, and his hands went still. "It would not be ill done if Máel Dúin were to lay aside vengeance," he said slowly. "But he must come to it in his own way." Diurán leaned down and kissed me. "Good-bye, little songbird."

He left, then, and after he had gone, I rose and donned my clothing. I knew the rhythms of the dún, and I knew the mind of Diurán. They would wait until the Lady had left upon her daily duty to hear the concerns of the isle folk and give them counsel.

When it was time, I climbed to the ramparts.

I watched them push the curragh to the shore, seventeen strong men straining, the curragh leaving a deep track in the coarse sand. There where the long green waves surged and broke into curls of foam, they launched their mighty vessel. I watched as the men splashed in the water and tumbled inside the curragh, scrambling to reach the oars. I could count their heads, brown and red and black, and Máel Dúin's like a helmet of gold. And then they were afloat and the oars came out, beating in a steady stroke, driving them away from our shore. An expanse of water opened as they rowed, growing ever wider.

In my heart, I felt empty.

Then I saw the Lady, riding along the shore on her grey mare. I saw her reach into her bodice, and the white gleam of her arm beneath her sleeve as she threw the ball of thread.

It flew in an arc through the air, unspooling as it went. And one end she held in her hand, and the other came loose at the end, fluttering down over the curragh. There was the flash of sunlight upon Máel Dúin's golden hair as he stood and reached out to catch the thread.

Once he had caught it, he could not let it go.

Winding the thread into a ball, the Lady drew it taut. The curragh turned its nose for our shore, and Máel Dúin stood like a statue in the prow as the Lady wound and wound, the silken thread taut above the waves, drawing them ashore. Then she took the end from Máel Dúin's hand and tucked the ball of thread into her bodice.

I do not know what words were spoken between them, only that the Lady turned her grey mare and rode to the dún, and Máel Dúin and his men followed behind her. So it was that they returned, and though my heart was full, I did not know whether I was happy or saddened.

All of us knew what had passed that day, but we did not speak of it, nor did we speak of it that night. Máel Dúin sat at the Lady's side, and he seemed content to be there, like a man who had won a reprieve. And Diurán played the harp and sang love songs as though he had never sung anything else and words of grief and vengeance and war had never passed his lips.

But he would not meet my eyes, and I knew they would try again.

In the morning, I went to the stable where my Lady was making ready to ride forth on her grey mare, and I touched the hem of her robe.

"Lady," I said to her, "perhaps you should not go."

The Lady smiled at me. "What, Cébha? Would you have me be idle? I have a duty to the folk of the isle."

And so she went forth and inside the dún Máel Dúin shook off his torpor like a dog shaking water from its coat and led his men to the beached curragh, and I watched them from the ramparts once more. So I was watching as they drew away from the shore and the green swell of the waves widened between us; but then the Lady came riding, and I knew she had not been fooled. Once more she drew the ball of thread from her bodice and threw it, and Máel Dúin caught the end, and it stuck fast to his hand. And this time, his men drew their swords and hacked at the thread, but it did not break, no matter how sharp their blades. So it was that the Lady drew the curragh ashore.

When it was done, she turned her grey mare and rode slowly back to the dún, and Máel Dúin and his men followed.

That night in the hall, Máel Dúin's men grumbled and said among themselves that there was no enchantment upon the thread and that Máel Dúin clung fast to it on purpose, for he did not wish to leave the Lady's side. But Diurán did not join them in their complaints, only sang and played his harp, and this night I felt his gaze upon me. When the Lady and Máel Dúin left the hall, he laid down the harp.

"Cébha," he said to me, "little songbird, I do not think you did me a kindness when you cut my hair. It was a greater offering than you made claim."

At that I was ashamed, and did not answer.

Diurán heaved a sigh, and it was such a sigh as held a world of sorrow. "Cébha, my Cébha! For your sloe eyes and sweet lips, I would be content to stay. And you know me, lass, I am one who would be content to honor your Lady. But the world beyond your shores is changing, and Máel Dúin is not hers to keep."

"Do you serve your master the druid or the monks of Duncloone in this?" I asked him bitterly.

"I serve Máel Dúin," he said and his voice was grave. "Tell me true, sweet Cébha. Will the Lady's thread stick fast to the hand of any man among us?"

And I thought of the fibers we had carded and combed with such care, straightening and smoothing each matted tangle. I thought of how the Lady had spun them, brown and black, red and gold, into a single thread. And it was in my heart to lie, but Diurán gazed at me with his dark poet's eyes, and my lips spoke the truth.

"Yes," I said to him. "It will."

He nodded, and I went away, for I did not want to know what he would do with such knowledge. Once only I glanced behind me, and Diurán was plucking rushes from the floor of the hall, smoothing them on his lap. Then I saw no more.

In the morning, I did not go to warn my Lady. Whether or not there would have been merit in it, I do not know, but I was sick at heart and had no wish for her to read the betrayal in my face. So I went to the ramparts and watched.

For the third time, Máel Dúin's men pushed the curragh to the shore and it left its deep track in the sand like the mark of some vast beast. For the third time, they launched their mighty vessel, and it rode proud atop the green swells, surging with each stroke of the oars. Once more I counted their heads, black and red and brown, and Máel Dúin's among them.

I saw him stand when the Lady came riding, and the sunlight gleamed gold upon his hair. Already, as her hand reached into her bodice and drew forth the ball of thread, he was gazing toward the shore. I wondered what look he had in his pale eyes. Was it the falcon's fierce stare or the tender gaze of the lover?

There, the Lady's arm moved, her skin white as foam. There, the mottled ball in a soaring arc, thread spinning out behind it, crossing the waves. There was the end, fine as silk, settling over the curragh and Máel Dúin's hand reaching for it.

I do not know which of his men leapt to catch it instead. He had a name, too, but I do not know it. It was too far, and there was nothing about him I knew at such a distance. I know only what I may guess. When Diurán held the rushes concealed in his hand and Máel Dúin's men drew lots, he was the one who drew the broken reed.

The end of the thread stuck fast to his hand. The Lady began to wind the thread into a ball, drawing the line taut, and the curragh's prow turned toward the shore.

And there was Diurán, and him I knew by the angle of his shoulders and the movement of his limbs, by his hair as brown as oak leaves in autumn, and everything about him. I knew there was sorrow in his dark poet's eyes; sorrow, and a warrior's resolve. The sunlight was bright on the steel blade of his sword as he swung it, severing the man's hand at the wrist.

So it was that the man's severed hand fell into the green sea, and with it fell the end of the thread that the Lady had spun, hour upon slow hour. And Máel Dúin and his men sailed away and Diurán was among them, and my Lady was left on the shore, bereft and weeping.

In the stories told by men, they say only what further adventures befell Máel Dúin and his men. In the end, he found his father's slayer, and forgave him. It was a monk, a holy hermit, who bid him to do so. When the tale made its way to our shores, the Lady heard it and smiled, though there was sadness in it. I do not know, in the end, if I served her purpose or hindered it. Although she bore me no ill will for what I had done, I did not dare to ask. Such boldness as I once had, I lost that day. I knew only that I was no longer worthy of speaking her name.

Of me, the tales do not speak. Perhaps it is as well.

My name was Cébha.

The Cat with No Name

❧

BY MORGAN LLYWELYN

The cat was Nuala's friend. The cat was the only living creature who was always happy to be with her. The cat had no
name because Nuala had not given it one. To name the cat would
mean it was important to her, and someone might have noticed.

When the weather allowed, Nuala played with the cat in the back
garden. The area they liked best was a scrap of neglected lawn behind
the sagging timber garage. A row of overgrown cedars ran from the
corner of the garage to the wall, out of sight from any windows in the
house. It was important to stay out of sight of the house, as Nuala
explained to the cat. Close to the ground, where some of the cedar
hedge had died back, a little hollow had been formed. The place was
almost like a grotto; hidden behind a spiky bush with yellow blossoms.

The little hollow was Nuala's private world. Hers and the cat's. She had gathered twigs and leaves to make a carpet for the hollow so she would not sit on damp earth and stain her clothes. If she went into the house with mud on her clothes, someone might notice.

It was important that no one notice, she explained to the cat. Nuala had much rather be in the hollow than in the house. The house was filled with shadows and cold with tears, and although the windows were large, sunlight never seemed to reach all the way into the rooms. The windows were fitted with window boxes but the flowers in them had died years ago. They had never been replaced. Only a few sere, withered stems remained sticking up from the dry, caked soil.

◆　◆　◆

WHEN NUALA FIRST SAW THE CAT slinking out of the garage one morning she had known immediately that it was a stray. It was easy to recognize a creature who had no loving family of its own. The animal was very thin and dirty, with patches of bare skin where the fur was rubbed away. The fur was lost to disease or fighting, perhaps, but it did not look like the sort of cat who got involved in fights. It was far too small and weak. Without enough fur to keep it warm, the cat shivered in the damp wind.

Nuala had two grown-up brothers and a sister, but they never came home. Not even to visit. They lived far away. Between them and herself had been the Dead Babies, who had been given names but were always just called the Dead Babies. There were so many of them, and their deaths were new and recent in the house every morning.

Since the cat had no family, Nuala began feeding it. She carried bits from her own meal outside in her pocket. She always fed the cat behind the garage, so it would not get in the habit of coming to the house and crying for food. Without anyone to love and care for it, the cat had stopped caring about itself. Nuala found an old hairbrush and started brushing the cat's dirty fur, and in time the creature began washing itself. She watched, fascinated, as it licked its paws and rubbed them all over its face and neck, then twisted its body into marvelous positions so it could clean every part with its rough pink tongue.

Sometimes that tongue touched Nuala's hand, and she was surprised at how rough it was. The pointed pink combed the cat's fur and made it clean, until all the dirt was gone, and the cat was revealed as being a lovely cream color. The missing fur grew in again; the animal became fat and sleek, like the cats Nuala saw sitting in other people's windows, looking contentedly out through the glass. Cats with loving homes and families.

Curled up in her hollow, Nuala would open her arms, and the cat would come into them. It would lie against her chest and purr, a deep rumbling that resonated through both their bodies. When the cat purred Nuala felt as if the two of them were singing together.

Sometimes the cat would twist around until it could look up into her face with eyes the color of green grapes. Words passed between them then. Not spoken words, but words Nuala could feel inside herself and understand. Trust, said the cat. Love, said the cat.

Nuala did not know what the cat did when she went off to school every day. She walked away from the house each morning very slowly, so the cat, if it was watching, would not think she was running away from it. There had been a time when she could ride to school on her blue bicycle with the little wire basket for her schoolbooks. But the bicycle had gone to pay for drink.

Once the bicycle was gone she walked everywhere. Other girls in her school, those she thought were her friends, had bicycles. But they soon tired of riding slowly enough so that she could walk beside them. They pedaled away and left her by herself. Their laughter and chatter floated back to her on the wind.

Nuala walked alone, gazing at the cottages and bungalows she passed. Wondering what it would be like to live in one of them. Here on the fringes of Dublin, the country was fighting a last stand against the sprawling city. Many homes still had traditional cottage gardens overflowing with flowers. Cats sunned themselves on stone doorsteps. Cheerful little dogs with friendly tails barked hello. Nuala heard snatches of music from a radio, or a mother calling out lovingly to her children. In fine weather when the windows were open she could smell bread baking. It was a warm, loving, tummy-rumbling smell.

When Nuala got home from school the kitchen of her house was always cold. There might be some leftover casserole in the refrigerator, gone hard and crusty, or a bit of dried cheese. Sometimes she could not find anything to feed the cat and had to wait until she was given her own meal, which might be very late. If it was dark, she must wait until no one was watching so she could sneak outside the hollow under the cedars. But the cat was always waiting for her there.

It did not reach for the food first, however. The cat had good manners. It rubbed against Nuala's ankles and told her it was glad to see her, then held up its head so she could scratch under its chin. When formal greetings had been exchanged it ate very daintily, no matter how hungry it was. In the morning she brought out part of her own breakfast, bread and a rasher or some of her egg, if she had one. She always fed the cat before she went to school. She never forgot. There was a tap behind the garage, and she had found and washed an old bowl, so she could give the cat fresh water every morning before she left. She always kept the garage door open just a little bit so the cat could go inside if it rained. No one would look in the garage. The car had been gone for a long time. Gone as the bicycle had gone, Nuala explained to the cat.

She did not like to go into the garage. It was as full of ghosts as the house. Car, bicycle, lawn mower, ladder, tools. Without them the garage was very empty.

When Nuala hid beneath the cedars with the cat there were no ghosts. They sang the purring song together, and she talked about her day at school, and the cat watched her face with its big green-grape eyes. Nuala spoke in a very soft voice, so soft that her teacher at school was always telling her to speak up. But the cat could hear her. It liked a soft voice. Loud noises hurt its ears.

Loud noises hurt Nuala's ears, too. Sometimes when there had been too much drink taken, there was shouting in the house. Then Nuala wished she could hide under the bed like a cat. The shouting beat against the walls and made her afraid. Sometimes blows were struck. Sometimes things got broken. The house was not a safe place.

Nuala explained that to the cat. She did not want it to think she was keeping it outside to be mean, when it might have been warm and cosy inside, curled into a fat ball in front of the fire. The cat understood what she said and never tried to follow her all the way to the house. Nuala loved the cat for listening to her and understanding.

She was surprised how little it took to make the cat happy. A little food, and it did not even need to be hot or well cooked. A dry place to sleep. Enough fur to keep itself warm. Nuala's company. With only these riches the cat was content.

Nuala's own unhappiness swelled up inside her like a balloon. She thought about all the things she wanted, like another bicycle, and a First Communion dress hanging in her wardrobe like a memory of beauty, and hot sticky buns waiting on a plate when she came home from school, and a house with geraniums in the window boxes. Sometimes she thought it would take all of those things at once to make her happy, to make her throat stop aching with unshed tears.

But she knew she would never have all those things at once. She would never have any of them. She would just get older and taller and have less and less. Someday there might not be a house at all, even one with shadows and ghosts. Nuala heard the word "redundant" mentioned many times, and there was more drink and more shouting.

She ran outside to the cat. When she was curled up in the hollow under the cedars the rest of the world went away. She could not see the house or the hungry cold sky. She could see only the spiky bush with the yellow blossoms, and the rough bark of the cedar trunks, and the green-grape eyes of the cat. Safe in their sanctuary, she and the cat shared their own world. Together they counted their other possessions. A shred of meat and a boiled potato in her pocket. Clothes for her and fur for the cat. A place that was their own, where no one ever shouted. "This is all the world there is," Nuala whispered to the cat. "Really. This is all the world there is. The rest is just a nightmare. Someday I'll wake up. And when I do, you'll be with me."

Curling itself into a neat ball, the cat began to purr.

Nuala stayed in the safe hollow until the evening shadows gathered. There was a brief spatter of rain, but not enough to cut through the sheltering branches of the cedars. When the rain passed, the setting sun came out and filled the sky with glory.

"God is looking for us," Nuala told the cat. "He's hung red lanterns in the sky."

Scrambling out from under the cedars, she stood up and brushed bits of leaf and twig from her clothes. The cat followed her, looking up into her face. It did not seem interested in the flaming beauty of the sky.

Nuala picked up the cat and turned its head toward the sunset. "Look," she insisted. The sky was even lovelier than a happy house with geraniums in the window boxes. Nuala needed to share that beauty.

But the cat would not look at the sky. Its eyes were made for seeing things closer to itself, for seeing mice and birds and dogs and Nuala. The cat was made for the small world of the cedar hollow and the circle of Nuala's arms. It purred and rubbed the top of its head against her chin, assuring her that it had everything a small animal needed.

Gently, she put the cat down. Slowly, one foot at a time, she walked toward the house. Walked through air dyed rose by the light of the setting sun.

When she reached the door, Nuala looked back. She could just see a small part of the cat, sitting almost hidden by the corner of the garage. The light stained its creamy fur pink, so it looked like a magic cat.

"I'll come back to you tomorrow," Nuala promised, shaping the words silently with her lips.

Then she went into the house. The rosy light glowed in through the windows, but no one had noticed. There was shouting and there was crying, and Nuala ate a cold meal by herself and curled up in her bed, wishing she was in the hollow under the cedars.

Next day there was no school. That was just as well, because the weather was dreadful. A hard rain rattled the windows and pounded on the roof.

"You must stay inside," Nuala was told. "Find something to do and leave me alone. I have a headache."

The little girl wandered from room to room—trying not to look into the corners, where the ghosts lurked—seeking something to occupy her time.

There was a television set, but it was broken. Otherwise, it would have gone the way of the bicycle. There were a few books, but Nuala already had read them. She had carried them out to the cedar hollow during the summer and read aloud to the cat, who had sat and listened though it was no more interested in books than it was in sunsets. But because it loved Nuala, the little animal had listened.

Now the cat was outside during a cold rain, and she was inside, hoping the cat had gone into the dry garage rather than waiting for her under the cedars. The wind began to blow very hard. When Nuala looked out the window she saw something very strange, something she had never seen before. The rain was going sideways instead of falling straight down. Dying leaves skittered frantically across the lawn. Dying branches broke off from the trees and pursued them, clawing the grass with giant fingers.

From moment to moment, the voice of the wind increased until it became the roar of lions seeking prey; the roar of a train rushing through a tunnel. Something was approaching at a terrifying speed. Nuala peered through the curtains of rain, trying to see.

Then she heard a sound like cloth ripping. As she watched in disbelief, part of the garage roof lifted up and blew away.

The cat would be terrified!

She ran out of the house. "Come back here!" someone yelled at her, but Nuala did not go back. The door slammed with a bang behind her. Thinking only of the cat, she plunged into the storm.

The wind hit her like a fist. She could barely stand up; she had to walk sideways, leaning against the gale. She could hardly breathe because the greedy wind tore the breath from her lungs to add to its own mighty voice.

When she reached the garage she could see that the door had been blown off its rusted hinges. Inside, in the dark shadows, two green-grape eyes glowed. A frightened voice said, "Miaowl!"

Nuala ran forward to pick up the cat. When she lifted the little animal she felt its frightened back claws briefly rake her chest. At that moment the wind hit the garage with all its strength. The tired old timbers gave up the struggle to stand bravely erect. Wood splintered, nails screeched. A great weight fell on Nuala, driving her to her knees. Choking dust billowed all around her. She could not see anything in the sudden darkness. Somehow she kept her arms around the cat, so that the animal was safely pressed against her heart when the rest of the roof collapsed upon them.

◆　◆　◆

SOMEONE WAS CALLING her name from far, far away. She tried to answer, but it was too much of an effort. She was very tired. A pale greyish light was swirling around her, making her dizzy. The voice of the storm was still roaring in her ears.

There should not be a storm after a red sunset, Nuala told herself. What was that saying? "Red sky at night." She tried to think clearly but she was so tired. It was easier just to drift into the greyish light and spin around and around, letting everything drift away. Darkness, blackness. Black velvet replaced the grey.

Someone was calling her name again. Not shouting this time, but sobbing, the way Mammy had sobbed year after year for the Dead Babies. And someone was holding her hand, not to slap it but to stroke it. She could never remember her father stroking her hand.

When Nuala tried to open her eyes she discovered that material was fastened over them. Her whole head was covered in material, with holes left for her mouth and her nose. Her nose smelled strange, bitter smells she did not like. The cat would run away from such smells.

The cat!

Nuala tried to sit up. At once hands were pushing her down onto the bed again. It was not her bed, she sensed, but a hard, narrow one. When she tried to pull away from the hands she discovered a metal railing holding her in.

There was a fresh buzzing in her ears and the greyness closed around her again. Her last thoughts were of the cat. She had to ask how it was, where it was. But how could she speak of the cat? No one knew it existed. It did not even have a name, she could not say, "What happened to Fluffy, or Snowball, or Creamy."

The next time Nuala woke up some of the covering had been removed from her head. She could open her eyes, though at first the light was so bright it hurt. She closed her eyelids almost all the way and peeped through her lashes.

She found herself in a long, narrow room with a number of beds.

Some of the beds had screens around them. Nursing sisters moved between beds, bending over, murmuring softly, doing things for the people in the beds.

Beside Nuala's bed was a straight-backed chair. Mammy was sitting in it with her eyes closed. Behind the chair stood Nuala's father, and Mammy was leaning her head against him. With one hand on her shoulder, he was staring across the room. There was no smell of drink coming from him, but he was very pale. There was dark stubble on his cheeks. The hand on Mammy's shoulder appeared to be trembling, but that might have been just Nuala's dizziness.

She made a small sound that was supposed to be a word, but it would not come up through her throat. Her parents turned their faces toward her at once. She could not remember when they had looked at her so eagerly. Love, their eyes said.

"Don't try to talk," Mammy told her gently. "You've had a bad time, but you're going to be all right. There's no damage done that won't mend, the doctor says. You just have to lie still and rest."

Nuala could not understand why her voice would not work. When she tried to ask about the cat, her throat closed up. At last she did manage to make an awful croaking sound that appalled her, but at least it was a word. A sort of word.

Her parents responded with tears of relief in their eyes.

"If we had lost you, too . . ." Mammy began. Then she put her knuckles in her mouth and turned away. But she said nothing about the Dead Babies, though once she had spoken of nothing else.

Her parents stayed with Nuala until she fell back into the greyness. Her last thought was to wonder if seeing them together like that had been a dream.

It was no dream. Mammy was there when she next woke up, and Nuala's father came to the hospital every day. He never smelled of drink. His hands shook and his mouth trembled, and sometimes there was an expression in his eyes that she recognized. But then he would smile at her in her bandages, and she knew he would not go out to the pub when he left the hospital.

The sight of his daughter's living face meant more to him than drink.

Bit by bit, Nuala learned what had happened. The garage had been blown down on top of her. A piece of planking had hit her head, which was why it hurt so. The storm had done much worse damage elsewhere. A tree had fallen across a car and killed a young man. Nuala had been very lucky, everyone said so.

In the house, the big window where she had been sitting had blown in moments after she ran outside. Shards of glass had sliced across the room like knives. If she had stayed where she was, she would have been cut to pieces.

"What on earth made you go outside just then?" Mammy kept asking. But when Nuala tried to explain her throat closed up, and she could not answer.

Her father was looking at his wife as he said, "I'm beginning to realize how much we have to be thankful for, if we don't let it slip away. And how little it takes to make us happy after all. Like knowing you're alive." He turned and smiled down at Nuala.

"My cat!" Nuala cried out at last. Her parents looked startled. She bit her lip, then plunged ahead in a funny rusty voice she hardly recognized.

"The cat I take care of. It was in the garage with me when the roof blew off. I went outside to save it." Her words began tumbling over one another in their eagerness to be said. "Where is it? Is it all right? You have to find the cat, it will be so frightened and hungry!"

"There was no cat, Nuala," her mother said soothingly. "You must have dreamed it." She looked around for a nursing sister; her little girl was becoming too excited.

"But there is a cat. There is!"

"What's its name, then?" asked her father. "I'll go home and call the cat and try to find it."

Nuala felt hot tears burning behind her eyes. "I never gave it a name." The new tenderness in her father's voice made her want to cry more than the shouting had ever done. "But I caught it before the garage fell down. I was holding it very tightly; I felt it scratch me because it was afraid. Look, I can show you."

She tore at her hospital gown and bared her chest. Her parents bent over her.

There were not any scratches.

Her father said, "When we shifted the timbers off of you, we didn't see any cat."

"You must have missed it, then."

He shook his head. "That's hardly possible. We moved every stick in that garage to get to you. We would have seen a cat if one had been in there. But I'll go back and look now if it will make you feel any better, if you'll promise to be quiet until I come back."

Nuala clasped his hands between hers. "Please."

Mammy stayed with her while he went to look for the cat. The nursing sister brought tablets for her headache, and a glass of cool, sweet orange juice.

"My daughter has dreamed of some cat," Mammy told the sister. "I'm afraid she's been a lonely little girl, but things are going to be different when we get her home."

"I didn't dream it!" Nuala protested. She was surprised at herself for being so bold. "It's a cream-colored cat with green eyes. I ran outside to save it."

"Then I think the cat saved you," said the nursing sister. "From what I understand, going outside is all that kept you from being mutilated by a shattered window."

Nuala's mammy thrust her fingers into her mouth. Her eyes were very large and shiny with sudden tears.

Nuala's father did not come back until visiting hours were almost over.

When Mammy heard his footsteps she looked up. For just a moment Nuala saw the old worry in her eyes, but there was no smell of drink on him. He only looked tired.

"I searched through every inch of that garage and shifted all the debris," he told Nuala. "I didn't find even a bit of fur, and no blood. If there was a cat, it must have run away after the garage collapsed. But I still think you made it up. You always did have an active imagination." He did not seem angry, though. He did not hit her.

"There was a cat," Mammy said softly. "Except I think it was an angel."

Daddy drew up a second chair beside Mammy's and sat down with one arm around his wife's shoulders.

A rosy glow seeped into the hospital ward.

"What a beautiful sunset," Nuala said in her rusty voice.

Pushing a strand of hair out of her eyes, her mother glanced toward the nearest window. "It is beautiful," she agreed, sounding surprised. "I had forgotten about sunsets." She lifted the child higher onto the pillow so the three of them could watch together, with the glow reflected on their faces.

◆ ◆ ◆

WHEN NUALA WAS WELL ENOUGH to go home she looked everywhere for the cat.

Her parents had promised her she could keep it; she could even let it sleep on her bed. She made out a list of possible names and carefully selected the very best one to give to the cat when she found it. She looked in the hollow under the cedars; she searched the fields beyond the house. She asked all the neighbors. She put up a notice in the local shop. But she never found the cat. No one in the neighborhood had ever seen a cream-colored cat with green-grape eyes.

No cat.

There was only the deep, happy purring that Nuala felt within herself when her parents smiled lovingly at her and at each other.

In the spring, the three of them planted new geraniums in the window boxes.

About the Authors

DIANE DUANE has been writing for her own entertainment ever since she could read (having written and illustrated her first novel in crayon at the age of eight). Her first novel, *The Door Into Fire*, was published by Dell Books in 1979. On the strength of this book, she was nominated two years running for the World Science Fiction Society's John W. Campbell Award for best new science fiction/fantasy writer in the industry. Since then she has published some thirty novels, numerous short stories, and various comics and computer games, appearing on the *New York Times* Best-seller List and garnering the occasional award from such organizations as the American Library Association and the New York Public Library. She is presently best known for her continuing "Young Wizards" series of young adult fantasy novels about the New York-based teenage wizards Nita Callahan and Kit Rodriguez. Works now in progress include the last novel in her Middle Kingdoms series (*The Door Into Starlight*), the seventh "Young Wizards" novel (*Wizard's Holiday*), and the completion of her present Star Trek/"Rihannsu" sequence of novels (*The Empty Chair*). In the rest of her spare time Diane gardens (weeding, mostly), studies German, listens to shortwave and satellite radio, and dabbles in astronomy, computer graphics, image processing, amateur cartography, desktop publishing, and fractals. She is trying to learn how to make more spare time.

BORN IN 1947, TANITH LEE began to write at the age of nine. In the early seventies three of Lee's children's books were published. But in 1975 DAW books of the USA began her life as a professional writer. To date she has published seventy-five novels and short-story collections. Four of her radio plays have been broadcast by the BBC, and she wrote two episodes of the TV series *Blake's 7*. She has won various World Fantasy awards and was short-listed for the Guardian Childrens Book award with her novel *Law of the Wolf Tower*. Lee lives in England with her partner, the writer and artist John Kaiine.

JANE YOLEN is a two-time Nebula winner for short stories, and the author of over 250 books for children, young adults, and adults. Called the Hans Christian Andersen of America by *Newsweek*, her many other awards include a Caldecott, three Mythopoeic Society Awards, a World Fantasy Award, a National Book Award nominee, two Christopher Medals, and three honorary doctorates. The reading room of the elementary school library in Hatfield, Massachusetts, has been named after her, a singular honor. She and her husband live part-time in Massachusetts and part-time in St. Andrews, Scotland.

ADAM STEMPLE is an author and musician who lives in Minneapolis with his wife, Betsy, his two children, Alison and David, and a very confused tomcat named Lucy. He spends his days watching the children (and the cat), his nights playing guitar with his Irish band, the Tim Malloys, and the few hours he may once have used for sleep, he now spends writing. He has just sold his first novel to Tor Books. Adam Stemple is very tired.

JUDITH TARR is the author of more than two dozen novels, including World Fantasy Award nominee *Lord of the Two Lands* and, most recently, *Tides of Darkness* (Tor) and *House of War* (Roc). Her mother comes from a large Irish family, and her grandmother, Mae Ryan, had the Second Sight. She has kissed the Blarney Stone and been addressed like a native in the streets of Kilkenny. She lives in Arizona, where she breeds and raises Lipizzan horses—some of whose relatives shared the role of the magical white horse in the wonderful Irish film, *Into the West*.

ELIZABETH HAYDON's debut novel, *Rhapsody: Child of Blood*, in her internationally best-selling fantasy series "The Symphony of Ages," was selected by Borders.com as one of the top ten novels of 1999 across the entire literary field. Each of the subsequent books in the series has made the "Year's Best" lists of Barnes and Noble, Borders, and Amazon.com. A longtime editor in the educational field, Ms. Haydon is also a harpist and madrigal singer, and has published over one hundred texts. The first novel in her fantasy series for young adults will be released in the fall of 2004.

CHARLES DE LINT is a full-time writer and musician who presently makes his home in Ottawa, Canada, with his wife MaryAnn Harris, an artist and musician. His most recent books are *Spirits in the Wires* and *A Circle of Cats*, a picture book illustrated by Charles Vess. Other recent publications include the collections *Waifs and Strays* and *Tapping the Dream Tree* and the trade paperback edition of *The Onion Girl*. For more information about his work, visit his Web site at www.charlesdelint.com.

RAY BRADBURY is one of those rare individuals whose writing has changed the way people think. His more than five hundred published works—short stories, novels, plays, screenplays, television scripts, and verse—exemplify the American imagination at its most creative. Once read, his words are never forgotten. His best-known and most beloved books, *The Martian Chronicles, The Illustrated Man, Fahrenheit 451* and *Something Wicked This Way Comes*, are masterworks that readers carry with them over a lifetime. His timeless, constant appeal to audiences young and old has proven him to be one of the truly classic authors of the twentieth century. In recognition of his stature in the world of literature and the impact he has had on so many for so many years, Bradbury was awarded the National Book Foundation's 2000 Medal for Distinguished Contribution to American Letters.

ANDREW M. GREELEY is a Catholic priest who teaches at the University of Chicago and the University of Arizona. He is on the staff of the National Opinion Research Center. Among his sociology books are *The Catholic Imagination, The Catholic Revolution*, and *Priests: Sociology of a Calling Under Attack*. His fiction includes the "Blackie Ryan" and "Nuala Anne" mystery series and the O'Malley family saga. He has an honorary degree from the National University of Ireland/Galway.

JANE LINDSKOLD has long been fascinated by the Irish poet and playwright William Butler Yeats. Indeed, her second published academic paper was titled "The Autobiographical Occult in Yeats' 'Second Coming.'" When she started research for this story, she was resolved not to write about Yeats's doomed romance with revolutionary Maud Gonne, but the story insisted.

Lindskold is the author of fifty or so short stories and over a dozen novels. The most recent of them are *Through Wolf's Eyes, Wolf's Head, Wolf's Heart,* and *Dragon of Despair.* She is always writing something, and enjoys doing so very much. You can learn more about her work at janelindskold.com.

FRED SABERHAGEN has been writing and selling fantasy and science fiction for a bit more than forty years, and now lives in New Mexico with his wife, Joan Spicci. His mother's maiden name was Monahan, but he has never been to Ireland.

PETER TREMAYNE is the fiction-writing pseudonym of Celtic scholar and writer Peter Berresford Ellis, whose work has been published in nearly twenty languages around the world. His work has received much critical acclaim and in 2002, being born of Irish parentage, he received the accolade of being only the second living writer to be bestowed as an Honorary Life Member of the Irish Literary Society at the hands of its current president, Nobel Literary Laureate Seamus Heaney. Nobel Laureate W. B. Yeats, Charles Gavan Duffy, and other Irish literary personalities formed the Irish Literary Society in 1891. The award was given in recognition of Peter's "notable con-tribution to Irish literature and cultural scholarship." He began to publish fiction under the Peter Tremayne pseudonym in 1977 and authored many books in the fantasy genre, based mainly on Celtic themes. In 1993 he began a series of short mystery stories featuring a seventh-century Irish religieuse—Sister Fidelma—which were instantly acclaimed. There are now twelve Sister Fidelma novels and one volume of short stories published. The books appear both in the UK and USA and are translated, so far, into six other European languages. Peter's work covers a wide field and demon-strates his many interests. There is now an International Sister Fidelma Soci-ety, supportive of Peter's work, with members in twelve countries.

CECILIA DART-THORNTON graduated from Monash University with a degree in sociology. Her interests include writing music, reading nonfiction, the welfare of animals, and environmental conservation. Her fantasy trilogy "The Bitterbynde" is published in twelve countries and earned high praise from reviewers across the world. "The Bitterbynde" comprises *The Ill-Made Mute, The Lady of the Sorrows,* and *The Battle of Evernight.* Currently Cecilia is writing a second trilogy entitled "The Crowthistle Chronicles," beginning with Book #1: *The Iron Tree*. Her grandparents were born in Ireland, but she now lives in Australia with her husband and two dogs. Her Web site can be visited at www.dartthornton.com.

L. E. MODESITT, JR., has published a number of short stories and technical articles and forty novels, many of which have been translated into German, Polish, Dutch, Czech, and Russian. His latest novels are *Darknesses*, the second book of the "Corean Chronicles," his newest fantasy series, and *The Ethos Effect*. His first published story appeared in *Analog* in 1973. Born in 1943 in Denver, Colorado, Mr. Modesitt has been, among other occupations, a U.S. Navy pilot; an industrial economist; staff director for a U.S. congressman; director of congressional relations for the U.S. Environmental Protection Agency; and a consultant on environmental, regulatory, and communications issues.

JACQUELINE CAREY was born in 1964. After receiving B.A. degrees in psychology and English literature from Lake Forest College, she spent time living in London and working in a bookstore, returning to the U.S. to embark on a writing career. An affinity for travel has taken her from Finland to Egypt to date, and she currently resides in west Michigan. She is the author of the critically acclaimed "Kushiel's Legacy" fantasy trilogy, including *Kushiel's Dart*, which received the *Locus* Award for Best First Novel and the *Romantic Times* Reviewer's Choice Award for Best Fantasy in 2001. Other previous publications include a nonfiction book, various essays, and short stories. Further information is available at her official author's site, www.jacquelinecarey.com.

MORGAN LLYWELYN, who is an Irish citizen and lives north of Dublin, has published thirteen historical novels about Ireland and the Celts. These include the international best-seller *Lion of Ireland*. Work in progress is *The Irish Century*, a five-volume series chronicling Ireland throughout the twentieth century. The first three of these novels have already been published to wide acclaim: *1916*, *1921*, and *1949*. Llywelyn's novels have been translated into a total of twenty-seven languages and five have been optioned for film. Her work also includes a nonfiction biography of Xerxes of Persia, four books for children, and a substantial body of short fiction for various anthologies. She is a founding member of the Irish Writers' Centre, past chairman of the Irish Writers' Union, and a cofounder of the Irish Children's Book Trust. Among her literary awards are the Washington, D.C. Cultural Achievement Award, the Best Novel of the Year Award from Penwomen International, the Poetry in Prose Award from the Galician Society, Book of the Year for Young Adults from the American Library Association, the Saint Brendan Medal from the Brendan Society, and the Readers' Association of Ireland Biennial Award. She has been named Woman of the Year by the New York Irish Heritage Committee, Exceptional Celtic Woman of the Year by Celtic Women International, official bard of Clan O'Brien, and an honorary member of Clan Kavanagh.